Frederick Boyle

**On the Borderland**

Frederick Boyle

**On the Borderland**

ISBN/EAN: 9783337335861

Printed in Europe, USA, Canada, Australia, Japan

Cover: Foto ©Andreas Hilbeck / pixelio.de

More available books at **www.hansebooks.com**

# ON THE BORDERLAND.

BY

## FREDERICK BOYLE,

AUTHOR OF " LEGENDS OF MY BUNGALOW," " THE GOLDEN PRIME,"
"CAMP NOTES," &c. &c. &c.

LONDON :—CHAPMAN AND HALL,

LIMITED.

1884.

WESTMINSTER :

NICHOLS AND SONS, PRINTERS,

25, PARLIAMENT STREET.

# CONTENTS.

# ON THE BORDERLAND.

## A STRANGE WOOING.

I DARE not precisely name the scene of this story. Somewhere betwixt the tropics stands a mud-built ruinous town, very mean, dirty, and unwholesome. Low green hills and woods lie behind it, and a grey sea before. In times not long past fleets used to ride beyond the surf, and rich caravans started daily for the inland wilds. That glory has departed, but its ruins amaze the stranger to-day. Amidst the ragged, sun-bleached thatch of negro hovels, lofty walls stand red and crumbling, with windowless eyes that blink towards the ocean. Down at the water's edge, built upon rocks that clang and strain under the beating of the surf, stands a castle. The guns are honeycombed, the pavements broken, the walls

／ 5                           B

bear a crop of jungle-weeds; but it rises hoar and stately, a marvel of antique grandeur. Neither time, nor siege, nor tempest have reft one solid stone from another. When storms roll high the thundering surge without, a rainbow spans its seaward front; when winds lie hushed of an afternoon, and the rocks burn white, its lofty keep and surrounding galleries throw a giant shadow on the strand.

The jungle has crept in steadily and softly. Lank goats and sheep of peculiar breed graze in the streets. Through the middle of the town a ditch, half-dry, sluggishly oozes and reeks between embankments of ancient masonry—a foul ditch, though mantled with velvet rosettes of pistia. They catch wild beasts of prey therein—creatures that make night clamorous pursuing scared poultry and belated lambs. But amongst the ragged palms and dusty india-rubbers ten or twelve great houses still tower above the wilderness of thatch; outside they have high garden-walls and big gateways; within, cool colonnades and balconies, parqueterie floors, and the rest of it. Most of them are tenanted by officials, but the impoverished heirs still occupy a few. Amongst those who keep the family mansion is a widow named Rudger. Her late husband had been a clerk, with whom his master's daughter fell in love. She was a half-caste, but her yellow hand brought Rudger this house and a business not yet wholly destroyed by the vigilance of our cruisers and the competition of younger settlements. The lady bore two daughters, and then, after several years' interval, a third. The circumstances of the family were still such as enabled Rudger to send the eldest girls away to school when they reached the proper age. But he died whilst little Mary was still too young to go from home, and the widow's resources scarcely availed to pay for the girls whose education was begun. Perhaps Mrs. Rudger's grief was not unconsoled when she saw Mary could not have foreign schooling. "The family," of course, should be in a position to meet any rival, whether at the counting-house or the piano; but Mrs. Rudger may very well have thought that learning is a great expense to parents and a great trouble to children. She herself had been brought up among slaves. Her English was shaky, and she had never been able to read what she did not know by heart. Yet her success in life had been notable—she had married a young man "all white," who never complained; Mary, a quadroon, with double her share of the superior race, might do as well, or better.

Mrs. Rudger naturally overlooked certain differences in the situation. Her own mother had felt for her child that respect which the negress instinctively yields to white or semi-white blood, though it be in what is else her own flesh. She resented familiarity in nurses and slaves towards her daughter, took counsel with her husband, and insisted that the girl's manners, if not her mind, should be pure white. And so the girl grew up quiet and demure, resembling the usual pattern of a young lady as much as circumstances would allow. No one would have suspected that her brain was full of charms and fetishes, omens, love-philtres; that she feared Obi, loved a negro song, a negro tale, all that is negro in ethics; that the principles and even the pleasures of civilized life were never appreciated, though endured. A veneer of training hid these impressions whilst her husband lived, but they worked through it as she grew older, and the necessity of restraint disappeared.

Little Mary however had no such influences about her as had her mother at the same age. The negresses took sole charge, and they moulded her spirit after their own. It chanced that there were no white children then in the settlement, and the household fell more and more into native habits. Arrayed in garments many-coloured, of the latest fashion which had reached that distant spot, Mrs. Rudger paid occasional calls, or sometimes gave a tea-party. The bright-eyed little girl was her companion, in silk stockings, flounces, and feathered hat. But on returning from these duties the mother donned an ample dressing-gown with nothing underneath, decked her head and arms with jewellery, and received native ladies for pleasure. The daughter meanwhile played with the slave children of the household, in the shortest of petti-

coats for her only raiment—less than that sometimes—
and thus she received, unconsciously as they were given,
such ideas of life's philosophy as a self-indulgent, lazy,
but not ill-disposed race of negroes entertain.

In the state to which such training would lead a girl,
the sisters found her. They returned from school young
women, and Mary was eight years old. Severe discipline, in an old-fashioned seminary of Cape Town, had
made them thrifty, pious, and proper. Every single
thing and person at home shocked them terribly. The
saucy slave-girls, three parts naked, but laden with gold
ornaments; the noisy men still more lightly clothed;
the dirt, the untidiness, made them bitterly ashamed.*
But worst of all was the degradation, as they called it,
of their mother and sister. The girls had been not a
little impressed by Mrs. Rudger's grandeur when she
came on board to welcome them; for their notions of
dress or taste were scarcely more correct than hers.
They vowed, as did all present, that Mary was a little
angel disguised in silk stockings and flounces. But on
reaching the big, shabby house, they saw with dismay
the usual transformation. Mrs. Rudger jumped out of
her stays, so to speak, and the little angel abandoned all
her disguises. It was too early yet to interfere. The
good sisters wept and prayed that night.

* In this country the mistress of the household takes pride in
adorning her female slaves with all the jewellery which she cannot
dispose on her own person.

No later than the morning they attacked the system. Mrs. Rudger gave way at once, agreed, lamented, promised—but never performed. Mary's condition, moral and spiritual, proved to be worse than the worst they had expected. She could neither read nor write nor speak English, beyond a few common expressions and a few sentences of the Catechism, to which she attached no meaning. Mrs. Rudger herself was alarmed and angry to learn the result of her neglect. It disgraced " the family." Going to the other extreme, she would have the child metamorphosed all round in an instant. And the child stubbornly refused. Whence it happened that, within twenty-four hours of her sisters' arrival, Mary was sobbing in bed, very sore, and full of evil passions. She tried to run away, but the faithless slaves betrayed her. More punishment followed, and, in short, the girl was whipped into submission.

But the change was all outside. The sisters could not keep her perpetually in view, and old companions crept in at the window, waylaid her in corners, and kept the spirit of savagery aglow. The excellent Misses Rudger were by no means fitted to change such a disposition. Mary longed for the time when she would be too old for the rod, and meanwhile she cherished hatred, always growing, against white people and their ways. The moment of resistance came earlier than might have been expected. Her sisters, so long removed from the climate

of their birthplace, withered under ceaseless fits of fever.
Her mother, satisfied with the progress made, stood
neutral. And Mary was a strong fearless girl in her
teens. She resisted the chastisement, and won a victory.

From that day the old life was renewed. Learning
was not to be shuffled off, but clothes and habits might.
The sisters, in despair, tried the influence of tears, but
it was too late. Possibly entreaties might have been
successful once; but, coming after severity, they could
but raise contempt. After a time, everything was
yielded, in shame and sorrow. For many months after
her triumph, Mary refused to touch a book, to speak
English, even to wear anything besides the native petti-
coat. Amusement unceasing was found in the sports
and gossip so long disused. The courtyard was always
full of girls, who laughed and shrieked from morning to
night. The Misses Rudger could understand not a tithe
of the loud conversation, which was lucky for their
peace; not that Mary would choose or tolerate vicious
companions. Her friends were the best of their kind,
but they spoke with the frankness of savages who live
always in a crowd together, and have not two words for
a spade. But I cannot honestly profess to think that
they did Mary real mischief. The bloom of a peach
is very pretty ; but the fruit is as sweet and pure
without it.

After awhile Mary tired somewhat of her freedom.

The earliest feelings of womanhood began to stir. Romping with other girls no longer satisfied her wholly. Once more she read a little, shamefacedly, and in private. Then she could be persuaded sometimes to dress, and visit such friends of the family as were " coloured " like herself. For years she would not willingly speak with a white woman, and the suggestion of meeting a white man would drive her back into barbarism. The sisters had learned some tact by experience, and they gradually brought her through this stage. But it was well understood in the settlement that the youngest Miss Rudger, when met by chance, was not to be addressed of malekind.

Mary was near eighteen years old when the town where she dwelt became our base of operations for a short but anxious war. At the house where I was quartered the Misses Rudger were intimate, and I soon met the elder pair. But my gentle hostess feared, above everything, lest Mary should be noticed and turned to ridicule by supercilious subalterns. When the troops began to arrive, she tried her utmost to keep the girl at home, but a further development now showed itself. Abating none of her angry shyness for mankind of white persuasion, she much fancied looking at handsome young officers, who were frequent enough in the streets. She wished only to see them; if they looked at her, as well they might, she trembled with passion. Never had the girl worn clothes so often, or so many hours at a time. It is true, as Mrs. —— told me afterwards, with a blush and a laugh, that she tore them off more fiercely than ever on returning indoors, and vowed that each walk should be the last. But nature had its way. It was accident which gave me at length the pleasure of a very brief acquaintance. A West Indian regiment was landing, and Mrs. ——, my hostess, had gone to see the show. I had returned, and I was sitting, very drowsy, in a long-armed chair on the verandah. Suddenly I became conscious of a fresh young voice, talking eagerly, and Mrs. —— replying. I gathered that the one asked if I was at home, and the other said no. It was my duty to undeceive them, but whilst thinking of it I dozed off. The same voice, much nearer, roused me again. In the prettiest of broken English, it was vehemently lauding the uniform of the West Indians—a burst of yellow, scarlet, and blue, which only a pyrotechnist or a negro could dispassionately admire.

"And what did you think of the officers?" asked Mrs. ——.

"Oh, beautiful! Fine men! How brave they look! And some of them will be dead!" The tones were so sweet and earnest that I remember imagining a face to match—dark eyes, wide with pity, a soft mouth drooping, and little hands outspread for emphasis.

" What! all handsome men?" asked shrewd Mrs. ——,
laughing.   " Surely not, Mr. Blank?"

" Oh, not Mr. Blank!"

" Nor Mr. other Blank?"

" Not that one, of course, either."

" Oh, indeed!   Then which of the officers was so
beautiful and so brave?"

This seemed the last moment for decorous eavesdrop-
ping.  Yawning loudly, I pushed back my chair, came
into view of the window, lit a cheroot, and entered with
all the surprise I could command.  The ladies were
taking tea; the younger, in fact, had suddenly buried in
the cup as much of her face as would enter that receptacle.  Upon Mrs. ——'s flurried introduction, she rose
and primly curtseyed, after the fashion of Cape Town
ladies in the last century.  I saw a girl, very pretty,
tall, and delicately shaped.  The negro strain showed
itself in crisply waving hair unglossed, dark complexion,
and full, tremulous mouth.  Miss Rudger had in its
utmost beauty that velvet eye which is peculiar to the
mixed breed.  Neither white woman nor negress ever
shows it.  Those who have not seen a mulatto girl of
the happiest type cannot imagine what is meant by
velvet eyes.  It is less a matter of expression than of
shade, tone, feature.  Mary did not lose it when she
positively scowled at me with bewitching ferocity.  Her

face was crimson, her lips quivered with anger and shyness. Vainly I tried to make her speak. To the extreme annoyance of Mrs. ——, she would not reply, and I withdrew as quickly as I could. My hostess then reproached her gently, and the girl's temper blazed. She rushed home, threw off muslins and laces, and vowed she would seek a friend no more among the hateful whites.

The sisters came moaning to our house. They doated on Mary, wild little savage as she was. Mrs. ——, scarcely less fond, sought her out. It was no use. The hint of a suspicion of a confidence which a natural enemy —a white man—might have heard, was enough to set the child's brain going. She collected her little negress friends, and renewed the old racket.

" At least," said Mrs. —— at length, " be persuaded to wear proper clothes."

" These are good enough for me," Mary sullenly replied. " I do not wish to be white girl."

" But, darling, there are soldiers everywhere now. You will certainly be seen."

" I am just as much dressed as any of my real friends. They are not ashamed if soldiers see them. I don't understand."

But Mrs. —— knew that she did understand, and persisted for sheer pride and temper. Mary would not appear in the courtyard until she saw the gates closed.

The West Indian regiment which had indirectly

caused these regrettable events was quartered in the castle.

I spent some pleasant evenings at mess there, the guest of a young lieutenant, whom I will call Pickering. A good soldier he was, and a good fellow, but one of those whom competitive examination does not distinguish. Failing even for the line, he accepted a West Indian commission rather than none. By family and fortune Pickering had the influence which can always help a man in the field, though useless in the "piping times." A brigadier named him " galopper," and so he escaped the garrison duty on which his regiment was kept back. The advance was expected from day to day, and Pickering hurriedly sent his traps to the general's quarters. He himself followed after tiffin. Perhaps the *vin du départ* had been copious; perhaps the sun was bewilderingly hot; anyhow, Pickering lost himself, at an hour when no one but the poorest negroes stir abroad. He wandered, angry and desperate, until he came across a house evidently European. Throwing himself against the crazy doors he burst them open. A bevy of native girls playing about the yard ran together and screamed. Pickering took no notice of them, but walked towards the staircase, which, as usual, opened on the court. So my friend says, and has said from the beginning. But malicious gossip declared that he ran straight into the arms of Miss Mary Rudger, who was attired in her usual

simplicity. I think that the truth lies betwixt these
stories. Mary was present, but her comrades shielded
her from sight.

Pickering marched upstairs, and presented himself
before the maiden sisters. Their confusion is not to be
told, but they gave him a guide and sent him on his
way. . Next day there was tremendous activity amongst
the purveyors of scandal. By breakfast-time every
mess was laughing at the adventure. But my hostess
was really alarmed. Hurrying to Mrs. Rudger's house.
she found the lady raving. This public disgrace had
outraged all the pride which a mulatto takes in respecta-
bility. She had knocked Mary down with a rolling-pin,
or some implement of that nature, and Mrs. —— found
the poor girl in bed, her forehead bound with dirty
towels, and she anxious to die and end the miseries of
existence.

Between the infuriated parent, who vowed she would
resume the discipline of the rolling-pin, and the maiden
sisters weeping helplessly, Mary's condition was pitiable.
Mrs. —— begged to have her for a while, and the
mother, in consenting, loudly hoped that she would never
return. The girl was brought to our house in a covered
hammock. I saw little of her. In those last few days
every one was busy. War ousted Woman.

We marched up the country; we fought some battles;
we marched down again, and re-embarked. Whilst

leave-taking, dining, and giving to dinner, I was scarcely more than conscious of our pretty visitor. She sat very prim and still, dressed to the chin and the knuckles. So the time passed, mostly consumed in bed and banquet. For in those six anxious months every one had contracted obligations of friendship which he hastened to pay. When my own departure was fixed, Mr. and Mrs. —— would not be outdone by the military. They invited the chaplain and the judge, the chiefs of police and customs, the doctor, all the civil authorities.

The night before, I dined with Pickering's regiment. Witticisms carefully stored and polished in our absence descended on his guiltless head. Themes for laughter were few in that dreary garrison. "For heaven's sake," he cried, "let me see this young lady! Where does one meet her?" On learning that she was resident in my quarters, he begged me to present him, and I promised, with great hopes of fun. On asking Mrs. ——'s leave to introduce a friend at the banquet, it was granted without inquiry. We descended so soon as my servant said that Mary had entered the drawing-room. Very soldierly and handsome Pickering looked, in his mess-jacket and white trousers, as I led him up to Mrs. ——. She gave me a look of reproach when I named him. Mary, who was beside her, would not even glance at us, but sat red and panting, a lovely little fury. Pickering took a place by her, and chatted gaily, asking no reply.

And when dinner was served he calmly appropriated her, talking all the while. Mary trembled with anger, but did not know how to resist.

If the youth's conduct was rather fast, the girl's was worse than rude. She gave him neither word nor look, though he was very pleasant and respectful. She would have changed her face to that of a Gorgon if she could, but the powers would not aid, and it remained bewitchingly pretty. Pickering nearly lost temper at her obstinacy. When Mrs. —— began her small warnings of retirement, he quietly said: "If people ask me the colour of your eyes, I shall not be able to tell them." No movement. " Is it not to be known of man? " No answer. " Of course I shall never learn it now!" A slight thrill of emphatic assent. " For you will run to your room, jump into bed, and cry your eyes clean out!" If his dazzled gaze could distinguish, Pickering received sudden enlightenment on the point at issue. But he smiled sweetly, and whispered at the door, " I feel easier! You have not tears enough to quench those fires!"

" She's charming!" he muttered, seating himself by me—"absolute perfection!"

" All that?" I asked, laughing.

" Every single bit that you can imagine."

" What? You don't mean seriously——" He nodded. It was no business of mine. " You have a strange way of wooing," I said.

" The girl is strange, confoundedly, and the circumstances are not exactly familiar. I have to tame a little
wild-cat. It's something gained," he said, slowly filling
his glass, "that the prey will not escape whilst the
hunter takes well-earned refreshment." I laughed.
"Bet you an even tenner that she is in the drawing-
room when we return, and that I make her speak?"

Done—booked—I lost! Certainly Pickering scored
his points cleverly.

In the drawing-room he leisurely approached, cup in
hand, and said aloud, " They declare, Miss Rudger, that
we have met before. I have given my word of honour
that we have not. I saw your sisters once, I believe,
but I could never have forgotten you."

All listened with amusement, saving Mrs. ——, who
blushed. There was a pause.

" I am not mistaken?" asked Pickering.

" Perhaps you did not see me," the girl murmured
painfully, yet not ill-pleased.

" I will vow I did not; and this is a subject on which
I'll permit no misapprehension in future." Then he sat
beside her, and I believe she spoke several times before
the evening finished. I know she smiled once, for I
remarked that her teeth were as pretty as all the rest of
her.

In the next three days Pickering was constantly about
the house. Mrs. —— and her husband liked the young

fellow greatly, but he seemed to make no progress in his love affair. So it appeared to us, but he was so perfectly content, that, when at length I sailed, an eccentric commission was entrusted to me. Some days after my departure in the cool of the afternoon, he called. Mrs.—— was walking, but her husband received the visitor.

" I have just presented myself to Mrs. Rudger," he began.

" A curious product of the country, isn't she ? "

" A type! If it were possible that old lady should undertake a voyage to Europe, I *could* not marry her daughter."

" *What?* "

" Love might run to it, but decency would forbid. Where is my little savage? "

" What on earth do you mean ? "

" Oh, haven't you noticed that I am over head and ears in love with Mary ? The mother smiles upon me. I feel it yet! "

" I don't doubt that you are serious and honourable," exclaimed ——. " Allow me to say, that, if you win this girl, you will have as brave and as good and as modest a wife as ever any lucky fellow gained."

" Yes—I know—but she is a desperate little savage."

Worthy —— proceeded in high excitement to deliver his opinion. Pickering is not distinguished for endur-

C

ance of platitude, and he yawned. "Thanks. You
are very good. I must do things my own wicked way."

Mrs. —— arrived with Mary, who coloured and
fumed. Pickering gravely advanced, seized her hand,
and addressed Mrs. ——: "I have asked Mrs. Rudger
to give me this young lady to wife. I think I know
her faults of temper and training, and they do not
frighten me. But you know her better. I cannot help
loving her; but if you, Mrs. ——, tell me that after no
time of probation shall I ever be proud to show my wife
to my mothers and sisters—I retire!"

It may be imagined with what a face Mary heard this
speech. So far as Pickering was concerned, she cared
not a jot for the verdict. But for her own self-respect
and womanhood she desired to hear, and waited, pale
and set, her unconscious hand resting in her lover's.
Mrs. —— hesitated, not in doubt of the sentence, but in
sheer surprise and bewilderment. Then she cried
heartily, "Mary is all good and pure, Mr. Pickering!
The man who wins her heart can make her mind what
he will. You it is, allow me to say so, whom I might
doubt."

Then, as was natural, Mary reasserted herself. Throwing away the hand that clasped hers, she looked Pickering in the face with even more wild-cat in her expression
than he had yet admired.

"You are a rude and impertinent boy!" And so withdrew, as hot and indignant, as stately and as witching, as you please. Pickering laughed softly.

Of course she refused to see him, and wept when Mrs. —— urged his claim to courteous treatment. He was only mocking her—besides, she hated him! Live with a white man, amongst "all white" people! she would die! or rather, she would kill herself and everybody! He spoke of a mother and sisters, awfully white doubtless! Oh, please, dear Mrs. ——, let her go back home, if this must continue. She was a wicked girl naturally, and something would happen if they teased her! "Something will happen you" is a negro threat of mischief, not to be disregarded. But Mrs. —— was not afraid.

Time went on, but Pickering's affairs did not progress. Mary would not see him in the house, nor would stir abroad. Exercise is not essential to creole comfort. But in a month or so arrived a number of boxes to the address of Lieutenant Pickering, which he forwarded to Mrs. ——, keeping back only one. She, in the secret, asked Mary to unpack them. All manner of pretty things were there, which I had been commissioned to buy at Funchal—dainty dresses, hats, and shoes, and linen simply and gracefully fashioned. The French *modiste* in whom I confided had entered with enthusiasm into our romance. Mary glowed with admiration, as box

c 2

after box displayed its girlish treasures. "Oh, how
pretty, pretty!" she cried.

"Try this one, dear!" said Mrs. ——, "and this,
and this!" The girl tried them, and blushed, and
nearly cried. "What beautiful things white ladies
wear!" she sighed, looking at her own bright image.

"Could you not bear to see Mr. Pickering, when you
are dressed like that!" asked Mrs. —— softly. The
thought was not resented. Mary only said, "It is the
dress. My heart is not changed."

"Then let us bleach it!" cried Mrs. —— gaily.
"The black colour does not go very deep!" Mary
sighed, and began to take off the dress, with sad glances
at her mirror. Mrs. —— saw the truth might be risked.
"The things are not sent for me, dear. You need not
disguise yourself again."

Mary's colour came and went. She looked an inquiry,
frowned, shivered a little, and began to cry. "It is
silly of him," she sobbed, "and wicked, when he knows
what I am." But there was no trouble in persuading
her to keep and wear the dresses. The concession,
which would have been difficult to obtain from a
modest English girl, was granted by this little savage
without one thought saving triumph and pleasure. She
did not understand that the giver might expect gratitude.
She felt no sense of obligation. A present descended, as it

were, from heaven, and she caught it. That Pickering should be concerned in the transaction was slightly irritating, but of course it did not really matter.

Possessing a wardrobe such as never yet had been aired in that settlement, Mary could not refrain from displaying it. Here the artful youth had placed his ambush. It need not be told how he gradually used the girl to meeting him, until at length he earned a customary right to escort her. His colonel strongly disapproved; his brother officers ridiculed whilst they envied him—for theirs was a dreary life. But little serious advance had been made even yet. If Mary lost something of her shyness as weeks passed by, she lost nothing of her mistrust. This shrewd lover perceived that it was time to strike again.

One day he carelessly complained of headache and sickness. Mary had heard with a cruel indifference of other mishaps, but these symptoms alarmed her. It is painfully droll to observe a mingling of pride with the horror which African creoles entertain towards their native disease. It is the deadliest of non-epidemic maladies, and it always strikes the white man—seldom themselves. To European science it is mysterious in beginning, course, and termination, while their rude arts conquer it, or they think they do. These facts comfort the negro and the creole under their consciousness of inferiority. The white man may be semi-divine, but

the fever is his master; the coloured man may be a dog,
but he masters the fever.  I am not sure whether Mary
would have suffered agonies worth description if Pickering had taken cholera; but this was a different case.
She displayed such a pretty interest and concern, that
the youth was almost tempted to rely on his own merits.
Luckily he resisted this impulse, and next day it was
announced that Lieutenant Pickering " had got the
fever."

The natural course of this horrid malady lends itself
to deception at the opening stages.  Mary was not surprised to see her lover waiting for the usual promenade,
pale and heavy-eyed, but able to take part in conversation.  When he suddenly, languidly, put his arm round
her, and took a piteous kiss, she blushed very much, and
gently repulsed him, but felt no astonishment.  It was
a bad sign only, and her eyes filled.  After a melancholy
dinner with my late hosts, Pickering grew worse.  His
glassy eyes began to shine, and he talked very fast.  Mrs.
—— would not hear of his returning to the castle.  She
and Mary would nurse him.  When that young lady
added tearful entreaties, Pickering consented.  If I have
rightly explained her feeling, it will be understood that
no extreme regard for the patient moved her.  It was
the fever she would combat rather than the lover she
would tend.  So a bed and things were brought, a room
prepared, and Pickering smoked and chuckled through

half the night, whilst his hosts sadly recalled the number of bright young fellows who had died, as he probably would die.

But Nemesis will not be trifled with. Before dawn, Pickering recognised with a cold thrill those pains which he had simulated. Getting out of bed to rouse his " boy," the agony of that movement made him groan. The doctor came at once, and "exhibited blue-pill." Mrs. ——, who knew so well the course of the disease, was greatly surprised to find her patient back in its first stage. He kissed Mary again when she entered the breakfast-room, and she neither blushed nor repulsed him. The counterfeit had not been suspected, but the truth was manifest. The arm round her sought support, the eyes that looked into hers had a wan pleading for life besides love. Pickering had room for no emotions save despair. Who was he to master and rule this fresh young creature, so strong, so cool and collected? He took her hands in his—where the veins already showed blue, and the sun-dye had vanished in a single night; he leaned his heavy head on her shoulder, and murmured with tears, " Love me, Mary! only say it, for I shall die in two days! "

You think my friend's behaviour contemptible? I do not draw on fancy. The African fever crushes a man's soul before it rots his body. I recall no case in my experience where the sufferer did not mourn his life,

and die each moment in anticipation. No other disease
has this effect. We saw a hero, a giant of stature as of
courage, who cried like a sick girl as he went home to
take the guerdon of his bravery. He died in sight of
land.

But Pickering was not so evil-starred. He says now
that Mary's whisper saved him, untruthful as it was.
Days of pain and wretchedness unspeakable, followed by
weeks of impotent misery, reduced him to the likeness
of a tottering old man. But he never lost consciousness,
nor mistook his love—signs that are fatal. A passion
which had been half-affected became absorbing; and
Mary felt the change. She saw that so soon as the sick
man recovered she must give him a serious answer.
Without telling herself what that should be, she wist-
fully studied Mrs. ——, and tried to learn her ways of
thought. When Pickering was pronounced to be out of
danger, she suddenly went home, and begged from her
sisters the instructions so long rejected. The lover
followed as soon as he could walk, but Mary would not
see him alone, nor would listen to his prayers. The
doctor ordered him to England, but he would not consent to go. Mrs. —— brought them together at length
by stratagem. Mary was pale, but resolved. " I am
no proper person for you to marry ! "

" Let me decide that."

"I cannot do so. There is your mother and the rest."

"They would adore you."

"It is absurd! I am not white, I am ignorant, and worse. Why you yourself——" She had not courage to finish the sentence on which she had placed great faith. Sudden blushes choked her.

"I?—oh! Well, if I didn't see you, it doesn't matter; and if I did, you can marry no one but me"

Her tone changed. "Oh, please go away to England, and never come back"

"Not unless you accompany me. I will never leave this coast without you."

"But you will die! The fever is returning even now. You cannot be so wicked as to throw away your life."

"Suicide is a less crime than murder."

"Oh! But you are not serious?"

"Look at me!" Shyly she raised her eyes and let them fall with a deeper blush. Her arguments all exhausted, she tried to lash herself to anger, but the wild-cat spirit was weakened. It vanished for ever in the wrathful flash of her eye and the shrinking of her lithe body as Pickering took her in his arms. He felt it, and murmured in sad surprise, "You do not love me at all then?"

"I do not!" Mary answered with emphasis.

He let her go ; the tears of weakness and disappointment came into his eyes. The woman's heart in her
swelled. She came near, and took his arm, and whispered,
with her downcast head upon his breast; " It was true !
But perhaps—I think—I may some time ! "

\*          \*          \*          •          \*

" But how can you possibly be married before the
steamer sails? " asked Mrs. —— in distress.

" There was another box from Funchal. Let us open
it while Mary is away." Everything needful was there,
from orange-blossoms to shoes. Mrs. —— exclaimed:
" How shall we deceive the child about the purchase of
these things? I don't believe there ever was such
impudence ! If Mary knew that her wedding-dress was
ordered within three days of your first meeting, she
would run into the bush again."

" Yes ! But see what a useful quality is conceit sometimes ! "

\*          \*          •          \*          \*

Pickering has exchanged into a cavalry regiment.
His wife is the sweetest, brightest, quaintest little lady
in the county.

# THE ROMANCE OF A MIRAGE.

THE romances encountered in real life are dreadfully sketchy and incomplete. It is the best and most interesting function of the imaginative writer to give true stories shape rather than to build up fictions ; or so at least I think, having no faculty of invention. The outline of a tale which I am going ;to fill in was given me by an official of the Telegraph Service as we steamed one morning across the blue bay of Suez. A slight mirage lay beneath the glowing hills on the desert edge. I observed that the phenomenon is nowhere so vivid as in the South African *veldt*, according to my experience. My companion's travels had not been so wide, though much more profitable. But duty had kept him stationed in many parts of the Egyptian desert, and he had witnessed such surprising illusions as eclipse all I ever saw or heard of. I suggested that a plain report of them, coming from an authoritative person like himself, would be valuable to science and most curious to the public.

Mr. Friar's modesty could not be brought to credit

that any experience of his might be worthy of record, but he told me what follows.

At one time Mr. Friar had charge of a station down the Red Sea, lonely in the extremest sense of the word. Himself, two native clerks, and two servants were the only human beings within a radius of unknown length. Bedouins did not come that way, for there is not a well nor a green herb for many miles round. Once a month a native vessel called to replenish the kegs and to bring forage for Mr. Friar's horse and a pony belonging to one of the clerks, Zohrab. If this supply did not arrive within ten days of its appointed time, the standing orders of the little colony enjoined them to embark and leave the place. They had a boat for the purpose.

That station, Um el Jemal, was the home of mirage. It displayed itself in every possible form, and in many which would be thought impossible. Often, when they turned out, the desert was a lively scene. Fishing craft sailed in pellucid rivers; sometimes a great merchant-ship or a man-o'-war appeared; villages stood out distinctly, camels and caravans stalked along, men prayed and marched. These visions changed from day to day. Sometimes the fantastic became grotesque; animals and men walked stolidly upside down, ships sailed in comfort on their trucks. But one picture appeared always the same, and very frequently. It flashed into sight directly behind the station—an ancient building of great size,

castellated, with a broad terrace before its massive gateway.  It did not glimmer into view, nor flicker in
vanishing, but burst on the eye complete, substantial,
remained about fifty minutes, and disappeared as suddenly.  So distinct was this phantom castle that the
clerks knew each of its windows as familiarly as their
own.  The terrace was often occupied by horses and
men, who presently walked out of the scene, melting
into air.  The moment of disclosure, and the duration of
the spectacle, varied with the season and with other
circumstances doubtless; but this was most constant
of all the mirage pictures.  Scientific people will regret
that my informant did not make precise observations
and note them down.  Civilised men have seldom opportunity to watch a phenomenon of the kind which often
recurs.  That there must be such is evident; several
others less conspicuous and less interesting haunted Um
el Jemal.

The gentleman of whom I speak is not a fanciful
person, and he had grave business to occupy his mind.
The clerks enjoyed more leisure.  They were young;
and, though an Oriental scarcely understands what it is
to be bored, that composure is not caused by lack of
imagination.  They took greater interest in watching
this apparition than their superior could have found,
since they understood much in it that would have
been a mystery to him.  The spectral mansion was

rather lively, as I have said. People came and went, and the very unusual proportion who were robed all in white, the frequent praying and preaching, told a political secret. Wherever this fantastic house might be situate, it was a haunt of the Wahabis, therefore a home of treason and rebellion, and therefore one of the clerks loved to observe it. When there were no visitors on the terrace, donkeys often paraded there, equipped with such housings as wealthy Arab ladies use. And presently ladies mounted, their sex distinguishable, though they sat astride, by trousers and veil, and the ugly, shapeless *ferijeh.* These demoiselles or dames rode out, but they never returned ; probably because the vision had disappeared before they got back. It was evident that the master of the house had a large harem.

About that personage the clerks could not make up their minds. Upon the one hand they thought they recognised him in a tall man who was present when the females of the household came on the terrace, as occasionally happened. It was deserted then, of course, by all males excepting this individual, who sat beneath the wall and smoked with some of the women, probably the elders. Amongst the bevy playing round, several were children and others quite young, as their lively motions suggested. They approached the man familiarly. One so privileged could only be the husband and father, or the eunuch; and the clerk's experience negatived this latter supposition. But, on the other hand, he wore a black burnoos, coloured clothes beneath it, and a head-handkerchief of the brightest tints. How should a leader of Wahabis dress himself like that?

Where this dwelling could be situate made a problem. Mr. Friar himself found time to indulge a mild curiosity. He looked up his maps and books, but they gave no suggestion. There was actually no hint to guide conjecture. Um el Jemal lies on the Arabian shore of the Red Sea, but the reflections in mirage came from every quarter. They were ruled by certain laws, no doubt immutable, like all of nature's framing; but what they could be one was more puzzled to guess the longer one's experience of them. The real boats, of which a phantom was projected into the desert, must be sailing on the west, or north-west, or south-west, if not on all these points at once. But they stood in the picture among trees and villages and caravans, which must be, the substance of them, in directions exactly opposite; unless indeed they were thrown across the Red Sea and the Egyptian desert hundreds of miles from the westward. It was mighty bewildering, and my friend gave it up.

His clerks knew nothing of science. Mirage was for them a natural feature of landscape in this lower world. But the number of Wahabis who frequented the house told that it must lie in Arabia somewhere. The elder of the two, a Mohammedan and discreet, did not want to

know too much about a spot which was evidently the
haunt of rebels and heretics. But the younger, Zohrab,
was a fanatic patriot, though a Christian. He hated the
Wahabi schismatics almost as bitterly as they hate his
own creed, but he was reluctantly inclined to think, as
do so many, that the supreme foe, the Turk, will only
be expelled by the aid of these bloodthirsty desperadoes.
He watched the house where, as he fancied, a grand
conspiracy was brewing, until it haunted him. Mixing
up together war, patriotism, politics, romance, and love,
Zohrab constructed new tales of adventure on every recur-
rence of the mirage. He had made a very distinct individuality for the Sheikh, the man in the black burnoos.
He had given him a name and provided him with a
lovely daughter, Ferideh, whom after thrilling incidents
he himself married on the day that Arab independence
was proclaimed in Damascus, and fifty thousand Turks,
including the Sultan and all his Pachas, lost their heads.
Though Zohrab was educated in Frank learning he did
not understand mercy to the Ottoman. His most
cherished wedding present would have been the false
Khalif's head.

He was a Syrian of Beyrout and a Christian, as has
been said. I picture a tall, lithe youth, small of bone,
but muscular, with large eyes and a delicate moustache ;
in short, a hero after the school-girl fancy when amiable
and composed. An æsthetic barber would have longed

for a model of Zohrab to exhibit in his shop window
had he seen him in that mood. But, if in conversation
somebody spoke well of the Turk, or alluded to the
great days past and the present degradation of the Arab,
this youth quivered and flamed like a war-horse tethered.
An Arab of pure blood is curiously like his steed in
peculiarities of nervous expression. A constant quiver
of the nostrils, an unconscious thrill of straining muscles,
an instant promptitude to take fire, are characteristic of
each. My portrait of Zohrab is but half fanciful, of
course; in drawing it I have before my eye a score of
models; amongst them, be it admitted with qualifica-
tions, that grandest of all savages I ever met, the Sheikh
'Mteyer, who betrayed his trust and did to death poor
Palmer and Gill and Charrington. But, if Zohrab was
like what that old traitor had been in youth, it was in
outward semblance only.

The stories he incessantly devised about the phantom
castle and its indwellers made pleasant fooling for Suleyman and the servants. They had no other diversion, and
they loved a tale. But all the while Zohrab was trying
seriously to discover where dwelt the chief who was
plotting for the great cause—who was also the father
of Ferideh; for his imagination had so mixed the two
threads of romance that they became one. From the
very first he had employed himself in urging the crew
of the supply-ship to make inquiries in all quarters; had

D

shown them the mirage, made a drawing of the castle,
with exhaustive notes, and offered a moderate reward.
The vessel hailed from Sûf, a very small Arabian port,
which desert Bedouins seldom visited; but it was the
only channel of communication with the world. The
Arabs were interested, of course, in a matter which had
the savour of magic; but for many succeeding months
they brought no suggestion that would bear scrutiny.
At length the Reis reported with delight substantial
news. A Bedouin, calling at Sûf, recognised the sketch
at a glance. It represented El Husn, the fortress-palace
of Sheikh Abou 'l Nasr (Father of Victory), which lies
four days' journey across the desert from Sûf.

With this fact in hand, the Reis asked no more. Who
had not heard of El Husn and the Sheikh Abou 'l
Nasr? Every Arab is familiar with those names. Zohrab
had heard them often, and he asked particulars which
any of the crew could furnish, subject to correction.
The Sheikh had been a Wahabi in youth, and taken part
in the grand struggles which would have broken up the
Turkish empire had the fanatics been less tigerish, and
Ibrahim Pasha, the Arnaout, been less shrewd. After
the collapse of that great movement, the Sheikh Abou 'l
Nasr retired to his fortress with his share of the spoils of
Mecca, Medina, and a hundred shrines plundered by
the Wahabis. When Ibrahim was preparing to follow
thither, Mehemet Ali recalled him for graver work.

Abou 'l Nasr rested quiet awhile, maturing his plans, and giving himself to the study of magic, in which he was proficient beyond all men. When the Wahabis recovered heart, he was ready, with patriotic devotion unaffected, with treasure beyond counting, and supreme wisdom. All Arab people consulted him as an oracle of God. The Sheikh Abou 'l Nasr said, " Fight here! Remove that man! Keep quiet there!" and always, when his command was followed, advantage ensued. He had ceased to be a Wahabi, smoking and drinking coffee, and doing what he pleased. The Arabs generally thought none the worse of him for that; and the Wahabis, though in their hearts resenting his apostacy, dared not quarrel with their great ally.

This detailed information stirred Zohrab to intense excitement. His daily thought and nightly dream were of visiting the Sheikh and offering his sword for freedom —and Ferideh. If the patriot chief were as tolerant as rumour reluctantly declared, his creed would be no bar to service. Whilst Zohrab was working himself up to action, a resolve was precipitated by events. His superiors invited him to join the Telegraph Service of Egypt, and they made so sure of acceptance that they despatched his successor the same day, giving Zohrab a month to arrange his affairs. That decided him. When the new clerk arrived by steamer, the supply-ship chanced

to be in port. Its return voyage carried this romantic
youth, his pony, and his carpet-bag to Sûf.

Disguised as a well-to-do Arab of the lower class he
drew little notice. Sûf is a miserable place, inhabited
by people calling themselves Bedouin, who live by fishing
and petty piracy. They also grow the most attenuated
crops recognised by science. But it is a central station
for feeding telegraph posts and lighthouses. A company of Turkish soldiers garrisons it, and a good
number of people, such as Zohrab seemed to be, is
drawn thither on business. He found his way to the
Medhafe, put up his pony, and visited the coffee-house
after a frugal meal. It was a horrid little den, windowless,
black all over with dirt and smoke. Coffee was dis-
pensed by a one-eyed negro, in cups that had not been
washed for months. Zohrab had fallen into English
ways so far, at least, that this return to native habits
sickened him.

An old officer came bustling in, and demanded papers;
he should have boarded the vessel, but he was asleep.
Zohrab assumed an air of dignity, and accompanied him
to the Medhafe. When the Captain read that this
stranger was an Effendi in Government employ he
became anxiously deferential—awkward investigations
impending! But Zohrab let it be understood that for
grave and secret purposes he was instructed to visit El

Husn, and asked for a guide. The officer looked startled.

· " Every man in this accursed place knows the way except my soldiers. The people arc rebels and heretics every one! No guide would serve you without the Sheikh's approval, and that perhaps you do not care to ask publicly? I thought not! Then, if I ordered one of these brutes to accompany you, I might as well send a burying party as a rear guard."

" I could go alone if the road is easy."

" Easy enough, if you met no evil-minded persons. You are acquainted with the Wahabi signs? No? Then it is madness to proceed, Effendi! "

" We were told that the Sheikh had abandoned his heresy."

" He? he's an infidel; may his father's name be cursed! But those who go back and forward to El Husn are nearly all Wahabis, and it's fifty to one you come across them."

" Can you not teach me the pass-words? "

" Oh!" said the Captain, suddenly blustering, " I've not neglected that duty. Wahabis have taken me for one of themselves—Allah forgive my sin! If you can recollect all I teach you, Effendi, there is no danger."

So Zohrab learned his part, carefully overhauled his baggage, removing all that could raise suspicion, handed it to the officer for keeping, and stretched himself upon the earth among the fleas. Then he stole away by moonlight. The soldiers, warned, let him pass the gate.

The first stage was long, but easy and not dangerous. Nevertheless to be alone in the desert is terrible. Not a shadow in the landscape, save the traveller's own, which his horse tramples wearily with shuffling, noiseless feet. When the moon sank Zohrab dismounted, waiting the dawn with his bridle in his hand. That is a solemn pause, even if no danger threatens. The still night is busy with sounds, soft and mysterious, high up in air. They gather sometimes for a rush as of a mighty wind, but no breath stirs. Then from the darkness comes a sudden clang, ringing and souorous, that makes the lonely watcher start to his arms. Zohrab had never known or had forgotten the rustling murmur of sand-grouse taking their early flight in thousands; the signals of wild geese and the sharp, metallic cry of zikzak plovers. Um el Jemal was too barren even for those strong fliers.

The dawn broke at last, and he resumed his way, followed it whilst the sun climbed higher and higher and pressed down on him like liquid heat. The sand-hills rolled away on either side so smoothly monotonous that their crests blended into one another, and the world seemed flat. No landmarks but the crags on the horizon, at whose feet the mirage glistened. The vegetation was all burnt and sapless, showing the sand through its spiky, brittle twigs. No colour there but

greys and browns and dusty yellows; but now and again
a bone gleamed white, and Zohrab's high-strung nerves
regarded it with a prescient thrill.

It was noon when he reached the termination of this
stage. The pious soul who dug or restored a muddy,
blessed puddle here had been commemorated by a Wely;
but the Wahabis had passed that way, and, after drinking, had overthrown their benefactor's modest shrine for
a superstitious monument. Zohrab plunged into the
evil-smelling pond beside his horse. Then, after the
meal, he lay upon the glowing sand to sleep. Evening
chills roused him suddenly, and they set off again.
The second stage was safely traversed, but with worse
alarms, for Zohrab thought he had lost his way. He
reached the well early, drank, ate, and lay down.
Wakened in the moonlight by the shrill neigh of his
horse, he saw a little cavalcade approaching.

In the desert one cannot hide, and Zohrab lay still.
The strangers drew up, looked at him, and dispersed to
their camp duties. They were not Bedouins, for no
camel followed them. After attending to their horses
they sat down to eat, but two armed men quietly
stationed themselves beside Zohrab. The moon vanished,
but in the circle round a smouldering fire torches were
lit. He thought out the situation, rose like a man from
sleep, and advanced with salaams. All eyed him gravely,
but did not reply. He tried a Wahabi signal, which

gained instant recognition. " Sal Khayr ! " said the chief courteously, piously avoiding the name of Allah. Zohrab sat beside this chief, and the questioning began, but much less eager than is usual. His story was pat, for he had little to conceal beside his creed ; and, whilst their meal proceeded, a frugal repast of bread and rice, the Wahabis listened with grave politeness. At the end all rose with a low ejaculation of thankfulness to Allah. Zohrab rose also. " Bind that spy ! " the chief commanded. In an instant Zohrab was stripped and tied, thrown upon the earth, and left there.

The camp did not stir early. At the hour of morning-prayer men released the prisoner, brought the carpet which he had thoughtfully provided, and went to their own devotions. Zohrab ought, I know, to have refused, and the story should end at this point with a harrowing narrative of his martyrdom. But my hero was not formed of martyr's stuff. He knelt and stood, folded his hands and spread them, touched the ground with his forehead, and so on. As nobody watched him closely, the performance did not cause suspicion. In the heat of the morning they started, Zohrab in the midst. To his questions the Wahabis replied very briefly or not at all. Indeed they scarcely spoke among themselves, and no stronger proof could be alleged of the influence religion has on character. That Arabs should be silent and self-contained seems incredible, but the Wahabis habitually display this phenomenon. Now and then, after long brooding over earthly wickedness and heavenly joys, a warrior cried sharply " Lah-Ullah!" seldom completing the formula. And others would take it up, half unconsciously.

At the halt Zohrab approached the chief, who heard his reproaches unmoved. " If you were going to visit Sheikh Abou 'l Nasr, you have no cause of complaint. I will conduct you to him!" No more words would he give, but the tone meant death.

The next march brought them within view of El Husn, so the Wahabis declared. Zohrab looked with all his power. Suppose that this place, to visit which he had probably sacrificed his life, were not the substance of his mirage dreams after all! So it appeared in truth, and his heart sickened. In the quarter where El Husn lay, as the guides alleged, nothing was visible but piles of crags; and there were no mountains in the vision. Zohrab keenly scrutinised the plain, but it lay yellow and bare to the very foot of those yellow barren hills. He had thrown away his life!

When still far from them, the party diverged towards a solitary mound. Two Arabs who had been lying on its crest rose to their feet and vanished. Presently they re-appeared on horseback, galloping from the further side. At a furious pace some young Wahabis rode to meet them, whirling guns but not firing. All went on

together to the well, talking eagerly. The remarks
Zohrab overheard suggested that action was at hand.
After spending the night at this halt, the Wahabis rode
in a straight course for the hills. The sun was high
when they reached a narrow gorge, so deep and so abrupt
that it lay in shadow almost cool whilst the crags glowed
and burnt above. Massive sungas, works of rough stone
piled up, flanked the entrance, and at every point of
vantage above the winding road such defences were
repeated. The Wahabis looked at them with interest,
and the elders told legends of fight this gorge had witnessed.

A mile or two beyond its mouth the fortifications
became continuous. Suddenly a valley opened, with
palms and green specks of fields, and huts and black
tents. At the further end, several miles away, shone
the white dome of a mosque. And in front appeared
the house of the mirage, on a terrace of the mountain.
Zohrab gasped! It was no trick of the eye! In real
stone and mortar, there stood the gateway and the
battlements and the windows he had daily beheld four
hundred miles away! There was the Sheikh in his
black burnoos and bright handkerchief. There were
the children playing on the terrace. Zohrab forgot the
peril in which he lay. What could harm the man to
whom such a miracle was vouchsafed!

Men clothed all in white came galloping from the

tents, and loudly welcomed their friends. Sheikh and girls vanished. Across the flat, up the hill-side, the Wahabis advanced. As Zohrab came out upon the terrace he wondered whether Suleyman was watching now and smoking by the station door. About this hour the mirage appeared at Um el Jemal.

Servants took the horses of the chiefs, who went in, whilst their followers lay in the house-shadow, eating, dreaming, and sleeping; so, many a time, had Zohrab seen the terrace occupied. Hour passed after hour, but he could neither eat nor sleep. Then two burly blacks called him. A few steps inside the arch, the roadway wheeled at right angles where a portcullis hung on rusty chains. Several meutrières in either wall allowed the garrison to make a last resistance, behind the portcullis, though the gate were forced. Under the further arch Zohrab saw a courtyard with stalky flowers and channels for irrigation; beyond it, painted arcades, where sat the Wahabi chiefs in their snowy robes. But his conductors opened a narrow door in the thickness of the wall, and threw him in. The dreary place he entered was a guardroom, used as a prison. Light entered dimly from the meutrières for a few hours on each side of noon. Eight or ten scarecrows in Turkish uniform lay round. Their eyes, feverishly bright, shone in the gloom. Zohrab addressed them eagerly, but they did not reply.

In a few moments the Wahabis passed, and smiled

grimly as they looked in. People came and went
through the archway. Then dusk crept over the fetid
den, though free men outside called it early afternoon.
After some hours of impotent storming, Zohrab grew
hungry, and asked his fellow-prisoners when food was
served. A big-boned Turk, who had been fat and jovial
perhaps in other days, answered bitterly from the darkness, "Those who enter here learn to live without
eating!" It was excitement rather than hunger which
Zohrab had suffered. But at the threat of starvation he
suddenly famished. The Turks would not answer again.

The prison had long been black as a mine when servants arrived with torches. The negroes entered first,
bound Zohrab, and threw him into a corner. Then the
others brought in food, a tiny mess of rice and a slab
of unleavened bread for each prisoner—saving the last.
They laughed to hear his cries for food and curses.
When all the Turks had done, the slaves unbound
Zohrab, and took the light away.

It is not strange nor painful for an Arab to fast a day
and night. Under ordinary circumstances he will sleep
through longer abstinence. But Zohrab's fervid imagination was moved here. That the realisation of his wildest
hopes should mean a fate like this was hideous, monstrous. He could not sleep. Standing by a loophole
he implored each passer-by to tell the Sheikh this and
that. An endless time it seemed before the show of

torches and the clash of the big doors told that real
night had begun, and an endless time of horror succeeded before they clashed again, opening in the dawn
which would not reach that prison-house for hours.
Perhaps he had slept, but it was the sleep that fevers.
All through the pitchy blackness, waking or dreaming,
he had seen the white eyes of his companions, who had
learned to live without food. Sharp pains transfixed his
body; blood rushed to his head with splitting vehemence
and left it frozen. Zohrab was still far from delirium,
but he heard familiar voices and raved in answer. The
Turks watched him anxiously as the dim light spread.
Horrid experience warned them that this new comer
might do mischief before he grew used to starve. No
one else heeded him, save by a mocking word thrown in.

Evening was heralded by its chills. Zohrab had
fallen beneath the loophole when the blacks entered
suddenly, and threw themselves upon him. In spite of
his desperate struggling they fixed the ropes, and food
was served to the others. Then they held the prisoner
firmly whilst a slave untied him, and when the last knot
was loosed they pitched him headlong with all their
strength. When Zohrab recovered his feet they were
laughing outside.

Such, then, was to be his fate—death by hunger, with
torment added! After a mood of helpless agony furious
raving got hold upon him. The Turks gathered in a

feeble heap to defend themselves. At midnight, or near
it, men came with lights. "The Sheikh summons you!"
they said, and led him out. That calmed him. Quietly
he followed across the moonlit courtyard, through dusky
alcoves, to an inner room, where sat an old but vigorous
chief, warrior and statesman every inch. He smiled,
took the narguilleh from his lips, and told the slaves to go.

"Health to you, my son! Sit down!'

Zohrab was trying to collect his thoughts for this
supreme crisis. But on the first effort of will he felt
them escape, fly round, transform themselves, and re-
appear, the same but in new shapes. They would not
be held. Frightened, awestruck, by this revolt, Zohrab
fell on the divan, without even kicking off his shoes.
The Sheikh started in surprise. That act told more
than he had looked to hear. The stranger was a
Christian and a "personage." He smiled in scornful
pity, but without change of tone asked whence Zohrab
came.

The youth began his story, very slightly and innocently falsified. He described how the fame of the great
Arab had reached him at Beyrout. But in this early
stage his attention wandered. He found himself talking
of home, of his mother and sisters—pulled up confused—
began to tell of the mirage, and described Um el
Jemal, with a minute but flighty sketch of his English
superior.

The Sheikh smoked and listened pleasantly. He observed, "You do not mention your father—may his soul have found peace!"

"He was killed by the Turks!" Zohrab passionately shouted. "When people told me of Sheikh Abou 'l Nasr, I said, He is my father and my lord! I will go and fight the Turk with him! Oh Sheikh, they starve me, and I could not get word with you! My blood is flame and my head a millstone with lightning in it! I am dying!"

"Who told you the way hither?"

"The Reis of our store-boat. I showed him your house and your image, and the Wahabis who came, and Ferideh——"

"You showed him?" began the Sheikh, astonished. "Who is Ferideh?"

"Your daughter! Oh, pardon me! I don't know what I say!" He threw himself along the divan, hysterically sobbing.

The Sheikh watched him thoughtfully, then clapped his hands and ordered bread and wine. Zohrab kissed his garments in the Oriental manner, not practised by this semi-Frank since childhood. He devoured the small cake, and looked for more. "Drink!" the chief commanded, and he swallowed the measure in one gulp.

"Now finish your tale, my son!"

" My head is whirling ! I do not remember ! "

" You have told me you are a Christian of Beyrout, employed in the service of the Porte. You invoked certain powers to reach me. What are they ? "

" Powers? You misunderstood, Sheikh, or I talked foolishness."

" Nay, my son ! " Then looking fixedly at Zohrab, and making strange signs, he spoke in an unknown tongue. The youth felt a deeper thrill of alarm as the thought struck him that his mind was giving way. He sat with eyes dilated, panting.

After several essays, the Sheikh paused in bewilderment. " What your power is I know not, my son, but it is inferior to mine. Instruct me, therefore ! "

" I swear I do not know what you refer to, Sheikh."

A sharp clang of brass resounded, and the negroes appeared. " Throw this Turk over the cliff ! " the Sheikh commanded; and in an instant Zohrab was overpowered and dragged out, yelling defiance and entreaties, through the archway to the moonlit platform. Lights gleamed at the window, heads appeared far above. Upon the very brink, Zohrab heard the Sheikh: " Tell the truth ! "

" By the God we both worship, I have told the truth ! "

" One—lift him on the parapet ! Two—his feet ! Throw his feet over. Well ? "

But Zohrab did not reply. He was looking to Heaven with prayers.

"Father—father! not before our eyes!" cried a girl's voice from above. And Zohrab saw a lovely face outlined in the moonbeams at a window.

"Lift him back! Put him in a room to sleep." And presently Zohrab, dazed and trembling in great shivers, lay on a carpet, with meat and wine beside him. It was long before he slept, and his dreams at first were of a thousand dreadful deaths. Towards morning he fell into heavy slumber.

The Sheikh sat beside him when he woke. After a moment's perplexity Zohrab sprang to his feet ready for a struggle.

"I have taken counsel. Now tell what marvels you please, and I believe!"

"You know I spoke the truth?"

"I know that and more. But explain how you saw me and my house if it was not magic?"

In the sudden brightness of his spirits a question rose to Zohrab's lips why the occult powers had not cleared up this mystery also. But he refrained, and told about the mirage. The chief was interested, but uneasy. If his dwelling could be spied on hundreds of miles away, why not his defences? Zohrab reassured him partly, and he said in conclusion: "Now, Sheikh, will you enlist an infidel?"

E

" If I enlist the Wahabi tiger for a good end, how can
I refuse a Christian dog?" he answered, smiling. " But
those who would be served by men must lower themselves to serve prejudice and passion. Call yourself
Aghile Agha of Beyrout! I put this garrison in your
charge, for other business absorbs my time. Lie quiet
to-day. I will send you books."

The Sheikh's library was small, but characteristic:
some poets, some works of unintelligible necromancy,
the campaigns of Zenghis Khan, and the autobio-
graphies of his great descendants, Babar and Ackbar.
The philosophy of these Moghul emperors, though
timidly rendered by an orthodox translator, had evidently impressed the Sheikh. In a dozen loose notes
Zohrab found its expression, which may be summarised
briefly: " There is no God but one; the prophets of all
creeds are his servants. There are devils beyond
counting, but the man wise and just can sway them."

Next day Zohrab took command of the garrison. It
was no honorary charge. Every dweller in the valley
capable of bearing arms was a retainer of the Sheikh.
Fifty of them in rotation served at the castle, and all
mustered for review at intervals. Drill is abhorrent to
the Arab as to the Turk; but these men, mostly veterans
of fight, performed to admiration the simple tactics
necessary for their warfare. They knew their place in
the ranks, and would keep it; they would advance or

retire as they got the word, obedient though not compact. Mechanical movements are not required in the
desert.

For awhile messengers and mysterious visitors arrived
more thickly. Every day armed men encamped upon
the terrace—Wahabi or other—whilst their chiefs took
counsel within. Owing to this invasion doubtless the
women of the household never came out on that side.
They had another space for airing, and Zohrab knew
they used it. In his room sometimes he heard merry
voices and scoldings, and the wail of little girls whose
ears are boxed. His apartment had windows, high above
the floor, that looked on the harem playground. Zohrab
was sorely tempted to climb up, and it was not the certainty of death if caught that checked him. He listened
for an individual voice that should speak to his heart,
and sometimes he thought to recognise it. Remembering
that, if he could not see Ferideh, she could see him at any
time, he kept himself neat and soldierlike.

After awhile the visits became less frequent. For a
day, then two days, no cavalcade was signalled from the
desert mound which Zohrab remembered so painfully.
He heard the men discussing this change, from which
they drew conclusions. One morning he sought the
Sheikh, who was pondering and reckoning as usual.

" My father, you won the name of the Victorious in
youth. Full of honours and renown you may rest at

ease, directing those who fight. But we are young!
Give me the untried warriors in your tents, and let
us go."

" Take two hundred, and march on Sûf. You may
have an opportunity to prove yourselves men, for the
Turks are reinforced to day. Hold that place to the
death, my son !"

" Do the Turks project a landing in force ? "

" You have a shrewd intelligence, Aghile Agha.
Yes! When they have put out the fire I have raised
they will march on El Husn. The result is in God's
hand. He has given me many years of peace."

" You speak as if the cause would certainly be
defeated, Sheikh ! Why do you despair ?"

" I do not despair, but I know. The time is not
revealed. We should hold out more than a year in the
South."

" Then we should hold out for ever if you took the
field, Sheikh," said Zohrab, timidly.

" No; I can command the Wahabis from a distance,
but I cannot serve with them, nor they with me."

" I understand. But if you know, that with such
instruments victory is impossible, why employ them,
Sheikh? I ask the foolish question of your wisdom."

" My son, the mason takes a rough tool to split the
stone which he will cut and fashion with tempered steel.
There are old guns buried in Sûf; the people will shew

them you. Fortify, mount them, have all prepared. When the time comes I will march thither with two thousand men."

" It is impossible the Turks should come by land."

" What Ibrahim Pasha dared not try Turks will not venture! And now," the Sheikh added with pleasant significance, " does Zohrab Effendi still dream of Ferideh?"

Zohrab coloured furiously, but he tried to answer in the same tone, " Aghile Agha dreams no more!"

The Sheikh smiled now. " Then let us look for Ferideh together with our eyes open."

Zohrab was transfixed. Such invitations are not unknown in legend or even in history, but those who gave them were reckless debauchees, or despots above the canons of propriety. The Sheikh waited with a dignified kindness as unlike the air of a drunkard as of a madman. Zohrab still hesitated.

" Why, my son, if I visited you in Beyrout would you not present your sisters to me? And if I visited the Queen of Frangistan would she not show me all the ladies of her realm? Are we Moslem beasts or our women unclean?"

" Oh, Sheik!" cried Zohrab, stepping forward, " there are no Moslem like you!"

" Nay, you do not know. Very many good Moslem

have broken a law, suited perhaps to the time, but foolish
now, to secure the happiness of those they love."

In speaking he led the way through bare stone passages with massive doors at every turning, useful if the
walls were carried by a rush of Bedouins, but valueless
against a disciplined foe. They came out in a grated
chamber, where girlish voices sounded close. Zohrab's
heart beat wildly as he took place behind the Sheikh and
looked. Five girls of different ages were seated on the
ground, vociferously playing at some game. Younger
children toddled about, and three women sat languid in
the shade. "Not one son!" the Sheikh bitterly muttered, but he recovered his good humour on the instant.
"Now, Zohrab Effendi, is Ferideh there?"

"Oh yes, father. That is she—the loveliest of all!"

The Sheikh laughed softly. "You must be more
explicit to a parent. Which is the loveliest of all?"

"Oh, you are mocking. She in the gold scarf and
blue trousers, with the snood of coins in her loose hair.
See! she has fallen over laughing. Her slipper has
dropped off. What a lovely foot!"

"That, Ferideh? Regard the others! They are
older and more beautiful!"

"Not for me. Oh, Sheikh, our souls are one!"

"But it was not your Ferideh who called that night
when you fancied yourself already dead!"

"She was not there or she was asleep! Oh, father, you will not break your word!"

"No! Perhaps it is best. My little Zireh will not be impatient whilst her betrothed is absent in the wars. Then let us go."

"You are displeased. Believe me I would choose another if I could."

The Sheikh laughed so loud that his old walls re-echoed. "I see how impossible it is now you are awake, Aghile Agha. Take comfort; the child is yours when these troubles are past, and you return."

"Oh, my father! Will you tell her she is destined for me?"

"No; for Zireh is young, too young for trouble; and no man can tell his own fate or another's when balls are flying. But you shall see her again the day you leave."

"Allah will be kind to you, Sheikh, who are so kind to men. When shall I go?"

"Choose your companions and bring the list to me."

All was ready in three days. As Zohrab stood upon the terrace after a last parade, the Sheikh took him by the arm and led the way to a chamber which he entered first. A little figure sprang from the divan, in a whirl of hair, to throw itself into his arms.

"Is this proper conduct in the presence of a stranger,

you wild gazelle?" said the chief, laughing. "Put on your veil."

Pouting and blushing, but not much abashed, Zirch covered her face; the proprieties becoming a young girl were not yet familiar. Zohrab saw again the features, lean and clear but not sharp, the eyes so dark and shadowed that light sparkled in them as on the facet of a black diamond, the pink purple mouth; the slender figure too, outlined in a robe of thinnest silk, crossed on the bosom, tightly swathed by a scarf upon the hips. Zireh looked at him when the veil was adjusted, with the boldness of petulant childhood, discontentedly, askance; but the young man's expression had such eager fire that she dropped her gaze, and raised it angrily, and looked to her father, bewildered.

"This youth, Zireh, is Aghile Agha, upon whose courage and discretion the safety of us all may depend. Now leave us, child."

Zireh looked puzzled as she withdrew, with a touch of her forehead and a bow to the stranger. At the door she glanced up under her thick lashes, caught his eye again, and hastily went out.

"I know—I know," the Sheikh ejaculated, "I hold a hostage dearer to you than life! Now to business. Three days ago I dismissed my Turkish prisoners secretly. You will hear from them on your road, I doubt not. When the swine have delivered Sûf into your hands, give them five hundred liras and help them to get away."

Had I dared to violate truth I should have liked to record that Zohrab's first act after gaining favour had been to procure the release of these fellow-prisoners. So an Englishman or a Christian would have behaved towards his bitterest personal foe perhaps. But my characters are Arab, with Arab ways of virtue as of error. Zohrab had given the Turks no thought of kindliness. He said, " Have they strength to reach Sûf ? "

" Oh, I have fed them till they are lusty as young camels, and Turks can always find strength for the devil's work."

Zohrab started next day. At the second halt he received a communication. Yielding to alarm and greed, the commandant betrayed his post. Before dawn next day the Arabs crept to a gate which they found unlocked, and carried the town. The Turkish soldiers fought and died; the superior officers surrendered, took the wages of their treachery, and embarked in the afternoon.

Then Zohrab began his work with zeal, repairing the old fortifications, building new, and mounting guns. Fortunately, the Turks were occupied down south, and their vessels only threw a dozen shells into the place in passing. Zohrab had a thousand cares and projects, but

very few hands to execute his schemes. Time went by
quickly, month after month. News arrived constantly
from El Husn, and rumours came by sea. The rebellion
followed its usual course. The Arabs, mustering silently,
overpowered small Turkish garrisons, swept the edge of
the cultivated land, and mastered the oases. The enemy
concentrated, yielding whole provinces to the rush.
Then the reaction set in. The wilder people of the
desert tired, and made off with their plunder. The
Wahabis, unrestrained, sacked mosques, overthrew
shrines, murdered priests, and persecuted the orthodox.
When the Turks began to move, no force remained to
oppose them face to face. Desperate forays were made
in their rear, and small parties were cut off, but district
by district they regained the country. After twelve
months, though the struggle was not finished, nor will
be so long as the Turkish dominion lasts, it had ceased
to be war. Then, if the Sheikh were well-advised by
his agents or his familiar spirits, the peril of El Husn
was nigh.

In his letters Zohrab had not breathed a hint of the
matter nearest his heart. And the Sheikh, though
liberal in his ideas, might have thought it shocking to
mention a girl. One day pressing news arrived. The
Turks were collecting an army to reduce the Wahabi
stronghold of Wady Afre, as they gave out. But Abou
'l Nasr was assured that they purposed attacking him.

On an advance by land nobody had counted. He had strong hopes of resisting successfully behind his desert barrier, but as a measure of precaution he sent his harem and valuables to Sûf. Solemnly the old chief commended them to Allah and his friend. Two days afterwards the caravan arrived, a score of women and children, with many camel-loads of property. The men who guarded it returned, leaving a few veterans to guard their master's family. Zohrab gave up his quarters to the ladies; amongst their dark eyes, still swollen with tears and alarm, he recognised Zireh's. But they did not look at him.

Of all the weary months of Zohrab's exile it was the longest that followed this event. He did not once see the girl now sleeping under his roof, and the merest propriety forbade him to seek communication with her, had any means come to hand. The Sheikh reported almost daily, and his news, though calmly told, was alarming. The party he had sent to destroy the wells upon the route the Turks must follow had been driven back by Bedouins. The schemes for a diversion had failed. None but his immediate retainers stood by the Sheikh, and the enemy were getting into motion. Forgetting all else in a generous enthusiasm, Zohrab begged to be relieved; that he might conquer or die with his benefactor, but the refusal was peremptory. At the same time the Sheikh wrote to his head-wife, Zireh's mother.

She came to the lieutenant, veiled and weeping, and
put into his hand the letter she could not read. He
pressed it to his lips, and brow, and heart. The Sheikh
enjoined upon his wife to obey Zohrab as she did himself, and to love him as her son; for he, as Zireh's husband, should be recognised as the head of the family.

"You to be our son! You!—a stranger who keeps
here in safety whilst my lord is struggling for life!" So
the fiery old dame went on. Zohrab read all the letters
to her, and at length she owned with sobs that the
Sheikh was wise; for the children's sake she would obey.

For a whole week there was silence. Scouts despatched
did not return. The garrison became demoralized, and
every night there were desertions. Zohrab made his
arrangements for the worst. The Sheikh had supplied
him with ample funds. He chartered the store-ship,
which no longer supplied Um el Jemal, and equipped it
for female passengers. Then he loaded the treasure and
baggage, in charge of trusty veterans, and waited.
At length two horsemen rode in with a brief letter.
After two days' fight, the Sheikh reported, the passes
had been forced. Whilst he wrote, the Turkish column
was pouring into the valley. Zohrab was solemnly
commanded to take ship at once and sail for Aden,
where, if by miracle the Sheikh escaped, he would
rejoin his family. But he bade them all good-bye, and
commended them to the merciful God.

The evil news had spread before Zohrab gained the
street. His soldiers were looting on every side. He
ran to his former quarters, and shouted for the head-
wife. Frightened slaves shut the door in his face.
Time pressed cruelly. As the soldiers gathered their
load of worthless plunder—each religiously avoiding
houses where he individually had eaten bread—they
made off for the desert; and as their numbers lessened
the townspeople became more threatening. Zohrab
hammered at the gate, and some score of Arabs swiftly
collected, full of mischief and revenge. Then he shouted
for Zireh; and suddenly the door opened—she stood
shrinking before him. " Where is your mother?
Quick ! " But the throng behind crushed in, and the
girl sank fainting in his arms. Zohrab shot down the
foremost, and, as the others pressed back, he caught up
his bride, ran to the zenana—and found it empty!
Dropping Zireh on the floor, he hurried out. But the
courtyard and the passages were now full of Arabs,
shrieking, yelling, rushing hither and thither. If there
were women's cries in that tumult they could not be
heard. Zohrab did not hesitate! Nothing remained
but to die, since he had failed to save. But, as he
gathered his weight for the rush, girlish arms caught
him fast.

" Oh, save me, Aghile Agha ! Save me ! Save me ! "
Zohrab looked. When love pleads with youth, honour

which commands to refuse and die must be stronger
than is found in the Arab's fiery blood.  Zohrab carried
her back, lifted her through a window, and they ran to
the shore.  There a boat was waiting, with half-a-
dozen of the guard.  Zohrab took four, and returned to
meet the whole body of townsmen, armed now and triumphant.  The struggle was brief and desperate.  With
one surviving comrade, Zohrab fought his way back.
He gained the ship, which set sail for Aden.

There Zireh was placed in charge of mission ladies
before her bodyguard knew what was doing.  A handsome draft on the Sheikh's treasure comforted their
bodies, not their souls.  They would have liked to raise
a riot, but the police damped their ardour.  When
Zireh's eyes had been opened to some elementary ideas
of life in this world and that to come, Zohrab confessed
himself a Christian.  The surprise was not painful; for
experience of English ways had shown the girl that
Christians are not unclean and miserable outcasts of
humanity.  So soon as he assured her that the Sheikh
knew his religion, Zireh was quite content; and in no
long time she professed herself a Christian—a bad one,
I fear, regarded dogmatically, but gentle, compassionate,
and pure.

They remained twelve months at Aden; but no news
came of the Sheikh or his family.  When that date was
passed, Zohrab spoke of marriage, and he met no plea for

delay—that would not occur to an Arab maiden if, by such unheard-of chance as this, she were left to speak for herself. The ceremony was performed in the garrison church, amid such universal interest, such attentions to the pretty bride from the highest quarters, and such military display as would alone have made it the happiest event of their lives. A week afterwards they sailed for India, and Zohrab is now high in the Telegraph Service of the Nizam, where he finds a few Arabs to talk with and many to avoid.

# LYING IN WAIT.

This description of a " Man-eater " crouched in ambush on a jungle-path was furnished to *The Illustrated Sporting and Dramatic News* in explanation of an engaving.

" Your drawing is admirably spirited, and—a rarer quality—correct.  The artist has made a careful study of feline attitude and  expression.  The head down-pressed below straining shoulders, the lips pendent with excitement at the jowl, rigidly curled over the front teeth, the eyes shining round and clear as lamps, the hind-quarters gathered for the spring, are true as beautiful.  I feel sure that, if the tail were not hidden, we should see it gently waving at the tip.  As  a  general rule, of  course, the man-eater is old, faded of colour, mangy.  So much had been observed even in  Pliny's day; but there are exceptions, of which an artist has the  right to  avail  himself. The one criticism  which I diffidently put forward has reference to the stripes upon  the belly.  Are they quite accurate?  I do not raise  objection, nevertheless, for every one who has tried to draw  a  tiger  without model has learned how unfaithful is memory or preconceived idea to recall its graceful marking.

" No less happy is the delineation of the dâk-runner. One would not pronounce what type or nationality is intended, but the expression of a man of low caste, such as are these runners, is truthfully caught. Trotting and shuffling through the jungle, this poor fellow sees before his path the white rag upon a pole, which warns him that a burra bagh sahib has lately made a victim close at hand. Not manfully by our ideas, but steadily and honestly he will push on—the tears and sweat running down his pallid face, eyes rolling, mouth agape and dry. He makes an inarticulate moaning as he goes, yelling now and again, propitiating the demon with slavish prayers. At a sudden noise his heart stops, as with a crash, and he falls prone. All the while his fingers, cramped but trembling, jingle the rings upon his lati. Still, somehow, he gets over the ground, and his bag is delivered safely at the next dâk-office. Nay, more ; he will return to-morrow, undergoing the same terrors, braving the same fate.

" Unless it befall him on the way, as your artist has represented. That dâk-runner is a dead man ! His wife, poor soul, is unromantic and sordid, harsh of tongue probably, despised by those canny people of her village who are well assured from which limb of Brahma's body they may claim their illustrious descent. But there will be compassion for her when the hours go by, and her husband still delays beyond his time. Presently, strangers

F

arriving in the dusk will report fresh signs of evil under the white flag—blood and broken branches and shreds of clothing. They have not delayed to look, whilst the darkness gathered round. But those deep round footprints in the moist earth, that trail of a heavy object dragged through the corinda bushes headlong, are marks that have but one significance. Then the widow bursts out howling and tears her face. The affrighted screaming children swarm about her. Never will they find their parent's corpse to burn with the holy rites, and his ghost will haunt them. All those kindly people sympathise with neighbours smitten with an awful curse, and they display their feelings so far as caste will permit. And, meantime, the patel draws up his report for the Zillah-Collector-Sahib.

" Everybody knows how it happened, and so do we. The dâk-runner snatched his staff, and clashed the rings thereon incessantly, pounding it upon the soil. For an instant the tiger paused. But he had heard that sound before, and it had not wrought him harm. He let the postman hurry by, glancing right and left with eyes distended that saw not. Then, with a roar, not grand like a lion's, but as terrible to hear, he sprang. A blow of the right paw, quick as thought, heavy as an axe, dashed the man's head upon the claws outstretched to catch it. As he tumbled, another pat broke in the skull, and the tiger lay along his prostrate body growling, lashing his

tail from side to side. No word had the victim uttered—
'Ai, ai!' he cried in agony, as the death-blow fell.
Presently, when all was quiet, the tiger moved, gripping
his prey by any limb convenient, and trailing it to the
darkest shade, whence came the noise of crunching and
rustling and rasping of the bones; with starts and snarls
of fierce alarm.

"I once saw a corpse brought in, that of a man I
knew, killed by a tiger. It was a sight to recollect with
shuddering, so hideously strange. This poor wretch
went out to track the brute. I met a small procession
in the road. Attended by a throng of awe-struck natives,
the body was carried on a charpoy, under a cloth. I
raised the covering and started, sick with horrified surprise. Many dreadful sights have I beheld since then,
but nothing which equalled that in unnatural ghastliness.
The wretched face was not injured. Dark plastered
lines of blood traversed the features, but they stood out
unmutilated. The long moustache passed behind the
ears, and, knotted on the crown, had its accustomed curl;
but the head lay lower than the shoulders! In place of
rising from chin to forehead it sloped back! I could
not hope to make a reader understand the effect of that
hideous and shocking reversal of all laws.

"When we came to examine—I, at least, had not the
nerve—we found that the tiger had struck with his
right paw outspread, carrying away the back part of the
F 2

skull, and leaving, so fragile is the Hindoo structure, jagged intervals between the claws. The blow had descended plumb, not sideways, as is the habit, for the left paw had torn the shoulder on its upper surface.

"If the use of the right hand by man be purely matter of convention, why do all animals, so far as I know, strike by preference with the right paw, and grasp or return the object with the left? I should think, in two out of three cases where facts have been recorded, the telling blow was given by the right limb, whilst the left steadied or threw back the object. I incline to think that when the smaller felines leap upon an animal, twice in three times they bite the neck on the right side, whilst forcing the victim's head downwards and in by pressure of the left paw on the nose. If this be so, it would seem that both the striking and biting creatures instinctively use the right hand.

"No class of men furnishes so much food for tigers as the dâk-runner. All beasts of prey have the instinct to observe the time and places where a meal may be secured with regularity and safety. The wells by lonely villages, the roads used by jungle-cutters, are particularly favoured by the man-eater. If he be too old, or indolent, or stupid, or decrepid to find an unmolested hunting-ground of this sort, he lies in wait for the postman. It may be suspected that the jingling of the lati is rather a signal than an alarm after awhile. Frank Buckland somewhere mentions the case reported of a man-eater which had destroyed forty persons in six months, of whom sixteen were dâk-runners. It is probable that in every instance recorded, where the den of an old offender has been searched, some remains of this unfortunate class have turned up. Speaking from memory, I think that the last returns of the Zillah department showed a total of 10,000 persons odd killed by tigers, leopards, lions, bears, and the like in India. Rather more were killed by snakes, I think, but I have not the figures. If we divide sixteen by two to make a general average, relying on Frank Buckland's authority, it would seem that 1,250 postmen are sacrificed yearly to wild beasts. Rather a startling estimate, most people will declare, but certainly not exaggerated on the statistics given.—Yours very truly,

" FREDK. BOYLE."

# WHY CAPTAIN RAWDON DID NOT GO TO THE WAR.

---

" You know, Clem, that my appointment is gazetted. If I could help in any way I would give you my last hour, but there is no room for anybody's interference, least of all mine. We may have our opinion of Damer, but a lady sees him from a different point of view."

" You have not been attending. I say Lucy is not in love with the fellow. She admitted as much to my father. Though of age, and a widow, she is only a child. Lassalle died within a month of the wedding, you know."

" Leaving her no fortune, I understand ? "

" Not enough to be an object with Damer. But it's no use talking about it under present circumstances. Arriving only yesterday, I had not heard your good fortune. You'll come to see the governor before you start ? "

" I'll come to tiffin to-morrow. Now let us have a peg."

The two men had been leaning over the balcony of the club at Simla. On the small terrace below, lit by the windows of the dining-room, a score of syces sat on their heels, bridle in hand. The rays of light streaming past touched here a pine-bough, there a scaly trunk; and vanished in the abyss. Far below twinkled the lamps of the bazaar. Between the darkness of earth and sky the highest tip of Jacko hung like a jewel, silvering in the first moonbeams.

The elder of the pair, Sir Arthur Rawdon, was almost too good-looking. Girlish features he had, large blue eyes, and a soft moustache, of which every golden hair knew its place and kept it. I imagine that if this young baronet had been rich, his natural indolence and his good looks would have led people to think him a fool. But necessity drove, and, in the process of development from a spoony youth to a smart captain of artillery, Rawdon sacrificed some of those charms which, if they fasci- nate bread-and-butter maidens, prejudice a cruel world against men too pretty. Sharp lines formed about his eyelids, and his voice learned the tones of decision. The smile lost its too great facility, but it gained in meaning. Indian sunshine creased his brow, and burned the colour out of his fair skin. Before Rawdon himself had quite decided that a young lady in her teens is not the supreme effort of the Creator, his more youthful partners mur- mured that, though dearly handsome, he was not

entirely nice. No long time afterwards they espied a
grey hair, and explained all their vague dissatisfaction
by the mutual assurance that Sir Arthur was getting old
—as a matter of fact he was in his thirtieth year, and he
had attained to the anomalous functions of an artillery
captain.

The other man, Clement Dawson, was a pleasant
young civilian. The two had been schoolfellows, and
their friendship was renewed in India. Dawson, accustomed to rely upon his comrade, wished him now to give
advice about the "entanglement," as he called it, of a
young widowed cousin with an officer of the 100th B.C.
Rawdon, however, had an excuse unanswerable. He
was just gazetted A.D.C. to a general on the frontier.

Ruefully the latter called to mind his engagement
next morning. He had meant to tiffin at the Fernery,
where, as was silently understood, bright eyes would
look for him. When his *bearer* came sadly and in great
concern, as if he did not carry a like message two days
out of three, to say there was no water for the sahib's
bath, the usual formula was not accepted with the usual
good temper. Honest Koda fled in haste to warn his
colleagues of the dining-room and stable that they should
defer their little bills that day.

"Unlucky day for presenting little bills," says imaginative Koda; "Mem sah'b writes that husband sah'b has
found all out, and is going to cut off her hair!"

Rents in Simla are monstrous, and Judge Dawson had to consult economy. Sons and sons-in-law, tutors, and school-masters, kept the pagoda-tree always aquiver. The pretty house discovered at length had drawbacks. It lay at the very bottom of Annandale, beneath a rock so loose and shattered that no one had ventured to occupy it for two seasons past. But Judge Dawson had stout nerves, and a limitless belief in his own opinions upon every subject. He surveyed the rock from above and below, poked a stick into one crevice, threw a pebble into another, and declared it firm as the Colosseum.

Rawdon could not find the path to this secluded spot, and rode hither and thither, with a growing sense of ill-usage. As he trotted round a corner, he met a lady carrying a basket of ferns, which she dropped with a little shriek. Rawdon jumped down, of course, and picked up the scattered leaves, the lady standing silent. " I hope there is not much harm done," he said, whilst busily engaged, with his head down. " I stupidly for-got that a horse's hoofs are unheard in this dust. I think they are all there." Turning to restore the basket, he looked up the road, round the corner, over the precipice, and amongst the rhododendrons, but no one was there! The lady had vanished. Rawdon turned out the ferns, seeking a name or a sign ; but there was nothing at the bottom except two pretty little gloves. He folded them up carefully and put them in his pocket. " It will be hard," he thought, " if I don't get some fun out of the joke;" and looked for marks in the dust. Among the prints of hoofs and naked feet he speedily discovered "sign." A little boot, fit match for those little gloves, had left its impression here and there. Rawdon followed the track some yards, until he came to a very narrow path almost hidden amongst rocks and bushes. Winding along a precipitous incline, he presently found a road which led him to a long, low bungalow. An ill-kept garden, full of roses and flowering shrubs, stood before it. A couple of *chuprassies* lounged about the wooden portico, brilliant in long red coats, trencher turbans, and twisted girdles of orange and scarlet. They rose and salaamed. Clem bustled out,

" It's awfully good of you to come, Rawdon," he said, leading the way. " The governor and mater are round here. Let me take that basket."

" Don't trouble ! Mrs. Dawson, I know you will not be surprised at a curious question. How do I look? "

" Like a very conceited and impertinent young gunner who has just been named aide-de-camp to General Blank and expects to be congratulated."

" Well, I'm glad it has not produced any outward marks," muttered Rawdon, quietly putting the basket on a chair, as he saw a young lady approaching.

" What *do* you mean ? Lucy, this is my pet hero, Sir Arthur Rawdon, and he is talking the most delightful nonsense."

" I shall try to laugh it off, but, when a man is going on campaign, it is unpleasant to see these things."

" To see what, Arthur?." asked the grave judge, who approached.

" I dare not trifle with your curiosity on such a subject, sir. My dear friends. I have seen a spirit."

" What, at the club? "

" No, here, on the road above your house."

" Dear me," said Mr. Dawson, anxiously, " who is your doctor? "

" I must tell the story. As I rode along the path—having missed the direct way to your house—at the corner something happened. My horse stopped suddenly—I heard a cry, not alarming, but awfully sweet. My eyes were dazzled. A form stood before me at which I dared not look. What followed? I found myself on my knees in the dust. There was a soft rustling, whether before, behind me, or in the air, I could not say—I turned—the road was empty ! Understand that all this passed in a moment. I looked about, and on the spot where the apparition had stood—if indeed it rested on earthly limbs—I traced the impress of two delicate little feet, or, I should say, hoofs ! Perhaps they were a sheep's—perhaps a spirit's ! That is all.

When I recovered myself I came down—you will not ridicule me for telling you? A man cannot hold his tongue about such experiences!"

Mrs. Dawson stood open-eyed, uncertain whether to laugh or to console. Clem looked amused, glancing at the basket. The judge cocked his head on one side, preparing for a solemn cross-examination. Lucy bent her face down, and gravely contemplated a tiny boot which she thrust from beneath her dress.

"Let us say no more about it," observed Sir Arthur. "What a charming view of the Snows you have here, Judge."

Every householder in Simla on this side holds it as an article of faith that he, and he alone, gets the Snows in a proper focus—at the other end they make a speciality of their Pines. Whilst the elders were explaining how and why this prospect was superior to that of everyone else, Rawdon watched from the corner of his eye. He saw Lucy take up the basket and search among the ferns. Not finding her gloves she looked at Rawdon with a bewitching air of hesitation, and caught his glance. That decided her, of course, and she moved resolutely forward to speak. But the *kitmutgar* announced tiffin, and Sir Arthur promptly offered Mrs. Dawson his arm, talking volubly. The opportunity passed, and Lucy perhaps did not regret it; for she saw that everyone would laugh at her, since Rawdon, of course, would deny all knowledge of the gloves. In truth they might ' very well have been lost.

He confessed long before this that Lucy was the prettiest creature he had ever seen. A catalogue of her features would be easily made, but I do not see the purpose. Arthur had no small experience of women—experience comes thick and early on Indian service—and the same glance which convinced him of the little widow's unequalled charm told him of danger. The charming eyes brimmed with life and spirit. The delicate lips could frame themselves to obstinate temper. Very little of the saint was there, but, as Rawdon thought, an illimitable store of love for him who could find it. Meanwhile, a consummate little flirt, eager for enjoyment, and very badly ballasted to go straight. Rawdon thought none the worse of any daughter of Eve because she might be frivolous or coquettish, provided, that is, she owned no commanding officer and her letters of marque were honourably registered.

" We asked Mr. Damer to meet you," said Mrs. Dawson, " but he could not promise; Damer of the 100th B.C., you know."

" I have often met him," Arthur replied, glancing in some astonishment at Clem. He understood the hasty ʌnd complicated signal despatched in reply to mean that the old lady was innocent as a babe of the family anxieties. Mrs. Dawson, an excellent creature, passed her life, so to speak, outside of things.

"When you are both out of sight I cannot decide which I like the best," continued Mrs. Dawson. " We always say that you are the two most charming young men in India."

" I insist upon an explanation of that 'we.' Which of the ladies of Harrypur go to make up the multitude?"

" Oh, I get into a habit of speaking for Lucy and myself, but she never saw you before this very minute, so I was talking nonsense, as usual."

" Delicate and judicious flattery is not nonsense, is it, Mrs. Lassalle ? "

" I don't know what flattery is——"

" No! How could you?"

" But I know what nonsense is, and talking of spirits on the Annandale Road is nonsense."

" It is not flattery though. What is a spirit? A messenger from Heaven charged to comfort men and give them nobler thoughts, sweeter aims, and hopes. One might meet them, or think we met them, on the Annandale Road as elsewhere." Lucy coloured, hesitated, and kept silence.

Mrs. Dawson placidly returned to her subject. "They tell me that many persons dislike Mr. Damer. I can understand why the Judge does not take to him, for he *is* a little noisy—I admit that. But such a manly, clever fellow, and so amusing in all society! He seems to beat everybody at everything."

"Not everybody, mother," said Clem. "I would back Arthur for all I have at anything Damer likes to propose; but he wouldn't take the bet."

"Oh how delightful!" exclaimed Mrs. Dawson; "we will get up matches, and all the best people in Simla will come. It is a charming idea of yours, Clem."

"The Annandale Pet against the Club Chicken!" muttered Arthur. "You forget, my dear Mrs. Dawson, that in five days I shall be on the frontier."

The Judge had been preparing a weighty speech for several minutes. He addressed Clem with his "prisoner-at-the-bar" swell. "I trust, sir, nay, I believe, that in some late remarks of yours you were employing heedless and unmeaning expressions, which are unfortunately current amongst young men in India. You could not propose to degrade the meritorious and honourable officer who flatters you with his friendship by treating him like a racehorse or coursing-dog, to be trotted out, matched, tested, and publicly exhibited for money——"

"O! of course not, John dear. Clem did not really mean that he would stake all he had on a chance. He is not a gambler; not that I myself have seen much harm come of gambling, and Harrypur is an awful place for

cards, you know. Indeed I was quite shocked to hear
the losses of some people—people one knew, I mean—
ladies. There was Miss——"

"Oh, aunt!" cried Mrs. Lassalle, excitedly, "I do so
much dislike those old stories! No doubt they are
dreadfully exaggerated."

"No doubt, dear, and I forgot she was a friend of
yours. I was just going to say that no mischief came of
all this gambling that I heard of. It is unlady-like,
because excitement gives a disagreeable and indeed an
objectionable expression to the eyes, and people's hands
get dirty at cards—I don't know why. I have always
strongly disapproved it, but there is nothing to ser-
monise about."

The dear, dull, honest old Judge was positively pale
with shocked surprise. "Do I understand, Martha," he
said, slowly, "that ladies whom we know at Harrypur,
who come to our house perhaps, are in the habit of
playing cards for money?"

"Oh, of course, John! Don't be so severe. Everyone knows it. People must amuse themselves somehow
in this wretched country."

The Judge continued solemnly, "Will you think for
an instant whither this practice may lead a female? As
a rule, she has not money within her reach. It is her
husband's, or her children's, which she risks, and, of

course, loses to a vicious man. As a counsel I have seen what this leads to, and the recollection is one of the most painful in my experience. I——"

" There!" interrupted Mrs. Dawson, as Mrs. Lassalle left the table, " you are always so serious, John. Lucy could not bear to listen, for some of her own friends in Harrypur used to play an innocent game at cards."

" Which of them? I insist on knowing."

" Take the evidence *in camerâ*, sir!" cried Rawdon, laughing.

" Your delicacy rebukes me, Arthur! But I am much disturbed by one thing or another. We shall see you again before you leave ? "

" As often as you like, Judge!" Rawdon answered, heartily.

The young men retired to smoke. " Well ? " said Clem, after a pause.

" It would be a shame if any one could stop it. Your cousin is a child, as you say. The man she loved could do anything with her, but he must use a silken bit. It is a mighty tender mouth, and a mighty restive disposition."

" What a happy thing it would be if you could break her yourself ! " said Clem, with some embarrassment.

" Aren't you ashamed !" cried Rawdon, laughing and colouring, "to bait a trap for a friend in your own house? Tell me what sort of a man was Lassalle."

" A noble fellow! Everyone loved him excepting
Lucy, who, short of that, was as fond as a woman can
be of a man. He did not intend to marry on such terms,
but his health suddenly gave way. I remember the
dear old fellow talking of Lucy much as you did just
now. He said she was not a girl to live in this Indian
hot-house, with her impulsive disposition and flighty
head. It was, I believe, as much for her sake as for
his own that Lassalle married her before sailing. He
had no idea how ill he was. Lucy made no sacrifice at
all; you will recollect that she had not a farthing.
They would have been as loving and as happy as they
deserved, but Lassalle died in Italy on his way home."

" A sad story! Here, if I know the voice, comes his
successor."

"*Absit omen!* But it's Damer; all alive, as usual!"

The study looked towards the approach, where no one
yet was visible. But a mellow voice lilting an old-
fashioned song preceded the visitor, who quickly came
into sight, riding down the breakneck path. " No
question of the fellow's pluck!" murmured Clem. " He
would gallop down the *khud* as soon as not."

Rawdon looked at the man approaching with new
interest. Familiar to him for several years past were
the thin, well-cut features, the eyes clear and keen as
a hawk's, and the light, vigorous frame. What Rawdon
sought was the token of a mind which would guide and

control the wayward impulses of a high-spirited girl. He sought in vain. Damer's intellect answered every call he made upon it. None more shrewd to see where interest lay, to grasp the means of securing it, and to circumvent the adversary. With him such operations of the brain seemed instinctive, and the cleverest schemers seldom triumphed over this noisy athlete. But when personal advantage was not concerned he seemed incapable of thought. Imagination easily pictures the married life of a soulless being, all vivacity and " go "— fits of eager passion and then forgetfulness, neglect the more galling because unconscious, reproaches met by blank surprise, sullen anger and impatience; worst of all, the passion-fit again. How long would Lucy endure this?

" Sell arms and like 'em!" cried Damer, throwing his leg over the pommel. " That's Arabic for how d'ye do! Here, you nigger, take away this precious, blessed pony, and worship him in the stable, but don't take the saddle off! So old Blank has made you his A.D.C., Rawdon! What luck! I should have liked to back myself first spear at the Pathans! Where's Lucy, Clem?"

" Listening for the echo of your footsteps, no doubt. You're training her for a steeplechase, aren't you?"

" No chance! Lucy could sit in a saddle before I

G 2

knew her, but she will never ride. Too jumpy! Doesn't understand a horse!"

" How?"

" Well, at the start she runs away. The poor brute thinks he is to gallop in earnest, and then Lucy squeals! You bring him up—five minutes later she is off again, to renew the same performance. Ask her if she'd like a jump? Oh, above everything, the biggest that ever was faced. At it she goes, as bold as Assheton Smith, but saws the horse's head round as he's taking off, and squalls. One might teach Mrs. Dawson to ride, but not Lucy! I was just telling these men that you are the most hopeless pupil I ever had."

" That's what stupid teachers say. I'm sure Sir Arthur would make allowance for a lady's nervousness." Damer glanced at the baronet angrily. The latter replied: " I'm sorry I cannot prove upon the spot that you do me no more than justice."

" You are not going to ride with us?"

" Unless you go towards the club, it is impossible."

The little widow curled her lip scornfully, saying: " I publicly retract my late opinion, advanced upon insufficient knowledge, as the Judge would say. Can you spare the time to help me to mount?"

" I could almost wish you set me a less pleasant duty," murmured Rawdon, as he offered his arm, Damer turning sulkily away. " Pleasures should be given to those who deserve them."

" Is it such a treat to toss a lady into the saddle ? "

" Under certain circumstances it may be."

" What are they ? " asked Lucy, with her pretty foot in Rawdon's hand. " When the lady has *hoofs* ? " And she rode away.

Sir Arthur was dining that night with one of the hospitable magnates of Simla—at a table exquisitely appointed, with fountains, fishponds, goddesses, forests, looking-glasses, and I know not what. The *menu* was worthy of Paris; the ladies if not beautiful, were beautifully dressed, and full of talk. There are a few great houses in Simla where the most captious can scarcely hit a fault, and this was one of them. The arrival of the Dawsons was judiciously put forward as a topic by Sir Arthur, and from the ladies first, afterwards from the gentlemen, he obtained certain hints and suggestions. They grieved but scarcely surprised him. Later in the evening he found Damer in the club cardroom, playing high, as usual; but losing, which was quite the reverse. Upon whispered consultation with the " gallery," Rawdon learned that this run of ill-fortune had been constant since Damer's arrival. In three days he had dropped much more than ten thousand rupees, and report said that this loss only followed heavy reverses on the turf.

When he first joined the service Rawdon was an enthusiastic player at all games of skill. A poor man, with those artistic and luxurious tastes which are more expensive than rakish living, he soon found that his gains at whist, billiards, écarté, and so on, came in very usefully. The fascination of gambling never mastered him, but he became known over India as a *grand joueur*. As such he had met Damer often, and, upon the whole, had won from him; this was some years before. A very sad event, with which he was innocently concerned, put a sudden end to Rawdon's play. From that hour he had never touched a card nor made a bet, and the excitement was considerable when, at the break-up of the whist party, Rawdon took Damer's challenge addressed to the whole room. They played écarté till the sun was up, and a member of the committee interfered. Damer had lost a very large amount, and he reeled like a drunken man; though never in his life had he tasted aught more stimulating than soda-water and Worcester sauce—a Simla drink, which I earnestly commend to a generation tired of " lemon-squeezes."

Upon awakening at the unholy hour of 9 a.m., Rawdon found Clem sitting by his bed. " Is there anything new ? " he asked.

" News enough when Arthur Rawdon takes to cards again. I've heard of your tournament last night. Are you so wideawake yet as to talk with a man who has three hours in the day the start of you? Well, then, I want to tell you what took place last night. When they returned from riding, Damer had the sulks, and Lucy was absurdly upright and dignified in a way that I remember when we were children. After dinner I took an opportunity to ask again whether she had anything on her mind, and she burst into tears."

" A lover's quarrel, perhaps!"

" Wait. I offered consolation, as you may suppose, but she only sobbed, ' No, you are too good, all of you. I have played the fool, and I must pay.' There was something in her manner that alarmed me. Rawdon, I should not tell you this had you not taken my words yesterday as you did. I think you are interested in our trouble."

His face showed that he was. Clem went on, " I could not say what I suspected. Something, no doubt, appeared in my face, for Lucy rose suddenly, pushing me away with all her strength. ' How dare you?' she whispered. My mother was asleep in the room. I never saw the girl so lovely. I muttered something, I don't know what, following her to the door. There she put out a trembling, hot hand, and said, ' I have brought it all on myself! It is not your fault! But don't—don't talk about me to Sir Arthur?' I break my promise for her good."

Rawdon lay silent for a little while, observing with
interest the proceedings of his *bearer*, engaged in the
absorbing task of putting studs into a shirt.   This operation apparently gave the baronet extreme and concentrated pleasure.   He said at length, " I fancy, Clem,
that I have discovered something ; but it is only fancy.
The worst is that I have so little time before me.   I
hope to carry this affair through myself ; but you will
be glad to know that, *if* I am right, you can take up
the cards after my departure—there, see how one night's
relapse has deteriorated my conversation !   I will call
before tiffin."

Clem arranged that his cousin should be alone in the
drawing-room.   She stood at a window, so fixed in
thought that Rawdon approached unheard.   " Is it the
Snows or the roses you are admiring so intently ? " he
asked.

" I don't care much for either.   Both are common
here ! "

" One soon exhausts the novelties of life.   How did
the riding-lesson progress ? "

" Mr. Damer lost his temper.   He says I have no
courage."

" Would you not have liked to sit on a balcony and
see a score of poor wretches break each other's heads in
honour of you, as ' the Queen of Beauty ' ? "

" Dearly! That is, they needn't actually break heads."

" A good make-believe would be near enough? And would you give your hand to the victor?"

" I know I should, but I might repent afterwards. By-the-bye, Sir Arthur, I have lost my gloves."

" I will order some from Phelps."

" Thank you. I prefer my own. And I fancy you know where they are."

" I? If so, why should I not return them?"

" I cannot imagine. But the spirit you saw yesterday tells me they are in your breast-pocket."

Rawdon displayed the lining. " I wish," he said, " that sweet spirit could read my heart."

" It would find my gloves there!" she exclaimed, stretching out her hands like a child, and withdrawing them with a blush.

" What sort of gloves are they? Describe them."

" Oh, the commonest things possible! Only fit to be worn on hoofs, hooves, what is it? Seriously, Captain Sir Arthur Rawdon, you have no right to keep my gloves. It is stealing!"

" And seriously, Mrs. Lassalle, I will not part with my talisman."

Lucy turned away, vexed to find that she was not vexed. And Mr. Dawson entered with Damer. No misfortune could depress that buoyant spirit. Watching him with new interest, Rawdon saw that he was not consciously or wantonly bad. He had no more sense of propriety than has a hawk; that was all.

That night Rawdon gave a farewell dinner at the club. The dignitaries who attended left early, and the remaining *convives* adjourned to the card-room. It was silently understood that Damer and Rawdon meant a duel *à outrance*. As they sat down to écarté, the former named stakes unusually high even in that high-playing community. Rawdon bowed, and the match began. Needless to follow its chances. After a run of luck which his adversary's skill reduced to a minimum of profit, Damer fell back into his evil vein. Chit after chit he drew, withdrew, and tore up, until the carpet was whitened with paper; but always the chit exchanged grew to a larger and larger sum. When turned out of the club, the maddened gambler seized the chance of "breaking his luck," but ill-fate pursued him to Rawdon's bedroom. Clem and two or three more looked on.

At seven o'clock Rawdon put down the cards. "Enough," he said; "if you gentlemen of the gallery will square your accounts, Damer and I can settle in private." Five minutes afterwards they were alone. It was an ugly picture which the dull morning lighted. Rawdon was calm but very white, his tie hung loose down the crumpled shirt-front, and the flowers at his button hole looked like a bunch of withered leaves. Damer's face was purple, and he rested it on closed fists, black with dust. " This is the amount you have lost," said Rawdon, " and here is last night's chit. You can discharge the sum without inconvenience, I suppose; but, if you desire it, I will suggest a means to escape the trouble of raising so much money at short notice. Shall I go on? "

Damer nodded. His mouth quivered so with hope that he could not speak.

" I believe," Rawdon continued, " that certain chits, signed by ladies of Harrypur, have fallen into your possession. Hand them over to Dawson, here present, and I burn these papers."

" I refuse!" screamed Damer, springing up. " You have cheated me out of all I possess, and with the swag you would buy Lucy from me. Never!"

" Very well! You know that I leave Simla the day after to-morrow. ' I shall take the usual steps before going, and in my absence Dawson will act for me. I warn you that the first moneys paid in will be devoted to the redemption of those papers."

" No, no!" cried Clem, snatching out his cheque-book. " I shall pay the amount this instant. How much is it, sir? "

" You cannot mean this, Rawdon? I am ruined, and, if you press me, I must leave the service! "

" The woman you have persecuted may show you mercy, but men will not."

" Then do what you like! Lucy has sworn to be true
to me, bound or free! And I would hold her to it,
though we both died on the instant."

" If you can trust her," said Clem, disdainfully, " why
not give up the chits? They are no more use to you,
now the truth is known."

Damer saw that instantly. After one moment's hesitation he took a sealed envelope from his pocket-book,
and threw it on the table with an oath. " Debit me
with the amount, Captain Rawdon!" he cried, and went
out bareheaded into the rain.

Rawdon went to bed, but Clem could not sleep till he
had acquainted Lucy with her deliverance. Wondering,
she came to him in a dressing-gown, with her beautiful
flaxen hair about her shoulders. Clem kissed her, and
gave her the envelope, which she opened, trembling.
Her joy did not take the form expected. Too shame-
faced to look up, she whispered: " How did you get
these shameful things? "

" Rawdon guessed your secret, and he made Damer
give them up."

Lucy burst into tears. " Oh! Clem, I would rather
have died—or married that man," she sobbed. " I can
never see him again! When did he guess? Before he
came here? "

" He guessed it the first day he saw you."

This assurance evidently gave comfort. " But I can

never see him again. I should die! And he is coming to-night!"

" It will be the last time. Surely you ought to thank him!"

" I would as soon kill him! I am very, very grateful, Clem, indeed, but don't ask me to thank him!"

" Well, I shall tell Arthur all you say, and how you look in a dressing-gown, and how long your hair is, and anything else that occurs to me as we talk over your conduct."

" You won't!"

" I vow I will, unless you promise to thank him."

" I promise!" But she never meant to keep her word.

" Now I am going to bed, child. By-the-bye, Damer is certain you will marry him all the same."

" I?" Laughing with a heartiness almost hysterical, she ran out of the room. *Fol qui s'y fie!* thought Clem. That silvery peal was not for Damer's wedding.

The Dawsons had a large dinner-party that evening, but one dripping syce after another rode up to present excuses for the ladies. Distances at Simla are very great, and such rain justified non-attendance even at a Viceregal dinner. When the only conveyance is a pony or a *jampan*, weather is a most serious consideration. Gentlemen arrived, some half-dozen, and amongst the rest Damer. The unexpected sight of him earned Lucy forgiveness from her cousin. That faithless little widow dressed elaborately, and made ostentatious show of descending, until Mrs. Dawson had left her, and the guests began to arrive. Then she sent a pretty note of excuse, donned a *peignoir*, and put her slippered feet upon the fender.

Everything is known at Simla, and all present saving the Dawsons were aware that Damer had lost a sum beyond his power of payment. They watched both winner and loser with great curiosity, but nothing happened at all. Damer was pale and hollow-eyed, but quite himself, laughing *à tort et à travers* with even more than usual volubility. Mrs. Dawson, the only lady present, withdrew early, and the gentlemen retired to that small room beside the porch already mentioned. As they laughed and talked, the rain softly pattered, and Rawdon observed that a few more such unseasonable days would make the bungalow an unsafe dwelling.

"Oh!" said the Judge, "I have examined the rock myself. There is not a house in Simla more secure."

At this moment a sudden smart blow upon the roof called every man to his feet, pale with alarm. Quick as thought began an awful din, rattle of pebbles falling, thud of great rocks, crash of breaking timbers. An instant before, the windows had been opened. Men threw themselves out, one on another. As Rawdon, the last, ran up the path, with a roar and heave as of an earthquake, the ponderous reef fell outwards. Flying pebbles knocked him down, but he rose, after a moment, bruised and bleeding. Ten yards further Clem seized him in his arms, springing from behind a tree.

"Lucy?" he cried, "your mother?" shouting in Clem's ear above the crash. The bewildered reply was scarcely audible. Turning, he saw light through a hurtling storm of missiles, and ran again towards the house. The rock had fallen solidly over portico and dining-room, and lay above their ruins. Pressing to the cliff, where the volley of stones flew mostly overhead, he made his way, clinging to roots and crevices. From the summit of the pile the candle-light was visible again, shining through a rugged gap in the party-wall. The flight of small stones had slackened, but boulders tumbling headlong down splintered on the rock like shells. Again and again Rawdon fell. Hours it seemed, but five minutes had not passed before he stood beneath the aperture, and entered.

The room was full of smoke and dust. He snatched up the candle and looked round. The girl lay close behind the door, white and lifeless. No hope of returning the way he came with that burden in his arms! Using all his strength, Rawdon forced the door open, caught her up, and ran down the passage. Ominous blows upon the roof distracted him. Black as a pit was the corridor. Letting the girl drop, he rushed back.

Little flames began to play amongst the boards, where embers had sprung from the fireplace. By the candle's light Rawdon found the back staircase, and tumbled down it somehow, his light burden resumed—out by the cook-house, and into the pine-wood. The ground sloped rapidly. A slip might dash them to pieces, and the soil was slippery with rain. Fifty yards from the house, he dared go no further in that darkness.

The clash of falling stones had not ceased, and the danger was undiminished. But, whilst Rawdon watched painfully, a dim glow spread over the ruin, the outline of the shattered windows shaped itself, and then in a few moments all that wretched scene was lighted by the burning house. Rawdon picked up his charge, still unconscious, and hastily carried her on, by the growing flames. They failed him suddenly. Another roar, another shock, which made the pine-trees tremble, and threw him headlong down ! The rest of the cliff had fallen.

To wake in darkness, not knowing where you are, and feel human fingers about your throat, is a test for nerves. Rawdon bore it stoically. He says that instinct kept him quiet. Though conscious, he said nothing, whilst Lucy passed her hands over his face. The noise had ceased. All was still in the wood. " Dead ! " he heard her sob. " Dead to save me ! "

" I am not dead, Lucy ! " Rawdon murmured. " Put your hand on my lips and revive me."

"Sir Arthur!" she cried with a little scream; "I thought it was ——"

" Never mind! Your gloves are on my heart, Lucy, and I can't stir a limb."

" If you would like to keep them ——"

" No! It was stealing."

" I give them to you."

" If you are in the mood to give, it is not enough. Put your hand in mine, darling. Will you let it rest there for ever?"

She made no reply, but cried softly. " Will you not answer?" he asked.

She whispered, " Am I worthy, Arthur?"

" You shall have no flattery from your husband. Kiss me, darling! I hear voices!"

She put her wet face to his, " 1 *will* be worthy of my hero!"

Torches gleamed among the trees above. Active little Ghoorkas, tall Sikhs, and Pathan mountaineers of the Viceroy's bodyguard were scrambling bravely down. Clem, the Judge, and Damer, were heard; but none ventured to pretend a hope he did not feel by shouting. " Call to them, Lucy!" whispered Rawdon, " my voice is gone."

" Oh, Arthur, I have not asked, I have not thought, of my poor aunt! How selfish and wicked I am!"

" I am almost sure she is saved. Cry out, dear!"

H

His fainting voice alarmed her, and she screamed for help.  Five minutes more, and he was being carried to the nearest bungalow, unable to restrain his moans.

So Captain Sir Arthur Rawdon, R.A., did not go to the war.  In the spring, when all the valley was aflame with rhododendrons, he married Lucy.  And on the same day, in a bleak gorge in Afghanistan, Lieut. Damer and his small baggage-guard stood in a ring of fire through the long forenoon.  He is recommended for the Victoria Cross; and Lucy vows, since that news came, her husband has put a new significance into his accent when he calls her " dear."

Ladies' gambling has been suppressed at Harrypur, though Mrs. Dawson declares that no mischief ever came of it.

———————————

# SEPOY AND ARAB.

VERY little has been published, so far as I gather, that even suggests the point of view our Indian troops adopted during the late war. But this question is, in truth, far graver than the mere issue of a campaign. It may reasonably be hoped that the British soldier will always emulate the deeds of his ancestry. Though he had sustained a check at Tel-el-Kebir, the issue would have been only deferred. But for the Sepoy it was all new experience, and more important matters lay at stake than victory in the field. It was not the first time he had left India for active service, but an Afghan war is a special thing for him. Even the Moslem Sepoy loses sight of the community of creed under the influence of inherited hatred and traditional wrongs. The only other case I recollect where operations were carried on for a length of time against Sunni Mahomedans was the Perak affair. But the Indian would not feel that a Malay was his co-religionist, nor could he get up enthusiasm for a people whose civilisation is so conspicuously inferior to his own. It was all otherwise in Egypt. The name of the land was familiar, sanctified in some

H 2

degree by constant allusion in pious legends. The language of the foe is a sacred mystery to the Faithful, the people are conspicuous as descended from the companions of the Prophet. Their civilisation is Moslem, modified by the same influences from Frangistan which irritate the Indian Faithful. It was a great trial of loyalty the Sepoy underwent, and his behaviour under the circumstances might well claim the notice of thoughtful men.

Government, no doubt, has confidential reports in abundance, showing what those best qualified to see and estimate the facts thought upon the subject. But the public, as I understand, has no information. This lack is owing not to want of " enterprise " in the press, nor, we may hope, to want of ability in the correspondents. It is due to the action of Lord Wolseley, which I have no need to criticise. He recognised but one army in the field, his own, to which one correspondent was allotted. " Indian Contingent " was a phrase he would not accept, and those members of the press who had left London expressly to join it, in the hope of marching across the desert, were enjoined to stay at Ismailia. The " Indian Contingent," if I may be allowed to use the words, went to the front, leaving its chroniclers behind. The single correspondent attached to Lord Wolseley's direct command had work enough, detailing the actions and feelings of the English troops.

So it happened that the special work of the Sepoys, and of their British comrades also, passed unrecorded. Who knows what took place on the south side of the canal during the fight at Tel-el-Kebir? In one or two instances, such as the seizure of Zagazig, the admirable service of the Indians could not be overlooked. But there was not, nor could be, any report of the Sepoys' behaviour, such as thoughtful people must have wished to hear. My own opportunities for remark were meagre, but I used them as I could. Let it be premised that I am not describing sentiments necessarily permanent. Reflection, possibly the charm of distance, and the influence of piously political superiors, may weaken the feelings prevailing at the time. I should not incline to think they will, but we shall see.

Generally speaking, then, the impressions of the Sepoys appeared to be contempt and dislike. For the Mahomedans amongst them, the consciousness of a common creed only intensified this feeling. It was a practice of the Egyptians, after we reached Cairo, to spread their carpets and pray ostentatiously in the neighbourhood of Indian troops; Pathans once displayed the same illusion. But they took little by the silent appeal. The Sepoys looked on with interest, but it was not friendly. Once I saw a group of soldiers belonging to the 20th N.I., who actually critised the performance. Probably they remarked some difference in the manner of genuflection.

For reasons that I did not understand, the Khedive personally was regarded with especial contempt. An officer suggested that this might be the outcome of Turkish intrigues in Hindustan, and it is possible. I have sometimes thought that if the Moslem Sepoys had been introduced to Cairo at the outset—its wealth, and palaces, and order—they might have been otherwise impressed; but their minds were made up before they reached that place. Though they delight in show, and respect costly appearance, Arab magnificence did not impress them. I remember the visit which Sultan Pasha and his suite paid to Colonel Sir Owen Lanyon in Ismailia. I chanced to come up whilst the horses stood outside. Their trappings were handsome, if eccentric to our eyes, especially those of the chief; blue velvet with gold and silver fringes, and what not. A number of Sepoys stood round, with contemptuous curiosity in their faces, making remarks. Said an Afridi sergeant, nearer seven feet high than six feet, with an oath so forcibly dramatic that I regret to suppress it—"I swear if that horse trotted into our village we should say the Ameer was coming to durbar; but when they saw its rider our women would laugh!" That observation gives a key-note to the sentiments prevailing before and after.

The least observant of spectators felt, as he saw the Indians traverse an Arab throng, "What gentlemen they look!" To tell the whole truth here, the same remark arose when the throng traversed was of English soldiery. But our men, dirty and pallid, in the hideous unserviceable dress supplied them, bore the stamp of qualities more important than good looks. The Arab has none of them—at every point he offended the Sepoy. Disregard of that elementary respect for others, which forbids a man to tramp upon his neighbour's toes in mere carelessness and brutality, must be resented the whole world over by men who carry arms, and are ready to use them. Accordingly, we find so much courtesy universal among fighting races. The Pathan, in his native wilds, is, perhaps, the very roughest of all animals, but he has a code of manners, suggested and strictly limited by the sword. A very brief service in our ranks, among the more polished races of the plain, enlarges his ideas. But the Egyptian Arab has no check outside, and no instinct within, to guide him. His nature, or his acquired nature, is more selfish and offensive than that of any people known to me, and it is unmitigated by the restraint of fear. None of his neighbours have spirit to cut him down, whatever vagaries he may play. And so he dances on their corns in cheerfulness of soul. More than that, he is sincerely astonished when susceptible people cry out.

The bond of religion must be stronger than we see it anywhere at this day to make an Indian Moslem feel that this creature is a brother. The contrast was just as striking as it could be. We hourly observed a working party of

Sepoys pushing through a crowd of natives. Their
loose jackets and trousers of fatigue dress were scarcely
more martial or even more picturesque than the ragged
night-gown of the Arab. The turban, indeed, or puggri,
with a loose end fluttering to the waist, is always superb.
But the faces, the manner, the expression, were a cruel
reproach to the African. Half-a-dozen Sepoys yonder
are pushing a cart. Perhaps they belong to that grand
regiment, the 20th N.I., distinguished by the black tips
of their puggris, stately Sikhs, or giant Pathans, or
lithe Rajputs. They are not working very hard. Half
their energy is expended on the rear, or on either flank,
where passing comrades fling banter, manly, though
indecorous, as is martial wit everywhere. They laugh
long and open-mouthed, throwing back their handsome
heads, displaying snow-white teeth to drive a dentist to
despair. Their eyes—large, well-opened—show the fun
of spirited schoolboys in their clear light. Though the
jokes they bandy are not refined, nor very witty, they
are the humour of strong men who respect themselves
and one another. When an officer-Sahib comes by,
decorous quiet supervenes. Those disengaged, salute;
the others gravely put both hands to the task. When
he has gone, the jest breaks out again. So they sweep,
without more notice than a shove and a frown, through
the sordid, leering, hideous crowd of Arabs, halt and
maim, one-eyed, foul, bestial of expression.

Observe that little group of Sepoys returning from their task—grave men these, probably Sikhs, superb in manly beauty. They walk hand in hand, talking among themselves. They laugh readily with each other, but seldom join the Pathan jokes. I remember once, when snowed up in the Kojak Pass, that a Sikh of the 26th N.I. was asked the name of his file-fellow, an Afridi. They had enlisted at the same time, and had served twelve years side by side; but neither would confess a knowledge of the other's name. There go half-a-dozen Madras Sappers, small men, broad-chested, and sturdy-limbed, soldiers every inch, and kindly fellows too. They have not the fine features, nor the large clear eyes, of the Aryan. Their skin is black like a negro's, and the whole type resembles the African on a smaller scale, but trimmer and brighter. In dark uniform, with a jetty handkerchief about their brows, a company of Sappers marching in the desert looks like a black square on the chess-board, moving. There are no better nor pleasanter soldiers in our army. A majority speak English, more or less, and many are fluent. When they went up the Khyber, in the Afghan war, our native troops stared to hear them easily conversing with the Sahibs, and emulation stirred not a few Aryan Sepoys to undertake a fitful study of English. I fear it is quite possible that, if we watched these good fellows closely, a grave and silent lurch might be remarked from time to

time, for the evil correlating their docile and excellent
qualities is shown in a partiality for the white man's
liquor.   But there are few troops whom one would stand
with so confidently as the Madras Sappers.

A very different type is the Beloochi, wild and picturesque, in dark green puggri and scarlet breeches.  He
has that wandering eye that marks the savage only half-
tamed.   We have few real Beloochis in our ranks, discipline is too strict for them ; but a crowd of natives from
the broken frontier clans—fighting men all.   The long
hair of some has escaped in the heat of work, and streams
behind in glossy ringlets, twisted amongst the flowing
drapery of the turban.   And there go troopers of the
Bengal cavalry, tall, broad-shouldered, slender of waist
and hips.   For martial bearing they have no equal in
the armies of the world, and their fine costume does
them justice.   The blue-striped puggri folded round a
scarlet peak, the long blue coat with scarlet sash, tight
yellow trousers and jack-boots, put to shame the fantastic frippery of European tailors.   In their ranks,
generally, we find the most devoted Moslem, for the
neighbourhood of Delhi is a favourite recruiting-ground.
A droll incident recurs to mind.  Marching once through
Scindh, our little party had a local chief for guide,
and a Jemadhar with two troopers for escort.  The guide
explained, as we rode along, certain abstruse questions of
the Faith, making a delicious hash of law and prophets.

Our Jemadhar was the most polite of men —what a lovely Arab he rode, by-the-by! But he loved Islam, and the ignorant rattle of this unorthodox Scindhi stirred his indignation. The troopers were not less angry, and they all pressed upon us, their very horses becoming unmanageable. Colonel Tucker ordered them back in vain. They would not retire until the puzzled Scindhi understood that he was talking nonsense, and then our little diversion came to an end. The path narrowing, he fell behind with the Jemadhar. It was but an instant's interruption. We heard murmurs, guttural in their emphasis, and, when our guide rejoined us, he said frankly, "I don't much of the subject we've been talking about. But, I swear, Colonel Sahib, that no respectable man in our neighbourhood knows more."

Among those Sowars passing, one should trace sympathy with the Arab Moslem, if it existed anywhere in our ranks. But they feel contempt for him almost furious. One trooper questioned would not admit they were his co-religionists, though mosques stared us in the face, and two believers were praying within a few yards. We did not insist on a burning question, and what the Sowar meant I cannot tell; he was a Pathan, and possibly Shiah; or, possibly, such a bad Moslem as not to recognise his fellows. One of the 6th B.C. summed up the opinion of the ranks concisely. Asked if his regiment had cut up many fugitives after Tel-el-Kebir, he answered with the strongest disgust, "How could men use a sword against stinking jackals? We rode many down!" The peculiar justice of the description may be appreciated only by those who have visited Egypt. The screaming and barking of an Arab crowd, all in full cry at once, the shrill snarling and foaming, make a din very like that of a pack of jackals. The adjective needs no explanation ; its simple truth is certified by the dullest of noses.

I had interesting talks with Monsieur Ninet, Arabi's Swiss friend, who avowedly counselled and sympathised, if he did not suggest, the uprising. He is acquainted with many Egyptians who, in all respects, would bear comparison with their fellows of the same class else-where. And he pins all his faith upon the fellaheen. I believe M. Ninet to be as truthful and conscientious as an enthusiast can be, and I would not join issue on this question. For, by his own account, these good people stay at home, crying woe and anathema, whilst the bad monopolise the sunshine and the public notice. As for the fellahs, the undistinguishable mass, the dumb mul-titude of toilers, perhaps they are virtuous. Rustics less hard-worked, better fed, find little time, if they have the inclination, to concoct villany. But they are not less brutal of manner than the townspeople, and they are, if possible, yet more strangely unconscious of such primi-tive decency as a well-bred animal exhibits. I do not

allude to the habit of stripping stark when there is work
to be done. So did their forefathers in every age, and
nothing more need be said. But the Sepoy was shocked
above all else by habits paralleled among the wild Pathans
alone in my experience of the world. And one cannot
readily believe that people who do not feel or understand proprieties instinctive with all but the lowest races
of humanity—or, as in the case of the Pathans, avowedly
cynical and vicious—can be trusted to possess more
recondite virtues.

I would not speak of the impression which the enemy's
behaviour in the field produced upon our Sepoys.
It was not quite the same, I think, in both arms
engaged. The cavalry had an unmixed joy—of gallop,
at least—in racing after foes who never professed to
stand, and they thought it, as one may say, a killing
farce. But the infantry were struck by that awful fire
which issues from the Remington, as from any breech-
loader. It was new to them in practice, and the horror
of that din confounded, perhaps, to some degree, their
just appreciation of the soldiers who raised it. They
certainly return with a deeper sense than ever of English superiority in *bandabust*—combination, arrangement,
strategy, which circumvented and nullified that hurri-
cane of balls. It is not to be understood that the Sepoy
flinched; I should feel shame to contradict such an
insinuation if it were hazarded. My whole meaning is

that the native infantry did not despise the Arab soldier
as did the Sowar.   One of these latter exclaimed, after
the gallant dash into Zagazig station, "What a gym-
kana, Sahib!"   He regarded the business as a series of
military larks.

So far as we can see, the effect of despatching Sepoys
to Egypt was all good—for the men themselves, for those
who stayed at home, and for the Empire.   But it was
prudent to remove them speedily.   To leave them
exposed to the influences of the country in peace-time
would be a hazardous experiment.   From remarks in
print at Cairo and Stamboul before the war, we may
feel sure that efforts will be made with increasing zeal
henceforward to inculcate the sense of *solidarité* amongst
all Moslems.   And there is an important class among
our Sepoys which would be likely to welcome it when
offered.   I refer to the Delhi Mohammadans, and all those
people immediately affected by the downfall of the Moghul Empire.   In strolling through the native town, after
the fall of Cairo, one saw not a few men, mostly belonging to the cavalry, who had established some sort of
intelligible relations with the populace.   Those who can
speak Arabic are very few, if any exist.   More Arabs
can make themselves understood in Hindustani, and if
time were allowed, at some expense and trouble, inter-
preters in abundance might be brought from the two
Hyderabads and elsewhere.   Persian is another link, for

a large number of Pathans speak that language more or
less. However it was managed, Arab and Sepoy did
contrive to talk before we had been established many
days in Cairo. We might observe knots of townspeople,
mostly well dressed, surrounding a couple of our native
soldiery in the Bazaar. Obsequiously they listened to the
strangers' remarks, and commented on them to a gaping
crowd. The rude and boisterous manners of the Egyptian are not to be repressed by any motive, since he
means no harm, and does not understand why his guileless brutality should give offence. But until the Cairenes
made this discovery they laboured under great disadvan-
tages. Opposite the Shoe Bazaar one day, I observed
two Sowars talking with earnestness, but with evident
difficulty, to a Sayyid. He was grave enough, but the
little throng crowded around laughed uproariously in a
sympathetic tone. The Sowars broke away in passion,
and went on, the Sayyid following. But such misunder-
standing would soon have been perceived and rectified
by shrewd zealots of El-Azar College and diplomatic
emissaries from Stamboul. It was well our Sepoys
departed. Their loyalty in the field lies beyond suspicion. It would be long before the thought of a
common cause to fight for, side by side with the
" jackals," could seriously be fixed in their minds. But
the seeds of a vague Panislamism would not be difficult to
plant, if teacher and taught had easy means of communi-

cation.   And, if they proved too feeble to overcome the contempt and disgust which Egyptian Moslem roused, they might ripen slowly under other skies to a perilous harvest.   But I feel sure that the influences of the campaign have been quite the other sort up to now.

# CAPTAIN WRENCH'S ILLUSION.

My friend Captain Wrench was thirty-five years old when some extraordinary events took place which he allows me to recount. His life to that age had been active and stirring; he did not understand what " nerves " are, he was quite incapable of poetry, and unfriends described him as a trifler—in short, a man very unlikely to experience tricks of imagination. He had returned from India on two years' leave for " urgent private affairs." The plea was no fiction. Although the season had long passed, business was so pressing that he found it needful to have a *pied-à-terre* in London. After trying a score of hotels, each less comfortable than another, he accepted an old schoolfellow's offer of his rooms in the Temple. Something of camp-life, as it were, a pleasing possibility of the unexpected, clung around those chambers. A man who dwelt therein was encompassed by enemies unseen, whose strategic movements round the door must be met by ceaseless vigilance. Wrench's schoolfellow, the best and almost the biggest of men, was more highly esteemed at the cover-side, on the cricket-field, and the river, than at the Temple Treasury—more warmly

I

welcomed in boudoirs and clubs than at his bank. Before
inducting Wrench, he frankly stated that some unreasonable proceedings of a tyrannous gas company forbade
him to include the use of their overrated monopoly in
the advantages offered. As a general rule, he advised
Wrench to distrust all raps at the " oak," and to defeat
such treacherous ambuscades by masterly inactivity; and
then the good fellow went his way.

The rooms were a fine example of that conscientious-
ness which distinguished our forefathers in all they did.
When masons of that period received a commission to
build, they raised a structure against which hurricanes
and floods would not prevail. Contemporary carpenters
had a like honesty. Their beams and panels matched
the solid walls. Not a joint had started in two hundred
years and more. It was quite a relief for the frivolous
modern mind to notice, amidst this display of virtue,
that every room of the three inclosed behind two massive
" oaks " led into another by two doors, one of which, if
not secret, was at least so contrived that even a suspicious
woman might easily overlook it; and as they all gave
upon the little hall, a client—let us say a client—could
choose a time to escape, though any two rooms of the
three were occupied.

The life Wrench had led rubs the freshness from all
novelty. A strange place was as familiar to him in half-
an-hour as it was likely to be in a month; and he slept in

a bed he never saw before as comfortably as in his own. He used these chambers once or twice a week for two months, without further thought regarding them. His habit was to dress there after business, and to return, if he stayed in town, long after midnight. So the summer passed, and autumn days shortened. One October evening he went home earlier than usual. Not a soul did he meet in those lonely courts. The wet pavement glistened in reflection of the gas, but there was no light in any window. Wrench felt it dull, very, and wondered why on earth he had left the club, where men smoked and chatted in a glow of cheerful firelight. The question recurred with greater strength whilst, after unlocking the heavy door, he searched for a candle in darkness that might be felt. When found, its feeble spark vainly contended with the black shadows. Disgusted with himself, Wrench entered the sitting-room, where no fire was laid, chose his book from a dusty pile upon the floor, and sat to read awhile. The Temple clock began to groan its usual lament before striking another hour from eternity.

Some instants afterwards Wrench looked up, thrilling awfully to a summons unheard. The room-door he had closed stood open; he saw the faint blue glimmer of the window in the little hall. On either side that pale reflection hung black nothingness. The candle-light fell dead there, swallowed up, though it touched the pictures and furniture on each hand lower down. It was not a cloud nor a mist that drooped around the door, but a sable blank. Not for a moment did Wrench think this an illusion of the eye. His forehead wrinkled and wet with fear, his eyebrows raised, he sat in speechless trance, waiting what should emerge from that unearthly void. It did not rest, but closed and gathered in, shutting out the still transparence of the casement, and opened again, like wings. Two sparks, keen and malignant, flashed and vanished above the blank. Then, where the doorway should have been, a child's face shone, pallidly luminous. Though twenty-five years had passed since he had seen those dead features, Wrench could have given them a name. Others followed, friends of youth and later years, all dead. Memory recognised each forgotten ghost. Some were there whose fate he had not learned. These visions did not seek his eye, but burned whitely for one pulse-beat and went out, as a firefly glows and disappears.

The procession ceased, and all was dark again—the wings closed—the baleful gleams returned. Then two faces showed, those of an old man and a girl. Wrench uttered an exclamation of dismay, and the black void contracted, took shape, closed swiftly round, crushed down on him. The two sparks intensified, burned into his very soul. And then, all was finished! Only the aching of the muscles in his face told Wrench what agony he had gone through. His mind was clear—he rose hastily and went out. The porter stared as he passed by, hatless, in evening dress, without an overcoat. He drove to the club. When the last member had gone, the steward lent him a cap, and he waited sleepless for daylight, sitting in one of the despised hotels. At earliest morning he sent a telegram: " Eugene Wrench to Colonel Innes, Bucharest. Are you both well? I have had a bad dream about you."

When the light was strong enough to search every corner of the haunted chambers, he entered, and brought away his clothes, dreading to look around the while. At evening arrived the answer : " Hagar Innes to Eugene Wrench. Quite well. Papa says, come here and we will nurse you." It was quite impossible to follow this advice—and yet—and yet—the impulse grew stronger, the conviction that in his full senses he had beheld this inexplicable warning became more clamorous as the hours went by. In short, Wrench started by the tidal train next evening. Three days' continuous travel brought him to Bucharest, where Colonel Innes was waiting at the Targovisté Station.

This old soldier belonged to the very small and secluded class of aristocratic Eurasians. His grandfather had commanded the armies of the Nizam, had professed el Islam, and married an Arab princess. The eldest son of this adventurer was trained in a military school at

home, where he distinguished himself alike in the study
and the playground.  He entered the Company's service,
and won no inconsiderable honours before his parent
recalled him to Hyderabad.  At the Nizam's Court also
he made his way, though he would never join the ceremonies of the creed to which he was born; opposition did
not go beyond this, however.  He married an Armenian
girl, also an heiress.  When the father died, Innes Sahib
was not nominated to succeed him, but he maintained a
position of great influence at Court.  Then came the
Mutiny, and this old soldier of the Company Bahadur
became very active and useful.  Besides aiding strenu-
ously to keep the Nizam quiet, he raised a superb regiment of horse at his own expense, and gave the command
to his only son.  This youth possessed all the qualities
which had made the fortune of the family, saving that
easy indifference about religion.  Educated in England
for a military life, though he had not joined the army,
he showed himself a brilliant officer, whilst his knowledge and skill with the native chiefs did the English
generals much service.  A young lady whom he rescued
from peril fell in love with him, swarthy though he was;
the Government recognised his services by granting him
an honorary colonelcy when peace returned, and em-
bodied his regiment.  With all his longing to pursue a
career so well begun, Colonel Innes knew himself un-
fitted for regular employment.  He married, and with-

drew to Hyderabad, where his father died within the year. And, before he could arrange the mighty and complicated matters of his heritage, his young wife also died, giving birth to a daughter. The circumstances attending her decease made this calamity yet more dreadful.

In her last moments, his wife had named the child Hagar, and so she was baptized. Colonel Innes was not a man to sacrifice his rights for the sake of nursing a baby. The widow of a comrade took charge of the infant, and settled with it at Simla on an extravagant allowance. The Colonel ran up to see them constantly. It was during this time, when Hagar was about five years old, that he made the acquaintance of Wrench, then a young subaltern. The liking on both sides grew warm. Five years later, Colonel Innes had settled his intricate affairs, and he withdrew to Europe, taking his child and Mrs. Ralph. The friendship of the old soldier and the young did not cool by time or absence. Whenever Wrench got leave he paid the Colonel a long visit, and he watched Hagar's growth in beauty with a feeling which he persistently described to himself as fraternal interest. The little girl's fleshless features, and lean, straight limbs rounded to more graceful symmetry each time he saw them, and Wrench found greater and greater difficulty in supporting his *rôle*.

Colonel Innes meanwhile waited with extreme impatience the moment when Hagar's completed education
should allow him to quit England. He suffered bitterly.
The "lick of the tar-brush" had haunted him from
school-days. He might have commanded that class of
society, larger and more amiable, which, being disconnected with India, would have seen in his Arab and
Armenian blood rather romance than shame. But he
never thought of seeking it. He could live neither with
his Anglo-Indian colleagues nor without them. At the
great military club which had elected him unanimously
at a moment of enthusiasm, he suffered tortures, but the
idea of joining another did not occur to him. At length
came the relief. All the professors declared Miss Innes
to be as thoroughly primed with accomplishments as
their resources could effect. Without difficulty the
Colonel arranged her "presentation" by an exalted
personage, and then the two escaped, joying like birds
set free. After several wanderings, they came to
Bucharest. The mode of life in that odd city commended itself to the father—saving the eternal bill-and-
coo; its ostentatious but not vulgar luxury appealed to
the daughter's instincts. They found a château to their
fancy some miles from the town, and the Colonel leased
it for three years. His expenditure, lavish even among
that vain and improvident nobility, attracted notice from

the first, and one glimpse of Hagar brought all society to his feet. Wrench had not visited them since they left England.

The fierce Roumanian winter had not yet set in, but, when the carriage turned into a bye-road, small sheets of snow lay in the copses and the sheltered slopes, and the wind was already bitter. Wrench had been delighted and surprised by the crowds and general brilliancy of Bucharest, as they drove along the Podoi Mogosoi, but this dull view checked his enthusiasm. They had been talking eagerly of India and old times, for the Colonel laughingly declared that he would leave the dream as a tale for Hagar. Wrench could not forbear remarking on the scene about them. "Yes," replied his host, "you see Roumania at its very worst. In a month we will ask your opinion again. But there is excellent shooting even now, as I will show you. Towards the end of November we will move to a small châlet I have in the Carpathians, where red deer and bears and wolves are abundant. As for wolves, if the season be early as they predict, we may have some sport here, for the brutes descend even on the villages. They are really dangerous, and one has to be careful in travelling at night. Two cadets were devoured in the Chaussée itself some years ago, between the barrier and the military school. What do you think of that? My house is just through the copse there. We have a gipsy village at our gates, with which I could well dispense, but Hagar cherishes the rascals."

They traversed the little wood, and suddenly came on a scene of popular rejoicing. Big bonfires blazed and every hut of a small straggling hamlet had half-a-dozen rushlights in its single window.

" Is there a fête?"

" I had not heard of it. Isn't this an extraordinary country, where the gipsy's special handicraft is house-building?"

"And where they live in the houses they build! What picturesque ruffians! They seem to be enthusiastically fond of you!"

" It's Hagar they love! She remembers Hindustani just well enough to talk to them, with the assistance of broken Roumanian and Italian and Latin, and I don't know what—an abominable mixture! Egad, here comes Si Miliu himself. You'll be able to understand him." Wrench wondered why.

They had gained the middle of the village, where two roads crossed. Here stood a little throng of men and women, better dressed than the others. They wore sheepskin coats, unfastened, showing the swarthy chests, fringed, not protected by a garment of linen. Bare also were their feet and legs, the wide white trouser falling little below the knee. Long black hair streamed on their shoulders, from a handkerchief, or a rough fur cap. Their wild eyes glistened in the torch-light. The women's costume differed, to all seeming, only in the gathering of the shirt at neck and waist, supposed by fiction to preserve decency. Their hair also streamed loose, and in feature, in the bold, laughing stare of the eyes, one could not distinguish one sex from the other at the same age.

Darker even than the rest was the village chief, who wore a sheepskin with embroidery on the breast and sleeves, which, cut short at the elbow, displayed a loose undergarment; he had high boots, too, and leather trousers. Saluting after the Hindustani fashion, he delivered an address in the same tongue. The poor gipsy folk rejoiced to see their seigneur's friend. He had come from a distant land that his father might not want a staff to lean on. Therefore the gipsy folk welcomed him, and would ever keep his name in mind, they and their children.

Wrench, much surprised, said a few courteous words, and they drove on, the villagers following with torches and tumult.

" How well that strange old man speaks Hindustani? "

" I am certain he is a gipsy of Hindustan—from Hyderabad I suspect. He scarcely speaks Roumanian to be understood, they tell me, and he has not been here long. In fact, my dear boy, Si Miliu is the most mysterious personage I ever met, and that is saying a great deal. Father, tell your young men to sing?"

At a word from their chief, the tossing, hurrying, noisy crowd fell into a sort of order. Six men in the prime of life, who were carrying violins, pushed to the front, behind them formed a number of youths, and after these the children. A storm of music suddenly burst forth. The air was in parts, distributed among bass, tenor, and alto, rising higher, thrilling more ecstatic, until the chorus struck in and raised it to a very frenzy of audacious inspiration; as suddenly, it paused and dropped and ceased, in a swift, short movement of the children's voices. Again and again the weird melody poured out. "I never heard music like that!" Wrench exclaimed, thrilling.

" It's like a composition of harmonious djins, isn't it? That is one of the battle-songs of Michel the Brave, by gipsy tradition. Here we are."

The château was a big, low structure, of no architectural pretensions, almost surrounded by substantial barns and outhouses. Two massive wings, protruding boldly from the façade, were evidently designed to protect these, as well as the central building, in case of a sudden foray. A stout iron grille running across from one to the other would delay a barbarous enemy the few moments needful for the inhabitants to take refuge in the wings. Its heavy, narrow gate stood open now. All the windows of the façade shone cheerfully, and at the gypsies' shout, before the carriage stopped, Hagar came bounding on the lawn. " Have you brought him, papa? How good it is of you to come, Captain Wrench! Go to the back, you gipsy men! " she continued in broken Hindustani. " Your supper is ready! " With a shrill cry they departed.

" Then it is to you we owe our grand reception," said Colonel Innes.

" What reception? There are only some neighbours and men from the barracks. Now, dear Captain Wrench, I must introduce you to some of our Roumanian fr—— acquaintances." A group of men, young and in uniform for the most part, stood about the door, and Wrench bowed like a machine at the recital of a dozen polysyllabic names. He would have described these youths, in his haste, as athletic barbers masquerading.

His young hostess was very bright and animated in talking with them when he descended to the drawing-room. In five years since he last saw her, Hagar Innes had reached the perfection of a strange and witching beauty. Hers was not the rounded prettiness which comes to its zenith at eighteen, but an aquiline delicacy of feature much more slow to ripen; she had nearly reached her twenty-first birthday. What might have been too severe in the moulding of the face was deli-

ciously broken by the contrast of golden hair, English;
with cream-white skin, Armenian ; and large, eager,
black eyes, Arab.   Bucharest excels in the beauty of its
women, and nowhere is public taste more critical.   But
the native poets had exhausted earth and heaven, Christian and Moslem, to find objects to compare with Hagar
Innes.

She ran up to Wrench and took his arm.   No one
else obtained a word willingly, and the Colonel was
hard put to it entertaining guests who spoke only French
besides their mother tongue.   Unlike her father, Hagar
subordinated Indian interests to the absorbing question of
the dream.   " It must have been very awful to make you
remember us !   We had not heard for a month !   I have
engaged Si Miliu to interpret it.   He is the most delight-
fully dreadful old man you have ever heard of—a real
necromancer !   Papa is afraid of him.   You know we did
awful things at Hyderabad, and Si Miliu can peach
upon us ! "

" What has he told you? "

" Oh, he doesn't tell me scandal.   But he has given me
lots of information, some of which papa owns to be true.
My great-grandmother was an Arab princess, you know,
and Si Miliu declares her mother was a gipsy.   But tell
me your dream? "

Wrench protested there was nothing to tell, and on
being pressed began some lame story, which Hagar

interrupted. " Keep your secret, if you like," she said, offended. " My necromancer can read thoughts as well as interpret dreams. He will tell me. Don't be frightened, that's all."

The exclusive attention of the hostess to one guest gave special offence to a gentleman on her left hand, who did not conceal his vexation. A tall fellow he was, profuse of moustache and eyebrow, handsome certainly, but rather sullen of expression. The others called him " Prince." His anxiety to please had been undisguised until he found that, after each few words which Hagar gave him on polite compulsion, she resumed her talk with the stranger. Then he glared and fumed in silence. But when Miss Innes, vexed with her friend, addressed him kindly, he warmed up, and plunged into discreet love-making. Her irritation soon passed, however, and with a smiling apology she turned away again. The white wrath of the Prince at this treatment was homicidal.

Coffee and cigars were served in the drawing-room, where Si Miliu had already installed himself, cross-legged upon a sofa; his high boots exchanged for spotless shoes of felt. He rose and bowed very low, touching eyes and either breast. " It is one of our magician's peculiarities," Hagar whispered, " that he will never come to you—you must go to him, even though he be summoned."

Wrench now saw the old man more plainly, and he was not struck. The face was of common Hindoo gipsy-type, but a certain look of intensity dwelt in the large heavy-lidded eyes. The hair and beard were dyed with unbecoming effect. He had doffed his sheepskin, and wore the common peasant dress of summer.

The Roumanian officers were deeply scandalised to find a gipsy seated in the same room with themselves. The Prince relieved his feelings by exclaiming roughly, " Stand up, slave, when great people are present! " Si Miliu rose and stood, with hands pressed closely together as in an attitude of prayer.

" Prince! " exclaimed Hagar, red with passion, " you forget that this old man is the guest of your host."

He started at the keen reproof, and stood speechless. Hagar put her hand upon the gipsy's arm, and gently forced him down. " I beg your pardon, Si Miliu. This is an English gentleman's house, where you are always welcome and honoured! Now here is your coffee, and when you have drunk it I have a great question for your skill. This friend of my father's—and of mine when he is not stupid—was induced to come here by a bad dream, which he will not tell me. I have promised him you will read the secret. Don't disgrace me, Si Miliu."

" I will do what is possible, missy-baba. Beg him to approach me."

" Now, Captain Wrench, imagine that the bugle has

sounded, and you are leading a forlorn hope. Draw near."

Wrench obeyed, saying, " I shall rather imagine that I am going to be photographed. Will he operate coffee-cup in hand ? " .

" Profane being ! Whatever happens, your fate will be deserved for blaspheming my idol ! "

With a deprecating gesture of the hand Si Miliu apologised for staring, and whilst he drank his coffee in small sips, like a Turk, he looked Wrench steadily in the face, then bowed, and turned to Hagar with a smile.

" You know it already ? " she eagerly cried. "You have read it."

" No; but, if the Captain-sahib will allow me, I will discover his secret."

Hagar swiftly removed the coffee-cup. " Now, Captain Wrench, dear Captain Wrench, show yourself a man. Give this delightful old creature your hand."

" Must I cross it with silver? "

" I don't hate you, because I know how ignorant you are, and that your humorous remarks are only intended to hide the faltering of your courage. Now, Si Miliu."

The gipsy studied Wrench's hand with intense scrutiny for a long time. "It is a good man !" he exclaimed at length. " A brave man, Colonel-sahib. Worthy to be heard though he asked for your greatest treasure ! " The gipsy looked meaningly at Hagar, who returned the glance with bewilderment; she suddenly blushed, and exclaimed, "But Captain Wrench's character has nothing to do with his dream."

"The dream?  Beg this young man to kneel down."

He did so.  Si Miliu put one hand on his neck, and with the other held his right hand firmly.  After a pause he said, "Listen now.  I dreamed I saw a man reading in a dark room.  It grew darker.  He looked up awfully at the door.  He remembered many friends who had died, and he feared for the Colonel-sahib and his daughter.  His pulse stopped, and for an instant there was peril.  But the good powers were watching.  They strengthened his failing nerves.  He rose and came out."

"It is not enough!" Wrench cried.  "Tell me more."

"I can tell only what you know."

"What does it mean then?"

"If you do not understand, how should your drogman?  Ask the Colonel-sahib!"

"I see you are convinced now," said Hagar in a frightened voice.

"May I tell all to the Colonel?"

"Why else have you come here?"

"Brought by you?"

"By a dream, as I understand."

"O, be frank!  Is the danger imminent?"

"Danger is always imminent over this house."  The old gipsy rose and stretched out his hand, whilst the deep eyes looked into vacancy. "This dream of yours, sahib, I knew nothing of it! I am frank to you and all! Let those who understand take warning."

As if in answer to the challenge, a furious blast of wind roared suddenly without. The window-frames shook, the candles blew out, the logs blazing on the hearth sent a fiery tongue that seemed to sweep across the room towards Si Miliu. Hagar, screaming with excitement, threw herself into her father's arms. But in a second the commotion passed.

It may be imagined that the Roumanian officers were bewildered by what had already passed, incomprehensible to them. But they guessed that the gipsy had been practising some art, and their superstitious natures thrilled. Crowding together, they threatened Si Miliu, who bowed in deprecation. Colonel Innes kept his presence of mind. He said, laughing, "If your dream signified that my house was to be burnt down, it is in a fair way of fulfilment." Lights were brought, liqueurs handed round, and the laotorei made their appearance. Absorbed in listening to the strains which have such an effect on their volcanic nature, the Roumanian officers forgot the offence of Si Miliu. Tranquillity was restored. Hagar laughed at her panic, and bantered the Prince on his alarm at a gust of wind.

Si Miliu was first to leave, rising stealthily with a

general salaam.  Wrench stopped him.  " When shall I
ask for more explanations ? "

" When it is necessary you will be told, I suppose."

A little before midnight the Roumanians went off, on
horseback, or in well-appointed carriages.  Hagar retired,
and Colonel Innes led the way to his den.  Wrench told
all his story at once, the old soldier listening in silence;
every pause was filled by the eldritch screams of the
gypsy fiddle in the servants' quarters, and the barbaric
chant of their fine voices.  Just as Wrench concluded,
a soft tap at the door announced Hagar, in dressing-
gown and bewitching little cap of lace.  Her feet were
naked in their little slippers.  So, many a time in years
gone by, had she slipped down to her father's study
when Wrench was there.  It gave him a shock to find
that she would still take the same innocent liberty.

" I could not bear the suspense, papa," said Hagar;
" and I knew Captain Wrench would be talking to you.
Please tell me what it all means."

So Wrench went over his story again.

" I understand now," murmured Hagar thoughtfully.
" You have been summoned here to protect us.  But
who wishes us ill, papa ? "

" I will tell you, darling, as it has come to this.  My
grandfather had other sons and daughters, of whom the
Princess was not the mother.  He provided for them

handsomely; but they were not satisfied. All through my father's life, and until I left India, they intrigued against us. I am afraid there is nothing of which they are not capable—indeed, I know it too well!" he added bitterly. Wrench knew he was thinking of his wife's death, which Indian rumour attributed to poison.

" But do you believe they could reach us here?"

" At every great crisis of our life in the old days we were warned by visions. For many years past nothing of the sort has happened, and I thought my enemies were disheartened after I had driven them from Hyderabad. But it is not so. I am quite sure this apparition which showed itself to Wrench was sent by the powers which protect us now as they used to do. A moment of peril is at hand."

" And what has Si Miliu to do with it, for some part he has, I am sure?" asked Hagar. " Who is he?"

" I do not know. That he is acquainted with all our family history has long been evident. Now, child, go to bed. Whatever is coming, we can only wait and trust and pray. Good night, darling!" Hagar put up her pale face to be kissed, and silently they parted. Going to their rooms, they heard the gipsy chorus ringing as the laotorci sought their village: "Goodnight, seigneurs! Good-night, dames! Sleep safe! God is watching!"

Next morning all the country was white with snow,

and a frosty sky above raised their spirits. Hagar was
not less beautiful for the dark lines round her eyes which
told of a sleepless night—so beautiful she was that
Wrench felt himself a presumptuous old fool who had
even thought, in the watches of the night, that such a
creature might be his.   This despondency deepened as
they rode into Bucharest to ask about the sleigh which
the Colonel had ordered from Vienna.   Hagar said
frankly, " You are not at all like what I remembered,
Captain Wrench.   You used to make me laugh when I
was dull! "

The words stung him.   " I was not so old then, Miss
Innes, and you were younger."

" Oh! " she answered carelessly, "if that's it, I will
be as young as you like, only set an example! "   That
was just what Wrench could not do.

In the afternoon, as he stood with the Colonel at a
window, they saw Hagar slip past in her furs.   They
hurried after.   She entered a hut in the gipsy village
and remained till dusk ; the Colonel confessed he had
been there in the morning, but had learned nothing.
After dinner, he asked if Hagar had been more fortunate.

" No," she answered, colouring.   "Si Miliu talked as
usual, but he gave me no information."

Day followed day, and nothing happened.   The snow
was deep enough for sleighing, and merry parties
assembled at the house, or followed from the Chaussée

for dinner and an unceremonious dance. The Prince was always on hand, and Wrench watched his flirtation with dismay. Though Hagar could not be his, he hated the notion of her marriage with a man like that. The Colonel, so shrewd and so devoted to his daughter, was not unbiassed here. After being lightly esteemed in England, he contemplated a match so illustrious with complacency. To himself the Prince was all that could be wished, respectful, attentive, loftily modest. His family had been distinguished before the fall of Constantinople, his wealth was immense, his person handsome, his intelligence regarded on all hands. Colonel Innes might not be trusted to check his daughter's inclination in such a case.

Wrench often met Si Miliu, who salaamed with eyes cast down, and went his way, obviously unwilling to talk. One afternoon, as he strolled moodily through the copse, Wrench came across the gipsy face to face.

" I cannot endure this, Si Miliu. When is the danger coming? "

"I told the truth, sahib! Why you have been brought, we do not know. But there is a danger, if you will use your eyes."

" Here—where?"

" You think yourself too old, and ——" he paused, respectfully contemptuous.

"You can read my thoughts, Si Miliu! Do I guess right?"

"You are a good man, and a brave, but too old!" Si Miliu laughed with quiet sarcasm. "Too old! Listen, Captain-sahib! We protect only the son, and the son's son! The danger of this young lady is no concern of ours! But I love her, I, the poor gipsy, and I would see her happy!"

"What am I to do? Tell me, for Heaven's sake!"

"Too old, this Captain-sahib. Too old! I do not deal in philtres, sir."

"I implore you! ——" But Si Miliu went off chuckling.

From that interview Wrench took hope, and changed his tactics. Since there was a chance, he would not be beaten without trying. A study of Hagar's character satisfied him that it was the respect and masterful disposition underlying all the Prince's humility which impressed the girl. His Highness took it as a birthright, like his title, that he should excel all other men in what he undertook. His despondency gone, Wrench shook off his laziness, and set himself to overthrow this good-looking idol. He found again the spirits which made Hagar laugh, danced with her, met the Prince on his own field. She did not hide her pleasure, resuming on the instant those easy relations which had been so agreeable in times past.

Then a brief thaw interrupted the eternal sleighing. A gymkhana which Wrench had been preparing for days past, with the hearty goodwill of a bored noblesse, was held before the château gates. A fine show of lovely faces and costly toilettes was there; the Colonel surpassed his famous hospitality at the lunch; and there was a ball in the evening. In every trial of skill Wrench was victorious of course. As he expected, the Prince could not endure this superiority, and, in a desperate effort to win the prize for tent-pegging, he twisted himself out of the saddle, sustaining an ignominious fall. When he recovered this shaking, a paper-chase was on, and the gipsy fox, cunningly directed, found a score of ugly places, all close to the road, whence the ladies could see the sport. The Prince rode well; but this sort of thing is not practised at the school, and he had another " cropper," supported with outward pluck and inward fury. Si Miliu was passing the gate as Wrench came by, muddy but heroic, laughing with Hagar in her barouche. His demure smile had a very kindly magic.

After dinner that night the Colonel fell asleep. He had ridden with such spirit as becomes an old gentleman, shirking no obstacle, but cutting off all ugly corners. Hagar was virtually alone in the drawing-room with Wrench, whilst her father slept.

" Will you confess, Captain-sahib? All those sports

and exercises were designed to show off your accomplishments ! "

" I will confess anything you like, and more."

"I distrust a criminal so glib in admitting his offences.
Why couldn't you leave the Prince happy in his conceit? "

" Because I am jealous, Hagar. I have presumed to
love you."

" Well, but that is no reason."

" You do not understand me. I ask you to be my
wife."

" Oh ! "

" I am too old and too worn for your bright youth?
Say so at once, and put me out of my misery."

" Too old !—There ! don't say any more to-night—
please don't ! Let us laugh."

" I cannot laugh till you have spoken. Give me an
answer, Hagar."

" You want to marry me? I understood you came
to preserve us from danger ? "

" The greatest danger for you would be to marry a
man who could not love you as you are worthy to be
loved."

" Would that be the very most terrible fate that could
befall me? And who is the man ? " asked Hagar,
colouring.

" Any man ; for no one could love you as I do, as I have done for years ! "

She was thoughtful for a time. " Papa, dear, you have been trying to give us a laotorei performance through your nose, and oh ! words could not tell how conspicuously you have failed. Tea is ready ! "

Next day the Prince arrived for lunch, with several comrades. He laughingly pleaded his bruises as an excuse to stay the afternoon indoors, while Wrench paid an expected visit to the barracks. A wolf-hunt on the grandest scale was projected by the officers, in requital of the Colonel's hospitality. When Wrench got home, after discussing details, Colonel Innes looked grave, his daughter excited. Neither professed any more interest in the wolf-hunt. Hagar withdrew early. As she kissed her father, she whispered, " Remember your promise ! "

Wrench heard the words, and put his intepretation on them. The Prince was accepted, and Hagar, of course, wished to spare his feelings as long as possible. A wretched evening. He could not command himself to hide his grief; Hagar looked surprised, then offended.

That night the frost returned, and preparations began for the great event. From noon to midnight the house resounded with clank of sword and jingling of spurs. The Prince did not appear, and Wrench learned that he had taken leave of absence on urgent private affairs ; to arrange for the marriage, doubtless. Si Miliu also was away. Wrench did his best to resume his frank intercourse with Hagar ; but she remained cool, sarcastic sometimes, quite pitiless.

It had been her intention to assist at the battue, though every one dissuaded her; but as the day drew near her wilfulness grew fainter, and at length she announced, with unnecessary vehemence, the resolve to stay at home. Upon the fatal morning, a great breakfast assembled all the hunters, and the hostess played her part with charming grace to all but Wrench. He, poor fellow, received the coolest good wishes, whilst for all others she had smiles and pretty jests.

For twenty-four hours the beaters had been out, searching the woods, and converging towards a valley, some ten miles from the château, where the sportsmen would be ambushed. None but women, children, and invalids were left in the gipsy village. The beaters could not yet be heard when the Colonel and his party had taken their positions. An hour passed, and a second. The Roumanian officer who kept watch with Wrench swore strange oaths unceasingly, as he clapped his fur-gloved hands. Towards three o'clock, faint and distant halloing told that the beaters were astir.

At this moment a gipsy boy came stealing across the snow, from one black trunk to another. He called Wrench, and speaking with difficulty, as one who has learned a lesson, he said in Hindustani, " You are wanted! "—And ran off.

The horses were stationed a mile behind. Again and again Wrench tripped in the snow, running at full speed through the woods, but he held to his rifle. Mounting, he galloped along the beaten track, till a heavy fall made him cautious. It was dusk when he passed through the empty village. All was still at the château, where no groom remained to take his horse. He ran upstairs, and in the drawing-room found Hagar.

" Has there been an accident? " she cried, starting up.

" No! I was summoned, by whom I do not know, if it was not Si Miliu. A boy said you wanted me."

" It was good of you to obey, but indeed I see no danger, except that gun you have brought into the drawing-room."

" Pardon me! It may be wanted."

" Why, what danger can there be? " said Hagar, rather frightened. " Look! All is quiet! Ha! what is that?"

Wrench sprang to the window where she stood, which looked on the back courtyard. In the half-light he saw dusky figures creeping and vanishing in the shadow of the outhouses. Their movements were stealthy and sinister; all friendly neighbours far away! Hagar clung to him, panting with fright. " Oh, they are brigands! Save me! " she cried.

"I will save you or die! Nerve yourself, darling!"
But she was wild with fear.

Wrench took her in his arms and carried her to the
small inner room. Whilst hindered by her panic clinging, he dragged furniture before the door and blocked
it. Hagar became almost senseless with excitement and
fear. He laid her down, looked to his arms, and took
station by the window, which gave on the front expanse,
where the snow, still untrodden, made a glimmering
twilight. Dim and confused movements on the lawn
were visible rather to his consciousness than to his eyes.
Suddenly a voice was raised, speaking angrily; a gunshot
answered it from the house! That flash lit the scene.
A score of armed men surged round the hall-door, all
clad in sheepskin, with tangled hair upon the shoulders.
Raising a yell they bounded forward, and the tumult
of a fight burst suddenly upon the stillness. By the
glare of random shots, Wrench saw an indistinguish-
able medley. At the same instant a fray began upon
the other side, crash of firearms, cries and shouts, and
the breathless din of hand-to-hand encounters. The
instinct of battle thrilled Wrench's soul. He dragged
away the barrier he had raised, but soft arms caught
him in a frenzied clutch.

"Do not leave me, do not leave me! I shall die!
Oh, what is it?"

" Our defenders are fighting down below, and honour calls me! Not while I live shall any one reach you!"

" No, no, no! Stay with me, or let me go with you! We will die together!" She put up her lips to his; he gathered her triumphantly in his arms. " My darling, we will not die but live together!"

Wrench led her to a couch, and she sat trembling, her head upon his chest, her arms about his neck. The noise outside diminished, passed into the distance, but no one disturbed them for an hour. Hagar sat paralysed with fear, convulsively shivering, heedless of her lover's consolation. At length the hall below resounded with hasty steps, and the Colonel's voice was heard shouting for his daughter's name.

" Here, sir, here!" Wrench answered; and the old soldier burst in.

When Hagar had been put to bed, and the doctor had reassured them, some explanation of these events was forthcoming. Two prisoners confessed themselves to belong to a brigand troop which had descended from the Carpathians, hearing of the Englishman's wealth. They said, however, that a half-dozen strangers had joined in the attack, with the approval of their chief, who was dead. They expected to find the château empty, but the gipsies, secretly recalled, held it in superior force. Not one of the strangers was identified, either amongst the slain or the captured.

The Colonel also had his story. As the beaters approached, a gipsy boy crept up to him and muttered in Hindustani, " Si Miliu says this place is dangerous. Go home!" The first wolf came prowling by at this moment, and the Colonel rolled it over. The boy, excited, took him by the arm, repeating his words, but shot after shot told that the fun was quickening, and the excited sportsman would not heed. At length the messenger shook him hard, volubly directing his attention to the rear. In the gathering dusk the Colonel saw a number of ruffians approaching, with treachery in their movements. He turned and ran. Several bullets whizzed about his ears, unnoticed in the fusillade.

Not till next evening did Hagar appear, pale and weak, but divinely beautiful in Wrench's eyes. She avoided his glance even whilst speaking to him, but the time of self-distrust had passed by, and he knew that this pretty confusion boded no ill. After her retirement, Si Miliu was announced; he had not shown since the fight. They found him in his usual chair, cross-legged, and gravely courteous; their thanks and questions scarcely got reply; the gipsy breathed short and deep in excitement. After half-an-hour's broken talk, he started— with a thrill, Wrench saw again that shapeless blackness, and the malignant sparks above. It divided. Through the gap, in faint and tremulous outline, he beheld the glimmering of marble columns, with rich stuffs between, a ceiling fretted in gorgeous hues, and sparkling with bits of mirror set therein. Although the candles on the table seemed to burn undimmed, all the light of the apartment came from that opening. The scene fixed and moulded as they watched; figures appeared. On a marble seat, inlaid with many colours, sat, cross-legged, a swarthy chief, bearded, clothed in gems from neck to waist. His turban flamed with diamonds, and the shawls on which he sat hung in splendid folds about the throne.

A little crowd of dignitaries, superbly robed, stood or sat with eyes downcast around him; prostrate on the ground in front lay three old men. Their raised hands moved tremulously, as in supplication; they beat their heads upon the floor. The chief waved his hand. A dozen armed men advanced, lifted them roughly to their feet, and dragged them out. Glimmering palace and sable curtain vanished. "It is over!" said Si Miliu. "The true God bless them all!"

He went out while they sat entranced. Hagar rose, sobbing hysterically, and threw herself in the Colonel's arms.

"You saw that?" Wrench began.

"Hush! Never speak of it again!" And they busied themselves restoring the girl to composure.

The next morning Si Miliu was gone from the village, and they heard of him no more. After rewarding his gipsy-defenders beyond their dreams of peasant wealth,

the Colonel hastened to leave Roumania.   He returned
to India with Wrench and his wife, and there died.

Of the Prince's fate all is a mystery.   After his refusal
by Hagar, he had remained solitary at his house, brooding revenge.   On the morning of the wolf-hunt he left
home with two servants, taking, as there was reason
to believe, a large sum in gold.   This fact is adduced
by some as evidence that he may still be living; but
others draw just the opposite conclusion.   The bones of
a man and horse were found in the track of the escaping
wolves.   The doctors pronounced an opinion that both
had been killed by sabre-cuts before the animals found
them.   Some suspect that this unfortunate man was the
Prince.

Long years have passed in quiet happiness for Wrench
and his wife.   They talk now of those events, and they
have convinced their brains, if not their superstitious
instincts, that they were all an illusion.

# COURAGE: A CHAPTER OF EXPE-
# RIENCE.

THIS is no essay. At Alexandria the other day I heard of a seaman who cut off two wounded fingers— his own—with a jack-knife, and turned up for duty as usual. The jack-knife had been lately used for shredding tobacco; and, when the mutilation was discovered, this poor fellow's arm had fallen into such a state that the doctors feared they must cut it off.

The story reminded me of an incident which occurred within my knowledge more than twenty years ago, and that suggested others. I am not going to argue or theo- rise, but simply to hold the pen whilst memory drives.

A match to the sailor's plucky deed was that of Grim- bold, a sergeant of Rajah Brooke's police. When the Chinese attacked his post, after a gallant resistance, he jumped from an embrasure, and cut his way through the crowd. A bullet shattered his forearm. Grimbold bor- rowed a native sword, with which and a small pen-knife he amputated his limb at the elbow, tied it up, and marched nearly two miles in an effort to join the Rajah. Under custody at the fort when the Chinese appeared was

a madman. Him Grimbold armed and posted; but the
maniac refused to crouch under shelter. He swore that
to hide was unworthy a brave man, and planted himself
in the verandah, alone against a thousand. There he
blazed away like the sanest of invulnerable epic heroes.
When Grimbold decided to evacuate the place, the
madman, unhurt, obeyed his call. But he refused to
jump from a window, and the others left him eagerly
unbarring a door that he might sally forth like a gentleman.

This man evidently understood the danger, but did
not feel it. Some infirmities are great aids to nerve. I
remember a war correspondent, stone-deaf, whose recklessness in pushing under fire and coolness when the
bullets flew thick impressed the Turks, who watched
him with a superstitious feeling. Wholly bereft of
hearing, he could not recognise one quarter of the peril,
and the awful din of battle affected him not at all. This
gentleman made several campaigns, and was killed in
Armenia, I believe.

The tricks imagination plays on courage are endless,
sometimes kindly, more often cruel. Once on a time—
the date is recent—a small English force lay for some
days in a terribly exposed position. Experienced officers
did not talk publicly of the ugly chances round. Two
young fellows shared a tent: the one had seen much service in little time, the other was quite fresh, full of con-

fidence, only longing that the enemy would show. He chaffed his comrade on his nervousness, until the latter. being also young, was tempted to open the eyes of inexperience, and show how desperate would be their case under certain most probable conditions. After that explanation he went to sleep; his fire-eating chum declares that he slept no more until circumstances changed. Of these young men who behaved so differently one has now the Victoria Cross; the second displays a medal with two clasps, and he won his company before his beard was fairly grown.

There are those incapable of fear, be the peril of what sort it may, savage man, disease, accident, death itself— the assured cessation of living. But they are very, very few; personally I have recognised but one. Many men and some women are proof against most dangers, but they dread one form, or perhaps several. In thinking of such persons, Scobeleff naturally recurs to one's mind. He once declared to me that he was terribly afraid of mere death. He said also that his fearlessness was a habit, which, if poverty and a sense of ill-usage had not made him desperate, he would never have found courage to acquire. But Scobeleff loved a paradox; a reckless talker upon every subject, he was specially untrustworthy about himself.

I should rather incline to think that mere courage is more general amongst Russians than amongst any other

people nowadays. I mean the unreasoning, irresponsible
readiness of a dog to risk life and liberty upon provoca-
tion. Not more volunteers rush out, when a desperate
enterprise is mooted, than from our own ranks; more
than all is a mathematical absurdity. But the Englishman stakes his life in another, a grander spirit. He feels
and reckons with the peril. Before meeting it, so far as
I have seen examples, he is quiet, thoughtful, contem-
plating the worst, and making his arrangements. A
Russian scorns all that, does not even think of it. After
assuring himself, rather roughly, that the needful dispo-
sitions have been made, he becomes the lightest-hearted
of the company to which he hastens. I do not say,
affects to become, for it may well be that deadly danger
stirs him to mirth, as it stirs another man, equally brave,
to self-commune. I cannot forget an instance on Radi-
sovo Hill, the morning of the great attack. An infantry
regiment stood at ease in the rain, waiting the order to
descend into that valley blind with smoke, echoing with
thud of guns and angry crackle of musketry. The
colonel and a staff captain approached and asked us to
accept charge of letters for their wives, to be forwarded
in case of accident. Then they stood chatting of London
and Paris with the warmth of men whose hearts were
there, though the battle raged closer, and a ball now
and then musically spun above our heads. They asked
the precise story of a scandal half-forgotten now, and

their shrewd comments told they were attending closely, when an aide came galloping through the mist. Three minutes afterwards the doomed regiment filed away down towards the valley of death.

Baker Pasha loves to recount an instance of the courage we are used to think truly British. During his grand retreat, which the greatest of living soldiers declared " a master-work," it became necessary to fire a large Bulgar village. Baker sent a company to do the work. Time passed, but no smoke arose. One after another he dispatched four orderlies to ask the cause of the delay; none returned. Then the general turned to his aide-de-camp: " Go, Alix," he said, " and see what those fools are doing!" Alix went full gallop, a Circassian behind. He did not come back, but the smoke appeared in thin wreaths. Every moment pressed. Baker sent another company with another English officer. At the entrance of the village they found two orderlies dead, and no sign of troops; but the village, full of lusty Bulgars, was buzzing like a hive. They pushed on. In the middle space the Chirkess stood, holding two horses; Colonel Alix, alone in a maddened throng, was moving from hut to hut, setting the thatch alight with matches. So the village was burnt, and the retreating Turks gained that delay which saved them—saved perhaps Stamboul, and so saved England from a desperate war.

I do not know that this story has been printed, though

many have heard it. No one is more disinclined than I
to single out persons for adorning my tale, when the
name has not been officially announced ; but the valiant
deeds of a soldier in performance of his duty are excepted from the rule.

Of a class quite different was the fine devotion of Lord
Gifford during the Ashanti war. He undertook the
scouting for our advance, under conditions as unlike as
could possibly be to those which usually attend such
duties. We scarcely saw him after he had entered the
woods. At the passage of the Adansi Hills, Lord
Gifford paid us a visit, and he turned up, of course, at
the battle of Amoaful, gaining his V.C., nominally, for
valour displayed in the assault of Bequoi next day. But
the reward was won before that, when he led his gallant
little company miles in front of our outposts and advance-
guards, creeping round the savage foe, cutting off
stragglers to get information, watching from the bush at
midnight such awful scenes as the bloody burial of
Amanquattiah. Lord Gifford had with him, if I remember rightly, two West Indian soldiers, two Kossus, two
Houssas, and a miscellaneous collection of barbarians,
the wildest and most ferocious to be obtained on the
recommendation of woodcraft and devilry. As we
passed upon the march his lonely camps deserted, the
fires long extinct in the circlet of piled boughs and
entanglements of vines, the least imaginative felt a

shock—so lonely and lost they seemed in the shadow of the forest, between the savage enemy and ourselves.

Of all classes, the bravest certainly is the sailor. His way of life from childhood trains him to be fearless, to be very shrewd within a certain limited purview, to be open-handed of superfluities, to be instinctively conscious of his own interests and resolute in securing them. But all who have served with him ashore remark a character-istic of sailors, which, undiscussed and unanalysed, causes that want of confidence which nearly all soldiers feel in a naval brigade. English officers entertain it more than do others ; as for Jack, his careless pride of self has not admitted it possible that a soldier could look down on him. But in foreign armies and navies the same idea prevails, to a less extent only because fewer instances of common service have suggested it. I am sure I know the reason, and it is as simple as can be. The better the sailor, the more has he studied, and the more is he acquainted with the dangers that threaten him at sea. A storm sweeps down with insufficient warning or no warning at all; an enemy may appear on the horizon, coming out of space as it were, and in an hour he may be fighting for life. The safety of all in a troublous time may depend on the wakefulness, the judgment of one man; and, if there be a flaw in arrangements over which few or none on board have control, all is lost.

Trained in such ideas until they become an instinct, the sailor goes ashore to take part in military operations. He sees, as one may say, no man at the mast-head to give alarm. The position he is set to hold is isolated, or at least open on one side. The enemy is known to lie in overwhelming numbers somewhere about. Why should he not come down and overwhelm the post? With the preconceived idea that soldiers are all more or less incapable, the officers of a naval brigade in such case are doubly convinced that the ship must depend upon itself. They raise redoubts and works; they dig like gnomes; cheerfully, yet with an injured sense, they keep sentry and picket-guard in such extravagant fashion as only sailors could endure. The military officer observes them with polite derision. He knows, for instance, having studied the ground and the circumstances, that, to advance from the direction which those good fellows are watching so zealously, an enemy must march three days without water. He has confidence that, although no look-out be visible, shrewd heads are employing active means, not less efficient, to insure the general safety. He has no experience which teaches him to expect danger continually from powers and accidents unseen, unsuspected. In short, he is not used to storms, nor to the sudden appearance of hostile forces out of space, nor to a foe who carries with him wherever he goes all things needful for combat and subsistence; and he seldom reflects upon the difference of his education and the sailor's.

No one has ever questioned the supreme fighting zeal of a naval brigade, which in all countries, I think, is superior to that of soldiers. But again, if the rout come, after the seamen have done their best, their instinct betrays itself. I have never personally seen a *sauve qui peut* of sailors, but I am told that it is much more hopeless than that of an army, and I should be inclined to believe so; for, when the ship is obviously lost, men take to the boats, and that familiar discipline which keeps order in emergency at sea is absent under the conditions of land service. The individuality which a sailor's life tends to encourage, and to suppress which is the tendency of the soldier's training, obtains free control, and every man looks to his own safety.

The bravest race of savages, I think, amongst the many I have known, is the Montenegrin; but, whilst I write, competitors recur to mind. Every square foot of the Black Mountain has its legend of desperate fight, often disastrous, but always honourable. A little instance of Montenegrin courage, which came under my own eyes, is as pretty as any of the stories recounted by the wandering bard. Whilst Dulcigno was threatened by European fleets and Montenegrin armies, the Albanians holding it, a dense smoke arose one day in that quarter.

The news of this phenomenon spread widely, and caused a positive statement in all the morning papers of the civilised world that the Albanians had fired their town. At sunset, unable to get news, and the people being much excited, I hired a boat at Pristan Antivari for the purpose of reconnoitring. A young officer had come down on business from the camp at Sutormans. He said to me: " What is the use of your going to Dulcigno, when you are not acquainted with the language of your boatmen, and you don't know the country? Send a message to Buko Petrovitch, the general, telling him I have gone in your boat to inquire. I will bring you news."

So I sent a note to the general, and forthwith this young officer started. At morning the boat returned, without him, but the men were charged to tell me that Dulcigno stood just as usual. Presently the commandant came, laughing. He said: " Effendi, that youth ha$^s$ made fools of us. He wanted to see his sweetheart in Dulcigno, and when the boat drew near he swam to land. If the Ghegghes catch him, they'll flay him alive." I don't know whether they caught him, but he did not return whilst I stayed, nor did he rejoin the army, for Buko Petrovitch sent to ask about him, ten days afterwards.

Afghan courage is undeniable; but it belongs to the fervid class. In a headlong charge—for resistance to the death when that issue has been resolved beforehand—no people on earth excel the Pathans. But an accident will strangely disconcert their minds; they seldom fight a lost battle. The history of their wars is as full of panic defeats as of heroic victories. The Piper of Jellalabad represents a type among them. At a certain hour every evening he used to climb a hill at the very limit of musket-range, blow his pibroch, dance his jig of defiance, and then withdraw. An admiring retinue attended him, heedless of the shots which occasionally told. At length an English marksman killed the piper, whose renown will be preserved for generations in the name he gave that hill. After his death, not one of the hundreds who had seemed indifferent to peril challenged our fire. Cases of the same sort frequently occurred in the last war. At Jamrud fort the sentries were potted at every night by the same man, or at least by the same weapon, for its peculiar report was recognised. One night, as we sat in the mess-room, a detonation louder than usual drew our notice. In the morning we found a burst pistol, rifled, and from that time our sentries were no longer molested. Natives presently reported that the man was unhurt, but neither he nor his fellows resumed their firing practice.

In that reckless bloodthirstiness which contains, of course, a proportion of courage, but which is more pro-

perly described as devilry, the Pathan will not be out-
Heroded. I do not speak of Ghazis, or " martyrs for
the faith," who murder to win heaven, and accept death
as essential to the merit of the deed. The Afghan who,
without vows or illusions, sees an opportunity to perform
a desperate act which will bring him pleasure or profit,
is not easily deterred by the danger of retribution. And
he displays great presence of mind. Some English
officers riding through the Khurd Khyber heard shots.
They quickened their pace, and at a turn of the defile
ran into a brisk skirmish. Three men were defending
some loaded donkeys against an equal number who fired
at them from behind the rocks. The former pushed on
and claimed protection, declaring themselves peaceful
traders attacked by banditti. The latter left hiding and
hurried up to tell their story; whereupon the three first
rushed at them and cut them down, killing all before
they could speak.

It came out afterwards that these unfortunates were
the owners of the goods and cattle, looted first, and then
murdered. This ugly tale reminds me of the death of
General Maude's bheestie, who was filling his masak at
the well, not two hundred yards from Lundi Kotal camp,
when the general passed with his escort. The well was
much frequented, and some Pathans were seated there.
Before General Maude reached the tents his bheestie

overtook him, and fell headlong in the road, cut literally
into bits.  An impulse of homicide had seized the Pathans,
and they had allowed it play.

I do not believe in the courage of Bedouins, still less
of Egyptians.  But, though we admit all the confidence
which skill and tried success will bestow, it was a plucky
feat to drive forty oxen from the lines at Kassassin and
bring them into Tel-el-Kebir.  That the Bedouin scouts
performed this feat, as they boasted, has been vehemently
denied, of course, but I am afraid the story is true.  All
the prisoners taken on the 28th of September declared
it; some had seen the oxen, and they described them as
foreign—certainly not Egyptian.  They agreed, also,
that the Bedouins' report was the cause of the attack
which was made two days later—for it represented that
the English camp was unguarded, that the troops were
scattered, and so worn out by sickness that they could
not stand a serious onslaught.

For courage and skill in. looting cattle, no race of
scoundrels can make a show with the Marris and other
dwellers on the frontier of Sindh.  The ingenuity of
these people is almost uncanny.  They have a knowledge
of the bovine character well worth scientific attention,
and they use it in conjunction with a study of human
frailties which is equally minute.  The simplest of their
processes is to cut through the stable wall—cattle are
always stabled in a country so perilous for them—and

lead out the animals. Two or three boys are entrusted with a business of this kind, and they are expected to succeed, though it be needful to make the oxen step over a watcher's body. At one of our posts the commissariat cattle were lodged in a walled inclosure, which contained several masses of ruin. Every morning the tale of beasts was short. In vain the distracted go-master applied for more sentries and more frequent rounds. At length, by mere accident, the secret of the nightly disappearances came out. Thieves had tunnelled under the wall, shielding either exit behind ruins. Such engineering work is familiar to people who conduct water underground from the spring to the place where it is wanted. But to induce half-wild cattle to descend a steep incline, pitch dark, hot as a furnace nearly, and that without making a suspicious sound, requires either arts unholy or such influence as one would like to observe in action.

The Arab proper, neither Egyptian nor Bedouin, is very distinctly a brave man in the European sense. I do not believe that his part in history is played out. In a very few years he will be free of his incubus, the Turk, the field of emigration open to his most active and enterprising sons will be terribly narrowed, and an Arab civilisation may again appear. All the soldierly feelings are strong in them now.

During the Russian war a young Arab officer was

taken on the Lom. His gallantry in the action had been observed by admiring enemies, and one high in authority tried to get him freed or exchanged. He asked the prisoner's word of honour that he would not fight again if liberated, and it was given. Shortly afterwards a desperate opportunity of escape presented itself. The Arab seized it, and got away. In the Turkish lines he was received with joy, and promoted then and there; but he refused to serve, recounting his promise. The general would not admit it binding, and threatened to shoot him, as a coward, in the back; and shot he was. A relation of the youth told me this story at Constantinople. I believe one might find many Arab soldiers (not Egyptians) who would die rather than break their plighted word.

In the sum of military honour no army is so punctilious as the German. That superb machine is braced and upheld by a code of such minuteness and severity as no other people would carry out. Crack regiments in the Russian service hold themselves together, and preserve the honour of the corps with strict vigilance, but their rules are fantastic, and still more so the execution of them. The doom of suicide has been passed upon a German officer, if stories are true, but in Russia it has been pronounced not once, nor a hundred times. For some terrible scandal, a cavalry regiment was exiled to Central Asia. It held an inquiry upon the officers

M

implicated, and the one found guiltiest was significantly told that a man of honour would not survive the shame of bringing disgrace upon his uniform. In such a case a German would, perhaps, have taken his own life quietly, but the Russian did nothing of the sort. On parade next day he charged the colonel with drawn sword, and was promptly shot. I have been told that the proportion of officers who die a violent death in time of peace, in Central Asian stations, is enormous.

It is common clap-trap of the cosmopolitan philosophy, that every man is brave. The soldier and the traveller know better. Nearly every man can be trained to hold his place in the ranks, and most men will rush forward with their fellows, if there be enough of them, and they shout. But this is not individual courage. I am not sure we are as brave as were our forefathers, but, if so, other nations have deteriorated in the same measure, for we keep the relative position they held. Unfortunately, courage will not save a state, nor win battles nowadays, unless it be backed by force, and I am acquainted with no authority who does not admit in private that he regards the chance of a serious struggle with panic. If England maintained at home but a hundred thousand men ready for service abroad, what a blessed revolution that force would bring about! Free to ally herself on the side of right, whichever it were, she would be mistress and arbiter of Europe, which would needs disarm before this new power.

# A KAFFIR TOAD.

THE name of Wisden is grateful to very many of those who dwelt on the diamond-fields in my time. For years before "the rush," a family so-called had been settled at Yarrodale, half-way betwixt Hopetown and Dutoitspan. When twenty thousand diggers on one side clamorously bid for fruit and vegetables, whilst a brisk young township on the other demanded a greater allowance week by week, the farmer, a thoughtful man, divided his cares and responsibilities. He took his daughters into partnership, assigning them the dairy, poultry-yard, and garden, and, as the elders married, he brought from home new scions of his pleasant stock—girls every one. Happier maidens do not dwell on earth, nor busier, for they constantly struck new ideas, which always succeeded. "Wisden produce" was announced with an air when the market-master took his stand upon the table at Kimberley or Dutoitspan. How many young ladies dwelt at Yarrodale about the time of my story I do not recollect, if I ever knew. Not less than half-a-dozen certainly—all fair, young, quick of speech and smile, more or less pretty. Until supper-time, at five o'clock, they were

M 2

supposed to be invisible to guests. One fitfully caught a glimpse of clean cotton skirts pinned back, slender white arms bare; one heard musical cries and girlish bursts of laughter, and snatches of song. One time I met the eldest, Grace, carrying a milk-pail and a scrubbing-brush. She was not at all embarrassed, but much too busy for chat.

The house stood behind and between two large dams, or pools, formed, not by digging, but by stopping an outflow of the natural drainage. Their banks stood fifteen feet high over against the front door, sadly blocking the outlook. In a country less wholesome, fever and ague would have made their home in Yarro-dale. The approach led straight between these dams to a stoop mantled with creepers that ran along the house-front. Here, at morn and dewy eve, sat Grandfather Wisden, armed with a catapult. For shepherds and grooms, Totty servant-girls, drovers, diggers on the tramp, made rendezvous for gossip at the shallow end of the pools, where the patriarch bombarded them. To right of the building lay a garden, hedged with pome-granates, always in flower, as it seemed to us. Its walks were shaded with peach-trees; vines grew every-where, and bucketsful of grapes might be commandeered without the formality of asking. There was always sunshine and always shade, cool drinks, and glowing faces at Yarrodale.

Appreciative visitors were never lacking at such short distance from the fields. All the hospitable Wisden asked was a note of introduction from some person of responsibility, which successful diggers obtained with ease. Never did we hear of a guest misbehaving, drunken or quarrelsome as he might be in camp. Nearly all agreed in respectful adoration for one or other of the young ladies.

Grace was reckoned prettiest and admitted cleverest of the bevy. Among her worshippers I must name Skinner, of the Colesberg Kopje—" Bang Skinner," we called him—and Hutchinson. The former was a loud-laughing, fresh-coloured, happy sort of fellow, generally liked of men, and a favourite declared of the gods. He knew nothing of diamonds when he came among us, and he never learned a morsel. It was not necessary. Two men worked a hole, nine feet by four, adjoining my claim. The day after Bang's arrival at the Colesberg Kopje he fell in with them, and straightway bought their patch for nine hundred pounds, the sum remaining out of a thousand which his kinsfolk had raised—perhaps to get rid of him. After paying the registration-dues and the first month's licence, he had not a farthing left, and the sellers stood him breakfast. It was Satur-day, when no digger works. To amuse himself, Bang borrowed a pick and pail. What he brought to bank at dusk he had no precise idea, but the diamond-koopers did not suspect his ignorance. At dinner that night, in glee rather than triumph, the fellow showed us a roll of bank-notes—just nine hundred pounds they represented! Forthwith he took position in the set that called a six-carat stone a " tizzy." Pray understand that this tale is literally true.

Hutchinson I had known at home, when he was a subaltern in a Lancer regiment. What follies or misfortunes drove him into our society I have forgotten, but he did not find luck there. After working like a mole on Bultfontein, his health was broken by those ills the unsuccessful digger cannot escape—filth, exposure, despair, unwholesome living. Hutchinson fell back on the deserted river-camps. Pleasant scenery they gave him, and this at first was medicine for a lad who came from the sweltering, lime-white, thirsty veldt. But the fare is harder, the work has its own attendant miseries, river-boil and rheumatism, more painful if less deadly than those of dry digging. When I left the fields, eighteen months later, Hutchinson had not seen a diamond of his own—but what hideous heaps belonging to other people!

So far as we disinterested ones could judge, Grace did not care for either in especial. Hutchinson had advantages, however, besides good looks and pleasant manner. He came from the neighbourhood of Wisden's birthplace, and he brought an introduction very different to

those supplied by Cape Town bankers and Port Eliza-
beth wool-dealers. Grace remembered nothing of the old
country, but perhaps she loved it none the less for that.
The elder generation of the family were enthusiastic in
welcome, and Hutchinson constantly rode over until I
sold my horses, going home. Then he starved for a
month to economise the money for a coach-ticket to
Hopetown, and tramped to Yarrodale from the nearest
point on the high road. Such eccentricity might not
cause suspicion once, but it could not be repeated; the
man who walks fifteen miles across the veldt must be
mad or in love—and miserably poor anyhow. After
three blissful days, Wisden lent him a horse for the back
journey. Some weeks later Hutchinson found a Boer
who passed Yarrodale, and in his waggon got a lift,
paying for it by making himself useful with a drove of
sheep. Grace was absent visiting a sister. After that
disappointment—how hard nobody can tell who has not
been in love, and penniless, and ill, and despairing—he
gave up. Physical weakness and disorder quelled his
courage. What good, after all, to torment oneself for a
pleasure that turned to pain in the enjoyment! Miss
Wisden did not care for him.

To work single-handed on the river is mere tempting
of the demon rheumatism. The bucket must be filled
knee-deep in the stream, the cradle must be sluiced, and
then, dripping from head to foot, the digger must seat

himself at the sorting-board. But Hutchinson had no mate. A Kaffir he kept, such a poverty-stricken wretch as his means could support for a little while longer. Very ugly and stupid was this poor fellow, distinguished from all young blacks I ever saw by the irregularity and badness of his teeth. I could not describe the unpleasant oddity of Stump's appearance when, opening his huge lips to laugh, he showed jaws gapped and discoloured. But Stump was attached to the master he had served two years, and Hutchinson valued his dumb friendship. Dull master and scarecrow man were not ill-matched, people said. Day after day, month after month, their record of failure dragged its miserable length along. The time was now in sight, hourly approaching, when Hutchinson's last penny would be spent, and he must lie down to die. He would not return to the pitiless, feverish, dry diggings, though his legs could carry him. Better to starve here in his ragged tent beneath the murmuring trees. To that point had the wasting of sickness brought him; Hutchinson called it despairing love.

He sat at his table by the river brink, and sorted hopelessly. Stump brought a dripping-pail from the shallow, poured it clashing in the cradle, rocked and rocked, threw out successive trays, and emptied the residuum, wet and glistening, on his master's board. Lovely pebbles were there, of every hue saving the blurred white of the river diamond. Hutchinson worked mechanically, scraping from the margin of the heap, smoothing the shingle, and dropping it over the edge, between his knees. Meanwhile eyes and thoughts wandered.

Gems are not found by such a method as this, but the chances of diamond-digging are endless. On a certain afternoon, as Hutchinson listlessly watched his boy throw out the trays, he saw something that made his heart leap. In the next pulse it sickened—for when did luck visit that claim? But he rose, found the object, stared gasping, hugged it, and ran into a glint of sunshine. A diamond at last, of macle shape, weighing some twenty carats!

Stump showed his joy by dancing, whirling, and howling, with an awful frown upon his brow. When Hutchinson came to himself, he resolved to tramp to Pniel, whence a coach or a post-cart would carry him to Hopetown. Stump he left in charge of the ragged tent, the worthless clothes and tools, with a fortnight's store of mealies, and a shilling to buy offal for the weekly feast. Forthwith Hutchinson started.

Before emerging from the narrow fringe of trees that borders the Vaal river, he came upon a waggon of singular appearance. In place of tilt it had a roof and panelled walls, adorned with pictures of the most brilliant colouring. Wild beasts were there depicted alternately with black warriors and white beauties, alike

arrayed in feathers and nothing else. These works of
art had suffered shockingly from sunshine, and whirling
sand, and thorns of the bush. By a little tent alongside
a huge Boer sat smoking, and a bush-boy—dwarfed,
naked, misshapen—restlessly pried about. Everything
in the small camp declared the Kaffir trader returning
homewards.

In ten minutes more Hutchinson saw the blazing veldt
outspread, a grey expanse barred with stripes of white
and yellow blossom in the near distance, fading out of
sight. Where the horizon should be, stretched pools of
mirage. Flat-topped hills hung above them, like stains
in the pallid sky. No object in the scene stood out,
excepting a man's own shadow. Smooth as a floor
the waste appeared, though each of those shining bars
marked the crest of a wave invisible. Now and again,
though no wind blew, the sand lifted, whirled up to
form a little dusky pillar, danced a few yards, and
dropped. A melancholy land indeed to traverse in the
glare of African summer.

For the comprehension of those who have neither
digger's nor trader's experience, I must tell what is a
"macle" stone. This shape of diamond, unusual but
not rare, is formed of two triangles, the one lying
smoothly and exactly on the other, adhering firmly; a
slight blow on the line of junction will make them fly
apart. A large macle, unflawed, is commonly worth

more than a single crystal of the same weight, since there is small waste in cutting it. Diggers do not like this form, however. Flat on top and bottom, a macle is much more easily concealed by a dishonest servant than is the plumper stone.

Four mounted Kaffirs overtook Hutchinson before he had gone far, and paused at his hail. They were Dutch-speaking Battapins, of Jantje's Kraal, rough as burly, but not ill-natured. For a shilling they gave him a mount on one of the led horses, and he reached Jardine's hotel by nine o'clock. Forty-eight hours afterwards his gem was sold to Schlessinger, of Hopetown, for two hundred pounds. He bought some clothes, hired a horse, and once more dismounted at Yarrodale.

The Wisden family were so delighted to see him, so shocked at his pallor and thinness, so anxious that he should remain till his strength was quite restored, that Hutchinson reproached himself for certain doubts and hesitations. Within five minutes of arrival he had made up his mind to tell Grace how he loved her. The young man was not a fool. He knew that two thousand pounds would hardly justify pretension to Miss Wisden's hand, and he had less than a tithe of that sum. But his luck had broken. If Grace would only hear him, and wait a few months, he would outshine Skinner in the display of gems which was often laid upon the table after supper.

That favourite of fortune had been staying a week at Yarrodale, but he left early on the second day after Hutchinson arrived. During that time no opportunity arose to speak to Grace, and another day passed by, happily, but anxiously. Next morning, the young man went out before breakfast to shoot plovers. Wisden met him on the stoop returning, and took his arm.

" My dear boy," said he, "did you yourself find that macle stone you told us of? "

" Yes, in my own claim. Why? "

" I was sure you said so. Well, Schlessinger has brought a Dutchman who swears that he found it, the very same diamond, on Monday evening, and it was stolen from his tent that night."

" Confound his impudence! Where is he? "

" Keep your temper, my boy. These unfortunate mistakes will occur sometimes."

But it was too much that his single stroke of fortune should be suspected thus. Hutchinson went in raging. In the Boer he recognised the owner of that ornamental waggon left behind at the river.

" What's all this, Schlessinger? " he asked roughly.

" I tell you flat, sir, Mr. de Ruyter is my old friend and client. He outspanned near your claim on Monday, with his pack of Kaffir produce. In evening time he washed some stuff, just for pleasure, and he found a macle. Mr. de Ruyter is a trader, not prudent. He showed the stone in camp, and so that night his tent was cut, and his belt commandeered. After a fuss, Mr. de Ruyter comes to me at Hopetown, and tells me. Then I think it right to show him the diamond I bought from you. So here we are. That's all my say."

" I swear to him," the big Dutchman roared, " by his broke brads un' scrats."

" How dare you ask me an explanation of this cock-and-bull story, Schlessinger? You know that nine macles in ten have their angles broken, and all are scratched in the river."

" That's as may be!" he replied with warmth. " Mr. de Ruyter says your boy was creeping round his tent."

" Ya! Mine bush-boy see thy dom Kaffir skellum ! "

" Why didn't you bring him along if you suspect him?"

" Dom! Skellum not to catch. Look here, man, I take my diamond ! "

" Find it and welcome. But if either of you says another word I'll knock your heads together."

" Ugh, thou talk'st!" De Ruyter answered without moving.

Wisden gripped his young friend just in time.

" Make allowances," said he. " These gentlemen are honest, and one of them has been wronged. When did you find your stone ? "

" I am ashamed to offer an explanation, sir. At what hour did you find yours, De Ruyter ? "

" To sundown."

" And you lost it after going to bed, at nine o'clock, say. At ten o'clock, Mr. Wisden, I reached Jardine's hotel, in Pniel, as Jardine and twenty men in the bar will testify."

" I suppose you don't want a stronger alibi than that?" asked Wisden.

"Not at all," said Schlessinger hastily; "I apologise, sir. As matter of form we will inquire. Good morning, gentlemen. Where there's no ill-will there should be no grudge. Mr. Hutchinson, happy to do business with you at any time." He departed, dragging out Mr. de Ruyter, who wanted, with many oaths, to know why and how matters were thus settled. Arguing in high and low German, the pair rode off.

" No worse than a droll incident so far as you are concerned," said Wisden. " But I should be almost afraid the Dutchman was not quite out."

" I won't suspect Stump, sir. He has stood by me like an honest man through hard times—terrible hard times. I should begin to fear for myself almost if Stump went wrong."

" Well, I didn't understand that the bush-boy had seen the theft. Still, those imps are born spies and detectives. I should look up Stump."

" We don't even know that De Ruyter ever had a

diamond. The camps will roar from Gong Gong to New
Rush when they hear of his broke brads and scrats."

They had wandered into the garden, and seated themselves upon a bench. White arms round his neck, a
fresh face pressed to his, obstructed Wisden's reply.

"Good morning, father; good morning, Mr. Hutchinson. Did you intend those plovers for any one in particular? If so, it was injudicious to leave them about
in such a hungry house as this."

"I laid them on the stoop for our general benefit,"
said he.

"Then you won't suspect me of stealing them? Oh
yes, father, I have been listening at the window. Good
girls don't listen, which is almost a pity sometimes. For
I can tell you something, Mr. Hutchinson. Stump was
here yesterday morning."

"Are you quite sure?"

"Oh yes; I saw him from my window while I dressed,
talking to Mr. Skinner's groom. If you doubt me, ask
father."

This was a little household saying which imputed that
Wisden would always back his daughter Grace. He
said now:

"She may be wrong, Hutchinson, but, if it were my
own case, I should believe her right until the contrary
was proved."

"It's very strange, certainly. Stump has no business

here, and that he should stop twenty-four hours without communicating with me beats all explanation."

"I meant to tell you yesterday, but I forgot," Grace continued; "Stump walked away from the dam with Sinclair, and I've not seen him since. But we'll ask the Totty girls."

She ran away, eager and graceful as Iris. The South African household is terribly observant within its pur-view. Grace soon came back with a whole series of reports. The toothless Kaffir was resting at the dam when the servant-girls turned out. Whilst they chatted with him, Sinclair arrived with his master's horses, and the men met like old acquaintances. An hour after-wards Stump was seen going towards Pniel alone.

After thinking over this odd story, Hutchinson appealed to Grace; Wisden had been called to the stock-yard. She replied:

"My opinion is, that, in justice to all parties, you should find Stump."

"I will start to-morrow."

"I should start to-day."

"It is so hard to break up one's holiday. You cannot know how despairingly I have pictured this bright scene, and—and your bright face—hour by hour, week after week."

"But you will come back in three days," she answered, leading him towards the house, "with an easy mind, to stay as long as you please. Father and every one will be sorry to see you go."

" You also?"

" As much as any of your friends."

" I want more than friendship from you, Grace. It was you I dreamed of, you who made the place so bright, you who make it brighter even than I fancied."

" What is the use of this, Mr. Hutchinson?" she asked, looking at him steadily, not severely.

" No use if it annoys you. If you say that, I will never speak of it again."

" I asked what is the use; if you had annoyed me I should have spoken differently. Working-girls learn that it is no use to talk of things that can never be, even though one liked to do it. And I do not like to hear you in this tone, Mr. Hutchinson."

" Because it's no use? Oh, tell me that! Could you bear to hear it if things were otherwise?"

" You have no right to ask. But I will answer in perfect frankness and truth that I do not know. Don't misunderstand. If you were rich, I should have to think and observe, and to put questions to myself, which there is no need for now, and which I have certainly not thought of."

" Because I am poor?" he said, bitterly.

" Because you never used this tone before."

" But I do now."

N

"And now I say there is no need to think before replying." She resolutely walked into the house.

All through breakfast Hutchinson turned these words over, while the merry girls pretended to believe that conscience was preying on him. Grace had spoken sensibly from the point of view she chose. But, if prudence were the first question, he had much better have addressed her father. So he did. Wisden listened in some distress, but greater astonishment. He gently hinted that the lover had no prospects; then, more strongly, that Grace's fortune was not small; at length, when Hutchinson persisted, that Skinner was the destined husband.

"I don't believe it! That is—— I beg your pardon, sir. Miss Wisden would not have answered as she did if she meant to marry any one at present."

"I like you, my boy," said the father, laughing grimly; "but confound your impudence! So you've been talking to Grace? Well, I can venture to stand by my daughter's words."

"They came to this, sir, as I understood, that if I were rich she might think of it."

"Very proper; but not put in those words, I think? No, I supposed not. Well, what Grace says I stick to. You are a good young fellow, but you aren't rich; Skinner is a good young fellow, and he is rich, that's how the matter stands. Now you can't alter that, can you? Then what's the good of talk that may end in a quarrel, which would deeply grieve us all?"

No good, if such were the feelings appealed to. Very wretched was Hutchinson as he rode away at noon.

Wisden lent his guest a mounted Hottentot, under whose direction he rode straight across the veldt to New Rush with the purpose of examining Sinclair before visiting Pniel. The moon rose early, the horses were good, and by nine o'clock they brought him into camp. The first passer-by directed him to Skinner's tent, a fabric of three rooms, surrounded by canvas dependencies, stable, cook-house, servant's quarters, store-room. Bang was entertaining friends, as usual, though his blacks had but just begun to wash the driving-cart in, which he had returned from Yarrodale—for, travelling at leisure, he had stayed the night at Pniel. Sinclair, a big, fat-faced half-breed, showed in the visitor. Half-a-dozen men, flushed with drink and excitement, sat round the table in a room lined with green baize, carpeted, handsomely furnished. Pictures hung upon walls; the fire-place had a mantel, a glass, and a clock; only the absence of ceiling betrayed that this was not a substantial drawing-room. Heaps of gold stood at every man's elbow. The cards set out before Skinner were piled with sovereigns. He held a pack in his left hand, covered with his right.

"Are you all on? Eh, who is it?" to Sinclair.

" You're as welcome as drink, Hutchinson.    Take the
bank a moment, Spud."

As they entered the comfortable bedroom Skinner
said:

" I'm driving care away with a mild faro to-night for
a change.  What is it brings you to this Golgotha ?  All
well at Yarrodale ?   That's right !   What is it then ? "

Hutchinson told his purpose, which Skinner could
not assist in any way.  He called Sinclair, who had
never heard of Stump.   Oh, the Kaffir he talked to at
Yarrodale dam?   Never knew his name till now, though
they had been acquainted ever since Sinclair arrived
on the fields.  For the rest, he had nothing to tell.  Each
went his way after that gossip.

The " hotels " of New Rush were not abodes of peace
at that time, but Hutchinson was weak and worried and
tired.   He turned out at dawn, and rode to Pniel.   If
Stump had walked thither at a comfortable rate he had
probably arrived about nightfall of the day before; and,
though he had left the place, people who saw him would
still have a clear recollection of the toothless Kaffir.  But,
if Stump had travelled at full speed, he might have left
Pniel fifty miles behind.   Hutchinson reached Jardine's
at evening.   In the bar sat an acquaintance, Mr. Bean,
late trooper in his own regiment, now an Inspector of
the frontier police.  Most fortunate it was.   Mr. Bean
would understand the situation, and would follow

instructions. Forthwith, taking him apart, Hutchinson consulted the Inspector.

" Well, sir," said Mr. Bean, "I think I may say your business is settled, and so is Meinheer Stump's. Unless I'm greatly mistook, you'll find the man you're looking for in the police hospital, if he's not yet been taken to the dead-house. We'll see, sir, if you like."

Going along Bean told what he knew. At early dawn on the day previous " old Davy," the baas of a small canteen at the Drift—the ford—brought word to the station that a wounded Kaffir lay outside his door. He was carried to the hospital, where the doctor pronounced him dead drunk and mortally hurt.

They crossed the river, and Bean pointed out a miserable shed of canvas, some twenty feet from the path.

" That's the place," said he.

" What sort of a man is old Davy?"

" Why, I should say average for his sort. One don't look for much virtue in a canteen-keeper. Davy's not a chap you'd charge with murder, unless you'd something to go on. But in a general way his sort's a bad 'un. If you're going to ask him questions I'd wait till the morning if I was you."

They reached the police hospital. The face of the wounded man was so swathed with bandages and sticking-plaster that Hutchinson would have scarcely recognised it. But his ill-formed jaw was not to be

mistaken, and a strained withdrawal of the lips showed
it to the fullest. Stump had lain insensible for thirty-
six hours or more. Hutchinson waited on the doctor.

"I say frankly," replied that pleasant gentleman,
" that I can form no opinion. If the patient were white
he would be in his grave by this time; but I've not
been long enough in the country to diagnose a Kaffir.
Experience as yet has only proved my ignorance. Your
boy's skull is fractured, and he has two or three killing
wounds besides; but I should be not at all surprised if
he got over it."

" How long will it be before he recovers? "

" Mind you, it's a hundred to one he'll die; but, if he
doesn't—then I have no idea what will happen."

Hutchinson returned with the Inspector to Pniel. He
asked what clothes Stump wore, and whether anything
had been found about him.

" Oh, didn't I tell you, sir? He hadn't a rag on his
body."

" Then of course he had been robbed."

" Well, we didn't know he was anybody's boy, so the
nakedness was not particularly noticed. It would be a
strange thing in this camp if a man lay senseless for an
hour at night and was *not* robbed. Now, Mr. Hutchinson, I can talk to you free, for I didn't have the honour
of making your acquaintance yesterday. Here's a naked
Kaffir found by a chap we have nothing against, who

tells his story straightforward. Have us poor over-
worked police—who didn't enlist for any such employment, mind you—have we nothing more particular in
hand than to go crowner-questing on a dead nigger?
Why, sir, there was ten thousand pounds worth of
diamonds stole that night from Angus's store, and there
was two hundred Barolong Kaffirs fought a pitched
battle with as many Basutos yesterday morning, besides
smaller business. It's devil take the hindmost here, sir."

Next day Hutchinson visited the canteen. As I have
said, it was a rag of canvas stretched on boughs.
Behind the board, on tressels which crossed its width, the
sleeping-gear of Mr. Davy lay hideously conspicuous.
A blear-eyed, towsled giant was he, cunning and brutal,
but he did not look a murderer.

"I want you to tell me all you know about that
Kaffir. He is my boy."

Mr. Davy had told all he knew to the police. He
mixed a drink for the inquirer, another for himself, and
held out his hand for the money.

"Here's a half-sovereign," said Hutchinson. "You
may work out the change if you like—on oath——"

"This is a lonely place, mate, after dark, though it's
'twixt the two camps. I don't know nothin' as would
harm anybody, an' I can't lie. What is it you want?

"Had you seen that Kaffir before?"

"Yes, I had. He came here to ask a drink in the
afternoon ——"

" In the afternoon ?   At what hour ? "

" As near three o'clock · as might be, for I'd just
tumbled out of a snooze which I take arter dinner.   He
asks a drink, I say, an' he cuts away smart when I asks
him what the blank, blank, blank he means by showing
his blank black nose inside a 'spectable canteen."   This
violence of language showed Mr. Davy's enthusiastic
adherence to the law which forbids serving black people.
" But," he continued, " the nigger got his drink at some
blackguard hole, an' more'n one or two ; for when I see
him again, just at dark, he was in deep water, as they
say."

" And that's all ?   On your oath ? "

" Have ye ere another of them little things, mate ? "

" Yes, if you earn it ! "

" Well, I never broke my davy, though my Davy's
broke often enough—meaning myself—eh ? " with a
roar.   " What I say can't do no one any harm unless
they deserve it.   When that Kaffir was hanging round
at nightfall, a man came to him, a coloured man—I
can't say more'n that, I swear.   And they crossed the
drift to Pniel.   There, I've done."   ... ..

" You wouldn't know the coloured man again ? "

" No, mate ; I tell you fair I would not ! "   · ·

Hutchinson paid the sovereign, and went to inquire
about Stump.   Not the least change was reported.   For
three days he employed himself and Bean in seeking a

clue to his boy's movements, but none turned up. Out of patience, and satisfied now that Stump was a thief, Hutchinson thought of leaving him there. Bean and the doctor counselled him in a friendly way to deposit a sum for expenses and for the burial. At this suggestion he revolted.

" If I have to pay for the fellow, I'd rather have him under my own eye. Can he travel, doctor ? "

" I don't know that he can't. We want his bed badly. You'll take him in a waggon, of course? "

So one day Hutchinson carried off the interesting patient, a senseless bag of bones, for spoon-meat is a mockery to the Kaffir stomach. In the servant's quarters at Yarrodale, a group of huts not too near the main building, a pensioned old Hottentot was very glad to take charge of Stump, and she confidently promised to bring him round. Then Hutchinson sought Mr. Wisden, who did not object in the least. A Kaffir more or less, sick or well, made no difference.

Stump's adventure was not very interesting, when all believed that he had met with his deserts ; but the problem of his arrival at Pniel within nine hours of leaving Yarrodale challenged the wit of the supper party. It was a lonely road to travel, and, besides, what farmer, digger, or trader, would give a seat to a black ?

" One of my neighbours has lost a horse, I expect," said Wisden ; " that's what it comes to."

"And a near neighbour, too," Hutchinson added.

The next night, when they sat in the study, in which Grace alone was allowed to take a chair, she said :

"This matter interests me so much, father, that I have sent all round to inquire. No one in the neighbourhood has lost a horse."

"Then Stump flew, that's all! When he recovers he'll tell us the trick, perhaps."

Half-an-hour afterwards Grace asked:

"By-the-bye, father, has Sinclair sent back Cherry Ripe ?"

"One of Jardine's people brought her in yesterday."

Hutchinson was startled by a sudden thought.

"Did Sinclair go on horseback, then ? "

"Skinner had left his cart at Pniel, and they rode here. His boy's horse fell lame, and I lent him Cherry Ripe to return."

"May I ask, sir, whether you saw Sinclair's horse, or whether you took his word for its lameness ? "

"I didn't see it. Egad! this suggests a commoner trick than flying! Your boy has a diamond—Sinclair borrows a horse, takes him to Pniel, and then robs him ! It's as plain as could be."

"You forget, sir, that Bang Skinner was there. Did Sinclair start, leading his own horse ? "

"Yes ; I see the difficulty. He pretended to leave his own horse somewhere, I expect."

".Sinclair didn't leave him anywhere along the road," said Grace, quietly.

" You have sent to inquire?" asked Wisden, rather astonished. " Well, we may take it for granted that the fellow deceived his master somehow."

" And he was not long in working the trick either," Hutchinson said. " It's clear, if you reckon the time, that Stump must have travelled very quick. That Skinner should not have observed him on that veldt, which is as smooth as a floor, nor notice that his lame horse had been hard ridden, seems strange."

" What do you mean by that look? Upon my honour, Hutchinson, I would not have believed that one of your name could hint such a charge."

" I hint nothing, sir, but I mean to inquire."

" As deep as you please; but don't insult my friends with your jealous fancies! There, my boy, sit down; I can make allowance, but you must do the same."

Hutchinson sat down, and talked for a few moments constrainedly; then he said Good-night. An hour later, just before the bolts were drawn, he dropped his pack of clothes from the bedroom window. In that large household it was easy to slip through the front door unperceived. When all had gone to their rooms, Hutchinson spread his rug on the stoop and lay down.

Sleep would not have come to him that night though he had lain on rose-leaves without a crumpled petal in a

yard of thickness.    Since Skinner was chosen, he would
go, never to return.    But to him, feverish and distracted,
came a vision white in the moonbeams, beautiful as
love.

" Dear Mr. Hutchinson," Grace pleaded, " I beg you
to come in.    We don't allow even a Kaffir to sleep here
beneath the level of the dams.    You are ill!    Pray,
pray return to your room."

" There is nothing I could have refused you an hour
ago, Miss Wisden.    If this spot is dangerous, I beg you
not to stay."

" Then I will fetch father.    Please listen to me."

Hutchinson felt that his host's arrival would make the
situation ridiculous.    He had been sitting on the rug, but
now he got up, and instantly became aware of racking
pains, of phantasma in his sight, and singular indecision
in the use of his limbs.    Grace saw him falter, and
caught his arm.

" You have taken the fever, Mr. Hutchinson!    Oh,
how dreadful!    Can you walk in ?    Lean on me."

" I can walk, but not indoors," he answered with the
vehemence of heated blood.    " I would die in the veldt
sooner!    I'm honest, Miss Wisden, and it was not jealousy
made me speak.    God bless you!    Let me go!"

" I know it was not jealousy.    When father thinks
the matter out he will own there is cause for suspicion.
Don't give him more pain.    Oh, please come in!"

"Do you suspect Skinner? Then you do not love him?"

"I do not, and I never shall."

"Love me, Grace! Try! Promise this, or I would rather die here than live."

"How can I, Mr. Hutchinson? It is ungenerous to ask when you are in this state."

"I will go in and get well. If you are free—— You love no one?"

"No one in the world—like that."

"Then I will win your love. Now I obey you."

As Grace cautiously fitted the bars of the door, she watched his feeble progress through the dusky room. Presently Mr. Wisden came, cheerily penitent, with those simple medicines that alleviate the common fever. But, on returning at dawn, he found this was another kind. To the hot and eager fit had succeeded terrible depression, and the pain of his limbs was such that Hutchinson could not repress his groaning.

"I fear yours is rheumatic fever," Wisden said, compassionately.

"Give me something that will kill," he answered. "In the other world a man cannot suffer worse than this."

"Cheer up, my boy! I've known lots of fellows who worried through a bout of it."

"They had something to live for, then. I've had misery enough, and there's only misery before me."

When Wisden made his report downstairs, the girls all cried over their work. They picked wool for a bed, but when it was finished Hutchinson refused to exchange his hard mattress. The doctor came, but he would take no medicine. To treat a man in that state forcibly would be to kill him with sheer pain. Wisden argued and adjured, the girls pleaded and wept—to no purpose. In that mood and that agony Hutchinson wanted to die, as a relief from present sufferings uncheered by hopes for the future ; and he was likely to have his wish.

At evening Grace came to her father. She said:

" If I ask Mr. Hutchinson to be patient he will submit."

" Then go at once."

" If he recovers he will expect me to marry him."

" That's absurd ! However, save the boy's life, and refer him to me."

" I will not do that, father—whatever I do, not that; but I will beg Mr. Hutchinson to be patient."

" Manage it your own way, dear. Why is the lad so unlucky? He's worth twenty Skinners after all."

So Grace appealed, and even in that agony the sick man's brow cleared at her words. Then she had Stump removed to the house, and nursed him carefully. The Hopetown doctor examined him and reported.

" Why is that Kaffir like a toad, Miss Grace ? " he began, entering the room.

"Is he like a toad? I'm sure I don't know why."

"Because he's awfully ugly, and he bears a precious jewel in his head. Look at that!" The doctor displayed a fine macle diamond. "It was jammed between his broken teeth at the back. I'll bring my tools to-morrow for an operation, and he'll tell us all that has happened in a day or two."

More experienced and more attentive than his *confrères* of Klipdrift, the doctor fulfilled his prediction. When Grace had laboriously transcribed the wandering narrative, she went to seek her eldest brother, and found him chatting with Skinner, who had just arrived.

"Will you read that, Jack," she said, "whilst we take a stroll in the garden?"

Jack received the paper wondering, and Skinner, wondering, led Grace out.

"What I have given my brother," she began, "is Stump's declaration. He says that he told your groom how he had found a diamond which he was taking to his master. Sinclair assured him that Mr. Hutchinson had gone to New Rush, and offered him a mount as far as Pniel. Allow me to finish! At the first outspan Stump came up with you, and you, Mr. Skinner, asked to look at his diamond. But you told Mr. Hutchinson you had never seen his boy, and Sinclair said he had left him at the dam."

"I can't believe that you take this drunken Kaffir's word before mine."

"I do, Mr. Skinner, and everybody will. For he does not know your name now, he never saw you before that day, but he will identify you when the time comes as Sinclair's master who rode with him from Yarrodale."

" And you charge me with waylaying this brute?"

"He does not accuse you of that. But he accuses Sinclair, and my father will issue a warrant and execute it within ten minutes."

" I swear to you, Miss Wisden, that I knew nothing of Sinclair's villainy till next day. The rest I confess, and it makes no matter: I wanted money, and I hoped Stump would sell the diamond cheap. Mr. Wisden had made me a loan for a speculation as he understood. It's all lost. and my business now was to borrow more. The game is up! It's useless now, Grace, to say that I loved——"

" Quite useless. What shall you do?"

" I can't go back to the fields," he answered, sullenly, " with this charge over me. I shall run to the Free State."

" Are your claims clear?"

" Yes, except some business debts and your father's loan."

" Will you transfer them to Mr. Hutchinson for five hundred pounds down ?"

" Yes."

" Wait in the arbour for ten minutes."

Jack was approaching, very grave. Grace met and turned him, whilst she fetched writing materials.

" Now, Mr. Skinner, here is a cheque for five hundred pounds, and my brother will witness the transfer."

He wrote it and annexed the licences.

" It's a good day for Hutchinson," he said, viciously. " A man might spare the price of a wedding-ring out of that pile. Good-bye, Jack! Keep clear of the cards."

Twenty minutes later Bang rode off, not gaily, but not uncheerfully, to try his fortune in other scenes.

Mr. Wisden does not know the truth to this day, and Hutchinson did not know it till long afterwards. They understood that Skinner, in remorse, broken with debts and embarrassments, made over his claims. Mr. Wisden readily advanced what was needful to free them of lawful encumbrance, for it was gambling that swamped the first owner.

In twelve months' time Hutchinson married, and, final proof that his vein of ill-luck had passed away, he realised his claims in time, and bought a farm near Yarrodale. De Ruyter received his macle, but he is not to be persuaded that Hutchinson's fortune is not due, in some mysterious way, to his temporary possession of that talisman. Stump is fat and very much married. The last news of Skinner reported him to be winning and losing fortunes daily at Pilgrim's Rest, on the gold-fields

O

# A STICK.

RECORDING the story of my " Gun-rack," I casually mentioned, in a list of articles which at that moment lay across it, " an almond stick cut in the Arx at Candahar, and a thorn-stick from the Khoord Khyber."* A comrade of the Afghan war pointed out to me last night that I was slightly forgetful of the facts in this description. Major L. reminds me that he cut the almond-stick referred to, with others, in the garden of the kiosk where General Stewart had his quarters, whilst I strolled round keeping watch—for damage to the trees was rigorously prohibited. As he identifies the object, I submit to correction, observing only that I did cut an almond-stick in the Arx, which apparently is lost; and that I never claimed, as it chances, to have secured this trophy in person.

The pleasant controversy recalled every detail of a scene too long familiar to General Stewart's staff. For my own part, I left it after some weeks' stay, rode back

* Legends of my Bungalow—" A Gunrack."

to India, crossed the Punjab, and joined Sir Sam
Browne's force operating on the Khyber line.

During our first halt at Candahar we lived in camp
on the north-east side of the town, in position to repel a
foe descending from Ghuzni. After the occupation of
Khelat-i-Ghilzai danger from this point was no longer
to be feared, and the army sought more comfortable
quarters. In spring and early summer, before the stones
crack and the earth shrivels in heat nowhere more cruel,
the neighbourhood of Candahar may be pretty. But my
recollection of it adds no pleasing picture to the mind's
crowded gallery. All round stood the circuit of grey
naked rocks; beneath, the grey naked walls of flat-
roofed villages, among grey gnarled orchards. For the
space of a mile about the city it is all one Golgotha, a
field of bones, generation on generation. Thousands
of monuments dot the place, many of them large and
costly, but all ruinous. Funeral processions meander
through the waste at afternoon and early morning; all
through the night jackals and wild dogs and hyenas
clamorously search the new-made graves. Each few
yards one must jump a rapid stream, muddy with human
clay, embanked with bones.

The general appearance of a cemetery is enhanced by
groves of cypress which rise here and there, dark and
funereal. But in effect those trees mark villa-gardens,
inhabited by merchants of the town or officers. Colonel

St. John requisitioned one of them for the general and his staff. As we marched in from Khelat-i-Ghilzai, guides should have been waiting to show our new quarters, but they did not appear, and we lost ourselves. An amusing promenade that was for horsemen, who "larked" over the streams and walls, but the infantry of the escort swore in many languages a unanimous anathema.

After several excursions in a wrong direction, and much aimless steeple-chasing, we found our new abode. A solid wall inclosed it, perfectly rectangular, along the top side of which coursed a deep and broad irrigation channel, traversed by a substantial bridge. Entering the narrow gateway at one angle, upon the right, in a space between the outer and an inner circuit, were stables and servants' dwellings, strongly-built, pitch-dark, venomous with filth. By this arrangement, a mob or a band of brigands forcing the single entrance would have all the armed retainers of the household on its flank. Beyond the inner wall ran another stream, carefully embanked, and lined with sturdy willows ; beyond that a broad terrace—the dam, in fact, of this swift brook—and the garden sloped gently from its foundations.

The whole space within the walls may have been two to three acres. It was divided by a canal, some twenty feet wide, shallow, paved with flat blocks, banked with masonry. Hewn stepping-stones crossed it here and there. At intervals along the sides opened sluices for irrigation. The upper half of the garden was laid out in squares, ten feet across or so, for vegetables and flowers, each of them surrounded by its water-channel. A number of walks, broad and smooth, intersected the space, each lined with cypress ; and the smaller fruit-trees— pomegranates, oranges, and the like—stood everywhere.

In the middle of the garden the canal poured into a large tank, walled with masonry, and provided with steps on every face. Broken structures therein had probably been fountains. From this point the ground was devoted to orchard trees. Beyond the tank the canal still descended, till its waters fell into a stream, almost a little river, at the bottom. Very handsome trees met across it. Beyond ran the garden wall.

Three kiosks, or pavilions, stood in this pleasure ground, a large one at the top, one right and left midway down either side. Though built of mud, they were not inelegant. The principal of them, occupied by General Stewart, Colonel Hills (now Major-General), D.A.A.G., Major Chapman (now Colonel), D.A.Q.M.G., and the chief's aide-de-camp, Norman Stewart, had been decorated in the Persian manner at no small cost. Walls and ceilings of the reception-rooms were coated with stucco ornaments, brilliantly coloured, or were painted with roses as thick as they could lie. One chamber had remains of that curious panelling in fragments of mirror, symmetrically framed, which is seen, more or less, wherever Pathan architecture established itself in Hindostan. I do not know, however, that it is not borrowed from the Persian.

Furniture and carpets possibly had matched this splendour of the walls; but when we arrived, here as elsewhere, the Candahar populace had worked their will. For this dwelling belonged to Mir Afzul, the governor, who had given it as a residence to two ladies of his family. When he fled, therefore, it was looted. In a well-built suite of rooms beneath the level of the ground—an area, in fact—we saw evidence of an attempt to burn the house. These subterranean chambers are occupied during the heat of summer. In one of them I found a stock of bulbs, mostly narcissus, and seeds. It had been the gardener's storeroom.

In the day when those buildings were raised, and those waterworks constructed, some degree of public confidence evidently reigned at Candahar. I know not when that time was. In an epoch less happy, but more readily identified, the walls had crumbled without repair, all the glass had vanished, the fountains had clothed themselves in moss. But the garden had been cared for. At every corner stood such clumps of rose and jasmine as I never saw, the mass of stems three feet diameter, spreading fifteen feet on every side. The irrigated beds were green with spinach, the walks lined with iris and overhung with cypress, the orchard-trees well-trained.

This is a long introduction, but I fancy readers may be not uninterested in the sketch of a Pathan villa. Memory recalls one much more magnificent, that of Rosarbad, on the Cabul side, which a great Ghilzai chief had just completed. Details of the scene there dwell among the most charming recollections in my mind, but they are vague. For I stopped but a few hours, going up and returning. Many officers who served in that campaign will remember the graceful mansion I refer to—their first halt, I think, after leaving Jellalabad.

We rode into our new quarters with a fine appetite, and the mess-cooks leisurely began their preparations. What moral courage is required to check a digression on our mess-cooks, their ways and manners!

Before the meal was ready, a small group of natives gathered on the terrace, under sanction of Captain Molloy, our staff interpreter. They were people of condition, dressed in the Persian style—long coats of pushmina cloth, edged with narrow gold cord, beautifully embroidered on shoulders and chest ; fur caps, wide breeches, and high yellow boots. To them arrived Colonel St. John, political officer, now Colonel Sir Oliver St. John, K.S.I. Presently the general ap-

peared, eager for his breakfast. He listened with interest to their petition, and courteously dismissed them.

The chief of these visitors lodged a claim to the
house we occupied. Mir Afzul had taken it from him
by force. It appeared that the claimant was a partisan
of that brother of Shere Ali's who killed his nephew,
the Ameer's favourite son, and was killed by him, in
action. I forget the names and the place, but those
interested in Afghan politics know all the painful story,
and for others it does not matter. How impossible I
should have thought it, three brief years ago, that such
a grave event in history would slip my recollection,
abiding only in colourless outline! The place it then
filled is occupied by other facts to be in their turn
dismissed.

When Yacoob Khan took the city, he found there
the widow of his uncle, with a baby boy. They were
forthwith imprisoned in the Arx, or citadel, and remained there till we set them free. Every one at mess
was touched when Colonel St. John described his
interview with this young prince, now twelve or
fourteen years old, a captive from infancy. I know not
whether he still lives. Terror and solitude had crushed
the lad. His limbs, his complexion, reminded one of
plants grown in the dark. Suddenly brought into the
daylight world,—born, as it were, at an age to see, and
in a painful sense to understand, the million of strange

things around,—there was great danger that his intellect would fail.

I am aware of no modern instance like this. The imagination cannot fancy what must have been the feelings of this boy, intelligent of nature, when the door he had never passed was opened, and he stepped into the bustling, anxious, savage world of Candahar.

The young prince had not been absolutely deprived of a companion. With his uncle's widow and his cousin, Yacoob Khan confined the wife and child of this sirdar who claimed our quarters. His life was spared on that account, but he lost his property.

General Stewart ordered that the case should be examined, and an arrangement made, if it proved just. This news spread through the city, and forthwith arose a dozen litigants. The original pretender collapsed at once, for he had no better title than Mir Afzul's ladies, though one earlier in date. Colonel St. John was persecuted with all the modern history of Candahar, its invasions and confiscations, the alliances of its inhabitants, the laws of real property, and the decrees of successive governors. Having other complications in hand, he appealed to the general, and our stout old chief, laughing heartily, relegated this question to the native courts. There it would still be disputing hotly, I don't doubt, if the prospect of rupees had not vanished with the sircar. And meanwhile we paid no rent.

I heard an outline of several amongst these claims.
It was mighty dull, that long wait at Candahar. We
had left the arctic climate in our rear, and we could sit
in the mess-tent after dinner, chatting ; though there
was no drink but rum, and only a " tot" of that, *pour
tout potage*. One of these stories dwelt in my mind.
What I remember is here set down.

Our garden, as was alleged, once belonged to a merchant whom I will call Haidar Khan. He traded
largely in Central Asia, transporting Indian and European manufactures, and bringing back tea, saltpetre,
turquoises, cheap gaudy silks, and Persian goods.
Bokhara was his favourite market (may I here use
the licence of an expert to suggest that the accent of
this word falls upon the second syllable?). When the
governor of Candahar, in rebellion against Cabul,
thought fit to send letters and presents to the Ameer
of Bokhara, he naturally chose Haidar Khan to bear
them. No trader had such tact in dealing with the
robber chieftains on that long route ; no one had
suffered so little loss from disease of beasts and
slaves.

For some years past, Haidar Khan, now growing old,
had ceased to accompany his kafilas. He was rich.
His town-house, jealously protected by high blank
walls, contained a treasure in its plate and jewellery
alone. Very many thousand golden coins lay stored

in a secret place which no one knew except his confidential slave : Darics and Bactrian pieces, which to think of makes the numismatist feel tigrish, Venetian sequins, Austrian ducats, Russian imperials, English sovereigns, the spoil of every race and every age. Accomplished slaves and fair daughters amused the old man's leisure. One care alone oppressed him, and it was of a sort to which Pathans are used.

Haidar's sons had turned out ill, extravagant, undutiful, addicted to the muddy wine of Shiraz and the bhang of southern infidels. But few of his neighbours had a pleasanter experience, and, since the boys had not yet been detected in a conspiracy to murder him, Haidar had still reason to be thankful.

The command of the governor was annoying. In the first place, no respectable trader likes to compromise himself in political intrigue. There was not much danger truly on this score, since the authorities at Herat were friendly, and the clans along the road felt no interest in Ameer or Governor. But the journey would occupy twelve months at least, and Haidar left a thousand cares behind. His money would be safe under protection of the guild—as safe, that is, as money can be in Afghanistan. But the guild would not take charge of personal effects, silver dishes and gold cups and jewels. Who could be trusted to guard his slaves when the master was away, and his wild sons skirmished round ? Haidar resolved to bury his wealth, and to take the young men with him.

Do not think, be it said in parenthesis, that I exaggerate the riches of this Pathan merchant. It is recorded in history that when the English general made a call for funds on Shikarpore, forty years ago, thirty thousand pounds was furnished in two hours, and one hundred thousand pounds offered before night. Shikarpore is the next bridge, so to speak, of the Pactolus that flows through Candahar from Central Asia ; a place even now not half so large nor half so wealthy, a mere village in comparison two score years ago. No disturbance, no confiscation, no misgovernment can stop the supply of gold which pours down that channel. For ages Candahar has been plundered systematically, but the only misfortune which can for a while delay its recovery is the blocking of the road above.

So Haidar Khan set out, with his two sons, and his long train of camels. After many months' journeying he reached Bokhara. His usual good fortune attended him along the road. The most savage of robber chieftains accepted their black-mail without complaint, disarmed by his pleasant shrewdness ; they even made him valuable gifts in return. He delivered the letters and the nuzzur ; unloaded his merchandize at the serai ; took a house and servants; prepared for a long and profitable trade, whilst the Ameer was thinking out his policy, and considering what presents to return.

In some months of delay Haidar turned his capital over several times. At length all was ready. What reply Bokhara sent to Candahar upon political questions I am not informed. But the nuzzur consisted of Turkestan and Yarkhundi horses, Bokhara camels and slaves; beside, one may presume, such trifling souvenirs as silks and arms gold-fretted, turquoises, embroidered horse-trappings, &c. With these in charge, Haidar made ready to set back.

The conduct of his sons at Bokhara has not been recorded; probably, being Afghans, they did some successful trade, and in the intervals compassed as much wickedness as they could find to do. But when it came to ordering the march, Haidar found that the eldest had two Persian women—bought captives, of course—whom he proposed to carry down. This could not be suffered. In Bokhara the prophet's law against enslaving Moslems is not much regarded; and at Candahar they are not very rigid on the abstract question. But Haidar was a personage. The eyes of the pious rested on him. Useless, and indeed dangerous to plead at Candahar that Shiah heretics are not included amongst Moslem, for there are many Shiahs there, and the Kazilbashis are a powerful community. A hundred considerations made the old man firm in his denial, and the slaves were left behind; I do not know in what position. Very vicious Haroun looked as he took his place in the caravan.

The Ameer's offerings were all of the highest class. Turkestan horses so punchy, so large-eyed, so velvety of coat, so clean of limb, the Persian Shah does not possess. The heads of the Yarkhundi's were long as their pedigree; when they arched their necks superbly they could bite a fly upon their chests. The silken fleece of the camels almost swept the ground; and their beautiful eyes, shaded by thick curled lashes, shone through a mane as stately as a lion's. I think I hear a critic murmuring aghast, "What animals are these the Legender is inventing ?" In truth the descriptions would not apply to usual breeds of horses or camel. But they are true nevertheless.

Led by their syces, the steeds marched loose, their gorgeous saddles and accoutrements safely stored away, But each camel bore a gilded litter with silk curtains, and in each litter rode a slave —Haidar had not thought needful to ask whether Moslem or no, since they were destined for his superiors. He himself kept with this bevy, and his trustiest servants mounted guard at night. The young men, and especially his two sons, were forbidden to approach.

But elderly travellers sleep sound after the day's long march. Pathan youths are enterprising ; Eastern girls not less inquisitive, capricious, thoughtless, than our own. The effect of seclusion practised upon female kind is to make the prisoner especially liable to sudden gusts of admiration. To be quite accurate, perhaps, she is not more liable by nature than are her English sisters ; but these get so early used to check the feeling that it is regarded generally as household fun. The Oriental girl has no opportunity to use herself to this phenomenon, nor has she any practice of self-restraint. Also it is the instinctive bent of prisoners to cheat their jailor, of young women to rebel against discipline. This impulse is naturally felt more strongly by a pampered slave-maiden than by the free-born. For such a purpose bitter enemies will combine and keep a secret. More-over—I really must one day indite a brief essay on the conditions, sentiments, moral anatomy of womankind under Moslem rule. Upon no subject whatsoever is such ignorant nonsense current. In twenty years of travel—through lands, for the most part, where poly-gamy prevails—I have learned, by daily use and hearing, the pros and cons—something, at least, of the actual facts ; and on a topic so intensely grave those who think they know the truth should speak out.

From the considerations noted I can believe that Haroun established some sort of compromising relations with one of the slaves. Such a charge was made against him, or, rather, against Haidar. It is not necessary to imagine that the relations were criminal in any sort ; mere bowing acquaintance, so to put it, would justify a savage punishment in the eyes of the Candahar gover-

nor. Haidar Khan was not ignorant of what was passing, for he threatened his son with death if he did not
amend. Some time afterwards, next day perhaps,
Haroun vanished with his personal followers : the
younger son remained.

In due process of time the kafila reached that point
where the road from Farah gives upon the great trade
route between Hindostan and Central Asia. Every
school-boy knows—quite as well as he knows many
other facts attributed to his omniscience—that Farah is
a great strategic position in the midst of that quadri-
lateral—Herat, Candahar, Ghuzni, Cabul. Owing to
circumstances uninteresting to detail, but intelligible
enough, the garrison of this place is generally loyal.
Farah was held at the moment by a zealous partisan of
the Ameer. He was informed, no doubt, of the treasonable correspondence which Haidar carried—what secret
of the sort can be maintained in a land which has no
telegraph, no penny press, no correspondents, special or
other ? But his quarters lay some distance from the
caravan road, and in the space between dwelt lawless
tribes, Atahzai, Alizai, Durani, who will admit no authority to come amongst them. For they live by black-
mail, which government officials would appropriate to
themselves.

Haidar, therefore, did not dream of peril from the
governor of Farah. At the junction of the roads, never-

theless, his caravan was intercepted by overwhelming force. Without discussion of terms, the Ameer's officials seized him and marched the kafila across the hills. Incredible to relate, the robber clans cheated of their due made no resistance.

Arrived at Farah, the governor held durbar and tried his prisoners publicly. Haidar Khan, overwhelmed with the evidence and bewildered by the perception that treachery enveloped him on every side, could make no defence. The treasonable letters were produced. Every slave in the kafila knew facts enough to damn him. Nothing remained but to pass sentence. All Haidar's personal property was confiscated. The presents of Bokhara, slaves, camels, horses, and the rest, were despatched to Cabul—that is to say, so ran the decree. We may have our doubts whether the Ameer derived one rupee benefit from all this plunder.

Nothing more is said of Haroun and the fatal beauty. Our tale henceforth deals with his younger brother. The theory of Haidar's innocence towards the Governor of Candahar, his employer, is based on the supposition that Haroun concocted all the plot, negotiated with the chieftains, secured a free passage for the troops, persuaded the Commandant of Farah to try a dangerous coup. And so, perhaps, he won the stiputedla prize, whatever it might have been. But, from one's knowledge of Afghans, one is inclined to think

P

it more probable that the Commandant rewarded him
by cutting off the traitor's head—much more probable
still, that he poisoned him. And one may almost take
it for granted that the Helen of this strife was transferred,
with her comrades, to the governor's harem, together
with all goods and treasures that had not been already
looted by his faithful servants.

In consideration of his virtuous character and his high
position in the mercantile community, Haidar Khan was
not put to death. His captor held him to ransom—for
the profit of the Ameer, nominally. A large sum was
named, but one the great trader could afford without
serious inconvenience. Accordingly, he drew a bill
upon his guild. There was difficulty in finding trust-
worthy persons to receive the cash, since the best adhe-
rents of the Farah governor would have been massacred
at Candahar. At length the younger son was commissioned to fetch it, under surveillance of some neutral
individuals. He went, and did not return; neither did
his colleagues.

After waiting an unreasonable time, Haidar Khan
wrote to the guild direct, telling all the circumstances.
In the leisurely course of things prevailing in Afghanistan, the cash arrived, under charge of honest merchants trading with Farah. In the meanwhile, various
shrewd but painful processes had been tried to stimulate
the captive's ingenuity. The guild explained that

Haidar's son had duly presented himself, and had received the money ; a copy of his receipt was inclosed.

It acknowledged ten times the sum demanded; by the addition of a cypher this dutiful youth had obtained nearly all his father's fortune, and vanished with it into space.

In terrible distress and anxiety, Haidar Khan returned to Candahar. There he was instantly arrested as a traitor ; the main cause of suspicion lay in the acquiescence of the Durani sirdars to his capture on the road, to be explained only, as the accusers argued, by Haidar's strong personal influence with them. Long before this, the governor of Candahar had made up his mind and sequestrated all that was left, town-house, villa, accomplished slaves, fair daughters, and the rest. As for the silver dishes and gold cups, they may be buried yet, a treasure to be disinterred, with many more, when the Russians Haussmannise this imperial city.

After languishing some months in prison, Haidar Khan was tried and found innocent. The next step was to make the governor disgorge, if possible. Whilst Haidar engaged in the beginning of this hopeless task, the governor of Farah marched on Candahar, with a swarm of Durani tribesmen, who had suddenly turned loyal. They fought some successful battles, and the city capitulated. This was final ruin. From the Ameer's

lieutenant Haidar had no mercy to expect.    He died.
But the sentence of the court which pronounced him
guiltless of the crime for which he had lost his property
was the only legal instrument bearing on his case.    The
claim was not forgotten by his heirs when General
Stewart rashly talked of paying rent for our quarters.
But there were other pretensions, both older and newer.
I incline to believe, that, if the title of that garden had
been exhaustively gone through, some generations of
lawyers would have been harmlessly consumed in the
interesting task.

# A POPO BEAD.

THE sale of Ashanti loot at Cape Coast Castle dwells
in my memory as a very quaint and interesting experience. The scene was picturesque, the business was
amusing ; and the transaction as a whole closed our
campaign with such dramatic fitness as I have never
since beheld on any stage of actual and living history.
The melodrama had been played through, virtue was
triumphant—vice, defeated, had fled the scene ; and
upon the very spot where the " action " first arose the
meritorious performers received their visible reward in
the spoils of the oppressor. It was an ending to the
war-play complete and smooth and rounded off, as the
Latin grammar puts it.

Very little plunder was obtained in the Gold Coast
Expedition, saving that found in the palace. A few
soldiers, no doubt, snatched an opportunity to rummage
in the breech-cloth of a slaughtered foe ; fewer still discovered there a little store of gold-dust. Some, perhaps, as they burst their way through the teeming

jungle, wreathed in smoke, echoing with musketry, and
wail of cow-horns, and ringing snatches of the battle-
song, marked a bracelet on some corpse trodden under
foot, and wrenched it off. But two cases only were
rumoured in my hearing. At Coomassie itself, where
valuable spoil lay all around, our eyes were greedily
fixed upon Bantama, the sacred treasure-house, where
six generations of Ashanti kings lie buried, with their
accumulated wealth around them. That mysterious
and dreadful spot we were not fated to behold, but
those who expected an arduous march, and a despairing
fight next day, made the most of a blessed halt. And
every one was put upon his honour not to touch the
curious things lying masterless on every side. Midnight
had past when a general order to loot was issued, and
nineteen officers in twenty did not even hear of the
permission till the town lay in flames behind our retreating column. Had I known it in time, there would
be some graceful costly ornaments in my cottage that
now lie buried deep beneath the ruins of Coomassie.

Our prize-agents certainly did well to hold an auction
of such things as they secured at Cape Coast Castle.
Very many of the objects sold would not have fetched
pence in London which there fetched pounds. Aggry
and Popo beads, jewels on the West Coast, would be
despised by English children; though their parents, if
concerned with the African trade, might contemplate

them with a sense of despairing mystery. The native silks, though superbly wrought, are vague of colour, meaningless in design, and useless for our purposes. The Ashanti cloths have every merit, but at the price they reach upon the coast one might buy Oriental stuff much richer of effect for any object we could set them to. And there were rich men in our little army who ran up the antique plate and the thousand golden knick-knacks as high as any home enthusiasts could possibly have gone.

The best of scene-painters could not plan a more romantic, more fantastic edifice than Cape Coast Castle. I do not know who built it, and the date I have forgotten ; but he was a clever man, and that was a happy period of the picturesque in architecture. From the sea one beholds a huge central tower, its angles rounded off; with walls and battlements, turrets and curtains, bastions and roofs, standing pell-mell beneath its shadow. The main courtyard, protected by portcullis and huge gate-towers, is triangular in shape. Staircases mount from it, and verandahs jut out in charming irregularity.

Our sale was held in the Transport office, called the Palaver Hall in former times ; and since restored, I suppose, to its original purpose. This great chamber is fifty feet long, perhaps, by thirty broad ; it has eight huge windows, and a spacious balcony on either side. Great triumphs and panic-stricken councils that hall had seen, and its era of revolution is not yet closed, I fear, though in our haste we thought so then. For months past it had been the headquarters of Captain O'Connor and his busy staff, who all, in emulation of their commanding officer, strove to keep their wits bright, and their tempers cheerful, under the most irritating form of labour. Here, the long hot day through, an endless string of carriers filed in and out, divided by the neat policemen into smaller streams— this to the pay-desk, that to the registrar, that to the distributor of metal tickets. Voluble excuses and angry replies, shouts of men forcibly led out, giggling of girls, clash of labels tied in a ponderous bunch, jingle of money-bags, ceased not from dawn till dusk.

It was here that the prize-masters arranged their stock, and conducted the auction, mounted aloft on tables. In the front row beneath, officers strolled round and bid and laughed and chatted. At their rear stood merchants of the town, black as you can paint, but attired, more or less, in the costumes of Regent Street. Behind them the women of rank, not ungracefully dressed, and superbly ornamented. They wore massive gold combs in their wool, rolled up to a cushion on the head, gold butterflies over the brow, half-a-dozen gold chains about the neck, earrings, bracelets, anklets, rings of Aggry bead and gold. At their back a rail repressed the clamorous and excited crew of " common niggers."

Bidding was so spirited at first, and the "fun of the fair" so enticing, that I went rather beyond my means. In the pause for lunch, I discovered myself to be possessor of a very miscellaneous collection, expensive odds-and-ends which long since have been given away or lost. One object only I still cherish in a mutilated form. Upon a sideboard in the palace, with many another fine old piece of plate, stood the tankard which legend ascribes to Sir Charles Macarthy. Every one knows that he was defeated and lost his head in 1817. The head we did not recover, though we found the great drum on which it had been fixed with those of other luckless heroes; the tankard I bought. But it proved to be as fragile and holey as interesting, and I got tired of sending it to be repaired. So the venerable object was sold at length, for its weight of silver; but I kept the lid and the old-fashioned high-shouldered hinge. Mounted on a Doulton jug, this fragmentary relic is much admired as the claret-cup goes round upon an afternoon; and few seem to question, though they are surprised, that Ashanti artificers should rival Lambeth.

As these tales are nothing if not gossipy, I may mention a few other things bought on that occasion—two shells of massy gold, weighing near half a pound; a bracelet of nuggets, strung without fashion on a cord; an armlet of snowy shell, very singular and beautiful,

which passed several times round the limb, fastening
with golden tags and tassels ; a golden butterfly, more
solid but infinitely less elegant than the Fantees manufacture ; a bracelet of some hundred little discs, eight-
knobbed, strung through the centre. I forget the rest.

These pretty trifles mounted to a pretty sum, and I
surveyed my purchases with rueful admiration.    My
sympathising hostess observed confidentially :

" I will give you a hint.    Buy some of the royal
ornaments."

" Why ? " I exclaimed aghast, " they are selling for
their hideous weight in gold."

" Just so," she answered, " and that is the reason our
people cannot purchase.    But if you buy, for example, a
necklace, all the Aggry beads in it are given you for
nothing.    Every woman in the town will take as many
as she can afford, and you will be left with the gold very
considerably beneath mint price.    It is buying money
cheap."

Any supercilious pride which accident planted at
birth, and Oxford fostered, had been long since knocked
out of me.    I returned to the sale room, determined to
retrieve my extravagance.    On the way, I remember
well, the " prince " overtook me—a young Russian
dignitary, who arrived too late to see the war, but in
time to see the return.    What a gorgeous and incredible
thing of splendour was he at the review in Windsor

Great Park ! He also had bought very largely, and he also was rueful. I told him this project to retrieve my modest fortune, and he replied very coldly :

" Je ne suis pas marchand, monsieur."

" Et moi, altesse," I answered, " je ne suis pas prince."

The Russian was less cordial after that, but, undismayed, I carried through my little speculation to excellent result.

It doesn't matter what I bought ; indeed, I forget, for Mrs. S—— sold everything again before night, leaving me that handsome profit which commonly accrues to the wholesale buyer who sells retail, as I understand. Amongst other things, however, I purchased a bracelet of Popo beads—an odd sort of bunchy ornament ; the beads suspended lengthwise, held by a golden button at one aperture. In unstringing them, to secure the gold, I remarked that one had been encircled with a golden band, very neat and ornamental, to prevent a crack extending further. Foreseeing that people in England would not credit the value placed on Aggry and Popo beads, I preserved this bit of evidence ; and I have it now, mounted as a pin.

Both Aggry and Popo are glass, the former opaque, the latter clear but rough. There are many varieties of Aggry, some more treasured than others ; only one of Popo, I believe. Both are dug from the earth, where

the corpse with which they were interred is thought to
have long since perished, but I am not aware that the
circumstances of any such treasure-trove have been
recorded by white men. The Aggry is found, as they
say, all along the West Coast, far into the interior. The
Popo is rare in Ashanti and Fanti-land, becoming more
frequent near Lagos. It must not be understood, however, that either sort is common ; quite the reverse, as
prices show. Our Birmingham manufacturers, and more
especially the Venetian, have been trying these many
years to imitate the Aggry bead. To an English eye—
superficial and untrained—their success is perfect, but
the youngest negro is not deceived. For all their science
and study, for all the wondrous effects of the same kind
which they have produced in transparent glass, our
people cannot find the secret of running a coloured pattern through and through the opaque substance exacted.
They can make a fac-simile of the surface, but that is all.

The Popo bead, I am informed, has defied all attempts
of imitation, but I speak with diffidence. Its peculiarity
is that the glass looks blue in light, yellow in shadow.
This change puzzles our crafty workmen, who could turn
out blue beads or yellow, exactly like it, ten thousand
of them, for a less sum than a single tiny cube of the real
sort fetches. To conclude this dissertation—not uninteresting, I hope, to any reader, though he be not connected with the African trade—it may be added that the

best authorities suppose them both to have been Egyptian manufacture—ancient Egyptian, that is. Such glass is seldom or never found with mummies in the form of beads, but small bottles of material very similar are frequent enough. If this be so, it is not surprising that Aggrys and Popos are not discovered in Egyptian tombs. Made for a savage commerce, the civilised manufacturers disdained to use them, and one would only expect to find deposits in the excavation of a merchant's warehouse or of a glass-blower's works. The curious point of the matter is the evidence thus offered of a commerce very much wider than had been credited to Egypt. Chinese and Indian productions have long since been identified in the plunder of her tombs, and it would seem that she dealt, directly or indirectly, with negroid races on the shore of the Atlantic.

In such trade as that the enterprising pedlar constantly found it judicious to hide his merchandise. In many instances, as common sense suggests and experience proves, he never recovered it. And, when the ancient trader died, his comrades would be sure to bury with him some at least of his valuables. In this way, doubtless, little stores of beads became distributed about the jungle. But I have mentioned that no white observer has reported the circumstances of a case, so far as I ever heard.

How and when was my handful of Popo beads discovered? I don't know, but I can suggest an explanation.

At a date easily identified, though I forget it, the King of Ashanti resolved to build a palace, the real thing, a house of stone such as Europeans occupied at Cape Coast Castle and elsewhere. Certain obvious difficulties challenged his imperial project. Neither architects nor masons were found in the realm, none at least trained to such work as this. If there were stone suitable nearer than the Adansi hills, it had not been discovered, and the sovereign had neither tools nor skill to work it. These circumstances enhanced the royal grandeur of the idea. When the king said: " Raise me a palace! " there was real merit in obedience.

Shortly before this time, the Portuguese had resolved to fortify Cormantin, a settlement upon the coast, south of Accra, if I remember rightly. With the magnificent ambition and the patience which distinguished them in that age, they shipped cargoes of hewn stone, and artificers of every kind, gathered I know not whence. The architect commissioned to superintend these works was a young mulatto of Elmina, educated in Europe; I presume that the coast was not more healthful at that time than now to pure-blooded white men. He reached Cormantin, and began the clearing of the ground, while the vessels were unloading.

The generals and chiefs of Ashanti, who had it in

their honourable charge to execute the king's command,
watched these doings with keen interest. Their scouts
numbered the ships arriving, inventoried the cargo, calculated the growing heap of materials and the increasing multitude of artisans. In course of time, they reported that a mountain of stone lay on the beach, where
two hundred skilled labourers and a thousand slaves
were encamped under guard of a company of soldiers.
Forthwith a picked body of Ashantis crept through the
bush, travelling almost singly, giving no alarm, swim-
ming rivers, skulking past the villages at night, converging from a wide circle. They rendezvoused behind
Cormantin, five thousand warriors. And on a morning,
as the Portuguese turned out shivering in the misty dawn,
wrapped in their blankets and smoking papelitos, the
Ashanti yell rang out on every side, and they all were
taken prisoners without a shot.

A large force was waiting on the confines of the
royal territory, and swift runners posted along the track
bore this news without taking breath. All was ready.
The war-drums beat—the thigh-bone whistles and the
cow-horns decked with skeleton hands called the army
to advance. It spread out fan-wise, overrunning all the
country, and sweeping the population together 'as into a
net. By forced marches it advanced, for a Portuguese
ship arriving would have endangered all the scheme.
But none appeared in time. Reaching the coast with

many hundred Fanti slaves, it loaded up the building materials; and, before this audacious kidnapping was rumoured at Cape Coast Castle, the Ashantis, their prisoners, and their plunder, had vanished in the silent bush.

A dreadful journey was that for Manuele and his comrades. Their captors lacked sense to see that the skilled artificers upon whom they were dependent should be treated gently ; or were too brutal to spare them at any risk. Naked as the blacks they struggled on, carrying each his block of stone or beam. Several died, and none would have escaped had not the king, impatient, sent down orders that these prisoners should be forwarded at once to discuss preliminary operations with him. So man-carriages were hastily prepared, and on the heads of slaves, in a long procession, they rode into Coomassie.

Manuele was a bright young fellow who knew his business well, and he had skilful workmen to execute odd jobs. Whilst his majesty consulted and inquired about the palace, his prisoners turned out a set of furniture such as Ashanti had never seen. Then they built an ornamental kiosk for the favourite wife, repaired all the knick-knacks European monarchs had sent to their black brother, made a score of wonderful things ; so that they stood very high indeed in the royal favour, whilst the caravan of stone was toiling through the forest, leaving a trail of human bodies and abandoned yokes but never an abandoned load.

The question of the site was grave. Manuele wished to build upon the market-place, a smooth and gravelly slope ; but the king rejected this idea with warmth. His councillors looked askance at the rash projector. Not where the great founder of the monarchy had sat houseless under a tree—Coomassie means "under the tree"—where the earth is too holy to be robbed of anything that falls on it ; not there should a miserable stranger be suffered to dig and desecrate. His majesty chose the bottom of the slope, ground muddy and unstaple, at that time occupied by the densest bush. It was necessary first to drain it, and upon this task Manuele set the innumerable slaves provided for him.

Meanwhile preparations advanced for that bloody rite which should protect the building from assaults of evil genii. The king ordered a foray into Denkera, and all the chiefs summoned paraded their retainers, who danced before the monarch and set out. Five months they were gone ; Manuele had just completed his drainage system at their return. As is usual, the king received his victorious army on the market-square. Twelve tent-like umbrellas were planted, in due order of precedence, for the twelve grand caboceers ; that of royalty—velvet, silk, and gold—in front of all. The family totem of each great chief was represented in solid gold on the apex of

Q

his umbrella. A fine procession it was that left the temporary palace to occupy the square. Great officers of state went first, clad in silk, stooping under the weight of golden ornaments, or supported by slave-pages, one on either side gripping their lord beneath his shoulders, one carrying each outstretched arm. All were followed and preceded by their state domestics, in charge of stool, gun, pipe, spittoon, calabash, toddy-jar, and what not, all decorated with gold. In tumultuous array they pressed through thronging ranks of the populace, who applauded their favourites, jeered their butts, and shouted uproarious comment, as a free-born martial people have been used to do in every age and every clime.

The king himself was preceded by his chief executioner, bearing the sword and belt of office; the former a useless cumbersome blade, set in a block of gold, with four legs, as it were. We took several of these odd objects. A crowd of aides and tormentors, less fantastically armed, marched about him. The royal heralds followed, carrying a long staff, and a plaque of gold upon their chests. After them rode the king, in a man-carriage, fitted with gold and silver, covered with a leopard-skin, shaded by silken awnings upon golden stanchions. A hundred of his favourite wives noisily advanced around him. Behind came inferior personages, honoured with the invitation to take refuge under the royal umbrella. Manuele had his place among them. Men whirling guns, painted scarlet, decked with leopard-skin and fluttering bits of scarlet cloth, scurried up and down along the outskirts of the cavalcade.

When the king was seated in his chair, beneath his huge umbrella, a hoarse wailing blast of cow-horns anounced that happy incident. The troops lay waiting behind a screen of lofty reeds, échelloned along that dreadful ditch where bodies of headless victims lie piled one on another ;—has any one of us, who had nerve to approach that spot, beheld a sight like the ghastly spectacle displayed there ?—Dancing and curveting the head-chiefs sallied out, performing again in mimicry the feats of valour which had, or claimed to have, distinguished each of them in the past campaign. The people roared approval or derision, the great caboceers looked critically on, the king sat mute as an image, stretching his hand from time to time for the golden cup which a kneeling slave-girl kept a-brim with toddy. Then the bones of dead chiefs were paraded, each mass in its own square box, carried on the head of a favourite slave, to be immolated on the tomb at nightfall. Another series of dancers followed, nobly-born young men, recommended for gallantry. The plunder next, a poor and miscellaneous assortment, for Denkera had been swept bare again and yet again ; had the expedition sought booty it would have taken another road. Spoils more valuable

Q 2

followed, hundreds of wretched slaves, many wounded, or dying of disease and privation ; to be sacrificed at the next " Customs," or to wear out life till the executioner should catch and mark them for his own.

Then came the real trophies of the foray, two or three hundred maidens of marriageable years, whose blood should be poured on the foundations of the palace, whose unsullied spirits should watch over it for ever. They had been well kept and well fed on the march. Those whose clothing had suffered were neatly redressed; their wool had been combed and decked with flowers; they had been made as pretty as nature would allow. Pretty many of them were in truth, with that smooth, round, large-eyed comeliness, not by any means unfrequent on the coast, and more general as one advances up the country, where pure negro blood has less and less disfigured the negroid.

Each step carried these poor creatures nearer to their doom, but they gazed idly about them, like stupid girls at a show. Manuele thought they had been drugged, and it is possible. Half had gone by when he suddenly perceived a face among the listless ranks that startled him. The features were swollen and dabbled with crying, but no tears flowed now. The eyes, distraught with terror, had no vision. Comrades on either hand supported her, swaying and stumbling.

As this wretched young victim passed the royal stand,

she looked up suddenly, and caught Manuele's pitying gaze. That broke the spell. She screamed, struggled, crying in some unknown tongue that needed no interpreter, for life. Men closed round, the clamour ceased ; Manuele dropped his eyes, shuddering. What could he do ? The army marched by, amidst shouts of admiration and welcome. But he saw no more. That face haunted him.

The girl-prisoners were lodged within the precincts of the palace. No man might enter their stockade unless privileged, but Manuele now came and went as he pleased among the royal buildings. For many days he resisted the temptation to look on that poor child again, busying himself with work, but the faster his preparations advanced the nearer approached her doom. Time went on, the foundations were nearly dug. He yielded to a morbid craving, and entered the stockade.

In sun and shadow all about the space they were sitting, dumb, stupefied. Manuele recognised the girl he sought, crouched upon the earth, a bronze statue of despair. Her well-shaped features, not distorted now but vacant, her light skin, told of a home far off in the interior, whence she had passed from hand to hand of the slave-merchants, with many a thousand more. The small rosettes burnt lightly on her delicate young bosom and shoulder-blades revealed her tribe, could Manuele have recognised the mark. She did not see him, and he

left the dreary prison filled with yearning sympathy.
Wild schemes of rescue crossed the good young fellow's
mind, but he had not courage for a desperate deed, and
desperate to madness that attempt had been.

But to delay the tragedy was not difficult.   In solemn
and mysterious tones Manuele informed the king that the
last spades-full of earth must be removed by himself
alone.   His majesty was pleased with this proof of loyal
thoughtfulness, and condescended to declare that he
would observe the proceedings.   But time passed, bringing neither incident nor hope.   The day could not
longer be postponed, and with a heavy heart Manuele
invited the king to assist.   At dawn his majesty turned
out, with his early jar of toddy, his pipe, and a few
wives.   The royal party took their station on the pit's
edge ; slowly and seriously Manuele pressed his spade
into the ground, raised it full, and discharged the earth
into a bucket.   Thereupon the ladies up above uttered
a simultaneous cry, leaped down with fluttering robes
and waving arms, upset him over the bucket, pulled at
him, pushed him, jerked him hither and thither, screaming, laughing, quarreling, jabbering.   Manuele, panic-
stricken, was rolled most uncomfortably in a bed of soft
warm flesh.   But in an instant their royal lord, waking
from a spell of stupefaction, dropped like an aerolith
amongst them.   The early jar was yet untouched, the
regal mind was clear, his limbs comparatively all his

own. Howling and yelping those forward dames escaped, this with a damaged nose, that limping from a master kick, the other with a bald place on her scalp, and all wofully dishevelled.

"Let no one approach!" cried the king, and with his own royal hands he scratched among the earth, bringing to light a mass of Popo beads.

" Dig, dig!" he roared, wiping them with his robe; and Manuele dug. Beads turned up with every shovelful of soil, Popos and Aggrys of all colours. His majesty laughed and grabbed and wiped, and laughed again,—finally he danced! Upon this stupendous phenomenon the pages fled, screaming for the royal heralds. These turned out, received the news, and bore it, galloping, to every quarter of the capital. Their official clappers toiled behind, finding not a moment's pause of silence to ring a concerto on their instruments. And forthwith all the population set off running. Those caboceers who had the entrée dashed through the gates, flying to assist at this glorious occasion. The royal wives charged down from their quarter many hundreds strong, crashed against the barrier in a phalanx so compact that it gave way; and all the loyal populace burst headlong through the gap. So, in a mass tumultuous and ecstatic, all the king's loving subjects poured to the blessed spot. But before they arrived his majesty had stopped dancing.

Many readers may imagine that the traveller's pen has bolted with him here—that an incident so absurd as this is not possible outside the walls of a theatre at Christmas-time. But I do not go beyond the actual truth of fact.

Few caboceers had beheld the auspicious event, for supreme happiness and fortune are rarely bestowed on man. The king, quite breathless, climbed out of the hole and addressed Manuele.

"Your devotion is rewarded!" said he. "I name you caboceer of the first class! I give you a thousand slaves, a thousand ounces of gold, fifty women out of my royal household! Before nightfall your lands shall be apportioned. And I grant whateve you rask now!"

Manuele tore off his shirt, baring his shoulders to the waist, and fell prostrate.

"I had sworn the Powers by your majesty's strong name," he said; "they obeyed. To you the glory, king!—I am a slave! I ask one of the girls captured in Denkera."

"She is yours. Gather the beads and bring them in."

Manuele never recovered freedom, but he lived in great honour and renown at Coomassie; and his de-scendants by the Denkera slave are still reckoned amongst the foremost of Ashanti caboceers. I should like to add that all the other girls were spared, but I have no evidence to that effect—one must not ask too much of a Gold Coast mulatto. He built the palace, and a surprising structure it was before we blew it up.

# A SAPPHIRE.

In travelling through the realm of Barbarie, one picks up many precious stones, literally and metaphorically. I should not value the companionship of a man who did not like to see and handle and own jewels. He must needs be a creature without fancy, excellent maybe in all prosaic capacities, of thorough business habits, a zealous churchwarden, an efficient chairman of the local board. But, if gems have no fascination for him, I should not care to travel in his company, or long to sit beside him at dinner. Observe that I do not speak of wearing jewellery, but of owning and admiring jewels. That attraction is strong on myself and on all persons for whose brain and heart combined I have respect. He who loved the Arabian Nights when young, and all the dainty records of fairyland, imbibed a glamour which never wears away. Curious it is, when one thinks of it, that gems had such an insignificant part in the mythology of Greece.

At different times of my life, returning from one

country or another, I have owned—not for long—a
pretty little heap of pearls, emeralds, and diamonds.
At present, I think, my only treasure of this sort is a
small handful of turquoises, brought from Candahar, of
trifling value. I purchased them in the bazaar, the
largest on that fatal afternoon when poor Willis was
murdered. I was counting out the money when a
sowar hurried by, shouting to us how the Sahib Log
were standing back to back down the street, fighting for
their lives. What a fierce push that was through the
hustling crowd, as we forced a way to them! There
were eight of us—Capt. Molloy, Dr. Finden, Lieut.
Norman Stewart, and four others whom I forget. But
this is a digression.

I own a sapphire, a very handsome stone, to which I
have clung like an Englishman, " in spite of all temptation," for twenty years. I bought it in Cairo, at
Shepheard's Hotel—the old, historic, uncomfortable cara-
vanserai, which was burnt down, was it not? which, at
least, exists no more. The vendor was a young fellow-
countryman, just returned from the Nile voyage. At
that time it was roughly smoothed and polished in the
native manner, which exposed not a quarter of its
beauties. I recollect very well that I gave him nine
pounds for it, but since the gem has been twice re-cut
it is worth several times that figure, I believe. This
young traveller gave me a story with it, which has

almost slipped my memory. In those happy times I
did not own a note-book, and it would be impossible to
say how much of the following narrative is his, and how
much my own imagination has unconsciously added. I
have put the legend into the first person for convenience
sake; you may suppose it a story told by one boy to
another in the verandah of Shepheard's Hotel, when the
golden sunset is fading duskily over the Ezbekieh, and
the tinsel lights of the cafés are beginning to gleam
under the acacias.*

We lay one evening off a town which was either
Manfaloot or Osioot, I am not sure. There were white
walls about it, which descended almost to the river-
bank, with domes above them rosy in the declining sun,
and dark-green palm-trees, fretted with gold along the
edges of their leaves. Francisco, our dragoman, did his
best to dissuade me from landing, as was the habit of
that worthy man. He insisted on the danger, real
enough, you know—this was in 1863—of being belated
in the narrow unlit streets, where nothing stirred after
sunset but dogs and robbers and outcasts. But I longed
to stretch my legs on shore, and the mosques seemed
rather handsome. So a guide was sought, and presently

---

* I have seen Cairo once more since this was written. If
a reader be puzzled to understand from what point of view
one could see those " tinsel lights " under the circumstances
suggested, he cannot be more at a loss than I was.

appeared an ugly, dirty old Copt, arrayed in a night-gown and a blue and scarlet turban. Of all beards that ever grew on human chin, this fellow had the longest and filthiest; a mat it was, an unnatural growth. And he had only one eye.

Led by the guide, who spoke a few words of English, I strolled through the empty bazaars, fought some lively skirmishes with dogs, saw the outside of a mosque or two, and visited a coffee-shop, where the faithful eyed me silently askance. Whilst drinking the blessed preparation which I thought mud, though I pretended to like it for " form's " sake, night settled down, and the Copt became uneasy. He led me back by another route, an alley dark as a coalmine, under a lofty wall ; preferring that way, he said, " because dogs bite," a reason vague, but intelligible on reflection. I learned that the high wall on our left was that of the pasha's grounds. The one-eyed calender informed me that he could get permission to visit them next day, for a baksheesh of two liras. Thirty-six shillings seemed too much to pay for a stroll through a burnt-up garden, but my crafty Copt assured me that the ladies of the pasha's harem were occasionally espied therein. Of course he told a falsehood, and I knew it, but who would not catch at the off-chance, when twenty-one years old ?

Suddenly, as we stumbled on, for we carried no lantern, my way was blocked by a human form, which

met me breast to breast. I cried humorously, like the
donkey-boys : " Riglak, Effendi! Shumalek, oh Sheikh!"
and tried to pass. But a sharp word of command, the
thud and rattle of arms grounded, brought me to halt.
Half-a-dozen lanterns flashed out suddenly, and I saw
the narrow passage full of troops. It was the patrol,
and I stood face to face with the officer, a fair-haired
man, very soldierly in his blue tunic and silver lace.
By the lantern his orderly displayed he looked me over,
smiled, and glanced beyond. The Copt shrank back,
whilst the officer passed me with an unfinished salute,
and spoke with him a moment. One seemed eager, the
other embarrassed. After a few low words, the young
Turk seized my follower by his most venerable beard,
drew that ancient countenance to his, and—how shall I
put it? He treated my Copt as Antonio treated the
Jew.

The action was so insolently droll that I laughed out.
Without apology, I snatched the lantern, lighted a cigar
thereat, and turned. At a word from the officer his
men fell back, saluted, and we passed through. The
Copt offered no explanation of this incident. In answer
to my questions he muttered that Turks are very cruel
and hard upon his nation. Next morning the wind was
fair.

Several weeks afterwards, halting at the same town, I
remembered the pasha's garden, and the marvels to be

seen therein. My former guide arrived, but he did not show so much confidence about obtaining a permit. Some scandals had been discovered, he hinted, or were suspected, at the Konak. What scandals? I asked, but the Copt did not know. He was a poor man, and with the effendi's permission he would now retire, to see what could be arranged. At night-time, whilst I supped upon the poop, a small procession of lantern-bearers issued from the narrow street and halted. My dragoman presently informed me that the Kisla Aga, or some such personage, desired a few moments' converse. I had no objection, but it presently appeared that the insolent eunuch expected me to attend on him. Taking a bottle by the neck, I peered over the rail, and distinguished the creature amidst his slaves below.

" If the Kislar Aga does not come on board within three minutes," I cried, " I will throw this bottle at his head."

Heaven knows what message Francisco delivered, but within the time I saw before me a tall, lean, wrinkled being, with the face of a peevish old woman who gives herself airs. His flowing dress was handsome, he wore jewels on every finger, and conspicuous in his turban was the peculiar sign, less of office than of degradation. I took his offered hand with repugnance —poor wretch! Francisco translated.

" His lordship the pasha sends compliments. If you

wish to see the harem gardens, you must be at the gate by sunrise." And forthwith the Kislar Aga departed.

" What did he come for?" I asked of Francisco.

" To see if all was square, sir. There's been something wrong in the harem. I have agreed to pay one lira for baksheesh." The Copt had asked two.

Next morning I was punctual. A guard of Nubian soldiers stood at the Konak Gate, and presented arms. We traversed a dingy courtyard, full of ragged suitors, passed through a small door at the corner, and entered the gardens under charge of two or three eunuchs. There was little to see, of course. Flowers grew in a tangle where shallow ditches moistened the earth. The space was mostly occupied by shrubberies and thickets, intersected by winding walks. Here and there stood a statue of surprising deformity. The art of childhood, displayed upon a turnip with a dinner-knife, comes nearest to the style of thing set out here for the ladies' delectation. I have laughed at the figures in the Winter Garden of St. Petersburg, but they do not bear comparison. Through the midst of the grounds ran a turbid canal, shaded by fine trees and clumps of bamboo. It widened at the centre to a pool, embanked with marble, chipped and stained. Steps led down to the water. In the middle of the tank rose a wooden kiosk, gaily painted; but its shutters were closed, and the bridge leading to it had locked gates. Some windows on the ground-floor of the palace stood open. I saw rooms sparsely but handsomely furnished, in satin and gold embroidery. Glass chandeliers hung from the ceiling, and the walls were lined with mirrors. Those windows had been opened to impress me with a glimpse of the magnificence within, but I knew very well that this luxury was atoned by sordid wretchedness in the apartments not displayed. The ladies were invisible, of course.

Not disappointed—for I had expected little—I returned, after leaving a card and a courteous acknowledgment for the pasha. Reaching the dabeah, I found upon my table a small iron box, and summoned Francisco to explain. But a slender handsome man in Turkish uniform appeared from the inner cabin, and said earnestly, in perfect French:

"I put myself under your protection, sir! If you dare venture to help a man in desperate straits, I implore you to hoist sail."

In astonishment and delight I gave the order, and my men, fortunately, were all aboard. A few minutes afterwards we were scudding briskly down the river, and I returned to the saloon.

"The pasha has a steamboat," I said, "and the telegraph."

"There is a chance that he may not pursue me, and life is worth a struggle. What have I not gone through

R

in these last hours! Your crimson flag to me was like a thread of sunshine in a black sky."

"But at Cairo," I observed, "you will certainly be taken."

"No. My papers are all in order. Besides, once we reach Cairo, if I demanded the pasha's head it would be served me. You have asked no questions before extending your kindness to a poor soldier, but I will tell you the story as soon as I have swallowed my heart, which sticks in my throat at present."

All day and all that night my guest sat on the poop, watching the rapid river and the mud-built villages. Instead of anchoring at dusk, we kept on, urging the crew with a promise of baksheesh. When the forenoon following passed without alarm, my protégé recovered heart. He broke into snatches of song, slapped the one-eyed reis upon the back—all reises, and most other Egyptians, are one-eyed—and convulsed my futile valet with unintelligible jests. A being less Turkish in his ways could not be imagined, and I asked his nation.

"I am a Genoese," he said, laughing and colouring; "but call me Yusoof Agha.

"Have we not met before?"

"I thought you would not recognise me. Yes, I have to apologise for my treatment of your guide, but you do not know what a villain he is. After dinner, if you like, I will tell you why I am escaping."

IIe did so, with many reservations, doubtless. I
never learnt how Yusoof came to embrace Islam, nor
anything about him, excepting this adventure. It may
be confessed that his manner of telling it did not lead
me to take an absorbing interest in his history; but I
should like now to hear the beginning and the end of
this renegade.

"You cannot fancy," he began, "the monotonous
misery of life in these Nile towns. There is nothing
for the virtuous man to do save pray and smoke and
pray again, and foretell the re-conquest of the world by
Islam. I am a good Mussulman"—here he winked and
laughed—"but I had not the fortune to be bred to
these delights, and they pall. Before I had been a
week in yonder garrison I wanted to die—oh, seriously!
But one nail drives out another, and before I was quite
bored to death I found amusement.

"Two or three days running, wherever I went in the
afternoon, I met a certain negress. One knows that
sort of thing, and, as soon I was sure, I gave her an
opportunity to speak.

"'Effendi,' she said, 'a beautiful lady has seen you,
and her soul is melting like wax,' &c.—you know.

"I expressed polite regrets to hear of this disaster,
and asked if the lady was married. No; her young
charms were like those of the plane-tree. And so on.
I recalled as much poetry suited to the occasion as my

studies could supply at a moment's notice, and hoped
to hear again when convenient. But before retiring
my black Hebe produced a little gage d'amour, which
would have warmed a cooler fellow than I am.

"'Allah!' I exclaimed, 'it is no kefaji's daughter
who sends a present like that! Who is your mistress?'

"The slave drew herself away saucily.

"'She will tell you when she thinks proper, I suppose.'

"I might have waited; but it is always well to know
beforehand with whom one sits down to a game. Very
few unmarried girls in a place like that could spare such
jewels. But it is dangerous, as you know, to ask questions bearing in the most remote degree upon the womankind of a family. At length I remembered your Copt,
who, let me tell you, is as vile a wretch as could be found
in Egypt. He pretends to live by acting as guide, but
his real pursuits are vastly more lucrative. The most
honest of them is to sell antique gems, which he imports
from Paris, and not the most abominable is to trade in
secrets. The poorest fallaheen all stand in his debt, and
he crushes them betwixt the upper and the nether millstone. But I did not know him then.

"This rascal was delighted to give me details about
every family in the town. There was more than a chance
that something in his way would come of it. The knowledge that my bonne fortune was unmarried simplified

the inquiry. I found that she could only be a daughter
of the pasha. He had two of marriageable years : the
elder affianced to my colonel, the other, Nuzleh, still
unattached. The Copt knew all about them, their
appearance, character, and tastes. Both, he said, were
very handsome, but the elder was bold and self-reliant,
whilst Nuzleh had a timid disposition, very rare amongst
Moslem women.

" Of course I had made no confidences ; but the
wretch hinted strongly that if either of the girls had
communicated with me it was certainly the former.
Refusing the fellow's services, I paid him and went
away.

" A day or two afterwards the slave carried me another
message. Her mistress would visit a stall in the bazaar
at a certain time, and she begged me to be about the
spot. I obeyed—one must lend oneself to these tom-
fooleries. The lady was punctual, of course, and I had
no trouble in recognising her amongst the others. If
this poor head of mine were capable of forming a prudent
resolution and sticking to it, I should have broken off
the adventure there and then. For she never took
her eyes from me until I fled in alarm. They were
beautiful eyes ! Next day, as I stood thinking of them
—amongst other matters, ma foi !—under the palace-
walls, a flower dropped upon me from above. No one
was by. I let my gauntlet fall and picked it up. Gen-

tilesse oblige ! But I prayed Allah to grant my beauty some slight gift of caution, since my own share is limited. And meantime I did not lounge beneath the palace-wall again.

" Some hours after the negress handed me a note. I could not read one half of it, and she could not help me. I swore the Copt to secrecy by all the gods who ever ruled in Egypt, and he deciphered it. The letter contained only verses and girlish nonsense. I got a poetry-book and wrote the reply; but when the messenger came for it she brought another, just a second edition, but in clearer writing. So things went on for several weeks. I was not so impatient as you would suppose, for with every other letter came a jewel. But things could not remain at this point. Making love by correspondence, at the risk of your neck, is a fashion out of date. The negress saw matters with my eyes, for she ran almost as great danger carrying these harmless notes as introducing me into the konak. But Nuzleh did not even think of a pleasure greater than writing verses. She was rather compelled than persuaded to let the slave tell her name. To my suggestions for an interview the silly child made no reply at all, but transmitted me her evening dreams and morning raptures, her impressions at noon and her visions at midnight, with an obstinate volubility which would have been droll had it not been so dangerous. I began to be bored. The volumes of poetry which I could borrow were nearly all used up in our correspondence. So I wrote in plain prose that a man gets tired of making love to an abstraction ; that I would receive no more letters until I had seen her. For a whole week there was silence, and I kept on my guard, for female pique runs naturally to daggers and poisons. Then came the answer. Amidst reams of poetry I learned that if I was so cruel she would obey, but how the meeting could be brought about her innocent mind was incapable of devising."

The autobiographical form is wearisome; having shown my guest's cynical manner of telling his story, I will drop it.

The maid proved to be as uningenious as the mistress. It is generally supposed that for cases of this sort women have more wit and courage than their lovers, but it was not so here. If they tried, they did not succeed in devising a plan for the interview, and Yusoof, of course, was absolutely unacquainted with the premises and the habits of the harem. For the pasha, so liberal to foreigners—who would gratefully report of him at Cairo —suffered no native to enter his gardens. Once more Yusoof resolved to let the matter drop, but those compromising letters still arrived, and he had no lover-like pretext for stopping them. The pasha's daughter could be terribly mischievous if she liked, without resort to violence. At his wit's end, Yusoof applied to the Copt, keeping back only the lady's name. That useful being saw no difficulty at all. The uncharitable might suppose that he had often answered a similar inquiry; the pasha had many wives and slaves.

" Can you swim? " said he.

" Like a fish."

" Under water ? "

" Like a moor-hen ! "

Thereupon the Copt revealed that no sentries guarded the canal; that the eunuchs' patrol was a mere ceremony. If the lady did her part with discretion, the lover risked nothing besides a midnight bath. Suspicious of every-one at Cairo, the pasha thought himself in safety here. Yusoof did not by any means regret the absence of danger. He told his plan and received the lady's trembling assent. Only, the meeting could not take place in her apartment, where a nurse but too faithful attended day and night. Consulted once more, the Coptic Sir Pandarus was ready. He named the kiosk in the tank, which always stood unlocked, saving those rare occasions when the garden was visited by foreigners.

On the first moonless night, Yusoof gained the bank of the canal, dived noiselessly beneath the arch, and swam under water as far as he was able. Rising to breathe where the shadows lay blackest, in two or three long stretches he reached the pool. Here, to gain the most sheltered place for landing, it was necessary to pass half-round the island, a fatiguing effort. He landed at the further steps, and looked round cautiously. No light glimmered through the shutters of the kiosk, no one moved within. But the windows of the palace were all illuminated, throwing a perilous glare between the trees. Perplexed, angry, and alarmed, Yusoof made up his mind to return, when a figure suddenly appearing on the bridge struck him motionless with fear. It stopped a few paces from him, and whispered, in tones quivering with fright:

" Are you there ? "

Yusoof recognised the negress, and approached her cautiously. She opened a door. It was pitch-dark inside.

" Where is the Lady Nuzleh ?" asked Yusoof, halting.

" There, there ! For goodness sake, go in !"

Thus encouraged, the lover poured forth to his invisible divinity the rapturous salutation which he had composed for this event. For European critics the effect would have been most seriously injured by a sneeze, but they hold other opinions on this score in the East. The lady revealed her presence by a sweetly murmured,—

" Allah make it good to you !" but her politeness ended in a sob.

The meeting seems to have been vastly droll in Yusoof's opinion. Shivering in wet clothes, he played the castanet between each word of his tender protestations. The fair one's answers were unintelligible, and her stalwart negress, holding the lover by his hand, forbade him to approach. Not ten minutes the interview lasted, and Yusoof vowed betwixt oaths and laughter, as he noiselessly slipped into the pool, that such a stupid entertainment was not worth a cold in the head, much more a life.

For several weeks the memory of this ridiculous adventure made him deaf to all advances. Fools and children, he told the slave, ought not to play at intrigue, which is an amusement for grown persons. Then it was rumoured through the town that there was sickness in the konak, and presently an old woman visited the captain's quarters. She brought a message of such blind, self-sacrificing love as touched me when I heard even Yusoof's careless rendering. Nuzleh had taken her old nurse into confidence, and she, poor creature, fearing lest the child should die, consented to everything. Yusoof's resolution failed, and his visits were many.

You think that the tragedy is coming now, but it was still deferred. The weeks passed by, and Nuzleh's elder sister was to be married to the colonel. His officers prepared the customary presents. Yusoof, deeply in debt to the money-lenders of Cairo, and to any one who would accommodate him, could only raise the needful cash by selling some jewel which Nuzleh had given him.

Upon the day when I arrived he took it to the Copt, who, in the afternoon, left at the barracks an amount representing one-twentieth of its value, or thereabouts. You will remember that we met beneath the konak wall. Yusoof charged the Copt with his trickery, and was told that if he did not like the price the colonel would give more, no doubt, to recover his bride's ring —for he supposed her the guilty sister. The incident that followed I have told. The Copt sought no vengeance at this time.

The colonel was married, and gossips began to whisper of a match far more grand for Nuzleh. Messengers passed to and from Cairo, until, at length, it was officially made known that a prince of the blood had asked the pasha's youngest daughter. Women have no small voice in their own affairs out yonder; and, in a common case, Nuzleh's objections would have been seriously entertained. But this alliance was too honourable to be delayed for a young girl's fancy. Her vehement protest caused suspicion, but the preparations went on.

During the night before my second visit, an inevitable discovery was made. The ladies of the harem opened Nuzleh's jewel-box, to see what parures she needed for her grand trousseau; and they found it empty. What followed nobody can tell. Before sunrise, a letter with a stone attached fell on Yusoof's bed, and told him in one word to fly. He rose instantly, packed his valuables in a box which he hid beneath his cloak, and escaped to my dabeah by the least frequented ways. And on his road he met the Copt, also avoiding observation. He was robed in his best, and his face was set towards the konak. Yusoof guessed his errand. Something had reached the usurer's ears, and he was hastening to sell his knowledge. Had Yusoof doubted, the old man's conduct would have betrayed him. He fell upon his knees, and my protégé, with great presence of mind, as he expressed it, slung the heavy box, and crashed it on his skull. Leaving the body there, he gained my boat without encountering a soul.

We reached Cairo safely, and I bade adieu to my passenger without reluctance. Two days afterwards he called, no longer Yusoof Agha, but Yusoof Bey. Whatever the offence which caused his banishment, it was forgiven. He gave me this sapphire; I suppose it belonged to that poor girl.

A few days after the newspapers announced her arrival. She came with her father and a big retinue, to be married to the prince. The ceremonies in such a case are long, but they came to a sad termination. Nuzleh died, how, under what circumstances, no one can tell. Many rumours flew about.

Yusoof Bey is one of the pasha's equerries (1863).

# A WOMAN'S KNIFE.

FROM time to time, for a dozen years past, I have made a desultory hunt for this souvenir. of my Bornean travels. Upon such occasions I nearly always found some forgotten object which distracted me; but the knife, so well remembered, would not appear. Its haft was a slender rod of ebony, curved back to fit the bended wrist, as is the lazy, graceful fashion of hand-tools in the East. The length was six inches, and five silver bands encircled the polished wood, which at either end was fitted with a socket of repoussé work in silver. The blade, two inches long, broad at the base, tapered sharply to a needle-point ; the cross-markings discernible at the wider end showed it had been hammered from a fragment of English file. The exportation of such in-struments from Sheffield must have roused curiosity sometimes amongst our more thoughtful manufacturers, for it is greater by a thousand-fold than would be re-quired for the legitimate uses to which a file is put. The fact is that people in that stage of barbarism where

a man's life daily hangs upon the excellence of his
weapon entertain a wise contempt for our swords and
knives. They buy them as tools, cheap, if not lasting
They buy them also as "material" partly finished, to
be re-manufactured. But files are the only steel goods
which they work up directly, and the only iron goods
are the ribands of metal which surround bales of cloth.
But this is a digression that would lead me into a dis-
course on the hardware trade.

A few days ago, upon the top of a book-shelf, I found
a roll of ancient bills and odd documents connected
with my Mexican wanderings; wrapped up in the midst
of them was my long-lost knife, very rusty and tar-
nished.

It was given me by a woman of Kuching, from
whom I bought a kain bandhara of Siamese silk that
would actually stand upright, so solid was it, and so
thick with gold. The thing cost forty dollars, less than
the value of the bullion, I should think; but the vendor
agreed to sell me another, which she was wearing at the
time, for twenty-four. I remember very well the design
of that: a Malay tartan, the large squares black, embroidered profusely in silver, with lines of various
breadth and tone of red upon a silver ground. Of this
bargain, however, she repented; and one day, when I
sent my servant to demand the article, she forwarded
the knife as a peace-offering.

This woman lived in a neat house of the Chinese bazaar, close by the fort. Photographs given me by the present rajah display the change that has taken place in this neighbourhood, where not a beam nor a tile remains to show what the most prosperous quarter of the capital was like eighteen years since, so greatly is it improved. The dwelling she inhabited had a wide verandah looking on the street, where she sat all day. They called her Dayang something or other; let us say, Dayang Sirik.

Two or three years before, she had arrived in Sarawak from Brunei, possessed of means to live in comfort, and many fine robes, articles of jewellery, and knicknacks. The police thought it necessary to investigate her rather mysterious existence, and they ascertained the facts here set down. My memory is doubtless inaccurate upon many points of detail, but I can trust it in regard to the main events. They give a horrid picture of the state of things that ruled in Brunei twenty-five or thirty years ago, but I should be not less surprised than glad to credit that it no longer represents the truth. In speaking of the habits of the late sultan, and the condition of his palace, I scarcely expect to find belief, but nothing is stated for which published evidence and official reports do not give warranty.

A certain pangeran of Brunei, passing through one of his dependent villages, saw a Murut girl whom he fancied. She belonged to a family of some position, and the chief thought it prudent to use honest means. His suit was accepted, of course, but the girl did not like to quit her home, and the lover did not insist. Upon an understood condition that the bride should live with her father, the wedding took place. In course of time a daughter was born, and shortly afterwards came a summons for mother and child from the husband at Brunei. Suspecting an evil design, the father refused to let them go, pleading the stipulation mentioned. Upon this arrived a body of truculent retainers from the capital, breathing flames and slaughter. A marriage-portion had been paid for the girl, of course, and this the father offered to return if he were allowed to keep his child ; then he offered to double it; and finally the husband condescended to withdraw his servants and dissolve the marriage, on receipt of three times the money he had paid.

The luckless Murut woman considered herself free once more, divorced by her scoundrel lord. After a time she accepted a suitor, perhaps a first love, amongst her own people, and they were married. When this news reached Brunei, the pangeran was furious. He swore to have the life of every one concerned in such an insult to his noble blood, and started immediately for the village. Warned in time, father and daughter escaped, but the husband was captured, tied to a tree, and stabbed by the chief himself. It has been said that the family of the woman was not altogether inconsiderable. They appealed to the sultan for vengeance, and for the restitution of their property sacked by the Brunci swashbucklers. The noble was summoned to justify his proceedings. Arguing by the Cheri, or sacred law, he denied that a payment of money could release a wife from the marriage bond ; it was only a solatium for the loss of her society at his town-house. What he had done, therefore, was a legitimate vindication of outraged honour. The sultan did not agree, and the chief imam condemned such an interpretation of the law. It was solemnly pronounced that the pangeran had behaved very badly. And there the matter ended.

Meantime the wife and daughter had fallen into their enemy's hands, and had been placed among his household slaves. After a while, a second daughter was born, the offspring of the murdered husband. It occurred to the noble that a present might restore him into favour with the sultan, and one day he despatched the mother and her two babies to the palace, as a tribute to the offended sovereign. I do not know whether it mollified his temper, but he accepted it. The children grew up amongst the palace slaves, but the elder, being of noble blood, was treated with more consideration than the other. In course of time she attracted the sultan's notice, and was promoted.

A certain change came over the fortunes of the family in consequence. The younger girl, Sirik, was appointed attendant to her sister, and the mother was freed. She left the palace, and took up her quarters in the city, living I know not how. Perhaps her Murut relations supported her; upon what secret fund of Providence do thousands of such as she sustain a respectable appearance in the thriftless tropic lands!

The harem of the Brunei sultan is no splendid abode —I use the present tense for convenience, since there is no reason to think that circumstances have changed with a new sovereign. It reminds one rather of a barn than of Haroun Alraschid's palace. In a building some seventy feet by forty, fourscore women live—wives, concubines, and slaves. I do not know that any white person has beheld the inside of it, for his majesty carries jealous care to the verge of hypochondria. Besides, very, very few, European ladies have visited his capital. Report says that the half-dozen favourites are lodged comfortably enough, and they certainly possess fine jewels and clothes. But those less favoured have a miserable existence. Their daily ration of the coarsest food is barely equal to sustaining life, and for garments they receive one set of clothes a year. Those who belong to families at their ease may get an allowance. Others, who possess some influence with their lord, turn it to profit. But such as have neither friends nor favour are not unlikely to pine in slow starvation.

Under such circumstances it will be credited that intrigue is busy at the palace. Malay women are at least as fond of dress and show as their sisters. Putting aside the prosaic question of securing a good meal every day, inmates of a royal harem who receive but one set of clothes a year—and those of cotton or cheapest silk —will always be plotting to get finery and cash. The house is old, constantly needing repair, and the sultan will not allow even a carpenter to go inside it. I should speak in the past tense here, however, for of the reigning sultan, his habits and character, I know nothing. The old monarch handled tools himself, aided by the female slaves. It was very foolish and short-sighted policy of his majesty, for what those amateur assistant-carpenters secured, they knew how to loose again. Bitter and murderous enmities rose in the palace, but every soul was leagued against the master. Secure in the ready help even of foes, the royal women escaped at pleasure, and stayed abroad for days. As the building stands on posts above the water, a board quietly removed gave exit to these amphibious nymphs. The canoe in waiting lay unnoticed under a convenient shadow, and a few noiseless strokes carried them to liberty.

To return was easier still. Even a favourite, by choosing her time, might reasonably hope that an absence of some days would be kept secret from his majesty ; much more one of the rank and file. It was proved in a great murder case that the daughters of the prime minister, married to the sultan, took a month's holiday once without his knowledge.

The whole life of these miserable prisoners was made up of intrigues—twisted, complicated, worked, and moulded one into another; intrigues of love, of jealous hatred, of court favour, of public and private fraud, of family and trade. They had no other interest or amusement; some, as we have seen, must intrigue to live. That they should love or respect their master was absurd. Those who treat women as animals will find themselves treated as animals are.

There was a young noble about the court, famed for his good looks, his recklessness, and his wealth; we may call him Pangeran Momein. The ladies of Brunei were satisfied that male fascination concentred in this youth, who seems to have been a rake as finished as the most civilised realm could show. At the time I speak of he had lately introduced to the capital a brother, Pangeran Budruddin, who had passed his early years among the Lanuns of Tampasuk. Possibly his mother came from thence; I do not know. Earth does not contain a race more fiendish in its public acts than the Lanuns, and those of Tampasuk are worst of all, having more wrongs, as they consider, to avenge upon humanity. But these pirates have virtues at home well fitted to counteract the hereditary tendencies of a young Brunei noble. In their own village they show none of that ferocity which impels them like homicidal madness on the sea. Dignified, good-tempered, forbearing towards each other and towards their slaves, they reverence the sanctity of home. Perfectly truthful they are, to the point that a 'man will not only die rather than tell a falsehood; he will commit suicide for shame if induced by a moment's weakness so to err. They are generous, and deeply imbued with the spirit of the motto, Noblesse oblige; the noblesse being simply Lanun blood. Though gay of mood and enterprising, they respect woman, putting her upon a footing which she occupies, I think, amongst no other people of the Far East. And she recognises that equality by taking share in all their interests and concerns. Not unfrequently a whole ship's company of freeborn girls used to cruise with their male kin in search of booty and adventure. The practice is abandoned now, as I have been informed, simply because the activity of European cruisers forbids such large vessels to be used as formerly, and the girls do not like to go in small numbers together. We might be sure, if there were not terrible evidence to hand, that these " shield-maidens," as our forefathers called such bands, were not the last at fray or plunder. To their male comrades they were sacred, regarded somewhat as are nuns by zealous Catholics. In short, the existence, the ideas, of the Lanuns, at home and abroad, are singularly

like in all respects to those of our own Vikings ten
centuries ago.

Pangeran Budruddin was educated amongst this
manly but misguided people. At twenty years old or
so he came to Brunei. Momein hastened to civilise him
after the court model, but his efforts were not appreciated. Budruddin could not feel interest in the commonplace intrigues, the struggle for favours, the oppression of helpless peasantry, which made up his brother's
enjoyments. He had the Lanun ideal of woman, which
I would not have the reader exaggerate, but which, at
least, is very different from the Brunei. Accustomed
to rajahs and chiefs who are true leaders of men—or the
Lanuns would not follow them, but swiftly run them
through—he declared the Iang de per Tuan himself, the
blessed Sultan, a doddering old fool. Of course, this
young noble did not think Momein's pleasures wrong,
but they bored him.

It may be supposed that a youth of such a stamp,
brother to the famed Lothario, good-looking, I imagine
certainly of strong character, did not fail to attract the
eye of Brunei ladies. But he fell in love with none
until malignant planets led him across the path of
Dayang Madih, as I name the elder of the Sultan's
slaves. It was at the end of Ramazan, when his majesty,
in full state, visits the tombs of his forefathers. On this
occasion the dames of the harem get their new clothes.

About a dozen, closely veiled, wait upon their master, sitting beneath the shadow of a yellow awning in the stern of the royal prau.

Water pageants are always effective, even in the dull and colourless Occident. Our own muddy Thames roused poets' enthusiasm and painters' ambition so long as the gala business of the capital was transacted " betwixt bridges."

Brunei is a wooden Venice, immeasurably finer in all natural aspects and effects, as more brilliant and stirring in its population. But I need scarcely say that monuments and public buildings do not exist. Two large mosques there are, as ugly and as mean as they could be, and scores of fanes (djamis) like pot-works of the most miserable sort. But the lofty dwellings of the nobility crowd every stretch of shallow water, and on state occasions each is a study, from the banners streaming on its roof to the gaunt piles that uphold it, prismatic with ooze and shell. The balconies, hung with brilliant cloths and silks, are filled with an eager, clamorous, motley throng. Clustered here stands the harem of a chief, white-veiled, but robed in hues of sombre richness which glow and flash with gold. They laugh and chatter in unceasing motion, passing their siri-boxes from hand to hand, smoking cigarettes of maize-straw. There crowd the slaves, half-naked, a sheeny mass of yellow skin, topped by the gay head-handkerchiefs, and skirted by the tasteful, sombre plaid of sarongs.

The water bears a thousand boats, crushing and jostling at points of vantage, scudding swiftly to and fro. Larger praus, belonging to pangerans not authorised to accompany the monarch, are decked with pennons, and their crews wear livery. Others, bearing rich merchants and sea-captains, dare mount no flag, nor put their men in uniform; but they try to hide this deficiency by decking their wives and their own persons with extra splendour.

It is a daily marvel how the bankrupt state contrives to furnish such a show. Public and private revenues have been diminishing this century past with ever-increased speed, under a system of government compared with which that of Turkey is a model. But we have learned in other climes that solvency is not the condition which oftenest breeds extravagance.

In the procession itself, beside the Sultan and his household, all the ministers and high officials take their part. It may be interesting to enumerate some of these, for the order of things at this capital is not less strange than excellent in theory. But I must again recall that my information dates back twenty years. Matters had gone there unchanged for something like four centuries; but the world travels quickly nowadays, and it is possible, though improbable, that Brunei has moved.

First came the Sultan's barge, streaming with flags of yellow silk, urged by fifty paddles, to the clang of gongs and beat of tomtoms. All the crew were dressed in yellow. On a platform amidships, under a great yellow umbrella, sat his majesty, in a long yellow coat of richest China silk, white satin trousers, stiff with gold almost to the knee, and head-kerchief glittering with gold-lace. His officials, gracefully robed, lay about him, not cross-legged, but kneeling with their hams upon their heels, or reclining on one hip. At the stern of the vessel, under a yellow awning, sat the wives and women. The next prau, almost as large, was that of the Datu Bandhara, minister of state for home affairs, whose flags, liveries, and umbrellas are white. Following came the Datu Degadong, chancellor of the exchequer, whose colour is black. The Datu Pamancha succeeded, in green; he is chief functionary of civil law. Then came the Datu Tomangong, war minister, all red. These are the four grand officers of state, whose colours are attached to their respective dignities. But the sixth prau belonged to a plebeian personage, more important than they—the Orang Kaya Degadong, chief of the " tribunes of the people." Every quarter of the city elects a representative to uphold its interests with the paramount authority,—every quarter, I should add, is inhabited by a separate guild. These, in their turn, elect a head, who is invariably a man of talent and

resolution. It results from the system of choice that
the Orang Kaya Degadong is, in effect, that person in
whom the majority of Borneans put most confidence;
and this is so well recognised that the sovereign and the
nobles dare not oppose his will, so long as the people
stand by him. They may cajole, and they may sometimes murder, but they do not resist.

Following the Orang Kaya was the Datu Shahban-
dhar, minister of commerce, whose duty it is, amongst
other things, to look after foreigners and strangers.
The Tuahs, the tribunes mentioned, filled several smaller
praus, mixed up with inferior nobles, whose jealousy of
precedence made the tail of the procession rather a jostle
and a scramble. Every one of aristocratic birth may fly a
banner, but must not use colours devoted to the chiefs.

Pangeran Momein was one of the eight secretaries
attached officially to the Datu Bandhara, entitled to
seats in his barge, where he had obtained a place for
Budruddin. It was in the bow, and as the vessels
followed close, going and returning, the young man
stood only a few feet distance from the royal ladies.
Many eyes invited him, no doubt, to rash attempts;
many roguish words were uttered for his hearing. But
he saw only Madih, who sat nearest. With a coquetry
perhaps innocent, universal certainly wherever it may
be practised without too much risk, the girl had shown
her face for one second when she marked a handsome

young noble observing her. The sudden gleam of admiration in his eyes flattered but rather alarmed her. Though an inmate of that evil palace since babyhood, Madih had borne no part in its iniquities. I do not mean to represent her as a miracle of virtue—a condition whereof she knew no more, by experience of life, than the mere name. But he who travels open-eyed in countries where passion is more frank of speech, and less controlled by habit, must learn that there are natures which cling to purity by instinct, without understanding, or conscious affection for it—which repel evil things to the last, though taught, poor creatures, to regard them as the natural ways of man.

Madih had laughed and helped at many a deception of " the master," and had borne her part in many an audacious trick. But, laughing still, she had refused herself to mix therein.

Even now, though Budruddin's face pleased her, and his behaviour was such as gratified her fancy, she only laughed at the messages he contrived to send.

But the youth was in earnest. He longed to return to Tampasuk, and to carry with him this girl who had moved his heart. He went to her mother and declared himself. The old woman might well be tempted to run certain risks, which long impunity had made almost insignificant in her eyes, for such a chance of liberty and fortune.

She visited her daughter forthwith, and used all her
influence, all her descriptive power, to obtain the girl's
consent.   And she succeeded, at least so far as to gain
the lover a hearing.   For the first time, and the last,
Madih stole out of the harem, accompanied by her sister.

Budruddin put all his heart into his suit, and triumphed.   It was agreed that they should fly so soon as
a Lanun boat in harbour had discharged its cargo.   He
urged his future wife to hide until that time with friends
he could trust, not returning to the palace.

Unhappily she shrank from this course.   The fear of
detection influenced her to some extent—being unused
to hazard it—and also she had a childish longing to bid
the companions of her youth good-bye.   The mother
also desired, as slaves will, to secure the few bits of
finery presented by the sultan.   And so, after three
hours' absence, they went back.

An escapade so brief and innocent of ill-doing had
seldom been indulged by ladies of the palace, but fate
was malignant.   The sultan chanced to be hungry when
he entered the harem, and in a bad temper also.   He
tried and rejected the fare awaiting him, and called for
a special sambal which Sirik prepared—a sambal is a
condiment peculiarly Malay, of infinite variety in material
and mode of spicing.   Madih then suffered for her caution
and timidity.   She had confided to none her design,
and when the Iang de per Tuan summoned Sirik, half-

a-dozen slaves went to find her, without ill-intention
hunted for her up and down, made so much noise about
it—really perplexed to explain her absence—that the
sovereign's notice was drawn. Ready always to suspicion, he demanded Madih ; went to her chamber and
found it vacant, and satisfied himself that both the girls
were outside. Then he withdrew, white and tottering
with passion.

The difficulty of leaving the harem, no great matter
anyhow, vanished at the return. So many women
passed in and out during the day that with a slight
disguise any one could go by the purblind sentries.
Landing from their boat the three women went up the
steps, and through the door ; but, on the other side,
men seized them. The sisters, shrieking, were cast into
a chamber and locked up, whilst the mother was dragged
a few steps inside the salamlik (the men's apartments).
A door opened, and she was pushed in. There stood
the Datu Bandhara and two of his secretaries, Momein
one of them. The only furniture of the room, besides
the divan, was a table, upon which lay the strangling
apparatus. The woman fell on her knees at once, begging mercy in wild tones. The Datu Bandhara ex-
horted her to confess, but the fear of death closed her
ears. She cried and raved incoherently, until one of
the slaves present gagged her with her own loose hair.
Then the Bandhara, a feeble old courtier, delivered his

speech, which promised life if she told the name of the guilty man. Relieved of the choking mass of hair which stuffed her mouth, the old woman began her revelations. After the first words, implicating his brother, Momein sprang forward with an imprecation, slipping off his heavy sandal, and striking her with all his force across the mouth.

"Why waste our time?" he cried. "She is guilty of offence against the sultan's honour! Let her die!"

He seized the machine of cords and wood, tossing it over to the executioners. Before the Datu could interfere, or the woman utter an intelligible sound, the silken string was about her neck, drawn tight by a motion of the hand; and after one supreme struggle, wherein every muscle of the body was exerted, her head fell on one side, and all was finished.

It remained to deal with the girls. Ignorant of their mother's fate, they boldly protested innocence, declaring they had quitted the harem to visit their family connections, and this assertion appears to have been sustained by evidence. The Iang de per Tuan himself did not dare use torture—perhaps did not think of it. The notion is repugnant to Malay ideas. Upon one historical occasion in late times the chief of Johore justified his doings in this respect by the "sacred books of England," which he said had been followed strictly. A sultan of Brunei, head of all Malay people, would not have ventured, had he been inclined, to use such means of extorting confession, though it were in the sanctity of his harem. But he could and did condemn Madih to death and Sirik to perpetual slavery. This sentence was lightened in the former case by an organised petition of the harem. No such favourite as Madih could be found amongst all the throng of women, and they used their influence—so great in all countries where polygamy is exercised—to obtain a commutation. They succeeded of course. The sultan married her off to an old dependent, and I know nothing more of her.

Sirik returned to her old degradation, and Budruddin escaped to Tampasuk. Some years after he came back as head of his family, Momein having died in a scandalous brawl. Whether he sought out his former love, I have no information. But he obtained the freedom of Sirik, and took her into his own household, as chief duenna of the harem. Some months afterwards, under circumstances unexplained, she sought refuge aboard a Chinese junk starting for Sarawak. Such a store of handsome things she carried away that the police took note of her as I have said. But no complaint ever reached them from Brunei, and her life at Kuching, if eccentric, was perfectly decorous. Nearly all the hours of the twenty-four she passed in the verandah, shifting with the movement of the sun. Huddled up beneath a handsome sarong, with fine silks strewn about the mats,

she watched the bustle of the Kina-pasar as long as daylight lasted.  Then she lit two candles, and still sat,
chewing betel without intermission, but very seldom
speaking.  The neighbours thought her mad, and treated
her with kindly reverence as one afflicted by the direct
interposition of the Deity.  As I interpret the feeling of
Orientals towards the insane, it is based upon the argument that Allah changed his mind in their special case,
for reasons to be accepted with submissive respect.  After
creating a human frame which he endowed with consciousness, he thought proper to withdraw the soul.  A
being thus exceptionally treated by Heaven must not
be lightly regarded by man.  And Sirik enjoyed the
advantage of this most interesting and respectable sen-
timent.

# A CARPET.

I HAVE no need to describe the object in question, to which, properly speaking, no legend hangs. I bought it at Candahar, for lawful money of the empire, and any adventures that occurred in bringing it down have been chronicled elsewhere. There is nothing particular to distinguish it from other Persian carpets. The size is perhaps unusual, and the colour. These slight peculiarities attracted the notice of our young Brahui guide, when I chanced to unroll it at Bagh. He exclaimed at once, " I have a carpet like that at home! We took dozens of them once in the Bolan."

I like to sketch a background for my little pictures of strange men, strange incidents, and nowhere could a scene be found more striking than that before our eyes as we listened to Rahim's story—for a story he had, of course, attaching to his carpet. The place was Bagh, in the Kutchi desert. Government had built a row of sheds outside the filthy town, where returning troops encamped. Imagine us seated by the door at evening

T

in the shadow of the hut.    The foreground is occupied
by tethered horses, soldiers passing to and fro, wild
Brahuis and Beloochis reckoning their pay suspiciously.
Behind them lies a waste of sand, dotted here and there
with a solitary camel.   Our young Adonis of the Brahui
nation stands leaning on his jezail.   The horizontal sunrays outline his beautiful face, gild his silken ringlets
hanging nearly to the waist, and his flowing, graceful
costume.   Away upon his left rises that stately tomb
renowned throughout the desert.   Its great yellow dome
throws a shadow almost to our feet, obscuring those un-
sightly mounds of rubbish round its base.   Terrace upon
terrace the huge building rises to that well-proportioned
vault.   Graceful pillars and pinnacles, latticed windows
painted blue, relieve the dulness of the vast mud-pile.
Its solid foundations are walled in with blind arches and
pilasters.   Umbrella-like kiosks, domed with azure tiles,
bound the steps of the main entrance.   Beyond them,
mysterious and still, almost picturesque, lies the flat-
roofed town of Bagh, among orchard-trees in bloom,
and pale-green thickets of tamarisk.   People in bright
loose garments, saffron and white and pink, green, blue,
and purple, loiter on the road.   Horsemen go by,
rapidly pacing, their four-knobbed targets slung behind
the shoulder, their ready weapons glittering.

Upon the other side the tomb lowers a dark wood of
cypress, the burial-ground of this oasis.   A pilgrim

kneels upon the sand, gleaming white against that shadow. Far has he travelled to behold the sacred place. He prostrates himself and beats the earth with front and palms, veiled in his mane of hair—rises to press his hands together—falls prone again. What would be the conduct of that devotee could he glance into my portmanteau? Rahim Khan himself, our trusty friend, would scarcely draw sword for me in that quarrel. Three tiles from the very sanctuary, the grave of the holy man, are locked up there! It would be vain to urge that the chief moolah sold them me for a rupee apiece; tore them from the monument with his consecrated hands, after timorous scrutiny of the neighbourhood. Those three tiles now form a bracket in my drawing-room, and support the " Cross " of which you will shortly hear.

I asked the story of this tomb, a surprising structure in the middle of the desert. Unfortunately, I made no note, and it has slipped my recollection. The merest fragment remains. The building was erected, by whom I forget, in honour of two Persian saints, one of whom is interred there. They were great princes. Either the Shah or the Ameer sent for them, and one obeyed ; he never came back. I remember no more, and these legends would be valueless and uninteresting if they did not preserve the strictest truth of history, scenery, and manners.

When Rahim Khan was quite a child he often saw at his uncle's residence a Candahari merchant named Asaf Jah. Rahim is nephew of Alla-ood-dina Khan, head chief of the Brahuis, who kept the Bolan Pass, and levied dues on all who traversed it. With this potent freebooter Asaf Jah had an hereditary friendship. When setting out for a commercial trip to India, he always gave notice to the Brahui chieftain, and an escort of honour met him at the Dasht-i-be-Doulat. If Alla-ood-dina was at home, he invited his friend to the castle, where in feast and gossip he passed the time, whilst his kafila laboriously but safely threaded the Bolan. A smart ride upon the Khan's Beloochi mare carried him to Dadur in the twenty-four hours, where he overtook his merchandise. Upon these visits young Rahim, a lovely boy no doubt, had often perched on the Candahari's knee.

Things went on thus for years. Asaf Jah grew old and rich. Once, after some days' entertainment at the castle, he rode down the pass to rejoin his kafila, as usual. An escort followed him. But Alla-ood-dina's friend ran not the slightest peril, and his Brahuis lingered, discussing news with a party of their country-men just returned from the south. There is a rock by Mach, whereon Mahomet stepped during one of those unrecorded journeys of which every land in Islam keeps a tradition. His footprint may be discerned to this day,

if one have the eyes of faith. I haven't, and the holy
mark appears to me much like any other hollow in a
slab of stone. The footprint is clear enough, however,
to be venerated by Damar and Kakar, Brahui and
Belooch, for a hundred miles about. Asaf Jah was a
pious man, and he never passed this spot without adding
his stick and bit of rag to the fluttering memorials that
encircle it.

The stone actually overhangs the pass, some ten or
twelve feet above. A well-worn ascent leads to it,
practicable on horseback. Generations of pilgrims have
cleared a little space where a man may leave his horse
whilst paying his devotions. But in summer-time a
handsome pista-tree hides all this tiny area from below.
It is rooted in the pass itself, and at its foot bubbles a
spring. The basin has been enlarged, and a rude arch
built over it, beautifully hung with maidenhair and
common English ferns, plastered with liverwort—for we
are still upon the highlands. The waters of the spring
vanish at some feet distance, sinking in the mass of
pebbles, and flowing underground towards the Bolan
river, which has its reputed source some hundred
yards below. This is a favourite halting-place for
Kakar Pathans. The cross-road leading to their wilds
debouches nearly opposite. It is a long march the
kafilas habitually take to this their first camp on the
journey to India. The road is waterless for many miles.

By resting here several objects are attained. In the first place, they put themselves directly under protection of Mahomet, who chose it for a grand testimony; in the second, they water their camels in peace: in the third, they escape the danger of camping side by side with Brahuis, Candaharis, Damars, and all those people, mostly unfriends, who habitually halt at the source of the Bolan.

After saying his prayers, and putting up his pious trophy, Asaf Jah sat in the shade, to wait the arrival of his escort. He talked with his slave awhile, and then both dozed. A sound of voices disturbed the merchant, who recognised the Kakar speech, and the merry chatter of young women. Somewhat alarmed, he crept on hands and knees and peered below, through the close and twisted branches of the pista. At the middle of the pass, some hundred yards in width at this point, three donkeys stood in the blaze of sunshine. They were handsomely caparisoned for women's riding, and slaves held them. A number of horsemen, fully armed of course, waited at a distance. But the voices did not come from thence. At the spring, right beneath his eyes, Asaf Jah beheld three girls unveiled, scooping the water in their palms, and laughing at their awkwardness. In that glance the elderly and prosaic merchant lost his heart.

It would have stopped Rahim's tale at the outset,

offended him sorely, and embued him with scorn for us
never to be effaced, had we asked curious questions about
this incident. As matter of history he did not refuse
allusion to the sex, nor even to love. But the allusion
must be quite abstract, void of all personal reference.
I never forget the lesson in Moslem *savoir vivre* which
this youth gave me once upon a time. Against the
advice of an experienced companion, I asked him how
many daughters had Alla-ood-dina Khan—such daughters
being his own cousins. The concentrated frigidity of
Rahim's " I don't know! " the sudden pause in his flow
of gossip and bright talk, gave me a first, a final warning
that individual woman must not be referred to in any
shape or way with the Brahui.

But I can imagine the portrait of a handsome Kakar
maiden, high in rank. She is tall, white, stately, formed
like a mother of giants and heroes. Her great black
eyes are superb of spirit and intensity, not slow even to
laugh in those young days, but incapable of tears. The
mouth is rigid even now, for all its perfection of shape
and colour, its smooth fulness of outline. That face represents a character wherein love is very near to hate—
suspicious, pitiless, unrelenting, a wild-beast passion.
The girlish virtues are all missing, even modesty and
chastity. Some male virtues appear, indeed, at their
strongest: high spirit, dauntless enterprise, tenacity, and
intelligence. But others which should be common to

either sex have not a trace—such, I mean, as truth and
kindliness; whilst the germs of every bad passion are
lying in congenial soil.

You think I am sketching a monster, and the charge
is not to be denied.   Monsters the Pathans are, and have
ever been since history first mentions the race.   Of the
innumerable statesmen who have dealt with them in
ancient and modern times,—of the many writers who in
Persian, Hindu, Arabic, and English have treated of
them,—not one records a national virtue, saving courage.
Their own historians are bitterest of all in warning the
human race against this desperate enemy of mankind.

But Asaf Jah was used to the type of woman I have
drawn, and he looked at this Kakar maiden only to covet
her loveliness.   He sat still, hungrily gazing.   Presently
the girls resumed their veils and mounted, riding towards
Quetta.   When they had passed beyond sight, Asaf Jah
hurried to question his escort, and learned that the party
they had just encountered were retainers of Usman Khan,
a subordinate chief of the Kakars.   Asaf pushed on, resolved to sell all his goods at Shikarpore, and return to
woo this peerless beauty.

Yah Mohammad Khan, eldest son and heir-apparent
of Alla-ood-dina, chanced to be at Dadur.   Asaf had
known him intimately since he was a boy, and he delicately sounded the young chief.   There is fierce hatred
between Kakar and Brahui, but for the moment they had

a truce. Yah Mohammad gravely remarked that his father would regret it if his ally took a wife amongst his enemies, but he did not speak with anger. And Asaf drew comfort from this indifference; for the ugly, squat sabreur, whose acquaintance I recall with pleasure, speaks with terrible emphasis when he is in earnest.

Asaf went on to Shikarpore, after dispatching a note to Alla-ood-dina. He named his intention of proposing for the daughter of Usman Khan, adding that Yah Mohammad approved. At Shikarpore he sold his merchandise for what it would fetch, and within a month returned to Dadur. Alla-ood-dina's reply was waiting. It accused his friend of deception. Yah Mohammad had not understood that the lady was daughter of Usman Khan. With that chieftain Alla-ood-dina had a family feud, which for the moment lay at rest, but was not, nor could be appeased. No one who allied himself with one party could expect to keep on terms with the other. Perplexed and disheartened, but clinging to his purpose, Asaf pursued his journey home.

I did not interrupt Rahmin, but a question arose in my mind which may occur to others who know something of the country. How could a subordinate chief of the Kakars hold his own against Alla-ood-dina? This puzzle was explained to me afterwards. Usman lived far away in the mountains. The Brahui Khan could not reach him without disturbing powerful Kakar septs with whom he was at peace. But a more honourable motive was hinted, perhaps with truth. Alla-ood-dina scorned to use his might as supreme head of the Brahuis in a family quarrel. He fought Usman with his own clan; and his subjects, as a people, were uninterested.

Asaf replied submissively and gratefully, declaring that, since his patron held such strong views, he put away the thought. And so soon as he had passed the Brahui frontier he sent a message to Usman Khan with gifts. A professional match-maker was easily found at Quetta. To this old dame Asaf confided his means and intentions; authorised her to propose such and such terms; then he went on to Candahar. Usman Khan meanwhile returned an answer, haughty though polite, stating that he preferred a warrior son-in-law to a merchant. But the match-maker, well paid, came to his village. The precise declarations she carried were given, not to the Khan, of course, but to his wife. In speaking of the daughter— let us call her Raziah—I have tried to show what like are Kakar women. It may be believed that such persons have authority in a household. The Khan's wife was tempted. Of men and arms a Pathan chief has abundance, but he wants cash dreadfully as a rule. Asaf's proposals included, of course, a handsome sum to the bride's father. And Usman Khan approved the match when this was clearly appraised.

The negotiations came to Alla-ood-dina's knowledge.

He wrote to Asaf once more. Upon the falsehood practised towards himself the chief did not insist, perhaps he
did not think much of that. He appealed to the honourable feelings of his old friend. " Oh, my brother, let
not our fathers hear that for a woman's sake we have
wasted the legacy they bequeathed us! My liver is inflamed thinking of the disappointment and danger that
await you. The Kakars are false. Though this maiden
have beautiful colours and bright eyes, so has the snake
which bears poison in its lips. If your heart needs a
young wife, choose which you will among my people.
But, if you persist in marrying Usman Khan's daughter,
there is death between you, merchant of Candahar, and
me, Alla-ood-dina, Khankhanan of the Brahui nation,
and all of our kin."

Asaf wrote an abject answer, but without hope that it
would move the fierce old chief. The Bolan henceforward would be closed to him. No merchant would
undertake even to cover with his name the goods of a
man proclaimed enemy of the Brahuis—none, at least,
whom he could trust. But Asaf was consumed with
that fond, foolish passion of age which discounts the
years remaining. He determined to retire from business. And in due time Usman Khan rode into the city,
with his wife and daughter, and a ragged retinue of
dhuni-wassails ; in due time Raziah was handsomely
married to Asaf Jah.

" Some years after that," continued Rahim, " this foolish fellow was persuaded to take a great kafila through the Bolan, and——"

I could not restrain my questions here. " Who persuaded him? Why did he risk death almost certain?"

" I don't know!" Rahim answered resolutely.

I saw by his manner that our young guide knew very well, but there was no arguing with his sense of decorum. I do not profess to have had other means of information But, from the incidents suggested, I have formed a theory, a legend, to explain Asaf Jah's mad action. It may not be true, but I am sure that it is not improbable in that land, with those people.

Candahar was then in possession of Abdul-rahman, now Ameer of Cabul. He carried matters with a high hand towards the trading class, too well used to be oppressed. Among his great officers was Bahram Khan, of Kakar birth, but of a family long since exiled from its native seat. In some assessment of contributions, Asaf Jah was entered for a sum much heavier than was just. Bahram Khan had it in charge to execute the order, and to him the merchant appealed. Among the faults of a Pathan woman, indifference to a husband's affairs of business is certainly not to be counted. Learning who was the person in authority about this matter, Raziah primed her lord with various facts and details regarding Bahram's family in Kakaristan which were likely to

earn his goodwill. Asaf used the information shrewdly,
gained his case, and won the sympathies of this powerful
officer. Bahram Khan often visited the house to feast
and drink. We may fancy him a stalwart soldier, with
blue eyes keen as a hawk's, a slender moustache, straw-
coloured, shading his false, handsome mouth;—of such
types the Afghan army is full. Raziah saw him often
from the lattice of the zenana, through a hole in the
curtains; and she continually met him, superb on horseback, in the bazaar. She fell in love. For her elderly
husband, a Candahari, a trader, she had of course no
regard. The unaccustomed luxury which had given
such delight began to pall. No impulse or training held
her back. From childhood Raziah had listened to stories
of intrigue which none rebuked. Neither the modesty,
nor the sense of honour, nor the physical alarms that
restrain other women have influence on the Pathan.

Means lay to her hand, as they do to all in that
vicious city. Raziah wrote to Bahram Khan, and he
replied, not knowing his correspondent. But she did
not desire a mere intrigue. After assuring herself that
Bahram's heart—what they call the heart yonder—was
free, she turned to another thread of the combination.
The husband was now insupportable. She tried poison,
fantastic substances recommended by Pathan tradition.
But Asaf ate her powdered diamonds, her tiger's whiskers, and the rest, without inconvenience. I do not

mean to say that either diamonds or tiger's whiskers are harmless. But their effect depends on accident, and Asaf was lucky so far. Whilst Raziah cautiously inquired how to obtain more certain agents, chance assisted her.

Bahram Khan suggested an enterprise which promised great advantage. Some Persian merchants had been seized by Abdul-rahman, and their stock confiscated. Bahram obtained the offer of it at a price which must yield enormous profit, if the carpets and things could be transported to Kurrachi. His old instincts roused by this chance of profit, Asaf bewailed the ill-will of the Brahui Khan. He talked to his wife upon the subject, and she saw an opportunity. Taking up the question with the savage but cunning eagerness that belonged to her nature, Raziah taunted him with his fears. She worked herself into a storm of passion, declared she would be no wife to a man afraid of Alla-ood-dina, with whom her father had waged many a battle. Other merchants threatened had forced the Bolan Pass, without the aid which Usman Khan would give his son-in-law. And so they had a serious quarrel—all quarrels, indeed, are serious with that people.

Asaf endeavoured to explain that, in cases when the Bolan had been forced, Alla-ood-dina had not taken part in the affray. It had always arisen from illegal exactions of his officers, whom he left to fight it out. The case was different here. But Raziah would not listen, and the uxorious old man gave way. He bought the Persian goods, fitted out his kafila, and engaged a very powerful guard. But Asaf principally relied on a diversion which the Kakars promised to make. When all was prepared, with such secrecy as might be, another storm burst. The merchant had never thought of going himself. So soon as Raziah understood this, or pretended to learn it, she raved with scornful passion, called her husband coward, and used other epithets quite unrefined. This sort of objurgation is not patiently supported twice in a Pathan household. Asaf seized his riding-whip, and laid the knotted thong across her shoulders. Raziah sprang at him, forced him down, and drew the ever-ready knife. But in the tempest of fury these people do not lose their heads. Domestic affrays are common enough among them, but when they end in the murder of the husband Afghan law punishes them with the extremest severity ; for every man is interested in this matter. Raziah withdrew, sternly declaring that she would not see her husband's face again until he returned from India.

Such refusal of marital rights is not uncommon. Strangely enough, etiquette supports a wife in any such freak of temper. There are exceptions, naturally ; but as a rule the husband has no remedy except divorce, if a wife be obstinate. Asaf yielded after a time, and was restored to favour on conditions. He strengthened the

guard, and obtained a company of soldiers from Bahram
Khan. To deceive the Brahui, it was put about that the
kafila would rendezvous at Chaman ; a week before the
time appointed, it had all collected there. Asaf slipped
away at night, and reached the Kojak Pass in twelve
hours' hard riding. Forthwith, the kafila got into
motion. Alla-ood-dina was doubtless aware of its approach. But, if the elaborate arrangements for mislead-
ing him were successful, Asaf might hope he would be
taken by surprise, and that the caravan would escape
before he could raise men enough to attack such a powerful body. The return by Lahore and Cabul gave no
anxiety.

But Alla-ood-dina was informed of every movement.
He had, moreover, an assurance that the Kakars would
not stir, and that the troops would not fight if
let alone. So soon as her husband gave way, Raziah
made known to Bahram Khan who was his correspondent. The confidential messenger exhausted herself
in describing her employer's beauty and her wealth.
Raziah would not see the Khan ; but thoughtfully,
frankly, in business-like style, she suggested how his
friend, her husband, might be betrayed, that he might
marry the widow. And Bahram accepted, of course,
without a qualm.

The kafila marched rapidly. In four days it reached
the Dasht-i-be-Doulat, were Alla-ood dina's officers were

waiting, as usual, to receive black-mail. Their presence reassured Asaf. Taking it as a sign that the Brahuis had not been warned, he peremptorily refused to pay. The officers acted their part well, threatened vengeance, and drew off. For three days the caravan proceeded peacefully, passed the Kotal, passed Mach, and gained that plateau in the middle of the defile the name of which I grieve to forget. The Kakars did not join, as expected; but military combinations in that land may be spoilt by innumerable accidents. The more dangerous portions of the defile had been traversed. Asaf felt tolerably secure, with his armed guard and his soldiers.

But whilst the sirwans were mustering at earliest dawn, their heads enveloped in long rolls of cloth, a panic seized them. No sound could they hear through that muffling; the plain was dark and misty, but shadowy forms flitted all round. They shouted, and the camp awoke. Then rose the Brahui yell, chorused by hundreds. Rattling, clashing through the pebbles, a storm of hoofs burst in on every side, swept through the camp, returned. No sentry had raised an alarm—they were all soldiers of Bahram Khan, acquainted with the plot. Men struggling to their feet were cut down, lay writhing, trampled under foot. Asaf ran out of his tent. A dusky horseman met him—the mare, checked in her stride, reared upright amidst a splash of flying stones—and Asaf fell, cleft to the nose by Yah Mohammad.

U

There were cries for quarter answered by the vengeful yell,—ringing chases and savage laughter. But when the dawn, fast whitening, displayed the scene, no man of all the kafila survived. The soldiers, drawn up, stood to their arms. A knot of horsemen mounted guard over the merchandise; others, dismounted, went to and fro, searching for corpses not yet rifled, whilst their mares stood quiet on the very spot where they were left. Camels trooped in leisurely, driven by the victorious Brahuis, gossiping, laughing, telling their adventures, looking under every rock for loot. An hour afterwards all had vanished but the burying-party—these heaped pebbles on the corpses as they lay. A large cairn was raised over Asaf Jah. Every passing Brahui throws a stone upon it to this day.

The plunder was immense. Common men fed their mares on melons and dried apricots and figs. Such was the number of carpets that Rahim, Yah Mohammad's page at the time, received a bundle of them. Every woman of Alla-ood-dina's clan robed herself in silk.

Bahram Khan also obtained his reward. Within the briefest time allowable he married Raziah. But, as these events happened shortly before Yakoob's victory over Abdul-rahman, it is likely that the honeymoon was interrupted. One may faintly hope that vengeance overtook the treacherous pair; but it is much more probable that Bahram Khan ratted in time.

NOTE.—This story is repeated as Rahim Khan told it. But within the last few weeks I have seen cause to suspect that Alla-ood-dina Khan and his zealous family deceived me—and also persons quite otherwise important—as to his real position in the Belooch confederacy. An opportunity arose to consult Lieut.-Col. Sir Oliver St. John, K.C.S.I., lately Political Agent at Candahar, who sends me the letter following:—

" My dear Boyle,—Save on one point, the *couleur locale* of your story is as accurate as vivid. The solitary exception is your calling our venerable friend Alla-ood-dina ' chief of all the Brahuis.' This he certainly is not; indeed, he and his clan of Kurds are only Brahuis in a certain restricted sense. In the course of my travels in the country I have come across clans descended from Arabs of Aleppo and Nejd, Jats from India, Afghans from the Helmund, Leks from Shiraz, Toorks from North Persia, and Kurds from Armenia. Of a clan of these last Alla-ood-dina is chief. All the various tribes now speak a dialect of Persian known as Beloochi. Among them, but not of them, are the Brahuis, of whose history it can only be affirmed that they are not aborigines, and whose language is so unlike Persian or Pushtu that philologists cannot make up their minds whether it is Aryan, Turanian, or Dravidian. According to some, the Brahuis are descendants of a colony brought from the north by Alexander ; others believe them to be of identical origin with the Rajputs; while a third story has it that they are remnants of the last Scythian invasion of India. Wherever they came from, they are very remarkable people. Though decidedly inferior in courage and physique to their neighbours, with no genius for domination or for spreading over the land, they have not only held their own but have been the preponderating power in Beloochistan. Their two great chieftains, lords of Sirawan (the highlands) and Jhalawan (the lowlands), are the principal members of the Belooch confederacy, of which the Khan of Khelat is the head.

"So much for the Brahuis proper. To return to our friend Alla-ood-dina and his Kurds. It is not uncommon in Western Asia to find smaller and numerically weaker clans affiliating themselves, so to speak, to bigger ones. Thus it is the custom for lesser chiefs who are members of the Belooch confederacy to speak of themselves and to be spoken of as Brahuis, though they would be indignant to be thought of Brahui blood. In the western part of the country the term Belooch is used in the same way; the Belooch proper is a peaceful nomad herdsman. I remember, ten years ago, rousing the wrath of a stalwart chieftain of the Regis (dwellers in the sand), with whom I was trying to bargain for conveyance across the great desert to the Helmund. He excused himself by saying: 'What would you have?

This is not India or Persia. We are Beloochis!' I asked him, therefore, whether his was a Belooch tribe, and I was startled by the lofty and indignant air he put on. 'We Beloochis!—no! Regis are men of the sword, whose trade is fighting, not tenders of sheep!'

"Thus it happens that Alla-ood-dina Kurd, a descendant of the Karduchi who hampered the retreat of the Ten Thousand, and tried gallantly to stem the tide of Macedonian invasion, is styled a Brahui. If his family history could be known, I have little doubt we should find that his ancestors were expelled from their native hills as too bad even for Kurdistan, and found no resting-place till they reached the Dasht-i-be-Doulat; a convenient asylum, whence their descendants have been pursuing for the last few centuries the hereditary occupation of robbing caravans and cutting throats, as described in your story.—Yours sincerely,

"O. St. John.

"Army and Navy Club."

# A CROSS.

THERE is no little city in Europe, actually none, so curious, so interesting, as Ragusa. Persons better acquainted with that coast have told me that in quaintness other Slav-Venetian towns may challenge it. My own experience of Cattaro and Antivari confirms this statement in some measure. But Ragusa is unique in memorials of ancient state and wealth, above all in story. Of that story in truth I have learned but just enough to see that most students read it in a different version. It is one, however, of special fascination. This is the antique capital of that single branch in the southern Sclav family which has yet proved itself European in any sense other than geographical. It was a republic, the rival of Venice in arms and arts, commerce and enterprise, for ages. The winged lion finally overcame and enslaved it; but Ragusan patriots will not admit that their forefathers were conquered by Venice. It was the shadow of the Turk that vanquished them, the iron barrier crushing their small territory, the incessant

threat of a malicious savage. I have no opinion on
that matter. The legend of Ragusa thrills one like that
of a mysterious and silent ruin. Be it remembered that
this small sleepy town gave us the fine word "argosy"
for a great ship stored with costliest goods.

From one stately gateway in the massive walls to the
other is but a hundred and fifty yards at most, but at
every yard one may pause to admire. Just within, on
the right hand, is a fountain somewhat of the Turkish
style. On market-days and holidays it is a pretty sight
when the girls assemble at this place. Every village has
its peculiarity of dress, mostly bright in colour ; but the
Herzegovinian is so supremely charming that it kills all
others. The robe, of coarse black cloth, should be properly called a chemise. It has little ornament; but from
the round "turban" cap descends a veil, framing a face
often pretty, always pleasing to the eye thus set off.
This drapery is of thick white material, falling to the
bottom of the skirt, and so large that a girl can wrap
her whole body therein if she please. World-wide travel
has not shown me a dress so becoming in severe
simplicity.

Opposite to the fountain is a church, and then the
broad, fine street, smoothly paved, stretches to the other
gate. Its blocks of stone-houses date, they tell you, from
the fourteenth century; saving the tones, which age
alone can give, they might have been raised yesterday.

Tall, solid, exactly alike, and precisely aligned, they present that ideal of street architecture which we are now laboriously trying to introduce; but we shall not easily match these handsome structures. Between each block endless flights of steps climb the mountain-side, with a narrow landing at intervals where terraced cross-wise traverse the ascent. Many a house here has its mouldering coat of arms; many a fine remnant of departed splendour one observes. Ragusa and Cattaro have been little mines of treasure for Viennese dealers in *bric-à-brac,* and the supply has not yet failed. Danisch Effendi, the Turkish Consul-General, is still adding to his museum of lovely cabinets, carved furniture, embroideries, and what not, which every visitor of taste admires with astonishment.

The handsome little street is broken only by an antique statue on its pedestal, and by the twisted richly-ornamented columns of the Doge's palace. In a small square opposite stand other houses, finely proportioned, gracefully sculptured and decorated, abodes of Ragusan grandees in a happier time. Of these I do not speak, for I recollect vaguely, and are they not chronicled in Murray? All my wish is to give a background for my little picture.

One day I entered that church mentioned, opposite the fountain. It is a building full of story, doubtless, but an ignorant traveller must pronounce it dull.

Nothing there dwells in my memory save the cross, which is my present theme. It stood upon a little table by the wall, dusty, worm-eaten, splashed with wax, and showing many a black gap in its surface of mother-o'-pearl. The decoration caught my eye, for I had seen the like in ruder workmanship on Russian shrines. I asked the verger, who in black patched robe was following, how that sacred object came to be treated with such neglect.

" Oh," said he, " a peasant left it many years ago, and he is dead."

" If it does not belong to the church," I said, " I will give you fifteen thalers for it."

The verger held up his hands as one who rebukes a sacrilegious person, thought about it, dropped his indignant palms, and followed us out pondering. Half-an-hour afterwards he brought it under his robe to the small hotel where I was staying, outside the gates, a quaint hostelry with a grove of trees before, where market-peasants camped; the city-ditch and its mantled wall upon one side, a large courtyard in rear. There we dined under a vine-clad trellis; the standing dishes of our bill of fare, fried cuttle-fish and paprika huhn and pilaff. All the naval uniforms of Europe were exhibited, for the fleets were " demonstrating " off Gravosa at that time. The clang of swords, the tinkling of glasses, never ceased throughout the day, and pleasant, courteous

officers of the garrison sat in groups through the long
dull evening. I took some pains to learn what the
Ragusans thought of our naval demonstration. Some
enthusiasts may be surprised to hear that those ultra-
patriotic Sclavs disapproved and disliked it in general,
loathed it in particular. But if one think a little, aided
by some knowledge of the circumstances, their feeling
ceases to surprise. It appeared to the Dalmatian as an
outward sign of Europe's solidarity with Austria, and
the gentlest distrust Austria. Then it was designed to
support Montenegro. Towards that principality Ragusa
feels exactly as Edinburgh felt towards the Highlanders
of Rob Roy's time. A common bond of hostility to
the German is not strong enough to unite the civilised
Dalmatian Sclav with his predatory and ferocious kin
of Montenegro and Bosnia. Ragusa sympathises with
Cattaro and the districts on the frontier, which have
been exposed to invasion and outrage from those savages
as long as the memory of man records. It was irritated
to observe all Europe following Austria's lead, as it
understood the matter, in strengthening the hands of
brigands, whilst Dalmatia was left in slavery to the
stranger.

I could not exaggerate the abhorrence of these people
towards that kindred neighbouring race which has been
described as the Christian Hero, and so on. They
persist in declaring it a tribe of irreclaimable banditti—

bloodthirsty, mischievous beyond all others, an enemy
of human kind. With bitter and unanswerable force
they point to the farmhouses unroofed, black with
smoke, that line the Bocche, surprised in some night of
terror, the peaceful inhabitants all murdered, and the
soldiers only warned by flames that steal and creep and
burst in triumphant fury when the marauders have
regained their mountain side. They confess in truth
that things have not been so bad of late, but the old
houses stand for a testimony. And they bid you observe
the fetid, noisome giant slouching along their streets,
his mouth agape at the signs of a very modest civilisation which his vulture eyes burn to destroy. For my
own part I think they do the Montenegrins injustice,
but I am not surprised. They are foul barbarians, for
circumstances have made them such. But there is gallantry, and manliness, and shrewd intelligence amongst
them, which constrain the disinterested traveller to wish
them well. Thieves they are, because men fierce and
strong will always act upon the motto, " Thou shalt
want before I want! "—murderers, because they do not
feel the value of life, their own or another's. The
organised and desperate brigandage of Montenegro is
produced by want of food. Each nook and pocket of
its rocks has been cultivated for generations. It is no
extravagance to say that wherever fifty plants of maize
or potato can find room there they will be found, though

the nearest cottage be miles away. Bits of soil twenty feet square are treated as fields, and even this cultivation does not suffice to feed an enterprising and prolific people. They plunder to live, but it would be quite useless to urge this excuse upon the sufferers.

Ragusans disliked our demonstration in particular, because the sailors shocked them. Most specially their friends the Russians offended in this respect. Unlike other Sclavs—other Sclavs at least of my acquaintance—Dalmatians are sober and temperate to such degree that extreme indulgence is unknown. Drunkenness perplexed, irritated, frightened them, rather than disgusted. I remember a delightful little story told me by the aide-de-camp of the general in command. A noble dwelling at Ragusa, sent to head-quarters in desperate haste begging immediate help—Russians were attacking his mansion. A detachment of troops was sent forthwith at the double. It found two sailors, very drunk and very ill, leaning in a helpless manner against the house-wall, surrounded by the servants armed, with whom they exchanged most miserable repartees in a tongue unusually unintelligible. They were escorted or carried to Gravosa, and sent aboard their vessel. The Count protested that life was unbearable under such alarming conditions, and he withdrew to his country-seat that night. I am pleased to record that our English sailors made less scandal than any, less even than the

Italian. But it must be owned that none got leave
without most rigorous scrutiny.

I have wandered somewhat from my cross and its
legend. The trophy with its stand is two feet high,
made of some brown wood, nearly rotten, veneered in
front, inlaid at sides and back, with mother-o'-pearl and
ivory. The florials—is not that the correct expression?
—at top and half-way down the body are roses, very
prettily fashioned, engraved and shaded in black lines.
Above the Figure on the Cross is St. Mark, writing,
with the eagle at his shoulder. Various saints and
martyrs are depicted beneath it, with the Virgin at foot,
a dagger pointing to her heart. She is again represented on the stand in a medallion, holding out a string
of beads; the Crowned Child in her arms also offers
a rosary. A medallion smaller and lower, at each side,
presents, the one, a saint with a sword; the other, a
saint with a bell. Between them two arms outspread
before a double Russian cross complete the figures. The
sides, back, extremities of the arms, and interstices have
graceful inlaying of roses and arabesque.

The verger assured me that this relic had never been
considered the property of the Church. The parish
priest authorised him to sell it, when he named my offer.
Under all the circumstances I believed this, but he was
in a desperate hurry. I let him go, and at evening-
time despatched the trusty Spero with a thaler to buy

drink, and injunctions to extract all the history belonging to my cross. Spero was a courier, who never caused me five minutes' irritation or annoyance during six months of the roughest service. He may be heard of at the Saint George's Hotel, Corfu. Be the hint fruitful to those it may concern.

Spero brought me back the narrative which figuratively hangs about my cross.

Once upon a time, towards the beginning of this century as I understood, a Herzegovinian peasant of the better class made the pilgrimage to Jerusalem. He was accompanied by his younger son. Upon the way, in the Holy Land, it appears, they rendered some service to a monastery, the nature of which I did not ascertain. In recognition thereof, whatever it was, the grateful abbot presented Michaeloudovitch with this cross, esteemed of quite peculiar sanctity. He also blessed the old man, his boy present, his daughters, and all future generations of the family. But he inquired particularly why the eldest son was absent, and, when his father unwillingly confessed that this ill-regulated youth did not care to make the pilgrimage, the abbot specially excepted him from the benefits implored of Heaven.

When the pair returned with their sacred treasure, in no long time the influence of the holy man's prayers became visible. Michaeloudovitch's landlord was a young Moslem Bey, handsome and chivalrous, if master-

ful, as are many of his class to this day, in a region still
uncorrupted by the decadence of Islam. He fell in love
with the eldest girl, and engaged, if his suit were peacefully accepted, not to interfere with the bride's religion,
not to marry a second wife, and to let her bring up her
children unmolested, if only she would not resist their
fulfilment of the outward ceremonies of his faith. The
girl returned his love. The parents, though distressed,
and in some measure coerced no doubt, assented. So
their eldest daughter married the Bey, a man rich
perhaps, even by the standard of English country
gentlemen.

I hear an objector exclaiming at the outset of my
story that the match was impossible for both sides. It
would be so now, but it was not impossible, nor even
rare, a generation since. When Christians were hopeless
of deliverance, and Mussulmans did not dream of revolt,
they lived on much better terms. Neither party was
fanatical. Beys did not contest that their forefathers
had been Christian nobles, who apostatised to save their
property and lives ; peasants did not deny the argument
of flesh and blood. Both Moslem and Christian now
would foam to think of such a marriage, and the Bey
would scarcely be restrained from murder to whom those
conditions were proposed.

The younger son of Michaeloudovitch was forthwith
appointed overseer of his brother-in-law's estates, a

position of great dignity and emolument. His sisters became engaged to the handsomest and most substantial yeomen of the neighbourhood. Everything the father put his hand to prospered, unless it were of a nature to benefit directly the eldest son. The luck of this youth became so strangely bad that every one recognised the visible curse of Heaven. He grew bitter and dejected.

Meanwhile the cross had been deposited in the village church, where presently it began to work miracles. All the population of the district flocked thither on saints' days. The outcast son was unremitting in his devotion. He connected this relic with his ill-fortune, and spent days before it. To no purpose. Then he proposed to make the grand pilgrimage, but fell into a precipice at starting, broke his leg, and lost a valuable horse. As soon as he recovered he set forth again, but on the first day's journey he met brigands, Turkish renegades, who took all his money and beat him sore. Again he set out, and reached Trebinje the second day. There the hahn unaccountably took fire, and he escaped with bare life.

It is not surprising that such a series of mischances weighed on a superstitious mind. Stancho, his relatives, and all the village, conceived that Heaven followed him with hate. No one would advance him money for a fourth attempt, and his own resources were exhausted. After moping and pining, the rebellious fit more natural to a Herzegovinian peasant seized hold on him. One day the community was horrified to learn that Stancho had apostatised, and was lying at the house of a moolah in Trebinje. That practical toleration of a former age, to which I have alluded, did not extend to a case like this. Christian and Moslem lived peaceably together, because their stations, their religious boundaries, were exactly defined. All their instincts revolted from a change of creed. The Turkish convert to Christianity was murdered forthwith; the renegade Christain, if his former fellows dared not kill him, found no sympathy anywhere, and no help beyond the imam's door.

All communication with the family was dropped, of course, and its next news of Stancho came through his brother-in-law the Bey. Under the new name of Selim, he applied for a commission in the militia of the district — to put into English form the spirit of his request. It was scornfully refused, and Stancho vanished for many months. He had good cause to repent a desperate step, which had not bettered his fortunes on earth, and had forfeited his hope of Heaven. When next heard of, he had cast aside the turban, and was fighting on the side of Montenegro, engaged, as usual, in a war with Turkey. He distinguished himself in the field. But there were many Herzegovinian volunteers in the army of Tchernagora. One of them recognised Stancho, who promptly cut him down. But the secret

x

was out. In consideration of his services the mountaineers spared his life, but they dismissed him.

There is no race of men so dangerous as the fighting Sclav, the Montenegrin, the Bosnian, the Herzegovinian, the Croat. Austria knows too bitterly what a terrible antagonist is the civilised Dalmatian when he takes up arms. If those wilder people ever had a character resembling the Russ, and Serb, and Bulgar, circumstances have transformed them. The contrast now is striking. Quick of intelligence but stubborn, cunning though fearless, patient though excitable, the mountain Sclav is a very incarnation of man the perfected wild beast. Under a mask of soldierly frankness he is perversely treacherous, as a rule, but also he is bound to the death by his own shibboleths, if one know them. Pity does not move him; his brain is cool whilst his passions blaze to madness. And he has the physical advantages which give his character full play. Generally tall, often gigantic, he is always strong, for none but the vigorous survive. His features are handsome, his eyes, of palish blue or amber-yellow, have the keen look fitting to a warrior. A long fair moustache up-curled hides his stern mouth; his bearing is martial, and his stride full of arrogant self-confidence. Though rough with his fellows, a man of the upper class is superbly courteous to the stranger. And a manly costume sets off every advantage.

Stancho yielded to his longings and went home; he reached the hut unnoticed, under his Montenegrin dress. Old Michaeloudovitch was absent, and the mother disowned him. He refused to leave, claiming his position in the family; some village women overheard the dispute. Luckily for Stancho the men were all at work, but these stalwart matrons set upon the renegade, disarmed him, drove him forth with blows and stones. A rude antagonist is the woman of those parts, graceful though her costume. She has broad shoulders and sturdy limbs; she has seen battle, and much worse than that. What virtues remain are not those belonging to her sex.

Bruised, disgraced, delirious with rage, Sancho pushed through the woods. Climbing upward, he crossed the bridle-path which led from the village to the castle. A girl was descending—one of the Christian maidens whom the Bey's young wife kept with her. In days gone by there had been love passages between Stancho and this damsel. She recognised her former suitor, and ran back full speed. He overtook and seized her; she would not listen, but screamed for help; in the brute madness of his fury, Stancho lifted her and dashed her with all his strength against a tree.

When the poor creature regained her senses, maimed for life, she repeated his wild threat of smashing every soul that lived in his native village as he had smashed her. It caused some alarm, and the sentries at night

were doubled; but Herzegovinians are used to carry
menace of this sort lightly. The atmosphere of peril
and chance is that they are used to. Talking once with
Buko Petrovitch about the probability of an insurrection
before the late troubles arose, the Montenegrin general
said to me: " It will happen, not because the people are
oppressed but because life is too quiet, the Austrian
police too active in protecting them. Herzegovinians
like to protect themselves."

Time passed on, and nothing was heard of Stancho ;
the extra precautions were withdrawn. Two years
afterwards a band of brigands fell upon the village,
murdered all who could not escape—men, women,
children—and fired it. Michaeloudovitch and his wife
had died meanwhile, but the second son perished with
all his family. At morning the Bey pursued, with what
force he could gather. The brigands were numerous,
Turks, Pomaks, broken Montenegrins, blacks, ruffians of
the deepest dye, well armed. Upon the second day
Stancho sent a message, announcing he would stand at a .
certain place. But, as the pursuers threaded a defile,
they were suddenly overwhelmed. The Bey escaped.
Urged by the desire of vengeance, and by a wife of the
true savage stock, he gave himself wholly to the task of
hunting down these murderers, with no conspicuous
success, however. Brigands were killed from time to
time—some were captured and tormented; but Stancho's

audacious exploits won him a legendary fame from a harassed but sympathetic peasantry. Recruits poured to his band.

The cross had been saved. It was taken to the castle, and set ‘in the private apartments of the lady. Some considerable time after the destruction of his village the Bey learned from his spies where Stancho would be found on a given night. Relying on the information, he set forth with his armed retainers, leaving but a score of men in garrison. At midnight the castle was alarmed, sentries fired and shouted, there was scuffling at the parapet. In a few moments the corridors rang with a clash of arms, a tread of hurrying feet, the screams of the butchered, the yells of the victorious, the splintering of doors. Women-servants sleeping near fled to their mistress; she stood knife in hand, white and panting, but firm of soul. Death was present in that little group of girls, not threatening themselves alone.

Stancho appeared in the doorway, wearing the fez and a whisp of Broussa silk around it; half a score of eager pushing ruffians behind him were kept back by the outstretched handjar. “No one shall harm you!” he said. “I remain here!”

His followers dispersed about the room, forcing chests, casting out embroideries and linen, jewellery and precious things. Stancho, looking round, observed the cross upon a bracket, stepped forward, and took it in his hand.

"The charm did not protect our village," he said, smiling fiercely, "and it has not protected your castle, sister! Better to trust a sharp sword and a steady pistol, whether we be Christian or Pomak!"

His sister had quietly crept up beside him. She snatched a pistol at his waist, and fired point-blank, a few inches from his heart. The men around sprang on her, but with a trembling hand Stancho beat them back. He sat upon a rifled chest, drew his other pistol, and sounded it with the chased silver ramrod. Pale and shivering involuntarily, he thought awhile; then stooped to pick up an embroidered handkerchief, wrapped the cross therein, and silently laid it down.

Meanwhile the brigands had collected all the plunder of that apartment. They did not trouble the women, for by other means they probably knew where treasure lay. Laughing and hallooing, as is the nature of the Sclav triumphant, they noisily filed out, carrying their bundles. Stancho rose and followed, taking the cross. Without a word he left his sister. The dull firm tread of his sandalled feet was smothered in a wilder burst of cries and yells outside.

Horrible work was doing there, but the Bey's wife gave no heed. She threw on her clothes, and was ready in a moment. "Listen, you girls! If I miss my lord in the forest, tell him that these Pomaks stay at Radomir to-morrow! They said so!"

" I will go with you, hanoum !" "And I!" "And I!" they cried. But the mistress did not stay to hear. Taking a key, she passed into the dusky corridor, treading carefully, less for fear of stepping in the blood than of slipping and so raising an alarm, gained a secret stair, and reached the woods by an unguarded postern.

Upon the following day, towards afternoon, the brigands were securely sleeping. After a long night-march they had breakfasted copiously with their friends of Radomir. A line of pickets, with sentries thrown far in advance, protected them. One of these, retiring at the double, announced suspicious movements in his front. Whilst the picket dispersed for observation, a messenger ran to alarm the main body. He passed along the village street towards headquarters, summoning sleepers as he went, and sent a comrade raising the same cry from the other side. All the brigands started to their arms and mustered, but the captain was not to be found. His share of loot, his arms, were there, but no Selim Effendi. Perplexed and angry they set forth on their retreat under command of the lieutenant. But from every road came warnings of danger, and the band broke into small parties, to make their way through the tangled woods. A rendezvous was named, but few reached it. Till evening the fight went on, and this redoubtable corps of banditti ceased to trouble any more. But Selim Effendi was not discovered either amongst the slain or the prisoners. And his few comrades who got through looked for him vainly.

That miraculous escape, when a loaded pistol was discharged at his very heart, suddenly aroused the superstition, and a better feeling than superstition, of his early years. Holding the cross he was preserved from certain death. He took it as a first last chance of Heaven's mercy. With the instinct of a Sclav, Stancho kept his secret, directed the midnight march as usual, the portioning of the booty. So soon as the grumblings and mutterings of the band, perfunctory on such occasions, had subsided, when all was still he crept away with nothing but his clothes and the cross, still enveloped in its napkin. Behind the first bush he threw away his fez, and stamped upon it. The distant peal of musketry all the afternoon told him of another serious peril from which good angels had preserved him. At the nearest monastery Stancho took asylum, and there so punished his guilty flesh that the monks declared him a saint. Some of the brethren had near as much cause for penitence.

It was years afterwards that he passed through Ragusa, in the robe of an orthodox monk, on his way to Jerusalem. A vague tradition was still extant which recalled his burning eyes and long flaxen beard dashed with grey. What impulse led him to deposit his cross where it would not be duly honoured is a mystery. He never returned from the pilgrimage. Fanatics of his stamp often vanish on that road. They start without money, they take what they need under a plea, honestly advanced, of their sacred character. They insult the Moslem, and they quarrel with all Christians who differ from their views. It seems a paradox, but on reflection one perceives it true, that if the lands they traverse were more civilised the proportion which reached the holy shrines would be very much smaller than it is.

That is the legend attaching to my cross. I have filled up outlines, but added nothing to the incidents which Spero transmitted in a few brief sentences.

# SOME FINGER-GLASSES.

THE title is not promising, I admit. One does not readily think of an article less likely than a finger-glass to have a good story attaching thereto. But mine were not originally made for the purpose to which I have turned them. In fact, they are not glass at all, but silver ; that is to say, the metal of which they are composed may be called silver, since a medijie and a chirik are so called. The work which gives their interest and curious beauty is Circassian. Long ago the virtuosi of St. Petersburg admired this peculiar ornamentation, and they established a home for it at Tulla, whence the style takes its name. But European influence, a great demand, and exile, proved too strong for the virtue of Tchirkess artificers. Tulla work has steadily degenerated, crystallising to conventionality. At the present time it bears just the same relation to the bold free model of true Circassian design as modern Dresden does to old, a regulation sabre to a Damascus blade, a barn-door fowl to a woodcock. Imitation, also, Russ or French, has done mischief by lowering wages. I know that for a grand occasion Tulla can pull itself up ; but at the best the spirit, if not the skill, has departed. This fact is understood in Russia, though ignored by haphazard collectors elsewhere.

If one of these latter saw the finger-glass which I love and pride myself upon beyond the others, I think he would deny that it had much bearing or connection with the Tulla work whereof he believes himself to own some great examples.

Before describing it, however, I must say for what use these things were originally intended. Every one, nowadays, takes or has taken a Turkish bath, and he remembers the shallow brass basin which they give him there when he asks for water. In the harems of great folk at Stamboul, such plain coarse articles as that would not be tolerated. Basins much more costly the oda-lisques demand, and, as most of them are Circassians by race, they have a liking for the style of ornament familiar to their youthful days, though they saw it then only on the sword-hilt and scabbard-ornaments of their father or their brothers; and thus it has become a fashion in the richer households of Stamboul to have vessels connected with the bath in Tchirkess work—silver, of course. My finger-glasses are drinking-bowls. They have been used by hanoums and princesses, by laughing slave-girls and wrinkled eunuchs. If I set myself to dream, I could fancy a tale for each of them. But at this moment I will make no call on imagination.

It took me several months to collect the number sufficient for my purpose, since these luxuries do not often find their way to the bazaar. I bought them all from a fat Armenian in the Bezestan, excepting the handsomest, of which I will attempt to give you some idea. It is seven inches across, two and a half high. Upon a gilt ground, roughened with innumerable dots and lines, which give the effect we call " frosted," black designs are traced with singular freedom. Upon the bottom—I speak of the outside, for the inner surface is plain and polished—is a star of sixteen points, three inches across. The artificer had too good taste to make it wholly black. In the very centre is a circle, occupied by a tiny star, between the radii of which the rough gold ground shows through. And the sixteen long arms are black only at the edges, shading off to a dusky hue down the middle. Starting from each alternate point, figures shapeless but symmetrical, which I am powerless to describe in words, run with bold sweeps to the upper edge, four of them, with a device between which very distantly suggests a group of banners. These also are not black through, but judiciously lightened in parts by rubbing off the inky material. There is nothing finikin about this ornament. The outlines are deeply cut, of a design broad and massive. The Tchirkess who drew, and the Tchirkess who executed the work, were masters. My other basins are almost equally beautiful. One of them is not gilt, and the judgment of the artist makes itself perceived in the lighter tone of pigments which he has used for the decoration of a silver ground.

I had occasion to visit the Sublime Porte one bitter day, which marked the beginning of real winter. My route, of course, lay through the Galata tunnel and over the bridge. At that time every ship was bringing emigrants from Bosnia, Herzegovina, Bulgaria, and the Dobrudscha. The arrival of Lazis from Batoum had almost ceased for a while; it began again, however. Most of the European fugitives possessed some small means, or had relations at the capital; and so they lived, though at death's door, until something turned up.

To persons who had not beheld the awful misery of the Batoum emigrants, the plight of these would have seemed horrible. All Constantinople thrilled with pity when first the refugees displayed their livid faces in the street. Nothing else was spoken of. The least charitable made a sacrifice; the idlest bestirred himself. But the sight grew familiar. Starving Lazis or Pomaks became an institution, almost a public spectacle. Reaction and satiety began, and what charity survived after a while in the shape of almsgiving, was nearly concentred on the bridge. Curiously pitiful the sight at its either end. A certain copper coin was demanded as toll;

but, some time before, the Government had called in
the copper currency. Hence one had to buy the needful mite, and this small exchange business had been
seized by the emigrant children. They swarmed in
many hundreds about either exit, patrolled the streets
of the vicinity, clinking a roll of paras in the face of
every passer-by, and chanting a little ditty quite melo-
dious. The burden thereof was: " Here you have
money for the bridge ! Money—money ! "

Whilst summer and autumn lasted, though these waifs
were thin and pale, their song came cheerfully. The
greater number, perhaps, were girls under ten years old,
with plaits of flaxen hair escaping from the ragged old
handkerchief that formed their head-dress. Attired in
one skirt of Manchester cotton, barefoot and barelegged,
they could not be too warm in November, even though
the sun were shining and the south wind blew ; what
their shelter at night was a mystery of which the street
dogs, could they speak, might give an inkling. But on
that day we rose to find the streets ankle-deep in mud,
a chill blast driving rain and snow before it. The poor
little wretches had come to their posts as usual, to seek a
profit so minute that I never could understand where it
lay. But they could not keep the roadway. Sodden
with wet, blue with cold, they huddled together beneath
walls and entries. Crossing the bridge twice I only
heard one shivering parody of the familiar chant. But

all this class of children were the favoured ones. They
had clothes of a sort, and capital enough to buy six-
penny-worth of copper coins. Heaven knows their lot
was terrible; on earth few knew or cared. But there
were depths of misery among the emigrants far more
profound, which no Christian probably had seen. A
Moslem friend might sometimes hint unutterable horrors;
but the foreigner was mercifully forbidden to behold
them.

I think that most men who habitually crossed the
bridge had a certain number of small clients to whom
they gave a trifle. For myself, I had two special favourites, pretty fair-haired girls, full of life and fun whilst
the sunshine lasted. They speedily asserted a right to
the dole which I had innocently thought a free gift. If
I offered less than they considered becoming, they
would follow any distance, holding out a little open
palm with the insufficient pittance displayed therein,
and speechlessly appealing to my sense of justice and
propriety. It was necessary to feel in all my pockets,
and to engage, in pantomime, that the balance should
be made up at the next opportunity, before they would
leave me. Upon this miserable day neither of my
young barbarians was seen. I transacted my business
at the Porte, and strolled on to the bazaar. Hovering
about the entrance, as usual, was a Greek boy who had
once or twice executed commissions for me. He ob-

served, in his very independent English : "Tchirkess
man is here, what got basin and other traps as you like.
You come and see." With wary steps I followed.
The unpaved road was trodden into slime, as safe and as
comfortable to walk upon as ice. We turned down a
steep descent to the right, and found ourselves in the
jewellers' bazaar, where a fetid torrent was hurrying
through the middle of the passage. Traversing this
freak of nature without surprise—it was God's will!
Inshallah!—a turn to the left brought us to the gold-
lace-makers' quarter, which always fascinated me.
Beautiful are the combinations, delicate the tracery,
glowing the colour of their manufactures. I have seen
nothing like them elsewhere ; Delhi jewel-work, and the
famous embroidery made in imitation, have something
of the effect, but are less bright and transparent of hue.
It surprises me that when ladies search every country
under heaven for gorgeous trimmings and startling
accessories, none have discovered the very curious lace
of foil and precious metal produced at Stamboul.

Tearing myself from this glittering display, a narrow
alley falling to the right brought us to the heavy,
antique portal of the Bezestan. I am not going to
describe that strangest sight, strangest even to those
familiar with its type in many lands. Persons who
have not visited Stamboul know all about it from innumerable books. I should like one day to gossip of

some matters regarding Turkish life which are not obvious to the tourist; even in that article, however, I should not permit myself to sketch the Bezestan. Something must be said to give a background, but it shall be briefly put.

My guide led me through the dusty passages, heaped on either hand with ancient furniture, carpets, arms, embroideries; antique china, horse-trappings, old plate, skins; Damascus, Persian, Algerian trays; superb old braziers lately fashionable as jardinières; Indian and Turkish narguilleys, Albanian girdles and belts, inlaid work of Tripoli, and gold-fretted silks of Aleppo— briefly, with all forms and sorts of article which we are used to term a "curio." The merchants sat cross-legged among their goods upon a faded carpet, or a bald leopard skin—pushing Armenians, and noisy Jews in European dress or something like it, slow Turks, sallow, slender, smiling Banniahs, wax-faced Persians, neat and trim. My little Greek exchanged a word here and there, and upon the information he received we changed our course several times.

Amongst the oddities to be observed—by the observant —in this oddest maze, is the system of " passing a word along." It is kept secret, that is, a stranger does not easily obtain a clue to its mysteries. But so much came to my knowledge through watching, that I gained a general idea. My guide would ask somebody at the

gates—perhaps an individual stationed for that purpose
—"Where is the Tchirkess, in such and such costume,
who has a basin for sale?" And forthwith the inquiry
was flashed from stall to stall, from corridor to corridor.
One man saw him in such a spot, at such a time, and
sends back word to that effect; another saw him later
elsewhere. And so from point to point the initiated
catch a hint, and, quickly as they may go, the verbal
telegraph goes quicker; so that, in a few moments, the
person wanted learns that he is asked for, and turns to
meet his pursuer. I have marked the process a score
of times, for there was no fanatic more devoted to the
Bezestan whilst I stayed at Constantinople ; but there
were several who rivalled me.

If such a system did not exist, hunting for a stranger
there would be like seeking Mr. Smith in Cheapside.
Thanks to it we found our Tchirkess speedily. An ill-
looking man was he, with a red beard turning grey, a
tall fur cap, and a long coat, which had been white, with
ragged cartridge-cases along each breast. Many are the
costumes beheld at Stamboul, amongst which, for artistic
merit, one would choose the Ghegghe and the Tosk Albanian, the Montenegrin, and the Tchirkess; something
might be said also for the Persian, on the score of
gentlemanly quiet. The others frequent are not worthy
observation from the judicious, though they have colour
and quaintness enough. Of these four, perhaps, upon

the whole, the Circassian is most commendable. It has a manliness and dignity rivalled only by the Ghegghe Albanian, which—but I speak with hesitation—may be thought too prone to brilliant hues. The Tchirkess has no pronounced colour at all. This statement may be received with surprise by people who have seen the Czar's Circassian body-guard, the lining of whose pendant sleeves flashes out as they spur to the gallop, just as do the outstretched wings of a flock of parrots rising. I have seen no representative of the tribe from which Russian military tailors got this idea; it may very well be their own discovery. Wherever I have met the Tchirkess, he wore the long coat—white, grey, black, or dark blue; with hanging sleeves truly, if of rank, but no rainbow lining; breeches to match the coat, and boots half up the leg. The rounded crown of his high fur-cap may be scarlet or azure, with silver lace, but this is only seen from behind. The cartridge-cases diagonally stitched upon his chest are embroidered with silver, if that extravagance can be afforded; if not, with worsted or silk. They relieve in a charming manner the severity of a robe which has neither buttons nor cross-belt, but I never saw the gay devices of this kind which distinguish Circassian regiments of the Russian army. A belt of metal, silver if possible, encircles the waist; from it depends, immediately in front, at an angle judiciously chosen and always the same, a broad straight dagger, of which hilt and sheath are ornamented with black arabesques on a silver ground; a pistol or two, and a guardless sabre, similarly ornamented, hang exactly where they would be thought fitting by a trusted master of decoration, with smaller objects, of utility dubious, but grace incontestable.

But the glory of my Tchirkess had long been discounted at the pawn-shop. A single dag, a mere instrument of murder, hung by a rude steel chain at his waist. Filthy and frowsy was he, scowling like an envious beast of prey as he hustled the throng with ugly swagger. My Greek boy casually asked if he had anything to sell, and without reply he brought up against a stall, disclosing one of my small pensioners of the bridge. She recognised me with a saucy smile, and said something to the man, whilst untying a ragged parcel. His truculent manner changed, not greatly to its improvement. I should interpret the awkward unctuous smile of his red face to signify that, as robbery and murder were forbidden for the moment, he would gain his end by amiable means. Meantime, the child had produced this basin, my best-loved finger-glass, and a graceful priming-flask of silver, leather, and bone, which hangs on the wall behind me as I write. The purity of the latter article was attested by that queer stamp, resembling a grasshopper on a gridiron, which is the equivalent in Turkey of our hall-mark. I regret now—for the first time it occurs to me—that I never asked where, under what circumstances, by whom, this stamp is imprinted. I know only that the age of an object thus certified can be ascertained within vague limits, since every Sultan had his peculiar and distinguishing impression.

The flask I bought at once, but there was no proof that the basin also was pure. The Tchirkess insisted, however, that it should be taken at its weight in drachms, and I had to yield. He answered my objection scornfully: " Do you think a man would make a thing like that in any metal but pure silver ? " The argument had its value, but I am not sure it was not unjust to the conscientious artist. He would have done his best, I think, in any material, under any circumstances. However, I paid a hundred francs, and carried the bowl away rejoicing. My conviction was that the gay mountaineer had stolen it. One may suspect that most people who buy odd valuables up and down collect a certain number of which the story will not bear investigation.

The Tchirkess insisted on shaking hands, and we parted. Six weeks later, or thereabouts, I was asked to join some distinguished acquaintances on a visit to Dolma-Batche palace, for which they had a special firman. After repressing the impulse to describe the bazaar, none but a lunatic would yield to the inclination of describing that mongrel palace. It is very big, and

we saw every inch, saving the harem of course. This
is the upper floor, and the communicating staircase is
so mean that one would not notice it. But there are
lots of fine things at Dolma-Batche. We had even the
privilege of inspecting His Majesty's bath and dressing-
rooms, an astonishing extravagance in silver and precious marbles. The great hall and the state apartments
are shown without difficulty to any one who asks permission; and I shall only say, of the former, that it is
quite beyond compare the finest and largest chamber
I have ever beheld. The Escurial and the Kremlin
may show something to rival it, but I have not yet
visited their marvels. And the state chambers are not
unworthy of that superb hall, which the Sultan's diminished and impoverished court would scarcely people.
The furniture of them, if tasteless and uninteresting,
represents an enormous value. There are tables and
braziers there of solid silver, which, if melted down,
would yield a sum not unworthy of imperial acceptance;
jewelled knicknacks, costly odds and ends innumerable.

But we were most struck by the pictures. One found
in that unknown gallery great works familiar from
childhood by engraving. I made no notes, and I forget.
But every few paces we came to a stop in amaze, recognising a Cavalier, a Gerome, a Beaumont, a Corot, which
one would have declared to be in some famous European
gallery. They might as well be buried as lie here. And

amongst them hung the strangest caricatures of scenery and the human form divine that ever child drew with its first box of colours. The Turk sees no difference between a Raffaele and a theatrical "poster." To guard these treasures, and show visitors round, are multitudinous servants, hungry, ragged, barefoot; by ragged, I mean that their black cloth suits have been darned until they can no longer bear a stitch, and flutter helplessly in ribands. They told us they had had but one month's wages in three years. Was there ever such a palace as this?

It was still early in the winter's afternoon when we departed, with much to talk of. Two or three resolved to stroll back to Pera by the longest route. We walked to Bechichtas, and on past the mouldy dwelling where exists in mysterious seclusion the late Sultan Murad, deposed as insane. Turning there, we climbed the steep street running through that quarter which Abdul Aziz pulled down and rebuilt. He had a maniacal dread of fire, and this hill of wooden shanties, overhanging the palace, haunted him nightly. I am ashamed to forget how it is called, for a traveller's tales are nothing if not precise; but curious persons can easily learn the name, and it matters nothing to the casual reader. A very fine quarter Abdul Aziz built in place of that destroyed, tall stone houses, excellently constructed, street after street. The one objection to the suburb is, that nobody wants to live there, as it seems.

When the refugees began to swarm in thousands, the empty dwellings of this neighbourhood were granted them, or were seized. Most have a shop on the level of the street, which, in their unfinished condition, is merely a big shed, unglazed, unfloored, unceilinged. The Lazis, or Pomaks, or Tchirkess who took possession, built a wall of rubbish to fill the aperture, or stretched miserable cloths across it. With only such protection against the wild weather of the Bosphorus, they took up their dwelling on the bare earth, without food or cover. There they rotted by families, abandoned of Heaven and man—rotted and died, and cleared away for others. At this very moment (May, 1881), I doubt not, corpses are thrown out of those reeking dens, corpses of those too far gone with sickness undescribable to creep abroad in the summer weather. With the earliest chill they will be retenanted, all of them, and the deathly diseases, lying in wait, will spring from ambush.

I glanced into one or two of those loathsome sheds, not without risk. In the haze and damp one saw heaps of rags, motionless, a hand or a foot projecting. Little children wailed unseen. In a single den I noticed smoke, and some shapeless creatures moving slowly round it. Nowhere a vessel of any kind, a tool or implement, or household utensil; but reeks and stenches of human decay, of living putrefaction, which streamed in close volume through the frosty air. House after house, street after street, full of these perishing wretches, and thousands in every quarter of the city! Not more persons died in the Great Plague of London by a swift stroke of agony than have rotted on the Bosphorus by a three years' doom, and are still rotting.

We walked up the hill, sad and sick. Very few emigrants were visible, for those who could stir a limb had sought happier neighbourhoods, where to beg or to seek such miserable work as they had strength to do. But, as we passed along, my little Tchirkess girl came galloping round a corner. She turned at sight of me, and ran off, but presently overtook us, out of breath, holding a packet of embroideries. We recognised the trimming of Bulgarian petticoats, coarse and rudely designed, but excellently stitched and bright of colour. I use them to loop my curtains. One could too easily suggest how they might have fallen into Tchirkess hands, but perhaps one would do injustice. Pomak and Christian women alike use this style of ornament.

Whilst bargaining with the small pedlar—two of our party spoke Turkish with ease—we heard female voices raised shrill in anger, and presently a negress and a Lazi woman, hotly disputing, bustled into the street. So fierce ran the quarrel that an old zaptieh, keeping pace behind, had to push away first one and then the other to keep them from clapperclawing. A little crowd, mostly Greek boys and loafers, scudded about them, interposing humorous remarks. The little girl in our midst volubly explained what the disturbance was about, and those who could understand displayed sudden curiosity. Opposite the spot where we were standing, the zaptieh pushed the Lazi woman through a torn curtain into her home, and with the other hand sent the negress staggering. After a volley of abuse she went down the hill.

We interviewed that zaptieh, introduced by baksheesh. He told us a queer story. The woman, Moslem of course, had borrowed thirty pounds Turkish—say twenty-seven pound sterling—of the negress, Moslem also, upon the security of her child, some three years old. The pledge was delivered, and remained in the lender's hands, at Scutari, where she dwelt. I did not precisely gather the motive of this transaction upon her part, whether she loved the baby, or whether she took it merely in the way of business with an eye to its commercial value as a slave when somewhat older. For some twelve months things had quietly remained in this condition. But the Lazi woman meanwhile had learned something of human rights, sacred and civil, as they exist even in Turkey. A Moslem child cannot be pawned according to the former, nor any child at all according to the latter. She demanded her infant back, without payment of the loan, and was refused of course. After several applications she lodged a claim of restitution with the cadi of Scutari, who summoned the defendant to appear. In blazing passion she crossed the Bosphorus, sought out her debtor, whom she encountered in the street, and hence this little scene.

I begged a friend staying at Scutari to get me a report of the case if it ever came forward. Some days afterwards he told me that the negress, resolved to be beforehand, had made a claim for her money in the civil court. So the action found its way through the Annales Judiciaires to all the press of Constantinople. It became a *cause célèbre*. The tribunal could not decide without hesitation, but eventually it resolved that the child, which was in court, must be given up to the mother. Thereupon, as proceeds the report of the *Constantinople Messenger*, late *Levant Herald*, "a scene not easily to be described ensued between the two women for possession of the pledge. The members of the tribunal, who had done their best to come to a rational and natural decision in the matter, used all their influence with the enraged negress to endeavour to bring her to reason. All efforts were vain, however. The angry debtor would have her 'pound of flesh,' or her money. Nothing more and nothing less. Finally, after a scene of confusion and violence, the officers of the court were compelled to use force to tear the infant from the hands of the claimant and deliver it to its mother."

I know nothing further of the case.

# PERSONAL LIBERTY IN ISLAM.

FEW men are competent to write with authority on
the political relations of the Mahomedan system, and
fewer still upon its social and internal working. After
experience of El Islam in the Far East, India, Afghanistan, divers parts of Africa and Turkey, I make no such
claim. But there are matters I have noted which may
well have escaped remark from observers more learned
and more thorough, matters of everyday life which
people accept as things of course, which they think too
commonplace for mention to the inquiring foreigner.
One of such subjects I propose to treat here, the social
and religious restrictions affecting personal liberty in
Stamboul. Some of the facts stated may surprise and
interest a reader not unacquainted with Moslem customs.
And it is to be observed that, in so far as these restrictions are based upon the Koran and its interpretation,
their influence, stronger or weaker, is universal where
Islam prevails.

One of the very first impressions which strikes a man

in visiting Constantinople is the superiority of Stamboul, the city of the Turk, to Pera and Galata, the cities
of the Christian, in some of those matters which we are
used to think belonging to civilised administration. For
all that has been done in the last two years to widen
streets, to pave them, to supply gas, water, and so forth,
Pera would still be the filthiest, the most uncomfortable
of all towns, if Galata were not worse. No one who
has not seen would credit that in this age a wealthy
population could be so ill-provided, not with luxuries
alone but necessaries. In the Grande Rue de Pera
there are not fifty continuous feet of side-walk; where it
exists, the breadth is less than a yard in general. In its
widest parts the street may average forty feet, but there
are "narrows" where it diminishes to fourteen feet
from wall to wall. Up and down this alley goes the
traffic of a rich and busy population. Carts are absent,
but porters and pack-horses, pedlars, box-wallahs, patrols,
and sedan chairs are even more obstructive. Here and
there building operations are in hand. Whilst half the
street is blocked by hoarding, long strings of ponies,
attached head and tail, carry out the earth, and return
with loads of brick and lime. They carry enormous
panniers on either side, and, when things go wrong with
the foremost of the cavalcade, all the roadway is blocked
in a moment. Hamals, stooping double under a bale of
goods, stump blindly forward, with an uninterrupted cry

of "Guarda!" Six or eight burly Montenegrins or
Armenians, marching *en échelon*, bear suspended on
their poles a ton weight of merchandise, which they set
down each few yards to breathe. Neither horses, men,
nor dogs step aside for the pedestrian. But worst of all
are the carriages—public and private. There is a law
enjoining them to pass the narrows at a walk, but no
one heeds it. Through a crowd which may be imagined,
of which ladies and children form a large contingent,
cabs force their way at a trot. The police do not affect
to keep order. It may be believed that shopping on foot
is not a lady's pastime under such conditions. There is
indeed a way to secure an uninterrupted passage from
one end of Pera to the other. Find a hamal carrying a
dead pig on his back, and march behind him. The only
stroll I ever took with comfort was made under this
protection.

Fifty yards above the bridge of Galata all is changed.
The low-lying quarters of Stamboul, occupied by Christians, are indeed a counterpart of the vile Tophané, on
the opposite shore. But beyond the narrow colony
of foreigners, and the immediate purlieus of the bazaar,
lie roads broader than Pall Mall, macadamised, and
provided with roomy sidewalks; open spaces are frequent. Round the great mosques are trees and grass.
From every height one gains a glimpse of gardens.
Where there is such easy room to walk, porters

do not jostle. Beggars, though in plenty, are not importunate or offensive as at Pera. All the sights of the capital, saving the modern tawdry palaces, are here. There are delightful rides and drives, an interesting and amiable population. House-rent and living are much cheaper than across the bridge. The water-supply, such an anxious question there, has never failed in Stamboul, and it is brought within reach of all. Street outrages and burglary are unknown, unless some band of Greek malefactors shift their quarters hither for a brief foray, usually disastrous. Why, then, does not the large and wealthy class of residents in Pera who may live where they please migrate to Stamboul? Why, on the contrary, do Europeanised Turks migrate to filthy Pera? The explanation of these mysteries is, in fact, my theme.

It is a current truism that, under governments despotic and irresponsible, the balance of human happiness is struck by increased freedom of the subject in matters non-political. This may be true in general, but Turkey offers a notable exception.

To take, first, public amusements, there is absolutely nothing of the sort to vary the routine of life in Stamboul, since late sultans have preferred to worship in the small mosque of the Medijieh, outside Galata. A platform for regimental music rots in the square between St. Sophia and the At-Meidan, but I never heard of its being tenanted. Nautches are common in the harems, of a very inferior class ; but no Christian nor bachelor Turk is allowed that wearisome diversion.

The absence of amusement is a trifling loss, however ; Moslems do not feel it, unless corrupted by the Frank. More significant is the fact that no hotels exist in Stamboul, nor any restaurant where an English artizan would sit. Beside the horrid cookshops which send dinners *en ville*—very good ones, too, though strange of flavour, and best eaten blindfold—a man can get no food unless he buy semeet and saloop and cakes of odd confection from the wandering pedlars. There is not even a coffee house where Turks of any position can assemble. Some months since a few of the younger generals and officials dwelling in Stamboul timidly spoke among themselves of establishing a club. They broached the project to Fuad Pasha, asking him to sound the authorities. With the headlong good-nature of his disposition, he consented to do what more cautious favourites would have trembled to think of. The " hero of Elena," the one native general who gained a victory in Bulgaria, escaped with a passionate reprimand ; all his clients are marked men.

Casual observers attribute this dullness to unsocial habits, jealousy, pride of purse and rank. They do injustice to the kindly nature of the Ottoman. We know what a large part of the old Turkish life was associated with khans, coffee-houses, baths, and public places of assembly. The inclination to meet in friendly gossip is not extinct, but a new order of things has arisen. As power declines, it grows suspicious ; when misfortune threatens an ignorant oligarchy, superstition becomes its master. The political authorities of Turkey see treason in every whisper, whilst the religious authorities see blasphemy and immorality ; they unite in thinking that human beings cannot mingle without danger to the State and offence to Heaven. Spies are everywhere, maintained by departments of Government, by ministers in possession fearing for the morrow, by ministers yesterday dismissed seeking means to upset their supplanter. Above these private informers is the army of religious police, some paid, mostly volunteer inquisitors. And, above all, the private myrmidons of the sultan. I am assured, also, that the chiefs who hold, or have held, high office in the household, know where to get information of all that passes in every important family in the capital.

This condition of things does not tend to cheerfulness, but the Turk has other cares. If he be a bachelor, Church and State combine to make life miserable for him. He must live with his parents, and, whilst they still exist, the authorities content themselves with a general reprehension of his celibacy. But when they die, if they leave him homeless, his troubles begin. It is forbidden any householder to take a young man into

z

his dwelling without permission of the civil and religious magistrates of the quarter.   Before this is granted, the lodger must undergo a severe inquiry, which takes into account not only his personal reputation but that of all his kindred.   The landlord, moreover, must display his ability to have this young stranger waited on without offence to morals—that is, without employing his female servants, or the female members of his family.   If the bachelor be rich enough to occupy a house, or to rent "unfurnished chambers," he cannot possibly obtain that simple privilege unless he show that a woman of good repute lives with him therein.   Those who can produce a blameless mother or a sister have no difficulty when the identification has been thoroughly established; even an elderly aunt is admissible.   But, if a young man have no kindred, he may go homeless for an indefinite time.   The abolition of the slave-trade is a grievance he warmly feels.   In days when this edict was passed, one could go into the market and buy a female creature, white or black, ugly or beautiful, according to one's means, and thus fulfil the law.   Times have changed.   It may probably be the fact that slaves are still to be purchased by those who have cash enough. Many Turks have assured me it is so, though I have met with none who spoke, or admitted that he spoke, by experience.   But the cost is very high; the merchant would not deal with a young bachelor likely to be thus circumstanced; and the transaction would surely be discovered.

He has, therefore, to find a servant. If, for any reason, he will not or cannot obtain a Christian his case is pitiable. The injunction to wear a veil, neglected among the lower class of Moslem elsewhere, and trifled with by the higher class in Turkey, is rigidly kept by women such as he is seeking. When there is a lady ruling the household, a compromise is permitted where servants, being few, must work hard. Covering the hair in presence of male members of the family is thought enough. But the muftis and the cadis, the imams and the ulemas, would be horrified at the idea of such gross immorality, if it occurred in a bachelor's house. He must wait, therefore, living as he can, until some one will cede to him, for love or money, an ancient woman to do propriety; or he may hire a chaperon. This essential piece of furniture secured, he has a domestic spy in his house, who will report his every word and action in the interest of the state and of public morals.

When this is the case with men, it may be imagined that woman's martyrdom is painful. The widow of small means can find no independent shelter, whatever her age. I have failed to discover what on earth becomes of her, if kinless. A very great deal of nonsense, and worse than nonsense, is talked about woman s status in

Mahomedan countries, but into that question I do not
enter. It is certainly a fact that the whole system of
Turkish ethics is based on the assumption that woman
stops indoors. It seems to reckon that all of marriageable years are married, with home cares, and, as a rule,
they are, even the slaves—at a later age in their case.
We have seen how the graceless estate of bachelorhood
is rebuked and persecuted. The written law, and the
social code of propriety, discourage walks abroad. Many
Turkish ladies there are who despise their ancestral customs; some, indeed, who might be named, not satisfied
with driving about Pera in veils of thinnest muslin, un-
folded, have welcomed young foreign diplomats at their
weekly receptions. Of such rare cases we need not
speak. Sisters less " emancipated " cannot even go
about their business or their shopping in the leisurely
way affectioned by the sex. They may not stand in the
streets to talk with an acquaintance, or fo r any purpose
whatsoever. When making a purchase, says the law,
they must neither enter the shop nor stay outside. Upon
the wall of the English consulate hangs a memorandum
of this edict, which I transcribe in its quaint phraseology:

" As of old the sitting of Mahomedan women within
or in front of shops, both in the Grand Bazaar and other
places, was forbidden by the Government, the necessary
measures are being taken against those who admit women
into their shops in opposition to this prohibition, and this

prohibition extends to all the guilds, and it is expected that English subjects, tradesmen, are to be found in these guilds. You are requested to order them to avoid any action contrary to public morals and this injunction.

"(Signed)    MEHEMET, AGHIAH.

"Of the Stamboul Police."

What is a housewife to do when she wants a yard of cotton or a bar of soap? She may stand to buy it neither inside the shop nor outside. This is one of many mysteries which I failed to trace, but in practice it matters little. The bazaars are well frequented in spite of edicts, and the little money-changers' stalls, the jewellers', and gem-dealers', have always a throng of women round them. Most of these are slaves and confidential persons transacting business for their superiors. In general, at the present time, they are selling jewellery or plate, clumsy of form, bad of workmanship, and inferior of quality, though valuable for the weight of metal and the size of gems. But a vast deal of underhand business is transacted by the sarafs and the yaghliktchis, small bankers and jewel-brokers. As a consequence of the restriction upon women's free dealing in the bazaar, a large class of female pawnbrokers and usurers has arisen. Turkish ladies are at least as extravagant as their European sisters, and even more thoughtless than the most foolish. In these times of the decadence, the

majority have parted with their gems and finery ; and
when a marriage takes place, a feast of circumcision,
or what not, they hire valuables for the ceremony at
monstrous interest.  Some twelvemonths since the system and the abuses it necessarily carries were displayed
in a famous case.  Haïrié Hanoum, wife of Mizhet
Effendi, ex-defterdar of the villayet of Broussa, was
charged with obtaining money and jewels under false
pretences.  Occupying a good house, where she dis-
pensed a princely hospitality, she made it a business to
hire valuables from the female dealers, which she immediately pledged in the bazaar ; or she hired in the bazaar
and pledged in the harems.  Sometimes the jewels were
needed to deck herself and her slaves at a grand ceremony ; sometimes she pretended a visit to the imperial
princesses.  The prisoner also borrowed articles from
people of the first rank, such as the wives of Essad and
Husein Beys, the daughter of the Governor-General of
the villayet of Hedjaz, and even from the daughter of
Muchir Safvet Pacha.  The important element of this
detail is her emphatic declaration that all these great
ladies either took money in the shape of interest, or actually
" stood in " with her, receiving a proportion of the sums
for which she pledged their ornaments.  In particular
she alleged that the family of Muchir Safvet made a
regular business of hiring out their jewels when he was
from home.  These statements, of course, were vehe-

mently denied, and the judges appear to have passed them over with as brief notice as possible. As for the transactions with regular female brokers, they proved to be a maze of in-and-in dealing. Those dames immediately repledged the objects which Haïrié Hanoum pledged with them. The lady carried on her little game for many months, redeeming some articles with the cash obtained upon newer loans. But the enormous interest finally swamped her. At the moment of arrest she was found in possession of five diadems, thirty-six jewelled plaques or medallions, eight aigrettes of brilliants, one gold watch and chain, two half-diadems, seven pairs of brilliant earrings, three jewelled lockets, one bracelet, six diamond pins, five valuable rings, four brooches in brilliants or rose diamonds, one bouquet with jewelled leaves of flowers, one brilliant crescent, two valuable enteris, ancient robes;—the whole set down at over five thousand pounds Turkish—about four thousand five hundred pounds. Haïrié Hanoum was convicted. I forget her sentence. But the foolish system which en-courages a swindle like hers is unchecked. In the lower ranks of life it produces every form of immo-rality, as a sensible man of the world needs not to be assured.

Another great scandal occurs to my mind, as happening at Cairo in 1880. A Sheikh Hamuda Berda lived in a quarter of the town less fashionable than is generally

affected by wealthy saints who have gained public recognition.  With modest assurance he declared that Allah
had personally granted him authority to cure all diseases.
By the hand of Mahomet himself, the Merciful One confided to him drugs and lotions which restored the sight,
replaced an amputated limb, and so on ; as for mere
pains and aches he removed them at a word.  During
many years' residence at Cairo a vast number of persons
profited by his supernatural skill, but he specially laid
himself out for female patients.   In later times the good
man found his practice so large that he could no longer
attend poor people.   From every part of Egypt, Arabia,
and Syria, wealthy ladies came to consult the Sheikh,
and of course they brought a handsome present.   One
day, towards the middle of 1880, the young wife of
Izzet Bey, a colonel in the Egyptian service, proposed to
visit him for an affection of the eyes.   The colonel sent
her with a proper retinue of attendants, who returned, I
know not why, after depositing their mistress at the door
of Hamuda Berda.   She entered with a favourite slave,
but never came out again.   For some days her husband
was not alarmed, since surgical operations demand a
certain time.   Anxious at length, he called upon the
Sheikh, whose manner was not reassuring.   He protested that the young woman had left on the evening of
her arrival, cured.   The colonel was not satisfied.   He
appealed to the police, and they searched the dwelling

minutely ; I presume that Izzet Bey is a man of influence. Nothing was found in the saintly house, but a very foul and malodorous well in the garden drew their notice. Removing the cover they found the corpse of the young woman and her slave, among such a mass of putrid bones as showed that wholesale murder had been going on for years. Brought before the cadi, the saint confessed his habit of strangling every woman who came to consult him if her jewellery seemed worth the trouble. Such hideous stories now and then shock the grave, dumb population of the East.

To return to Stamboul. Of course there is a post there, and a telegraph, but nobody employs the one if he have anything particular to say, nor the other if he be hurried. I know by experience that a letter takes on an average three days in transit from Pera, and a telegram somewhat longer, if it arrive at all. This is not the result of stupidity or thoughtless indolence as most people believe, but a matter of system. The Turk is neither stupid nor thoughtless. I remember calling upon the Indian Secretary for Foreign Affairs one Sunday after- noon at Simla. He sat meditative over a chart of Central Asia, and the outcome of his reflections was presently delivered.

" A curious fact," said he, " has come under my notice. Look at this map! From Orenburg to the Chinese and the Afghan frontiers every reigning house is Turkish—we call it Turcoman. The Shah of Persia is no exception. Follow me!"

I did so, and Mr. L. went through the list with a display of knowledge—geographical, political, and genealogical—which filled me with awe and admiration. It is as he said; through all that vast area, the ruling family of every state is Turkish, if not of pure blood, at least by paternal descent.

Since the subject peoples, the Persians especially, hate the Turk or Turcoman with the bitterest animosity, we must conclude that there is a quality in that race which brings it to the front among its equals in civilisation. The Arab, the Tartar, the Kurd, and the Pathan, have made vast conquests in their time, of which nothing remains ; but the Turcoman, be he of Othman's sept or another, holds what his forefathers won, and makes advances in his turn. When he finds himself environed by more civilised peoples, much more when he is matched against them, he goes to the wall, but among his equals he takes the lead. The English race alone in modern days could make a similar boast.

It needs a certain time, and a concurrence of circumstances which seldom favours the passing traveller, to gain a true conception of the Turk. The first introduction to a statesman or a soldier of the empire is not impressive. As a rule, pashas are fat and pasty of complexion. Their ungainly clothes exaggerate the usual faults of build; they are ill-brushed, ill put on, and they commonly want some important buttons. His excellency's address is cold, slow, nervous, and uncomfortable, or effusive to a disagreeable pitch; I know better than most that there are conspicuous exceptions, but we are speaking of the general rule. The visitor's preconceived idea of Turkish ignorance and barbarism is more than realised. Unless his business be such that the dignitary is obliged to speak out, he retires with an impression that his excellency did not know much, did not understand what he heard, and did not feel any interest in what he understood. This opinion changes vastly after some experience. The Turk is patient of folly and attempted fraud, however bare-faced, but the charlatan seldom deceives him. It is really astonishing how shrewd and clear and well-informed are the men who come to the front under a system which appears to us haphazard and corrupt in the utmost degree. How quick and keen of perception they are—in their own affairs—nobody could believe who had not close and familiar dealings with them. And their cold resolution is almost fanatical. He who has seen much of the ruling Turk understands how it is they keep their place under certain conditions of society.

No argument is more commonly used to prove the dulness of the Ottoman than that based on his neglect of advantages unequalled perhaps in all the world. He is starving amidst every kind of national wealth, which foreigners are eager to develop at their own expense for his profit. But it is a grave mistake to suppose that this state of things results from mere dulness. Ignorance and stupidity would leap at the chances daily thrust before the embarrassed Government. The fact is that Turks of the governing class know very well that their native land is rich, appreciate the value of mines, roads, railways, ports, and forests the rest. But they say in plain words to a man who gains their confidence : " Wait awhile, and you shall see. We did not learn your Christian secrets in our youth. But we have established schools; we have imported European science; we have set our sons to learn. A generation is arising which will be independent of the foreigner. When it is old enough, then concessions will be granted, and then all the world will see great things." For that time they wait obstinately, delaying and postponing, as the oriental manner is, yielding one point only at a time under severest pressure. If speculators and capitalists would lay it well to heart that Turkey means to admit no more foreign enterprise if it can possibly be avoided, whatever the temptation, they would save themselves much time and cash, many disappointed hopes.

But, whilst Turks thus patiently await a new generation, the youth who should furnish it are growing up emasculate, bewildered, discontented. They learn West-

ern science at the schools, they read Western books—
mostly French novels—in an atmosphere of dulness and
repression such as I have described. The pride of race
and contempt for Christian nations which sustained their
forefathers have been utterly uprooted by events and
education. Their homes are no more luxurious nor
their minds easy in a masterful indifference to the European world. Their faith is utterly sapped; fanaticism
enough there is, but the fanaticism of envy and malice
and not of conviction. Under these conditions young
Turkey, on whom such hopes are based, is growing up
rotten. The parrot-learning it has acquired will be useful only for tricks and schemes. Very significant is the
fact that the grave and graceful ceremonies of social life
are almost forgotten. In no country were these so pleasant to observe, so dignified and mutually respectful, as
here; but the houses where they are still practised are
quoted by name. It is an interesting sight even now to
observe the gestures and compliments at a grandee's
*levée*; but the kindly reverence of a household towards
its chief is scarcely practised anywhere. Without intelligent sympathy at home, forbidden all amusement and
diversion out of doors, ignorant of boyish sports, even of
riding probably, the Turkish lad falls into dissipation.
For any kind of vice he finds liberty enough at Stamboul. No Christian have I ever met so bold even in
imagination as to draw a picture of the dark places in

that city. But several of these educated youths have assured me that the luxurious temptations of immorality in Stamboul—not Pera nor Galata—are unequalled in their experience of Europe—not inconsiderable.

The state of society was revealed to me with rather startling force one day. I called upon a young Mahomedan whose English education has made him one of ourselves in all respects, saving that it has not shaken his religious faith. He held in his arms a lovely child of two years old or so, who screamed with passion. A small Circassian boy, fair-haired, blue-eyed, was trying to distract her, but the apparition of the " Chelebi " was more successful.

The children were presently dismissed to the harem, and my friend observed :

" I dread to think of that boy's departure. My baby has the temper of a little fiend, and only he can manage her."

Knowing the small Circassian to be a slave, I asked why he was leaving.

"I must send him to Robert College soon," was the reply, " and get another playfellow for the child."

Robert College is the American school where so many middle-class youths are being educated—well educated, too, though perhaps the training is not in all respects the best.

I said : " The kindness of your people towards their

slaves is well known to me, but I did not think it ran so far as to pay their expenses at college."

He answered, laughing : "Not as a rule, of course. But my intention is to marry those two if Achmet turns out well. He is clever and well-disposed. The missionaries will keep him honest, I hope."

This was such a novel view of the relations between bondslave and mistress that I discussed the matter at length several times.

My friend told me that such matches, never rare in Turkey, are now quite usual. The state of morals is such in Stamboul that parents do not willingly take a daughter or a son-in-law from families of their own rank. They distrust all the world. It has lately become a common thing to choose a slave, boy or girl, to grow up under their eyes. The first expense averages, perhaps, forty pounds, and the female child costs little. She is taught truthfulness and virtue, fine sewing, the mystery of coffee-making and of filling a pipe—the arts of a very simple housewife. A boy is vastly more expensive ; as in this case, he must be sent to school, launched upon some kind of employment, and provided for until the parents are satisfied he will make their child happy. Then the pair are married, and the ex-slave becomes a member of the family, though that makes little change to him.

My Moslem friend is on such terms with me that I

speak of his wife almost as freely as I should speak of a Christian's. Remember, that he was brought up in England and speaks the language as well as we. Many readers acquainted with Constantinople will know whom I refer to.

To my question how the child's mother regarded this idea, he answered that it was her own conceiving. And then he related various stories of domestic misery and crime within her knowledge which had brought his young wife to a fixed resolve that her daughter should not wed a Turk of Stamboul.

I asked what she proposed to do if this little slave died before marriage.

"In that case," said the father, "we are determined to look out a husband in Syria, where there are still honest men."

Such is the view which a Turk, educated in the real sense, expresses of his countrymen—not the elder, but the new generation, of whom so much is hoped.

# A PUMA RUG.

COSTA RICA has changed vastly, no doubt, since I travelled through the Republic, with a comrade, in 1866. Its coffee is now an article recognised and esteemed throughout the world; and this distinction, properly translated into figures, means comfort, education, public works, and all those forms of progress so deficient in our time. There have been revolutions and troubles with the clergy; we have dimly heard of civil war; I rather think that a president has been · massacred. But the statistics of the coffee trade show unbroken prosperity in the mass. It is probable, therefore, that some kind of amusement other than gambling and drinking has been devised by ingenious and wealthy idleness. I have not had the pleasure to meet a Costa Rican travelling, and the reader may admit that as evidence not wholly unimportant of their home-staying disposition. We may reasonably hope, therefore, that a system of diversion, public or private, or both, is now in use. I should fancy that San José, or, better still, Cartago, might be a very

2 A

pleasant residence under those conditions.  The women
are pretty.  Fair hair, blue eyes, rosy flesh are common
amongst them, for neither Indian nor negro has mixed
the blood, and the climate of that tableland is as brisk
and healthy as the world could show.  But in our day
life was very dull.  Jungle-shooting of every description is to be obtained within a few miles of San José.
One might bag a jaguar before breakfast—or he might
bag you ; and jaguars mean abundance of deer and other
game, though one must start overnight to gain their
feeding-grounds.  But no one troubled about such
matters formerly.  What became through the day of the
bright vivacious girls one saw at market or mass, in
early morning, I could never learn.  Costa Rica had
already gone so far beyond other republics of Central
America as to found a club.  It was a gambling shop,
no more, where the Chancellor of the Exchequer kept
the bank.  This is not exaggeration.  My old friend,
Mr. Matthews, English Minister to the five republics,
congratulated me as the only foreigner who ever left
that capital a winner.  So I have no prejudice in saying
that life was intolerably dull at San José.

Amongst other changes in Costa Rica, the Serebpiqui
route has doubtless undergone transformation.  In 1866
it ran through a district practically unsettled, and the
road came to a sudden stop at the Disengagno, on the
edge of the tableland.  There was some talk in San José

when we young English travellers announced our intention of riding through that forest to the Atlantic. Not a few had done it when much pressed for time, but they were persons of small consideration. An adventurous female even had gone that way; but it was rumoured that she lost her wits, and it was quite certain that she was drowned before reaching the San Juan. A body of troops had marched along the track to surprise San Carlos Fort during the Filibuster war, and their bold enterprise virtually closed that struggle. But Costa Rican society had no personal acquaintance with any man so rash as to try the Serebpiqui route. And Costa Rican society advised us with warmth not to undertake the business of pioneer martyrs.

. It may be worth while very briefly to explain the situation. San José and Cartago, the twin capitals of Costa Rica, stand at a great elevation midway between the oceans, but at that time they had actually no communication with the Atlantic. All the commerce of the country went round Cape Horn, or across from Panama by railway, at enormous freights. People said, with what truth I know not, that the ferocity of the Guatuso Indians obstructed and broke up the old route to the Atlantic, by the Serebpiqui river, during the struggle of Independence, when the military posts were withdrawn; whilst the Talamanca Indians wrought the same mischief on the southern road to Limon. Upon the other hand, revolutionary individuals declared that the coffee-growing oligarchy had systematically spread reports to alarm, and had taken active measures to discredit these convenient roads, so soon as their growing industry discovered that the enfranchisement of the peons was obnoxious. Freed from bondage to the soil, labour showed an inclination to desert the coffee-grounds for the Tierra Caliente, and the landowners took fright. However that be, the fear of Guatusos and Talamancas seemed very real at San José.

A road of some sort is now open to Limon. Whether commerce have benefited or no, it is reasonable to imagine that the fabulously fertile land upon that route is occupied more or less, and no forays of the Talamancas have been reported to Europe. As for the Serebpiqui, I have not heard its mere name for sixteen years; but I conclude that it is now, to some degree, inhabited.

Our friends of San José did not exaggerate the dangers and discomforts of that journey. We started on April 3rd; we floated on the San Juan River, Nicaraguan waters, April 8th. Only six days! But to me now each of them seems a week. There is no jungle in the world more lovely than that where it laughs in young luxuriance; no mountain streams are more bright and musical. Great tree-ferns meet across the bubbling water, their fronds translucent as green glass where the sunlight flicks through a canopy of leaves. Every tree

is clad and swathed in creepers, huge snakes of vegetation, bare and ponderous, sunning their jewelled heads
at a windy height above; or slender tendrils, starred with
blossom. Here and there is a vast hollow pillar, reticu-
lated, plaited, intertwined—the casing of a parasite which
now stands unaided, feeding on the rotten *débris* of its
late support, and stretching murderous arms abroad, in
the world of leaves above, to clasp another victim. Other
trees are fading to a lovely death under shrouds of fern,
which descend from the topmost branches in a grey-
green cataract, soft as a pall, three feet thickness of
tender sprays. Great sheaves of bamboo make an
arch of verdant feathers overhead. A thousand tropic
blossoms, unknown to us, clothe earth and brushwood in
a veritable sheet of colour; foremost among them, always
associated in the mind with Central American scenery,
convolvuli, blue of different shades and shapes and sizes,
flesh-coloured, white. The forests of the New World
seldom show that dim and awful gloom so impressive in
tracts of oriental jungle; probably because all the land
was densely peopled when the Conquistadores came.
But in the older parts, where undergrowth is checked,
grey Spanish moss, drooping from the boughs, has much
of the same effect. I do not remember where I described
the trees thus solemnly caparisoned as "standing like
cloaked mourners in procession." I do not now think
of a better form of words.

Through such scenes we made our way, descending always from the tableland, over hills, through steaming valleys, beside the winding brooks, always in forest. The mud was sometimes chest-deep. Sometimes we enjoyed a steeplechase over fallen trees. We climbed up and we slid down, we crossed the treacherous stream a dozen times an hour. Every few moments somebody was down, falling soft in that moist earth, and never injured by the sagacious mules. To observe their cleverness was a pleasant study. After a short experience we resolutely dropped the reins, hitching them over the high pommel, that man's invention for guiding instinct—useless here at best—might not work absolute mischief. And we watched the brutes under us with disinterested admiration. In climbing they were cats; in descending, where they found themselves beaten, they hastily gathered up their legs and slid like trussed rabbits, till mere weight brought them gently to a stand.

By what instinct our Indian guides found their way is an old problem which constantly arises in such travel, and is never to be solved. After some days' journeying —which, as I have said, appear to have been such long days as were occupied with the Creation—we came to the Serebpiqui itself, at a point where it is navigable, with luck and Indian paddlers. Two of these were awaiting us, and we embarked. Within ten minutes of starting our canoe entered the great rapid—a howling,

screaming, tumbling waste of water. Oh, that was a
fright! A graze, a touch of impediment underneath,
would have upset us—and upset was death assured. No
man could stretch his arms to swim before the current
dragged him under, reived him, spitted him upon a snag,
beat him to pieces on a rock, tossed his fragments up,
and whirled and mouthed him. Rocks these Indians
knew, every one, but snags are formed from one instant
to another, and no practised vigilance can detect them in
that writhing, curling race of waves.

We shot down like a bubble, and in the foam-flecked
reach below our Indians stopped to wipe their brows, to
say a prayer of thanksgiving, and to babble with grim
laughter in their unknown tongue. I looked about.
Something moved by the waterside twenty yards away.
Upreared behind a boulder, with his fore-paws resting
on it, stood a chesnut-coloured animal, whose beautiful
green eyes, full of spite and mischief, were fixed upon
us. Its lips drawn back showed milk-white teeth, its
whiskers bristled ; it swore at us like an angry cat.
Such a charming picture that was, I never forget it—
the shaded grey rocks around, the little sparks of sunshine on the fulvous velvet coat, the large green eyes,
and the tricksy expression. A rifle stood between my
feet, but my right arm was jammed. With a forcible
nudge I warned my companion, who fired. The puma
bounded several feet, rolled over, showing his white

belly, and in two long springs went up the bank. He did not appear so graceful when the smallness of his head and the disproportionate size of his paws were revealed in action.

We landed and found blood, which the experienced Indians pronounced at a glance to be not arterial. At evening we reached the hacienda of La Vergen, where dwelt an enterprising individual who had gone in largely for stock-raising. His market, of course, was Nicaragua; and the two rivers—the Serebpiqui and the San Juan— gave him an easy route. Very pretty was the scene, as we viewed it at sundown. A wide savannah edged the stream, with neat loghouses and fences round it. Troops of cattle advanced from the forest edge, already misty, some galloping at clumsy speed, tossing and butting, pursued by savage vaqueros shrilly whooping, who twirled the lariat round their heads and launched its heavy circlet like a whip, or threw the unerring noose. Others moved quietly along, a serried, ponderous mass, outlined by the slanting rays. Each herd went towards its corral, where other horsemen were waiting by the entrance motionless.

We made for the principal inclosure. A very handsome woman stood watching us from the door while she nursed her baby. This dame was costumed in the latest fashions which had reached San José; it is probable, however, that she knew of our approach. Her husband came to meet us, less accurately but more picturesquely attired, in jacket of Guatemalan manufacture, broad scarlet sash, and high boots. He introduced us to the lady, took us inside, and forthwith produced green aguardiente of his own distilling. The walls were rough logs whitewashed; the floor was a creaking, rattling bed of planks ; the table and the stools were as primitive as they might be. But what epicure who has enjoyed that beverage of the gods, green aguardiente, can look at furniture or surroundings when his cup is full!

He was an amusing man, this cattle-breeder, whose name I quite forget. Many droll facts and stories he told us before bedtime, of which I noted down a part. We drew him to the subject of wild beasts, and our host was nothing less than an illustrated encyclopædia. He had a pair of tame pumas behind the house, and we sallied forth with lights to visit them. It was beautiful to see the creatures start from sleep, and rear themselves against the bars, their great clear eyes intent with curiosity. The master put in his hand and scratched them, whilst they arched their backs to press it, purring like cats. No animal has a prettier head, more graceful body, or more velvety paws; but the proportion is not correct. The head of the puma is too small; that of the jaguar, its rival, too large and broad. Its body is too long, and its paws are monstrous. These beasts were so perfectly tame that our host would not have confined them if there had been no children about the ranche. But none of their species can be trusted with children.

The puma and the jaguar are the ranchero's special hate ; he calls them lion and tiger. The homestead of La Vergen was surrounded by a narrow belt of forest, which hedged it from a number of savannahs where the herds pastured. All the large carnivora for miles about collected in this strip of woodland, lying in ambush for an ox that strayed beneath the trees. Some took up their quarters permanently until destroyed ; others returned home after the meal ; others paid a visit longer or shorter. We asked how on earth these facts were known, and the ranchero confessed that he had no proof; the authority of his Indian hunters satisfied him. Of these he kept a little staff, who turned out every day for service. He paid them wages, and a dollar a-piece head-money for pumas killed, half a dollar for jaguars.

The tigreros paraded, ugly, squat Indians, with big heads, small grave eyes, and a stupid type of mouth. They all came from Nicaraguan territory, for there are no Indians in Costa Rica, saving the wild tribes of Guatuso and Talamanca—so, at least, we were assured. The latter, I fancy, are known well enough. It is not dangerous for a pedlar to visit them, and those anxious to learn their appearance and their manners will find published material—that is to say, I think so, for our travels never led us near their country, and, personally, I know nothing. The Guatusos or Pranzos are much more savage ; and no man living in that day—I cannot tell how it be now—could give serious information regarding them.

A couple of spears, one long and one shorter, make the equipment of the tigrero. His dogs, big, slouching, light-coloured animals, are evidently related to the coyote. Dangerous rather than savage, not prone to bark, they perform the rôle of house-dogs badly. The Don assured us that puppies will not bark at all unless taught by others. But they learn at once, thus differing from the thorough-bred coyote, which can only howl and whimper in the first generation of domesticity, and seldom succeeds in learning a true bark until the third.

We asked why a dollar was granted for a slain puma, and but half for a jaguar, seeing that the latter animal is much more dangerous and destructive. It appears that in the fashion of hunting to which these Indians obstinately adhere, the less terrible beast causes the greater loss of life. Tigreros go in couples, the head man in advance with his two spears, the subordinate following with his machete, or chopping-knife. The jaguar is easily tracked, and he does not go far when roused. So soon as it is thoroughly conveyed to his mind that these intruders wish to see him personally, he turns with a roar that always gives sufficient warning to such practised shikaris. A moment afterwards he comes trotting up. The foremost Indian kneels, holding a spear in either hand, the long one farthest out—his companion stands at the side. The jaguar does not pause, but, gathering himself up, cleaves the air in a mighty bound, his forelegs wide asunder, and claws hooked to rend. Very seldom does it happen that the long spear fails to transfix his unprotected chest, or the shorter one his throat.

Such is not the puma's conduct. When disturbed, he skulks swiftly through the brushwood, and commonly escapes. In following a jaguar, dogs are seldom hurt, for he disregards them, and they have no need to press him. But the puma turns constantly, massacres a hound, and speeds on again. Even if wounded he is slow to stand; but when brought to bay at length it is a more deadly risk to face him. For this combat the spears are useless. Springing with his paws crossed, the puma would dash them aside. His feet firmly planted, knife in his left hand, machete in his right, the Indian stands forward. He has one blow in mid-air. If it fails, if the skull be not cleft like an apple, brute and man roll over in a hideous embrace. At such a time the comrade seldom wanted in jaguar-hunting would be invaluable. But when an Indian sets out intentionally to track a puma he goes alone. So did his fathers and so does he.

Very, very rarely a jaguar springs with his paws

crossed, and then there is wailing in the tigrero's hut. For the spears upon which he relied are twisted from his grasp, and the huge beast falls upon him kneeling. If the compadre with the machete be true, the tiger has probably two victims instead of one. The single chance of these poor Indians lies with their dogs, and it is but a very small one. Jaguars with this uncomfortable habit are scarce, however—if it be more than an accident. None of the ranchero's Indians had seen a case, though that fact proves little. Witnesses of the phenomenon rarely survive.

Still a third reason was furnished us for the higher reward, besides expenditure of dogs and greater risk. The puma has a horrid habit of following a human trail. The same practice has been charged against the true lion. There is no doubt that the former animal has it. The motive is not so apparent as might be fancied at a glance. It is evidently an instinct. Should this animal, prowling through the woods, come across man's footsteps, he follows them, though they be days old; provided, I imagine, that the scent have not yet dispersed. My own Indians pointed out to me an instance where—I took their assurance for it—the man had passed three days before, and the puma within t w hours. It may be the cunning creature knows it likely that where man has gone something eatable alive or dead may be discovered. He is not above gnawing a

stray bone. But I have no serious suggestion to offer.
Be the motive what it may, the practice leads directly or
indirectly to the death of many travellers belated in the
woods. And it causes the puma to be regarded with a
shuddering hate which the more ferocious jaguar does
not inspire.

When I add that the trail of these two animals is
distinguished one from the other by a small heap of
earth which the puma's forepaw throws up behind, I
think I have exhausted all my memoranda of the hints
which our skilful ranchero poured forth. There is
something characteristic in this detail of the footprint
also. The pads of either brute are almost alike in size,
though the tiger be so much bigger and heavier. But
he goes along with a free bold stride, whilst the other
crouches and crawls, his head down pressed between the
shoulders, all his weight thrown on the forelegs. Thus
they sink deep, and leave a tiny hillock of moist soil
behind them.

The lore of venerie unrolled by our kindly host was
illustrated with stories. He himself gave all his mind
to war against the puma, leaving the jaguar to his
tigreros. Caring only to have the brutes destroyed, insensible to the pleasures of the chase, he found this
system judicious. For, as he used a rifle, an immense
expenditure of time was saved. And the habits of the

puma mentioned divest its pursuit of danger if firearms
be used—as a rule, understood.

We had diverged to the subject of black lions, an
animal whose existence has been denied. The ranchero
had nothing decisive to advance on this disputed question. He heard with astonishment and contempt that
European savants doubted. Black pumas, he alleged,
are as well authenticated as black jaguars. He had
never killed one. Such skins as had come beneath
his notice were very large truly, as large as the black
jaguar's. But he laughed scornfully at the idea that
any woodsman could make a mistake. And the testimony of one so experienced impressed us.

" One day," said our host, " news came to hand that
two of my calves had been seized by a black lion. It
was at the furthest pasture, some ten miles out. In the
afternoon I rode thither with my dogs, to sleep at the
vaquero's hut, and follow the creature in the morning.
All the herd was brought into the corral. Soon after
dusk arose a great commotion, the cows running together,
the bulls charging and furiously skirmishing round them.
We turned out—beyond the corral-paling, you understand. It is a big inclosure, and the night was very
dark. Noise enough there was already to scare all
honest lions in the world ; but on a sudden rose such
tumult as sinful creatures make in purgatory. Cattle
bellowed and roared, women screamed ; then a multitude

of galloping hoofs shook the ground, and timbers crashed!
All my herd streamed through the fence, tearing over
the misty plain.   Fortunately, none of us stood in their
way.

"Nothing could be done that night, and I went back
mad.   That four-legged demon had sprung or climbed
the railing, snatched a young calf under its mother's
belly, and vanished ; you must know that she was
tied against the housewall.   Some Indian women saw it
fly down among them, as they said, its great eyes burning like lamps; saw it crouch a second growling, staring
at them, seize the calf beneath its struggling mother,
and fly back.   I knew too well that more of my young
stock would be missing before dawn.

"Sending to the ranche for more vaqueros, I went to
bed.   Next day all turned out early—the Indians to
search for my poor cattle, I to pursue the lion.   His
trail was followed easy enough."

"A moment!" my companion exclaimed.   "Did you
notice whether it was a puma's track by the sign you
have described to us?"

"No.   The dogs lifted it instantly, and I followed
at a canter.   At the forest edge I left my horse.   The
hounds had a long start—all but that old perro yonder,
who waited for me."   He pointed to an ancient dog,
grey and scarred, the only one admitted to the house,
of breed more European than the curs outside.

" I heard the pack quarreling and snarling a long way off, and I knew what it meant. They had found the remains of that black devil's supper, and were dividing the fragments. I was not much vexed, however; he would leave little of a sucking-calf. It took me more than half an hour to reach the spot, for there was an ugly bit of swamp to circumvent. When I got there not a dog remained, and the bones—not of one but of three calves—strewed the earth. It had been his regular dining-room for three nights, ever since he made his appearance on my land. That told that his lair was not far off probably, and I decided to search for it, though the one dog left me was rather demoralised by a scrap or two of meat, snatched on the sly whilst I was hunting round.

" I kicked him off, and he began to smell in a larger circle. The trail was struck in a moment, of course, and we set on. I knew I could depend on that faithful perro not to outrun me, and I was rather warm to face a black lion, when one has need of a steady hand. So I went quietly.

" It was further off than I expected. After two hours' tramp through the woods I saw it was probable the brute had his den by the river. But long before we got there my dog became anxious and uncertain. I could see the track quite plain, but he did not follow readily, looking behind him, pausing and growling. I thought

2 B

that taste of flesh disturbed his mind, and urged him
along, but more and more unwillingly he travelled, with
such odd movements as alarmed me, for I thought him
going mad. Suddenly he turned, rushed past me barking
savagely, his hair on end. Very glad to see him go, I
sat down to rest, while he took a long start, and I considered what to do.

" The perro's cry grew fainter and fainter. Then his
note changed to the querulous worrying and snarling,
with a loud long bark now and again, which tell the
master that his dog wants help with a dangerous quarry
I guessed how it was in that moment. Whilst I followed the lion's old trail, it had been following me! I
ran back. The perro was working further from our
path. Luckily I struck at once the spot where he had
branched away, but it was slow lifting his track through
the forest. I had made up my mind to return when the
clamour changed to yelps and howls—the lion had
faced about, struck down my dog, and perhaps was
tearing him. As fast as possible I hurried on.

" But if lions mean killing, all is over in an instant
when they have their victim down, and the perro's
miserable yells showed him to be still alive. After a
while I came up. See the marks!" We observed two
deep scars on the dog's left shoulder, and two slighter
ones; two rugged punctures on the right. There the
puma's claws had grasped whilst he struck.

" The children loved my dog, and no artery was cut.
I shredded some Spanish moss, bound up his wounds,
slung him in my scarf, and set out for home ; so far had
we wandered that it was nearer than the corral. I am
strong, señores, but the sun was hot, and a dog is heavy
on one's shoulders. No path led through the forest, and
I could not feel sure, not being an Indian, that I was
following the true course. A hundred times I thought of
dropping the poor animal, but I had not the heart when
he licked my neck, and I remembered what his fate
would be, devoured alive by ants and flies.

" Presently he became restless, and then he growled.
' It needs many lessons to teach a fool,' says the proverb.
I hit him with my elbow, but he would not be quiet.
He began to bark feebly, gathering up his limbs, poor
beast ! I suddenly caught the hint, and turned. At a
few yards' distance the bushes softly swayed beside my
track ! That lion was following again ! I looked to
my rifle, and set forward. In ten minutes the growling re-commenced, and the dog's excitement grew
stronger and stronger. The brute was creeping up ! I
cocked my gun, faced round, but that devil was quicker !
Nothing could be seen but the waving of the twigs. I
fired a chance shot to no effect, and resumed my way,
after loading. For a long while all was quiet. I gained
the river-bank, and was working down, relieved of all

anxiety, for the spot was familiar.  In an hour I should
be at home.

"Beyond a broad belt of reeds and swampy ground
lay the clearing.  That was an ugly bit to traverse with
a lion at one's heels, and I congratulated myself he had
run away.  One could not see a yard on either hand
when, half-way through, the perro growled and barked
and struggled in greater agitation than before!  I cried
to the saints, and the sweat poured down.  When I
turned, the reeds were all bending and quivering but five
yards away!  I shot, and hurried on, but the ground
was difficult.  In a few moments the dog again gave
warning, and the reeds swayed all about.  I shot!  But
now the dog did not cease to raise such feeble clamour
as he could, and I shot as fast as I could load.  Madre
di Dios, señores, what a run that was!

"The firing saved me!  Two vaqueros resting in the
shade knew the sound of my piece, and came to meet
me hallooing.  The perro was almost choked in con-
vulsions by this time, and I believe that lion had just
gathered himself to spring when their shouts alarmed
him.

"Now, señores!  What was the creature that pursued
me thus, in broad daylight, though I fired into its very
jaws?"

"Might it not have been a jaguar?" I asked, timidly.

"You are ignorant of our woodcraft, señor!  Why

should a tiger follow a man? The brute was not hungry, for it left my dog. And if a tiger had behaved in that way he would have sprung as soon as he came up. No! It was a lion—but a black one!"

" Did you follow its trail ? "

" I could not find a tigrero till next day. . Then the footsteps were tracked for miles after it left me, going straight for the hills. The Indians saw it was travelling, and returned. We have had no alarm of black lions since. And from that time, señores, I have understood how a kind action does not go unrewarded. For, if I had abandoned my dog, I should never have reached home that day."

When we left in the dawn, that excellent ranchero presented each of us with a puma skin. Mine is still an ornament of the bungalow.

# A BIT OF AN OLD STORY.

DOES a true drama of human life ever work to a climax and end fittingly? Does one romance in a million reach any end whatever, save interruption and oblivion? I fear not. Poetic justice, so my own expe-rience tells, is confined to poetic processes, and the only romance which terminates properly is that which began unperceived, unimagined, and unstudied. I have had occasion to observe many dramatic commencements and many dramatic conclusions. But all, though more or less effective of themselves, were disconnected.

Two years ago I told the story of a mantel-piece in my possession, how I ordered it from a potter in Multan, and how I gave him directions for an inscription which he did not follow.* When the object reached me, though it was pretty enough, I found that the Persian words were not those I had ordered. Upon inquiry, I learned that the Sunni fanatics of Multan raised a riot against my potter—a Shiah and a Persian—and smashed

* Legends of My Bungalow—" A Mantel-piece."

his stock. Foremost among the malefactors was an Afridi Pathan, whom avenging neighbours pursued. He took refuge in a garden and fell asleep. Heavenly beings appeared to him there, and when he woke he found two bracelets on his chest. The Afridi was arrested that night for his share in the disturbance, and in court he produced these jewels, of beauty more than human artificers can fashion, as he showed. They were his glory and his defence. Allah approved his deed, and it was for earthly governors to bow.

The magistrate did not question Allah's authority, but he impounded the bracelets. A rich merchant of the town chanced to be in court. His change of face when they were handed round drew the magistrate's attention, but he steadily denied all knowledge of them. This mystery remained undecided. For his disorderly conduct the prisoner was sentenced to a month's hard labour, and three months more in default of his share towards compensating the potter. Meantime, the bracelets were handed to Sayyid Farid-ud-din for exposure in some public but sacred place, where the owner might recognise them, if earthly owner they had. Farid-ud-din was chief of the moollahs who attend the Bahawal Hak, the tomb of the great Multan saint.

So rested matters when I told my story. Friends, whom I had begged to keep me informed, wrote that the things remained without a claimant when Zahad

recovered liberty. No further news reached me, and
I supposed that this romance, as usual, had broken off
at the end of the first chapter. But on returning from
Egypt the other day I found a continuation, very welcome, though it does not upset my sad theory.

On his return from jail, Zahad hastened to demand
his blessed prize. Imprisonment had left him no sense
of disgrace. It is the function of magistrates to perse-
cute. Zahad was fresh from his mountain home, a
shrewd and resolute young giant, quite unacquainted
with civilisation. He was not religious, few Pathans
are ; but superstitious, and fanatical, and overbearing,
as are all his kin. Islam is less a creed for them than a
banner and a token. But for it they are glad to die.

Farid-ud-din dwelt in a ruinous but substantial mansion by the Fort. The Bahawal Hak, of which he was
chief guardian, stands within the fortified enceinte, but
the old gates were never closed at this time. With
difficulty Zahad obtained an audience, for he was
ragged and dirty. But the Sayyid's tone changed
when he understood who was his visitor. He abandoned his air of lofty unconcern, uncrossed his legs,
and descended with grave and respectful salaams ; conducted Zahad to the corner seat of the divan, and called
for coffee.

"The blessed bracelets," said he, "are safe in the
Bahawal Hak, lying upon the sacred tomb itself. All

the faithful reverence them! Be not puffed up, oh youth! nor disdain the counsels of the aged. When I heard of this event, I sought in prayer and deep reflection why you should have been favoured above all the pious of the city. The Merciful One heard my anxious communings, and he revealed his purpose. Great and dangerous service it is your privilege to render Islam, oh Zahad Afridi!"

"Tell me Heaven's will, oh Sayyid!" exclaimed the Pathan, fervently. "Though it lead through flame and blood I will pursue it!"

"It is written that he who wins heavenly favour walks along the edge of hell! Allah has signalled you out for his service, and beware of slackness! Listen, my son! The infidels are full of boasting and vanity, under the accursed English rule! Beside our holy tomb stands their idol-house, where the dogs worship wood and stone. Our forefathers destroyed it again and again; but for money, and for the revenue it produces, they allowed it to be restored. Allah has judged them! Ranjit Singh, that Shaitan, turned it into a magazine, and the English blew it up when Mulraj Mal Khan—whose name is grateful!—defended the city. Under protection of the Christians the infidels rebuilt it, and deluded Kaffirs from every part swelled their torments hereafter by subscribing to make it glorious exceedingly. There is now a scheme afoot of incredible profanity. Those children

of the Devil point the finger at our sacred shrine.  They
say, 'The Faithful One, Sheikh Baha-ud-din—in whose
name all the world finds peace!—lies under a lofty
dome, whilst our foul and degraded idol-house is flat.
Let us arise and bestir ourselves!  The accursed English
are our friends and fellow-dogs!  There are great and
rich men of our shameful persuasion who will find us
money before passing to their doom!  Let us build a
spire ten times as high as the dome of Bahawal Hak!
So all the world shall see that our gods of human manufacture trample upon holy Islam, and laugh at the
Faithful!'  That is their project, oh, my son!"

Zahad started up.

"Where is this idol-house?  Where are the vile un-
believers?"

"Stay, stay, impetuous youth!  Nothing yet is done!
They are gathering the money and the stones, collecting
masons, preparing designs.  There is time to warn them
that if they persist in this unparalleled wickedness, brave
men and pious will sacrifice their lives before it shall
succeed.  To give them such notice is your first task."

Zahad undertook it at once.  He learned that a certain Manich Chanda was the most zealous advocate of
the scheme.  His blood aglow at this threatened insult
to the faith, the Afridi rose.

"Give me the heavenly jewels," he said, "and I
will be doing!"

" Nay, my son! Had the All-Wise designed you
should have them now, how should the Collector-sahib
have taken them from you ? They are a promise, not
a reward as yet. You may see and adore them as do
others, fervently, in this desperate time, but such an
inestimable gift has still to be deserved."

Zahad flared with rage sudden and deadly, but the
Sayyid put out his hands, and repeated the Fetcha, the
Beginning, that verse of utmost sanctity which awes the
faithful hearer though he be mad with passion. Zahad
went out fuming, and made his way to the house of
Manich Chanda. The merchant was away on business,
and his servants, insultingly suspicious of the big ragged
Pathan, would not say when their master was expected.
In fierce passion Zahad strode away. As he passed the
corner of the house a scarf fluttered down from the
balcony, and lightly veiled his head.

I picture the scene. Manich Chanda lived in a great
blank house, gaudy here and there with paint half-
effaced. Its windowless wall occupied one side the alley.
Within and above its high portal, carvings and fretted
ornaments of wood, cut almost as fine as lace in designs
of intricate beauty, alone suggested the wealth inside.
Opposite stood another gateway, as elaborate and as
lofty ; but the walls that held it were broken and weed-
grown, surrounding piles of rubbish that had once been
a stately house. Its demolition gave the sunrays access

to the overhanging balconies, of exquisite woodwork,
that adorned the upper story of Manich Chanda's
dwelling.   It was a glorious burst of light in the
shadowed alley.   Above and lower down, such balconies
almost met from either side, and the sky was a narrow
strip between.   But at the end lay an expanse, bathed
in blinding sunshine, with market-people in a thousand
tints of drapery.   And beyond, above them, towered
the lofty gate, pink in the sun, black in keen shadow,
its opening filled with the living green of trees beyond
the moat.   ˙

No soul was visible in the dark alley.   Zahad took the
scarf with awe, and stood, his lithe figure poised, his
blue eyes interrogating Heaven with rapture.   That
this was a second sign he never thought of doubting.
He did not glance at the balcony overhead.   Had he
done so, not even his hawk-eyes could have pierced the
small gaps of delicate tracery, behind which two girls
watched him, laughing and trembling.   No hint of
Allah's meaning descended from the radiant sky.   Zahad
examined the celestial scarf.   It was not less beautiful
than the bracelets, not less evidently work beyond human
skill.   So light and soft was the material that he could
crumple it all up between his palms; the gold woven
cunningly in its texture alone gave it weight to fall.

Zahad found voice.   As he feverishly twisted the holy
object round his head he recited prayers; and then he

strode towards the light and throng, with the gait of one who has a mission from on high. His cries grew louder. " Lah-ullàh—ul-lah-hu!" he yelled, bursting from the alley mouth.

An officer-sahib was riding by; with a quick movement he hitched his revolver more convenient to the hand, and undid the strap. The market-people gathered about Zahad in alarm and curiosity. An old Sikh policeman pushed to the front.

" None of that, Afridi!" he remarked in his equivalent for the familiar warning of our " Bobby," " or I shall run you in !"

" You will run me in, dog! Me, the chosen of Allah ! Listen to it, ye faithful ! Lah-ullàh—ul-lah-hu !"

The Afridi had no weapon, and the old Sikh cared little for his inches and his flaming eyes—he had faced such in youth, and had seen them cower and dim before the steady press of the soldiers of the Khalsa. Without more words he closed. Other police came running up. Zahad snatched a steel-yard from a booth close by, and slung its heavy weight round his head with giant strength. The policemen stood an instant. Zahad yelled without ceasing, and whirled his tremendous club. The crowd, three-fourths Moslem, began to take fire. " Lah-ullah !" many cried, and the ominous " Din! din !" began to mutter. It was an anxious time at Multan in the beginning of last year. The officer spurred his horse, broke through, and rained cutting blows on the Afridi with his heavy riding-whip.

Zahad was brave and high-spirited like all his race. At this moment he felt within him all the strength of Heaven's support. But for such attack he was not prepared. A very young man, brought up with severe home-discipline, yields by instinct to the whip, though swords and bullets would not daunt him. Quick as a pulse-beat he would have recovered his presence of mind, but in the moment's hesitation the police sprang forward and bore him down.

Next day he appeared again before the court, on a charge of disorderly conduct in the market-place. The sense of divine protection rather failed him now. A Christian in like case might not have been disconcerted, since he would understand it possible that the favour of Heaven should display itself in his humiliation. But such ideas cannot occur for a Moslem's comfort. Zahad perceived and humbly admitted to himself that he had made a mess of it somehow. Sayyid Farid-ud-din stood amongst the audience, and his grave face poured rebuke upon the prisoner.

The magistrate delivered a lecture which Zahad heard in silence, his head erect; wherever lay the mistake, this Kaffir knew nothing about it. He was fined two rupees, and bound over to keep the peace. Zahad did not own a cowrie nor a friend, but a householder unknown to him stepped forward, and did all that was necessary. When discharged, the Afridi asked for his scarf. Nobody had seen it. He began to make a disturbance, but the police closed in, the unknown friend took his arm, Zahad submitted, crestfallen and despairing. He said not a word, but his sighs were of that volume the Oriental alone can heave, and he walked in semi-consciousness. What unprecedented torments would be allotted in the other world to one who had enjoyed such blessed grace and had proved himself unworthy by acts of thoughtless indiscretion!

They reached the Sayyid's house, and found him just within the door, as if to receive an honoured guest. Zahad threw himself on the ground.

" Well said you, holy man, that he who is favoured by Heaven, walks along the brink of hell. I may not sit beside the lowest of the Faithful. Let me lie in the dust."

The Sayyid did not press the point. He sat on the divan whilst Zahad lay along the floor, and probably he thought their respective positions quite fitting. With great interest he heard of the new manifestation, and pondered it gravely.

" Allah has indeed marked you for great deeds," he said, " but not yet. Go to Gujrat and meditate in solitude six months. I will give you letters to Pir Shah Daula, the sainted recluse, who dwels in Gujrat. I will give you also money for the journey. Stay with that holiest of men until it is revealed to me to send for you. Go to-night."

" May I look upon the bracelets ? "

" You may hold them in your hand whilst I myself conduct the evening service."

The day was not Friday, and innovation on the fixed ceremonial of Islam is so rare that Zahad thrilled again. They went together to the Bawahal Hak. The heavenly tokens, wrapped in a cloth of gold, were placed in Zahad's hands, and the Sayyid took his station at the mihrab. News of the strange event had spread, and the mosque was crowded. What feverish visions and what agonising fears alternated in the Afridi's soul I am not equal to imagining. The words recited by the priest were unintelligible to him as to all others, but they were sounds that stirred the blood by fervid association. And then Farid-ud-din ascended the minber to preach. His sermon differed only from those the Faithful heard every week by a grander style and an air of significance not less impressive because vague. He spoke of the glorious time when this city was a bulwark of the faith ; when the infidel, though magnanimously suffered to live, dwelt in subjection and reverence. He alluded to the persecution of the Sikh conquerors, which many of his audience fired to remember, and he cautiously hinted that times of still greater humiliation might be at hand unless the Moslem turned zealously to Allah and his Prophet, who had promised that none should prevail against those who kept the faith. As he finished, every eye was glowing, every heart burning with passion. Most of those present knew what infidel schemes were referred to, and they vowed, in whispers and sobs, then in hysterical shouting, that the Moslem would all perish before their saint's dome should be overtopped by an idolatrous spire.

That night Zahad departed for Gujrat, and he dwelt for six months with Pir Shah Daula. The later time was one continued ecstatic trance. When, after long penance, the saint declared that Heaven was mollified, forthwith Zahad began to experience delights unknown. He saw and he felt the joys reserved for the Faithful after death—the flowers of unearthly fragrance, the black-eyed girls of beauty more than human, the majestic poetry of angels' converse, the light of the very sun itself, the jewels and gold; above all, the thrilling sense of life immortal won by virtue and devotion. Then he learned for a truth, that is felt not repeated, that this lower world is nothing, its pleasures and its pains of equal unimportance, contemptible alike. To him, in this frame of mind, came one day the order to return to Multan.

The Hindoos had been active there and successful. Their co-religionists had subscribed, masons and materials had been collected; the walls of the temple

2 c

strengthened to bear an enormous increase of weight
The Mahomedan population had petitioned Government
against this sacrilege.   They had gathered outside the
Collector-sahib's compound, and shouted threats.   Government was alarmed and embarrassed.   But it could
not stultify the principles on which its rule is based by
denying to one religion a dignity accorded to the other.
It could only return warning for menace, increase the
garrison, keep the police alert, and wait for overt acts.

The population of Multan, Hindoo and Mussulman
alike, have been in all time noted for the heat and
obstinacy of their religious convictions.   No district of
India has suffered persecution so frequent and so severe,
nor has any endured its fate with such ferocious obstinacy.   Although the Mahomedans were supreme for
seven centuries and a half, they daunted the fanaticism
of the subject race.   Again and again riots and outrages
against holy Islam caused an indiscriminate massacre.
On one occasion, Aurungzeb, out of all patience, ordered
ten thousand Hindoos to be slain, and the order was
zealously obeyed ; but upon his death disturbances began
again.   Nowhere else in India has Brahmanism shown
such spirit, though every district has its legend of heroic
stubbornness.   The Sikhs, who tamed Afridis and
Shinwaris, making the Khyber Pass as safe as a street,
did something to lay the devils who possess Multan.
In the reckless and scornful oppression which those

sabrcurs imposed on Moslem and Hindu alike, the sufferers learned in some degree that they were fellow-countrymen. But when the Sikhs perceived a faint *rapprochement* they exploded it with ease. A prudent fear of English magistrates, who do not massacre, but prosaically hang and fine, imprison and transport to the Andamans, have kept fanatics in awe more or less since the annexation. The police have promptly suppressed little rows and demonstrations which would have gathered force until they set the town ablaze. But in this matter of raising a spire on Prahladpuri Temple Hindoos stood within the law, though they acted in the old spirit, knowing well that a storm would rise.

Zahad made his way to the Sayyid's house through streets thronged with Moslem, sullen and threatening Hindoos exulting and defiant. No blow had yet been struck, but desperate elements were mustering. Excited groups of leading Moslem stood about Farid-ud-din's door. Zahad learned that the holy man had been summoned by the Collector-sahib an hour ago. He waited until the Sayyid came back with a train of Faithful. After these he pressed in, with many others. When the small room below and the court-yard were full, Farid-ud-din made a speech, which those could hear who could not see the orator.

He said in brief: "I waited on the Collector-sahib, the General-sahib was with him. The Collector called

on me to preserve the peace. I answered, 'How shall I
control the Faithful when their livers are inflamed with
a sense of wrong? I have no soldiers.' The Collector-
sahib replied: 'They have no wrongs, and, if they think
they have, it is you and your fellows who have irritated
them. This is no time, oh Sayyid, for a delicate choice
of words. The Sircar has been watching you, and, if
disturbances follow, it knows whom to hold responsible.'
What a monstrous charge, ye Faithful! Have I urged
any of you to seek justice for outraged Islam by means
other than legal? I said to the Collector-sahib, 'My
enemies have abused your candour, oh father of the
people! The Faithful of Multan need no hints or guiding
when their holy places are insulted. I, on the contrary,
have done my best to restrain their pious indignation.
We know the English rule—it is heavy on Islam, but
not unjust.' He answered, 'I have spoken!' And the
General-sahib added: 'I warn you that my soldiers,
Moslem and Poorbeah, will shoot without distinction,
let who will begin the riot! And do you look to it,
oh Sayyid, for a green turban will be no safety.' So
the General-sahib spoke, in contempt of that colour
which marks me, unworthy as I am, for a descendant of
the Blessed One. But, since such is the tone of the
powerful, in the hearing of you all I adjure the Faithful
to disperse and go quietly to their homes, relying on the
justice and tenderness and respect of the Sircar towards

Islam, which have been long apparent to all who can
see, and are now plain even to the blind. Go quietly,
friends! Allah does not need your arms. He can
avenge himself by ways mysterious to our feeble minds.
Go in confidence."

The crowd filed away murmuring a significant acquies
cence. They belonged to the trading class which naturally
prefers to entrust its cause to Heaven, if that may be done
decently, rather than make disturbances. Zahad remained
in his place. After awhile, those intimate friends departed who had stayed whispering with the Sayyid.
They looked at the Afridi curiously, but did not speak
to him.

Then Farid-ud-din came up with a weary air. His
foot was on the steps leading to the upper story when
Zahad called his attention. He hurriedly turned back.
" When did you arrive? Have you shown yourself in
the street? Come up!" The Sayyid added, glancing
round suspiciously: " The moment of devotion is at
hand! Hush!"

They went up the stairs, passed round the central well
which looked on the court below—protected by a balus-
trade of dainty carving—and through several apartments. The magnificence of them struck Zahad with
awe. To us they would have seemed close and unwholesome, tawdrily furnished, though many of the odd
articles were lovely and tasteful in themselves. To a

rich Hindoo they would have seemed commonplace.
But the Afridi was amazed.  Such things as he saw
there on earth were the plenishing of Heaven in his
dreams.   Twice a door opened suddenly, and a girl-
child's joyful face appeared.  At sight of a stranger it
vanished in alarm, and Zahad heard merry chatter, but
his quick mountain-eye remarked jewels, gold-wrought
silks, and dainty luxury, scarce, as he thought, terrestrial.

They reached a distant chamber, and then, after such
words as roused the Afridi's blood, the Sayyid disclosed
his plan.  It was radical.   He suggested that Zahad
should blow up Prahladpuri Temple, with means and
under circumstances arranged with minute skill which
could scarcely fail.   Zahad consented with enthusiasm to
play his part, and his host left him, sending in choice
food by an ancient slave-woman.

But although the Afridi agreed with warmth, he was
conscious that the proposal would have been otherwise
acceptable a few days before.   He had no longer real
delight in the idea of risking his life for the glory of
Islam.   The direct influence of Allah, so to speak, had
vanished from the undertaking, which became an operation of mere war.   As such the Afridi welcomed it,
but there are neither Houris nor ecstacies in such
work.   And as the hours passed by this scene of dis-
illusion grew stronger.   Zahad had been used to sleep a
great deal under the saint's tuition, and his dreams had

been divine. Whilst his eyes were open, and his senses abnormally keen, he enjoyed broken visions. But now he could not sleep, he had no waking visions. The desire of his body was to lie still, and his mind was flat as his limbs.

Two days he endured this misery, which became painful; then he confided his state to Farid-ud-din. If only he could get abroad for a few hours to enjoy the sunshine and the crowd it seemed to the imprisoned mountaineer that he would be all himself. The Sayyid would not hear of this—too grave interests were at stake, and the police too busy. He preferred to try medicine, and his remedies were potent. Zahad felt again the enthusiasm and the self-devotion which had thrilled him. He penetrated to the throne of Allah's self, and saw the utmost joys accorded to the Ghazi, the martyr. They were too keen for endurance. After raving and bounding in his cell, he rushed out and created dire alarm through the purdah. Farid-ud-din was powerless to control the fervid young giant. Consigning his household to remote and most uncomfortable places of concealment, he left Zahad free to roam through the mansion. And after awhile, when he had ransacked the place in a strange frame of shrewd observation and mystic extravagance, the Afridi fell asleep. He awoke infinitely more wretched than before, so depressed and incredulous that he thought his whole story an illusion. In pure alarm, the Sayyid consented to let his prisoner out for a few hours.

Events had ripened during the latter days. The building of the spire had actually begun, and the Moslem were waiting in despair, the Hindoos in confidence, for the Government's final answer upon the question of right. It was expected that afternoon, and a disturbance would so certainly follow, whatever the decision, that troops had been moved from the cantonment, and posted in central spots.

Zahad's feverish mind felt sympathy with the alarmed and excited throng. He strolled for hours, neither speaking nor spoken to. The consciousness of a superior fate inspired him with contempt for those fussy talkers. Whilst they were rioting and bandying sticks, he would triumphantly solve the question by himself. What feeble fools are talkers beside the man of action! But the man of action is generally pleased to see a crowd of interested lookers-on, whose mere helplessness is an acknowledgment of his supremacy.

Towards evening a rumour spread. The Lieutenant-Governor in Council had considered the Moslem protest, and given a final reply. The Hindoos stood within their legal right in embellishing Prahladpuri at their own cost. The Government would restrain any attempt to outrage Mahomedan feeling, and it invited the Faithful to await with patience its action in this matter.

Then the streets cleared suddenly. As by a word of command the Moslem slipped away, and the Hindoos, finding no one to quarrel with, retired in some bewilderment. Zahad roamed about till dusk. Then he betook himself, ready and determined, but unenthusiastic, to the Sayyid's house. He passed many little knots of his co-religionists, eagerly whispering and collecting. It was dark when he reached the alley where the last of Allah's manifestations was revealed. There he was stopped by police and questioned. Whilst replying impatiently, a sudden uproar distracted the inquirers. A turn of the roadway hid Manich Chanda's house, but the noise came from that quarter. The police broke away, and Zahad followed. Before they got sight of the building, a little column of townsmen burst from a side-passage, beat down the police with sticks, and ran along. Round the next turning they fell amongst a swarm of raving Moslem, who occupied the narrow wynd in a mass compact. Too closely pressed to advance, they shook their bludgeons in a swarthy flare of torches, crying, " Din! din! Lah-ullah-hu!" The spirit of the scene stirred the Afridi's blood. His height, his long arms and tough muscles, forced Zahad a way through the outlying mass. He came near the door, not unbruised. Here was collected wilder material than the city could furnish—Scindhis from the desert, Pathans and Beloochis, whose eyes gleamed through tangles of long hair, wet with perspiration. They all carried arms, and they yelled in frenzy.

Round the entrance was motion still more vehement. Great hammers whirled and thundered on the massive door. With a roar and a crash it gave way, and Zahad was carried in. There was no resistance nor any living thing in the house. By ways prepared in times more habitually perilous, every soul had got away. The building was rummaged from top to bottom in an instant, chests smashed, apartments stripped, and all that was moveable trampled or carried off. Those who entered first, the Pathans and Beloochis, understand looting as a science, and they did the business thoroughly in a few moments. Two cries, repeated by a thousand voices, disturbed them. It was a scream of "Fire!" within the house, and of "Soldiers!" outside. All tumbled headlong down the stairs, disposing their plunder as they went.

Zahad was among the last. As he ran from an apartment of the purdah—the harem—he saw a big Belooch escaping with a bundle. From an aperture therein trailed his blessed scarf! Zahad recognised it at a glance and sprang on the looter. Explanations were not asked nor offered. The Belooch, a heavier man, almost as tall, sustained the shock, but he had no time to draw a weapon. Clutching each other like wild beasts, rolling and roaring and rending with their teeth, they struggled amongst gathering smoke in a horrid din.

Moslem and Hindoo were fighting outside, whilst the soldiers, with fixed bayonets, drove all before them, and the police made indiscriminate arrests. The street was cleared in three minutes, and a score of daring fellows bounded up the staircase. At the same instant the Belooch came whirling down, head foremost. Zahad followed him, clutching the bundle. And presently they were both conveyed to the guard-room on stretchers.

The rest of the tale may be summarised very shortly.

The Belooch died, and half-a-dozen witnesses deposed that they saw Zahad pitch him downstairs. To the magistrate's eye the case was simple. Two plunderers had quarrelled, and one had murdered the other. Zahad was convicted. To the question what he had to say before receiving doom, he answered vehemently: "The Belooch was found in possession of a scarf which Allah had let fall from the sky as a special mark of favour"——and so on. The judge interrupted. He said:

"This is not the first time, prisoner, that you have pleaded a similar hallucination. Last year it was some Delhi bracelets which mysteriously reached you in a dream. Now you justify yourself by an incredible story about a scarf. If I could admit you sincere in believing that these things were gifts of Allah, the simplest inquiry would have disabused you. The bracelets are before me. They speak for themselves—a dozen like them might be bought any day in the bazaar. To make certainty doubly certain, here is the mark of a well-known jeweller. The scarf is Dacca muslin, embroidered by hand. In a score of houses you will find such articles ——"

"No, no, sahib!" cried the Afridi, distracted. "It cannot be. I myself saw ——"

"Summon an expert," ordered the judge, "and Manich Chanda."

. Manich Chanda drew the attention of all by his confusion when interrogated about this simple matter. But when asked generally if the scarf was not a common pattern of Scind embroidery he eagerly replied that in all rich purdahs such articles were common. And the expert, a Moslem, only glanced at the bracelets before declaring that he recognised them. They were brought from Delhi by a confrère, who told him casually that he had sold them to Manich Chanda. This statement made sensation. Zahad was overwhelmed. He sank down in the dock and heard no more. Had this evidence been brought at the first trial, he would have laughed in simple scorn. But it confirmed dim suspicions, unacknowledged and unshaped, which had been forming in his mind.

. After a pause, the judge continued:

"You have been convicted, prisoner, upon the clearest evidence. I shall instruct competent persons to inquire into your state of mind. But my duty now is to condemn you to penal servitude for ten years."

. Zahad paid no attention. The doctors declared him

of sound mind. He is now in the Andaman Islands, noted in the prison-books as " dangerous."

Manich Chanda suffered for his daughters' silly and improper freak. For years he had been out of caste, paying the penalty of a youthful voyage to Europe. It was this misfortune which caused all the others, for Hindoo girls brought up among the decencies of caste life would rather die than notice a Moslem, much more leave him gifts. But Manich Chanda had fair hopes of reinstation at a price. For this end he had subscribed largely to the fund for raising a spire on Prahladpuri, and had taken the most active part in collecting money. The disclosures of the trial ruined him and his daughters beyond hope. He is the richest citizen and the most miserable in Multan. They remain single.

The riots had their course. After a week of most intolerable disorder, the town was formally occupied, but a certainty of defeat and punishment did not stop the fighting. At length the leading people on both sides felt their religious enthusiasm cool before the stagnation of business. Through the mediation of the commissioner they reached an agreement. Prahladpuri Temple was to be embellished with a spire, but only thirty-three feet high. It is just finished. The Hindoos were to have a well dug at the municipal expense, and they waived their claim to draw at the Holy Moslem fount.

# A BUNDLE OF PHOTOGRAPHS.

It was my singular good luck to visit the South African Diamond Fields whilst their authenticity was still suspected, their marvels untold, their scenes and customs unreported. " Dry digging " was first incredulously whispered on the Vaal in December 1870; in February 1871 the rush took place.' Long before my arrival the colony had run mad; but it was not until the New Colesberg Kopje had been well proved, that Europe believed the dreadful truth. The discovery of this grandest of all mines occurred, if I remember right, in July 1871, and I reached the fields in October. As yet the movement was almost exclusively colonial. Government reports estimated the yield of diamonds at 300,000*l.* a month, 3,600,000*l.* a year, and the production was increasing daily. A very few European dealers, better informed than rivals, had agents on the spot. But the bulk of those interested in gems, and nearly all the public, still discredited, or resolutely affected to discredit, the truth of facts which must in their ultimate course reduce the diamond to the value of the garnet.

I saw the Fields, therefore, as very few English visitors
have seen them, at the most interesting stage, with eyes
unprepared. What they were like, what manner of existence diggers led, is shown in a packet of small photographs which turned up yesterday. Some of these faded
views—no great results of science at any time—I purpose
to illustrate like a conscientious showman.

First to notice is a picture of the house at Bultfontein, where I lived, a guest of my excellent friend
W——. Mud though it was, people called it "The
Residence," "The Mansion," and such fine names; not
unreasonably, for the wealthiest of diggers had but a
tent or a frame-house of canvas, the largest of traders
only a shed of planks, my Lord the Chief Justice and
Her Majesty's Commissioners but a tiny baize-walled
room apiece in an "hotel." There was another house
at Dutoitspan, used as the prison; one at New Rush
occupied by "The Company"; and a third at Alex-
andersfontein, five miles from camp, which was let to
Captain Rorke, Chief Inspector of Claims. No more.
And they tell us there are streets and villas now.

It was of this house at Bultfontein that a colonial
paper solemnly declared the walls to be set with diamonds. How they laughed at home! But the statement was untrue only in the sense that it was foolishly
exaggerated. One Sunday W—— asked some friends
to breakfast—a wretched, greasy feed enough, but deli-

cious to those poor fellows, for some of whom no feast had flavour or variety but a few months before. The meal finished, one of them strolled restlessly about the little room. Quick and suspicious eyes were there. The whole party rose on a sudden, threw their comrade across the table, and tormented him until he hysterically owned the finding of four diamonds in the plaster. They forthwith stripped the walls, heedless of expostulation. Nine more were discovered; and so effectual was the search that none have been discovered since, to W——'s knowledge. 'Some time afterwards he resolved to dig a cellar, and speculators eagerly bid for the contract; if stray diamonds were found sticking in the house-wall, there must be a new Golconda in the soil beneath. The successful competitor executed W——'s ideas, and paid him a large amount for the earth removed. But he found not a single stone. Such surprises, such disappointments, were common on the fields at that time. My shrewd host perceived that the plaster had not been made at Bultfontein, where there is no water, and he rightly judged that diamonds therein did not prove diamonds below the foundations.

Fancy a very small, low building, flat-roofed, without a window visible. Successive layers of sun-dried brick are conspicuous, for the surface of mud-stucco only clings in flakes. Strange articles undistinguishable lean against the wall, throwing keen-edged shadows which

make one feel hot only to recall the glare. Obtrusive in
the foreground stands that emblematic wheel-barrow,
containing pick and spade and bucket. There are three
doors of varying height and width. At one of them I
stand, not unpicturesque perhaps, in puggree and white
flannel; beside me a friend, dressed for this occasion in
his cherished suit of tweeds; well in the foreground,
burly J. F., with rolled-up trousers and uncompromising
boots, stuffing his pipe with a determined thumb. Beyond the house-wall appears a corner of the tiny stable,
where W—— kept two modest ponies. Further on, a
goat is perched upon some eminence resembling a shattered cart; then a round Kaffir hut, and the cook-house
beyond. Once upon a time that cook-house was annexed
by three Hottentot women, who expelled our female servants—we only, for miles about, had female servants—
and kept possession two days. One of them declared
she was Queen of Russia, and had come to see that the
diggers had fair play. After various manœuvres, quite
futile, we trapped them, as monkeys are trapped, with a
bottle of Cape Smoke, ostentatiously left unprotected.
They raced for it, and our Kaffirs lying in ambush
occupied the hut in force.

That demented allusion to the Queen of Russia was
based, no doubt, upon a curious incident that occurred
during my stay. A lady visited the Fields, travelling
with her maid and man in a handsome covered cart; she
was said to be a Russian princess exiled from Europe.
Mystery hung over her, and we were a good deal excited.
It is certain that Sir Henry Barkly, Governor of Cape

2 D

Colony, gave this illustrious stranger an urgent recommendation to the care of all officials; but his circular
contained no hint of her nationality or station. Our excellent magistrate of Dutoitspan was much perplexed
how to make things comfortable for the lady; but she
proved to be quite independent, with her cart and her
servants. His attentions finally concentrated in a solemn
stroll every evening, with the Russian princess upon
his arm. She bought many diamonds, and paid for
them.

The scene familiar to us when we stepped outside that
mansion is displayed in a panorama, consisting of four
views. The camp photographer had no large resources.
His pictures are all one size, four inches by two-and-a-
half. To take the landscape from Bultfontein Hill, he
has apparently aimed his camera at different points of
the horizon, and connected the shots together. But the
result is close enough for me. Spreading the small
sheets smooth, I recognise that unforgotten tableau. In
the immediate foreground, all along, are grey hills of
" sorted stuff," " siftings," riddled earth dug from the
claims. Not a man is working on all this side. The
fabulous wealth of New Rush, the superb gambling of
Old de Beer's, the staid prosperity of Dutoitspan, have
seduced away the thousands who used to populate our
hill. The veldt stretches unbroken to our left hand,
miles on miles of grey monotony. Beyond the sharp
edge of its horizon flattened mountains glimmer. Travelling towards the right, a solitary tent appears far off,
then two or three, then a jumble and a wilderness of

canvas. Our tree is conspicuous amongst them, with waggons and frame-houses round it. The panorama shows a width of four miles, and a depth of I know not how many ; but there is not another tree. That cameel-dorn bestows a glory on our camp whereof New Rush bluster cannot deprive us. With what chuckling did we see those plutocrats wander up and down, two hours by the clock, seeking an object on which to hang a nigger, and finding none ! Our tree is registered in maps and surveys. Distances are measured from it. History must refer to it. If anything happened to our tree, the geography of West Griqualand would be em-barrassed.

Under its shade I recognise a small canteen, notoriously unlicensed, yet ignored by the Excise. This privileged pot-house is kept by Duplat, the Boer who owned these farms, who sold them for about 5,000*l.*, and who would starve if the police stopped his miserable enterprise. In front of the canvas city stands another dwelling which I recollect—a pal-shaped tent, bellying on its ropes, patched and dingy. The man who lived there had a claim upon the other side of Bultfontein, which he worked with feverish industry. People thought him rich, but he never displayed his diamonds. In passing two or three times a day, 1 used to speak to him, and after a while he confided in me. The poor fellow was not looking for diamonds any longer; not one had he found, but hundreds of rubies unapproachable in colour. I saw the fatal mistake, and hinted it cautiously. He admitted that the dealers would not buy his stones, but he had an

ingenious theory to account for that.   The deluded man
showed me a jar full of lovely garnets, such as wiser
diggers put carelessly aside as presents for their children.
He was still deceived when I left the Fields, and I fear
he may have lost his senses when the cruel truth ap·
peared.

The second bit of my panorama shows the outskirts
of Dutoitspan.   The horizon is effaced by one huge
continuous mound, the barrier of siftings between Camp
and Field, the town and the mine.   It is almost a range
of mountains, as mountains go out yonder.   We have
not yet reached the magnificence of New Rush, but at
this rich digging there are groups of tents beyond the
crowded purlieus of the township, where a lordly comrade has his residence, his stable, his cook-house, and his
servants' quarters all detached.   Buggies and " spiders "
stand in the open here and there.   Farther on, in the
next picture, appears Dutoitspan Camp, an orderly
confusion of tents, frame houses, corrugated iron roofs,
sheds, and enormous warehouses.   Conspicuous lies
the dam, a shallow pool, with three dead cattle lying
suffocated in the mud.   That little train of horses
descending from the Market Square is probably sent by
the police to drag their carcasses away.   The water we
drink comes from the dam, stagnant and fetid at the
best, thick with the churning of hoofs, odorous with all
impurity.   We pay threepence a bucket, and we fetch
it ourselves.   No marvel that we seldom wash.   Pontak
wine comes as cheap, and is not more nasty.

So familiar was that scene half a score of years since,

that memory, stirred by examination of this photograph, identifies many an object. There is the great store of Sonnenberg Brothers, that Californian firm which tried to " hold " diamonds. It quarrelled with the banks, and vowed vengeance. Notices were posted that Sonnenberg would purchase every diamond brought to them. I do not know what arrangements they had framed to meet the run. For fourteen days they gallantly held out, while excitement grew, and bets mounted higher. Then they broke, with *nine pounds weight of diamonds in hand*, and a mob of sellers at the door! Of that incredible figure I am absolutely certain, but I will not guarantee that the struggle lasted fourteen days. I think, upon reflection, that it was much shorter.

There is the neat little house where Swelly Dave lived—he of whom I wrote in " Legends of my Bungalow." In that warehouse yonder, one stifling day, I took refuge from a thunderstorm which nowhere breaks so suddenly and so awfully as on these burnt plains. A woman in the street ran to shelter, calling her little boy. He delayed an instant—Heaven itself seemed to crack and burst above him; earth and air flamed in one undistinguishable blaze! Then our dazzled sight returned. The child lay in the roadway, smoking! The sluices of the sky broke open, the rain descended in a cataract. But we heard the mother's scream of frenzy, saw her run and drop grovelling in the mud and wet——

But I would dwell on pleasanter recollections

Benning and Martin's Hotel shows plainly—a large wooden structure on the Market Square. What larks we enjoyed in that hostelry, grim enough sometimes! The adventures of a Russian corpse there on Christmas night are not to be excelled for grotesque horror; ten years ago I had courage to print that story, but I dare not now. Harmless fun was always to be had at Benning and Martin's. The accommodation consisted of a bar-room with a humorous billiard-table; a vast shed behind, open to the roof. One washed in the open—if one washed—finding one's own water. Partitions of green baize on either side the shed made bedrooms. The central space was the dining-hall, but it had a double row of open beds, where diggers tired or drunk lay down, dressed or undressed, as they thought fitting. These public couches were reckoned by the hour, and Martin's factotum, George, held it his duty to rouse an occupant at every termination of his lease, so to speak. "Hi, it's daylight outside!" was his invariable formula. How many hours George counted to the day depended, so far as I could gather, on the number of his "pick axes," a beverage of pontak wine, brandy, and ginger-beer. After each relaxation of the sort he haled a sleeper out of bed, regardless of protest.

One day, as we sat down to breakfast, arrived an athletic youth, who had kept it up very late, or begun it very early. White as a miller with the poisonous lime-dust, scarred with Hebron boils, bare-armed, red-eyed with the glare of sorting, he looked a type of digger. This youth got into bed, high-boots, butcher's knife, and all, wrapped his head up, and lay quiet. "I'd give that chap his full time, if I was you, George," said somebody, and George looked as if the same idea had crossed his mind. But it was the good man's custom to take refreshment whenever he carried an order to the bar. Business was transacting after breakfast, and business there means drink. George forgot his prudence, and after a while he shook the muffled sleeper—" Hi, man, it's daylight outside !" The other's reply is not to be transcribed—a large proportion of remarks out there would not bear repetition. But George was persevering. Suddenly his victim jumped up, snatched off the blanket, twisted it tightly round George's head.

" Is it daylight in there, you blackguard—is it?" punching him.

" No, no, it ain't ! "

" Then don't tell a chap no more lies," exclaimed the youth, with a final kick.

What a grand display we had sometimes on that rough board ! From some mysterious receptacle ragged brigands would produce a store of diamonds which an empress would regard with interest. But the first warning of catastrophe was very near. It reached us in November or December 1871. What fortunes we missed, those who were on the spot in that earliest panic ! If we had only known ! But who could keep his judgment cool, his faith unshaken, when Sonnenberg accumulated nine pounds weight of gems in a fortnight, besides what he sold, what he refused, and what stood over? It was that startling fact which daunted us, I think. How could diamonds keep up, we said to one another dismally, against that flood? They did keep up, however, they keep up still, though the final smash draws nearer and more near.

On that black day, wandering as we all did from one closed dealer's to another, I called at the little frame-house above the dam, which I recognise in this photograph. It was occupied by my friend M. Mège, representative of a large firm in Paris and London. As we talked disconsolately at the door, a Dutchman offered us a perfect stone, very slightly yellow, of forty-seven carats, at 27s. the carat. He had taken it over all the camps since daybreak, dropping his price until it reached that incredible figure. And we refused! I feel savagely bewildered even now to think of it.

We have stayed long enough at Dutoitspan. My bundle of photographs is scarcely touched, and I meant to say a word of each. But before traversing those three miles of veldt—sprinkled with limbs and carcasses of oxen at each yard, busy with carts, dotted with bands of Kaffirs—which divide me from the promised land, I must call your attention to the fluttering rag of canvas, the shapeless objects standing there, all solitary, beyond the outskirts of Dutoitspan. They are the outward signs remaining of a curious incident. Once upon a time we had a deluge so copious and so long enduring that the most industrious knocked off. The river-camps were flooded. A happy notion struck two diggers of Cawood's Hope, thus reduced to idleness. Shouldering their cradle, they tramped hither, hired a cart, and went round New Rush, begging the nodules, "lumps" we called them, which are found in most claims—masses of

tufaceous lime, which will not crumble. Our diggers
knew very well that diamonds were as likely there as
anywhere ; but, if a lump refused to break under two or
three careless blows, they tossed it on one side, and used
it for building walls or such purposes as that.  No one
refused the men of Cawood's Hope ; some, in that idle
time, employed their Kaffirs to load up the cart.  By
noon they had enough to begin operations in the river
style, washing the lumps instead of pounding at them.
Next dawn the little tent, the cradles and fixings, stood
abandoned as you see them now.  Not half the lumps
collected had been touched, not a stick of their property
had they removed.  Those ingenious diggers of Cawood's
Hope were seen no more, but somewhere about the
world dwell two men in comfort if not luxury, who tell
their children a legend of the Diamond Fields even
more strange than others.   We laughed and we swore,
but very, very few took warning.   Henceforward men
would not give away their "lumps."   But they left
them piled on the roadside, until the sun dried and
powdered them.   Then a thirty-carat diamond rolled to
the feet of a passing Kaffir in sight of half-a-dozen people.
But still we would not trouble to investigate our lumps.

    Look now at the pictures of this wondrous jewel-box
It is lunch-time, and the claims are deserted.  So truthfully marvellous is the representation of that scene the
perplexed observer cannot say which is top or bottom of
the photograph.  At this present time, the roads and
walls so confusing here have vanished, and New Rush is
one pit, eight acres of area or so, bounded by "the

reef."*   I could not possibly give an idea of the former
chaos represented here.   After thoughtfully resolving
which is the right end up, one sees abysses apparently
unfathomable, crossed by broken roads, interrupted by
terraces and platforms, traversed by ropes like a gigantic
web, diversified with windlasses and suspended buckets
and wheelbarrows and endless machinery.   Minute in-
spection will discern a Kaffir whose attitude harmonises
finely with the scene.   Solitary on the brink of a murky
excavation, he has gazed upon that world of holes till in
perplexity and dizziness he rests his elbows on his knees
and clutches wildly at his hair to keep his brain from
whirling.

I understand the feelings of that Kaffir.   New Rush
was a place to stir imagination beyond all others on the
surface of the earth.   How many millions sterling have
been dug from that small field, no larger than one of
our great London squares!   How many thousands have
been enriched by it—how potent must be its influence
on generations unborn!   We troubled little about such
questions, but they arose as one looked upon that laby-
rinth from the hill of siftings that encircled it, a new
chain of mountains in the antique landscape!   Thousands
of men were toiling in the cool dark shade below,
scarce bigger than dolls.   Long before my time, white
labourers refused at any wage to descend those perilous
holes—fifty, eighty, a hundred feet sheer, with no support for the crumbling walls of lime.   Even Kaffirs

---

* All the reef has now fallen in, and New Rush is a big deep pond,
waiting for machinery to pump it out.

might not be tempted, after they had earned enough to buy a gun. But in the fever of avarice and rivalry men dug and sank, wasting no time in precautions. They sat upon a plank suspended in mid-air, and scraped the walls plumb-line in hand, whilst jealous eyes above watched every motion. They tunnelled beneath the roads, so weakening them that one after another they fell in, with result more or less disastrous. The walls collapsed incessantly. Then the reef itself, the hill against which they worked, toppled over bodily, and smashed the pumping-apparatus. But still the mad struggle continued. Still the Kaffirs poured their buckets on the sorting-table, and at dusk men stowed away their handful of precious stones, withdrawing to drink and gamble in those fine tents sprinkled round the outskirts of the township. Or, after working hard with their own hands all day, they retired despairingly. For New Rush is not all enchanted ground. There are parts of it, as I know to my cost, which do not pay for working. It startles one to hear that eight acres of ground return 300,000l. a month; such was the estimate of this kopje alone when I left; just the sum which all the fields together yielded at my arrival. But of this amount, four roads out of the twelve probably contributed two-thirds; one-sixth of the area was almost un-productive, Heaven only knows why. All things connected with the diamond become more mysterious the more opportunity one has of studying the question practically. I could talk by the hour on this theme without going beyond the range of my personal observation.

Take, as one detail in a thousand, the matter of chips—
they are common enough on the Fields—fragments split
from the crystal under circumstances which may be
variously suggested.   The size of the perfect mass may
be calculated if an angle remain upon the chip, and no
such gems survive as the antediluvian monsters which
we find in bits.   My friend W——- observed a flake
which, when whole, represented a diamond of 3,000
carats or thereabouts.   Now, these broken sections are
found at every depth, buried, closely enveloped in what
we call " stuff," tufaceous lime, just as any stone is buried
in the earth.   But, have two chips ever been dug that
fitted together?   One might naturally expect that the
discovery of a fragment deep down under the soil would
argue the presence of others within a reasonable distance ; but it does not prove to be so.   The exploding
diamond must have scattered over an enormous area.
What was the force so gigantic which hurled its parts
away?   All the world knows that our Cape gems split
even now.   I never saw a man who had actually beheld
the process, but it is evidently slow and gentle.

Enough of scientific problems.   Here is a view of
New Rush at work.   The photographer has chosen one
of the less crowded, less successful, roads, and he has
persuaded all the men about it to take an instant's rest.
You can fancy what bearded, brawny ruffians they seem.
European diggers had scarcely yet begun to show.   These
giants who overtop the stalwart Kaffir by a head are
Africanders, English or Dutch of blood, quiet and God-
fearing mostly, unless they think themselves aggrieved.

Unfortunately, that was an abiding notion. After the collapse of the Republic and the withdrawal of President Parker, no course the Government could follow satisfied them. Kaffir thefts and landlords' claims troubled these good fellows sorely. The latter they ignored with menace, but the former grievance embittered every day. What innumerable meetings gathered in the Market Squares of Kimberley and Dutoitspan to vituperate the Kaffir and his wicked doings! Every man who addressed his " brother diggers" from the market-table—where sat the chairman lawfully elected, high-poised aloft under an old umbrella—declared such abuses had been impossible under Stafford Parker's rule. And they spoke truly. For in those days men did not trust a Kaffir even with the spade unless they watched him. To send gangs of cunning savages, alone and masterless, into the twilight of the deep-dug claims whilst one lay in bed or smoked at the " Pig and Whistle"— to let them sort and bring their "finds" at evening—such confidence would have seemed a suggestion rather humorous than mad in the early time.

But we had come to that. I scarcely blame the Kaffirs if they yielded to such temptation. One did not need the thousand proofs advanced to convince one that they would steal under the circumstances. A piece of evidence as conclusive as amusing I remember. Until the English Government annexed the Fields, blacks were not allowed to work on their own account. When this regulation was annulled, many home-staying speculators made their venture. A colonial clergyman of the guileless sort

chose a little party of his converts, explained his vague
ideas, furnished the needful means, and started his Kaffirs
for New Rush. All they understood was that their padre
longed for some of those shining stones wherewith the
Bushmen used to pierce their instruments. On arrival
at the Fields, they hired themselves out, stole every
diamond they saw, and when they thought the store
sufficient they set off home rejoicing. Very cheerful
was that padre. After glutting his gaze with the pretty
heap of gems, he very injudiciously asked when and
where and how. Then the horrid truth came out in its
unblushing nakedness. Shocked beyond words, the innocent suborner of those innocent kleptomaniacs lodged
his ill-gotten treasure in the bank. And month after
month he advertised for claimants. I never heard of an
application. We were too busy to trouble about spilt
milk or lost diamonds.

But we were not too busy, the day's work done, to
indulge the sport of chevying, beating, hanging Kaffirs,
burning the tents of receivers suspected, and generally
playing mischief. It was a wild time, that of the New
Rush riots. After meting out justice on the thieves, a
natural impulse counselled the plunder of the landlords.
We sat under arms all night at Bultfontein Residence
time after time, expecting th summons to assist Dutoitspan or to defend ourselves. One afternoon, especially,
it was reported to the magistrate that 4,000 New Rush
diggers had vowed to march on a general crusade against
wrongdoers. He swore in special constables, but it was
too evident that the mass of diggers at Dutoitspan would

not interfere unless personally annoyed. That was an evening of excitement! A storm saved us, if I remember rightly.

In justice, however, it should be added, that pleasant incidents occurred during these paroxysms of unreasoning vengeance. The rioters burnt a canteen, smashed all its contents, nearly killed the Kaffirs there, in the master's absence. He returned before they left, and somehow secured a hearing, which convinced those well-intentioned persons that they had made an error. Forthwith they raised a subscription in diamonds and coin, which paid the money loss ten times over, and laid the foundation of that sufferer's fortune in five minutes. What was done for the Kaffirs I never heard.

What a contrast are such feverish scenes with that depicted in the last photograph I set before me! It represents a " wet digging," Cawood's Hope, or Blue-jacket, or Hebron, or Moonlight Rush—one of those sweet landscapes we beheld in " the depths of some divine despair" on a holiday run from the madding crowd and the sun-bleached desert. Four men, all white, stand by a shallow pool, barelegged, pausing with their simple instruments in hand. Fine trees overhang the little group. A hill clothed with brush swells up behind them, and before lies the swift pellucid water of the Vaal, making blessed music of its silver ripples, softly hurrying down great flakes of heavenly blue and cool green bars of happy shadow. The wives of those too fortunate adventurers are somewhere near, cooking the rude but welcome supper. Their children are playing

in the bush or bathing ; brightening their fathers' pleasant toil with merry voices.   At night all will slumber
quietly in the old waggon under the kindly trees—the
slumber of hard work well, not fantastically, paid.   To-
morrow, perhaps, the men will take a holiday, clean their
trusty roers, mount and scour the veldt, returning with
spring-bok and duyker, guinea-fowl and koraun.   Such
was diamond-digging once, before we dreamed of fabulous gains, of making fortunes in an hour, of the hurly-
burly, the mad merriment, and unheeded wretchedness
of the " dry fields."

www.ingramcontent.com/pod-product-compliance
Lightning Source LLC
Chambersburg PA
CBHW020234110726

47898CB00004B/1258